NEGATIVE OBSESSION

DAN CHAPMAN

Winsyatt
United Kingdom

NEGATIVE OBSESSION

Copyright © 2024 by Dan Chapman

All rights reserved.

The moral right of Dan Chapman as the author has been asserted. All work contained within is the author's own, unless otherwise stated. No part of this publication may be reproduced, distributed, or transmitted in any form or by any means, including photocopying, recording, or other electronic or mechanical methods, without the prior written permission of the author and publisher.

The story, all names, characters, and incidents portrayed in this production are fictitious.

Cover art & design © 2024 Dan Chapman

ISBN-13: 979-8340345868

First edition. 2024.

A story has no beginning or end: arbitrarily one chooses that moment of experience from which to look back or from which to look ahead.

Graham Greene, *The End of the Affair*

PROLOGUE
'A loss of something ever felt I'

The city lay under a thick blanket of snow, white and pure, smoothing out its jagged edges, silencing its usual roar. From above, from the soaring flight of a bird wheeling over the rooftops, London seemed a frozen landscape, a great still beast wrapped in winter's icy grip. The Thames ran black and sluggish through its heart, its dark surface occasionally disrupted by the line of a bridge or the blotch of a boat. From high above, as a falcon flies, where the rooftops and streets are swallowed in the monochrome stillness of snow, the city appeared strangely quiet, suspended in perfect time. A vast white expanse stretched out, muffling the sounds of life below, and it was only in the movement of people—tiny figures trudging through the snow, a scattering of buses, the rare run of a car—that the city betrayed any sense of its usual vitality. From this height, London felt vast, slow, and peaceful—an illusion created by winter's temporary dominion.

The snow lay thick on everything, from the dome of St. Paul's to the towering columns of Nelson's Monument, now coated in layers of white. The distant silhouette of Tower Bridge rose like a spectre over the frozen river, which itself had slowed, dark water flowing beneath a fine layer of ice in places, lethargic and burdened by the cold. The current pulled weakly at the detritus of the city—plastic bottles, discarded papers, or an empty takeaway container swirling lazily in the grey water. But even here, where the river pulses beneath the quiet surface, London's dark heart felt strangely sedated.

Across the city, below the bird's silent flight, life continues in minutia, little fragments and small moments preserved in the frosty air. Footsteps crunch as people make their way across the streets, bundled in thick coats and scarves, heads down against the biting chill. Children, faces red from the cold, run after each other, their shouts carrying faintly in the still air. A bus moves listlessly through the snow-covered road, its wheels spinning slightly before finding traction again. Snowflakes fall from the sky in slow, lazy spirals, drifting down like whispers from the clouds, blanketing the buildings and pavements below in delicate layers.

Near the riverbank, the scene is quieter still. The snow has piled high along the embankment, muffling the city's breath. Here feels untouched, save for the occasional footprints leading from one corner of a path to the next. A car lies abandoned by the river's edge, half-buried beneath the accumulating snow, its tires stuck in the deep frost, its roof and windscreen already blanketed in white. The vehicle is as still as the buildings, as though the world forgot it was ever there. No one moves near it; no one passes by.

But from a distance, from above, something in the scene calls for attention. A flicker of movement—or rather, not movement but a change in the whiteness below, a small disturbance in the flawless landscape. It is barely visible at first, just a subtle indentation in the snow, like tiny craters that pock the otherwise smooth surface. Closer still, the marks become clearer, like small, perfectly round droplets pressing into the powder.

And then, closer, the faintest sound. A rhythmic tapping, soft but insistent, like the ticking of an unseen clock. The source is unclear, but it grows louder the closer one gets, merging with the slow thaw of the morning sun. Drip. Drip. Drip. It is the sound of water—or something heavier—falling from the unseen above. The rhythmic tap, a steady beat, echoes in the air with a strange persistence as though, ironically, it belongs to something alive, something with intention.

The morning sun has begun to work its way through the winter's chokehold, and small rivers of thawing snow trickle from the car's roof. But it's not just the melting snow that falls. Dark, wet spots begin to appear on the ground beneath. Slowly at first, then more steadily, droplets fall from an unseen source, landing in the snow with a quiet plop, each leaving a tiny crimson mark in the white blanket below.

It drips steadily from somewhere within the car's interior, though no movement is visible from the outside. The door remains shut, the windows fogged and frosted over, concealing whatever gruesome secret lies within. The snow beneath the car, once pristine, is now marred by small patches of red, a macabre contrast against the stark purity of white surrounding. The small puddle grows steadily, each drop of blood absorbed into the snow, but leaving its mark, nonetheless, creating a dark and expanding stain.

And so, the rhythmic tapping continues, an ominous metronome, marking the passing of time in this forgotten corner of the city. But there is something unnatural about the way it sounds here, in this quiet place by the river, under the weight of the snow. It's as if the world itself has paused to observe, as if the city is holding its breath.

Across the river, life goes on as normal. People walk along the embankment, oblivious to the scene unfolding just beyond their view. The hum of distant traffic drifts through the air, muffled but constant, a reminder that the city is still alive despite the eerie stillness here by this car. The distant clatter of a train crossing the bridge breaks the silence for a moment, before fading again into the background.

Above, the snow continues to fall, though lighter now. The sky is a pale, washed-out grey, devoid of any real colour or warmth. The buildings along the riverbank are stark and solemn, their outlines softened by the snow that clings to their walls. The water flows beneath the bridge in slow, languid waves, each one carrying with it the weight of the city's history, of the countless lives that have passed through these streets, these moments of winter. But here, in this frozen corner, time seems to have stopped. The blood continues to fall, slowly but surely, mixing with the snow and leaving its trail. The tapping is unrelenting, each drop a reminder that something has happened here, something beyond the ordinary, something hidden from the eyes of those passing by.

In the distance, the faint sound of church bells is heard, their chimes floating through the cold air like a distant memory. The city, with all its history, seems to be waiting, watching, as if holding its breath for whatever comes next. But for now, all that remains is the silence, the snow, and the steady, rhythmic drip of murder falling into the winter's stillness. And the abandoned car, now a part of this frozen tableau, lies waiting, its secrets locked within, as the river flows quietly beside it, carrying with it the cold breath of the city, indifferent and eternal.

**

Across town, a dark-haired man stirs from his uneasy slumber to find a world that had changed in the night. Outside, the snow had fallen heavily, blanketing everything in a quiet so profound that it muffled the usual sounds of the city, almost as if it had been swallowed whole by the cold. He shifted beneath an old, worn blanket, stiff from the chill but offering just enough warmth to keep him from freezing, wiping his greying hair from his face. His breath came out in clouds, collecting in the fogged windows of the car, sealing him in a cocoon of his own making, cut off from the world beyond. His features are striking, a blend of refined sharpness and haunted intensity that makes his presence hard to ignore. His hair, a touch tousled and often left just shy of unruly, frames a face where high cheekbones give way to a jawline that hints at both determination and a subtle gentleness. The faint stubble he frequently wears softens the harsher lines of his expression, though there's an alertness to his features that hints at an underlying tension.

The windscreen had become a blank canvas, coated in layers of snow that obscured everything beyond the narrow, dim confines of his vehicle. It was as though the night itself had buried him under its weightless, silent oppression, too, and he was only now clawing his way back to the surface. He blinked, rubbed his stubbled face with numb fingers, and checked the dashboard for the time. His heart lurched. He would be late for his appointment.

A curse slipped from his lips as he fumbled with the keys, trying to start the engine. His fingers were stiff, clumsy, not yet awake. The engine sputtered, coughed once, and then roared to life, but the first breath from the heater was cold, icy air blasting into his face before it began to warm. Outside, nothing stirred but the steady, relentless fall of snow.

The man threw off the blanket and reached for the ice scraper in the glove compartment. The cold bit into him the moment he opened the door, cutting through the thin layer of warmth he'd managed to build. The snow crunched beneath his boots as he trudged toward the front of the car, and his breath puffed out in front of him, mingling with the snowfall. His hands worked mechanically, scraping at the ice that had formed on the windscreen, clearing a patch large enough to see through. The task was mundane, repetitive, the effort of moving felt like wading through something thicker than water.

In the stillness of the early morning, his thoughts drifted unbidden to the events of the past few week. A name floated to the surface of his mind—Murray—and with him came a cascade of fragmented images: dead faces, unanswered questions, and *that* girl's face. He shook his head, trying to banish them, but the thoughts clung stubbornly to the edges of his consciousness, refusing to let go.

His fingers, already numb, clawed at the frost, scraping away the remnants of ice. The snow had slowed though, falling in light, lazy drifts now, as though the sky itself had tired of its relentless task. He wiped his brow with the back of his gloved hand, feeling the cold sweat there, a reminder that no matter how deep the snow fell, the burden pressing down on him was not from the weather. It was something deeper, heavier—a load he could not shake.

With the windscreen mostly cleared, he climbed back into the car, slamming the door behind him to shut out the cold. His body ached, and the leather of the driver's seat, cold and unyielding, bit into him through the layers of his clothes. He reached for the stereo, his fingers stiff and slow, searching for something—anything—that could cut through the oppressive silence. The familiar strains of *Who Knows* by Marion Black filled the car, the melancholy tune wrapping around him like a shroud, its slow rhythm matching the dull throb in his chest.

The heater finally began to do its job, filling the car with a tepid warmth. He sat there for a moment, fingers wrapped around the steering wheel, staring through the patch of cleared glass at the world outside. The snow-covered streets stretched before him like a dream, empty and frozen, untouched by the usual bustle of the city. London, muted and still, lay beneath this thick blanket of white, its landmarks barely visible through the fog of snow: St. Paul's, the Tower, Nelson's Monument, all standing like distant sentinels against the grey, winter sky.

He sighed, long and low, then shifted the car into gear and pulled away from the curb. As the car moved through the empty streets, he let the music carry him, the soft croon of Black's voice filling the space between his thoughts. The words settled on him, pressing down like the snow outside, a reminder of all the uncertainty that lay ahead. He drove on, the roads slick and treacherous, but the real danger lay not in the ice beneath his tires but in the thoughts swirling in his mind.

The city passed him by, but with its familiar contours softened by the snow, and yet the man felt as though he were moving through something foreign, something impenetrable. The usual sounds of the city—buses, taxis, the hum of distant traffic—were distant now, swallowed by the quiet. But beneath that quiet, he could hear something else, something persistent: a slow, steady dripping, like the ticking of a clock. It followed him, unbroken by the weather or the passing time, each drop a reminder of something that gnawed at the edges of his awareness.

The man's hands tightened on the wheel as the buildings blurred into the background. Each turn feeling like he was stepping deeper into a dream, or perhaps a nightmare. There was a sense of inevitability about the way the snow fell, about the way the world had folded in on itself, and the man felt it in his bones—a sense that something was closing in on him, something he wouldn't escape.

By the time he reached his destination, the music had long since faded, leaving only the quiet hum of the engine and the distant rattle of the heater. He pulled up outside a modest building on a side street, unremarkable in its appearance, save for the memories it stirred in him. Sitting there for a moment, he stared at the entrance, knowing that once he stepped inside, everything would come crashing down on him again—the questions, the memories, the past that refused to stay buried.

He opened the door and stepped out into the snow. It crunched beneath his boots, the sound too loud in the stillness, as though the world had been waiting for him to move. The cold air bit into him, but he barely noticed. His thoughts were elsewhere, tangled up in the knots of guilt and fear that had been tightening inside him for days. He walked toward the building, his footsteps slow, each one heavier than the last.

The man wasn't ready for what awaited him inside, but what choice did he have? The past was catching up to him now, faster than he could run, and he could feel it pressing down on him, relentless as the snow that still fell, steady and unyielding. The slow, steady drip followed him to the door, echoing in the back of his mind like the ticking of a clock, counting down the moments until everything would unravel.

**

A few miles away, the man with the rough, short beard and blondish-brown hair moved briskly through the snow, his boots making shallow impressions in the white powder that had gathered overnight. His build is athletic yet understated, with the look of someone who moves through life with purpose, his strength hinted at in his stance rather than flaunted. His face is striking in its quiet depth, with light, piercing eyes that seem to mask as much as they reveal, often shadowed by a brooding thoughtfulness that's difficult to place. There's an inward quality to his gaze, as though he's both present and absent, watching from a distance even as he engages with the world. His complexion appears ruddy from the cold, cheeks slightly flushed beneath his beard. He wore a dark green jacket, its corduroy collar turned up against the biting air, and jeans that had begun to gather a fine dusting of snow along the cuffs. He contrasted sharply with the muted greys and whites of his surroundings. The jacket had seen better days, its fabric frayed at the edges, but it clung to him like a second skin, a reminder of the warmth that felt so far away. His jeans were well-worn, the fabric faded and soft, while sturdy boots crunched softly over the thin layer of snow that coated the ground, each step stirring up small flurries of powder that danced briefly in the air before settling back down. His light blue-grey eyes, sharp and restless, scanned the scene ahead of him but not with the urgency of someone in a hurry. No, his movements were deliberate, steady—purposeful, but not rushed.

With one hand, he fumbled at the phone in his pocket, the screen lighting up as he typed a quick message, eyes flicking between the device and the street before him. The other hand stayed in his pocket, curled into a loose fist as if guarding some inner tension, something coiled beneath the surface. His footsteps slowed as he reached the row of warehouses, structures long abandoned by whatever industry had once thrived there. The buildings loomed, silent and vacant, casting long, uneven shadows across the snow-laden ground. There was an air of dereliction about them, of forgotten purpose, their brick walls crumbling in places, graffiti scrawled across their facades as desperate splashes of colour against the monochrome of winter.

The man stopped in front of the one furthest down the line. It was the most intact, though the windows were coated in grease and grime, and the entrance door—heavy, rusted iron—stood slightly ajar, its edges crusted with frost. He glanced at his phone again, his thumb flew over the screen, the small light illuminating his face in the dim light of the early morning. The moment felt suspended in time, as if caught in a frame of a forgotten film, the noise of the outside world dimmed to a whisper. He glanced up, and the sight before him held him for a moment—a massive, heavy iron door framed by crumbling brick and peeling paint. Rust clung to the metal like old scars, a testament to years of neglect and abandonment. The door had an imposing presence, a watchman guarding the dark secrets held within. With a resigned sigh, he slid the door open, the iron groaning under the effort, the sound of metal scraping against concrete echoed in the empty space, a hollow, metallic groan that carried through the stillness like a falcon's cry in an open canyon.

Inside, the warehouse stretched out before him, an expanse of desolation. Shafts of weak light filtered through the grimy windows, illuminating dust motes suspended in the air, like fragments of memories caught in a web of time. The interior was a labyrinth of shadows and shapes, piles of debris littering the ground, forgotten artifacts of a bygone era. The air was colder still here than outside, untouched by the warmth of the pale winter sun. His breath came out in small, white clouds that lingered briefly before dissolving into the dimly lit interior. He paused just inside the entrance, turning back to grip the iron door with both hands, his muscles tensing as he dragged it shut with a loud, resonant clang. The sound reverberated through the warehouse, filling the space with an eerie silence after it faded. It was the sound of abandonment, of a place long devoid of life, where even the echoes felt hollow, detached from any living presence.

He stood there for a moment, still, listening to the space around him, attuning to its strange ambience, before stepping further inside, slamming the hefty door shut behind him with a finality that reverberated through the space, a sound that seemed to awaken the ghosts of those who had once toiled here. The atmosphere was thick with a palpable sense of history, of lives lived and lost in the service of industry. The iron beams overhead, rusted and flaking, spoke of the glory days when this place had pulsed with life, when it was a centre of production, a vital cog in the machine of a colonial empire that had spread across the globe.

Yet, here it lay, abandoned, a forgotten relic of London's industrial past, echoing the tales of colonisation and exploitation. The walls bore the scars of a forgotten time, the brickwork mottled with the marks of history. What had once been a hub of activity, a place where people worked side by side, was now a hollow shell, a husk of its former self. He felt that history, a burden that reminded him that the echoes of the past lingered still, threading their way through the fabric of the present.

The air was thick with dust and the scent of rust, a reminder of the iron that had once fuelled an empire's ambitions. He brushed a hand along a rusted beam, feeling the rough texture beneath his fingers, and for a moment, was transported back to a time when this space was filled with the sounds of clanging metal and the shouts of workers, a cacophony of life. Now, it was just silence, punctuated only by the soft drips of melting snow from the roof, each drop hitting the concrete floor like a heartbeat—slow, rhythmic, inevitable. The iron that had once signified strength and resilience now felt like a chain, binding him to a legacy of both triumph and tragedy. As the sunlight filtered through the grime of the windows, it illuminated the contrasts that surrounded him; the beauty in what once was, and the decay of what had come to be. It was a painful metaphor for his life.

He moved through the warehouse, each corner revealing remnants of the past—broken machinery, forgotten tools, a rusted cart overturned in a corner, as if abandoned in haste. The shadows stretched long across the floor, mingling with the remnants of snow that had drifted in through gaps in the walls, the cold creeping in like a memory that refused to fade. In that moment, he felt the profound connection between the space around him and the world outside, the past and the present intertwined like threads in a frayed tapestry.

Outside, the city continued to bustle, unaware of the stories contained within these walls. The industrial heart of London, once beating loud and strong, had shifted and evolved, yet remnants of that age now still lingered like ghosts. The man paused, his breath clouding in the air, contemplating the paradox of the warehouse: a space that spoke of both glory and decay, a testament to a time when the city had stood at the centre of a colonialised world, a hub of ambition and exploitation, and he felt an unsettling kinship with the place. The echoes of its history resonated with the complexities of his own existence, the way one life intertwined with another, each a delicate brushstroke in the larger painting of human experience. It was a reminder that perhaps there was not much difference between the world of the past and the globalised reality of today—a cycle of ambition, loss, and the relentless pursuit of something just out of reach.

The man took a deep breath, steeling himself against the chill that wrapped around him in an unwelcome embrace. He was not merely a visitor to this abandoned space but a participant in a narrative that spanned generations, a thread woven into the fabric of London itself. As he moved deeper into the shadows, history settled upon him more greatly, and he felt the eyes of the past upon him, watching, waiting. The falconer stood poised, aware that every step taken echoed not only through the empty warehouse but through the annals of time itself. And as he took that step, the rhythmic tapping of dripping water melded with the silence, a reminder that time, like the blood that fell in droplets onto the cold concrete, was an inescapable truth—one that bound the past and present in a relentless cycle of memory and consequence.

**

The suburbs, too, lay hushed under the snow. In one of those quiet, leafy enclaves, a street stood in starker contrast to the sleepy grandeur of the rowhouses. The tall, elegant façades, dark red brick stained with history, looked undisturbed, every window still drawn, shutters closed, as though nothing ever stirred behind them. But outside one, something shifted—a flash of movement, barely perceptible, but enough to disturb the stillness.

The young woman moved quickly but carefully, slipping through the alleyway that led around to the back of the building. She was in her mid-twenties, slender but strong, dressed in a worn leather jacket that clung to her shoulders. Her rich, chestnut brown hair frames her face, with expressive, blue eyes edged by thick, arching brows, she possesses a piercing gaze that shifts fluidly from warmth to razor-sharp focus, depending on the demands of the moment, and there is an undercurrent of urgency here—something fragile beneath the surface that belies her cool, methodical movements. She radiates a blend of determination and warmth that makes her both approachable and formidable. Her skin is fair, her cheeks often flushed with a natural colour that gives her a lively and accessible appearance, though there's no mistaking the intensity that lies beneath her calm exterior. Her features are strikingly delicate yet possess an underlying strength, with high cheekbones, a defined jawline, and a slightly upturned nose that gives her expressions a touch of spirited charm. Her lips, often pressed in thoughtful concentration or quirked in a slight, ironic smile, complete the look of a young woman who's seen her share of hardship, yet remains unwavering.

Behind her trailed a man, close in age but younger, his expression less assured. His pale face was tight with hesitation, and he kept glancing over his shoulder, as if waiting for something—or someone—to interrupt them.

She worked quickly, barely hesitating as she reached the door to the upstairs apartment. Her hands, slim but steady, moved with a precision that hinted at practice—perhaps more than she would care to admit. With a quiet click, the lock gave way, and she pushed the door open, a faint draft of cold air following her into the apartment.

The young man paused at the threshold, swallowing hard before stepping inside. His boots left faint, muddy tracks on the polished floor, and his breath, shallow and uneasy, mingled with the coolness of the room. The woman barely gave him a glance, already moving deeper into the space, her eyes scanning the walls, the furniture, every corner as though she were trying to gather as much information as possible in the shortest time.

The apartment was small but neat—lived-in, yet curiously devoid of the warmth one might expect. The furniture was minimal, the décor modern and restrained. There was nothing ostentatious about it, just an unsettling sterility to the place, as though whoever lived there hadn't quite managed to make it their own.

The woman's attention was pulled to the wardrobe in the corner. She yanked it open, fingers brushing hastily over clothes on hangers—neatly pressed shirts, jackets, and trousers that hung there with a kind of detached elegance.

She rifled through them quickly, her movements growing more frantic as she found nothing of interest. She turned to the shelves above, pulling down boxes, tossing their contents aside as if searching for something she couldn't quite name.

The young man lingered near the doorway, shifting from foot to foot, his brow furrowed. "What are we even looking for?" he asked in a hoarse whisper, as if the very walls of the apartment might betray them.

The woman didn't answer immediately, moving on to the bookcase. She ran her hands across the spines of the books, not bothering to read the titles, just searching for something—anything—that might provide a vital clue she was right. Her fingers brushed against framed photographs, knocking one to the floor in her haste. The glass shattered with a sharp crack, but she ignored it, moving on as though nothing had happened.

"Come on," urged the young man, his voice louder now, and tinged with frustration. "This is pointless. What are you even—"

But he stopped when he saw her face, her sharp focus suddenly locked on something else. Across the room, on a simple wooden desk, sat an old 35mm camera, its body sleek and black, worn at the edges with use. The woman's eyes narrowed, and she crossed the room in two quick strides, picking up the camera with both gloved hands as though it were something precious, fragile even.

She turned it over, inspecting it with a kind of reverence. The young man moved closer, peering over her shoulder. "What is it?" he asked, softer now, as though sensing something significant.

Again, she didn't answer him, her fingers too busy tracing the contours of the camera, the lens, the worn leather strap. But before she could open it or examine it further, her attention was drawn elsewhere—something on the wall. She turned, slowly this time, her breath catching in her throat as her eyes landed on a large black-and-white print framed on the far side of the room.

The young man followed her gaze, and the moment he saw it, his face paled even further. The image was stark, a haunting composition of light and shadow that dominated the wall. There was something about it—something unsettling in its simplicity, in the way the dark shapes bled into one another, the way the angles didn't quite make sense, yet drew the eye in all the same.

Neither of them spoke for a long moment. The woman took a step closer to the photograph, her eyes widening as if she were trying to make sense of what she was seeing, as if the image itself had some hidden meaning that only she could understand. The young man shifted beside her, his voice barely a whisper now. "Is that... what is that?"

The woman didn't answer, her breath coming in shallow gasps. She stared at the picture, her heart pounding in her chest. It was as if the image had reached out and taken hold of her, refusing to let go. Something in it, something indefinable, had sparked a deep, primal fear within her.

"We need to go, Tobes," she finally said, her voice noticeably shaky. "We need to get out of here now."

The young man hesitated, his eyes darting from the photograph to her face, but he didn't argue. He could see it in her eyes—that look of realisation, of understanding that came with the knowledge that something terrible may be about to happen. Without another word, they both turned and hurried out of the apartment, leaving the haunting image behind. Unbroken by weather and circumstance and slowing with every passing second, a grim metronome continued to play its tortured tune.

1

'A narrow Fellow in the Grass'

Jack Miller awoke with a throbbing ache behind his eyes, as if the night had left a residue of guilt woven into his skull. The words, *Every man shares the responsibility and the guilt of the society to which he belongs*, reverberated through his mind like the toll of some distant bell, heavy with the burden of half-forgotten things. He turned his head, squinting at the slant of morning light filtering through the curtains, and saw the woman beside him, her back gently rising and falling in a shallow rhythm. The sight of her stirred a sadness within him, sharp and brief like the bite of winter air. Then came the guilt—deeper, slower—a familiar ache in his bones.

He stretched, feeling the tug of pain along his spine, a dull reminder of age or perhaps just consequence. Virtue, he mused, had always been bound to pain, but the connection seemed tenuous this morning, fragile and frayed. His thoughts wandered, as they often did, on a journey that often led nowhere. Questions swirled, offering no solace, only a vague unease that clung to him like the remnants of a bad dream. He had lived in this place, this mental fog, for over a decade now, drifting through time without tether or purpose.

A memory surfaced, older than the rest. It was distant, blurred by the years, like peering through the cracks of a weathered fence, catching glimpses but never the full picture. He remembered the hand—a gnarled, aged thing—

on his shoulder. It had been Professor Stephens' hand, though the man it belonged to had seemed older that day, more worn than Jack remembered. Outside the walls of the lecture hall, in the unforgiving daylight, Stephens had looked every bit the relic of his own cultural philosophies, the years etched into his face, his skin pulled taut over his brittle bones.

That day, outside a small café not far from The Strand, Stephens had joined Jack and a fellow student—a bright-eyed psychology lad named Charlie, a couple of years Jack's junior. The meeting had been unplanned, unexpected, like so many things in Jack's life. Stephens, notorious for mingling with his students, had asked if he could sit with them, and Jack, half-flattered, had obliged. The professor launched into a casual lecture, the topic drifting unexpectedly toward Epicurean pleasure. Jack could still hear the professor's voice in his mind, rasping through those ancient tenets: freedom from fear, the absence of pain.

The words had stayed with Jack, fragments of a legacy long since reduced to dust and scattered letters. But there had been something else—something Charlie had said as Stephens left, leaving Jack to foot the bill for his espressos.

"So, the gods do not punish humans," Charlie had mused, almost absently. "But neither do they reward them. I wonder how Stephens feels about that. He didn't mention judgment, did he?"

It had been a passing comment, the kind of thing that lingers in the air for a moment before drifting away, but it had stayed with Jack somehow, somewhere on the periphery of his thoughts. Even now, as he lay in the half-light, staring at the ceiling, he could hear Charlie's voice, clear as if it had only been yesterday. Or maybe it had. Time, for Jack, had long since lost its shape, stretching and folding back on itself, blurring the line between memory and reality.

Jack's attention drifted to the dresser where the metronome continued its quiet, persistent quest. It marked time in a way that seemed both arbitrary and precise, each second distinct, as if they existed in separate universes. He imagined it—each tick a solitary figure, unconnected to the last, floating in that fourth dimension, where time did not concern itself with the past or the future, simply marking the present, second by second. Time, he thought, was more than the grass, more than the surface it hid beneath. It was a snake in the grass—the narrow fellow that slipped between moments, dividing one from the other, unnoticed until it suddenly reared its head.

He tried to hold onto that thought, but like so many others, it wrinkled and faded as soon as he reached for it. The metronome, oblivious to his philosophising, continued its steady, tireless journey, casting tiny flecks of dust into the sunlight that crept, sly and insistent, through the blinds. The sound didn't wake him—nothing did, not really—but it was always there, a quiet barrier between him and sleep.

He stood, his limbs heavy, his body slow to respond as if his bones were made of lead. They always told him it was simple: just put one foot in front of the other. The top of the mountain wasn't important, only the next step. So, he moved, each step a conscious, deliberate effort. His head pounded in rhythm with the ticking metronome, a double-time march as he made his way through the apartment. The bottle of whiskey on the breakfast bar caught his eye—nearly empty—and the sight of it in the morning light made him wince in a way it hadn't the night before. He had been too tired to notice, then. Or, too tired to care.

Now, even in the dull light of morning, he was too tired to see anything that mattered. This day would not be different from the others, he thought. Perhaps a handful of small moments would set it apart, but it would blend into the rest, a single note in a song that never ended. As he opened the fridge, his thoughts wandered. For a brief moment, he saw himself as the metronome—a small figure in the vast field of time, moving from one second to the next, caught in the same inexorable rhythm. He was a snake in the grass, too, seeing his life laid out like blades of grass on either side, but unable to change his course.

Without taking anything from the fridge, he let the door close, reaching instead for a glass and filling it from the tap. He drank quickly, the cold water doing little to clear the fog in his head. Placing the empty glass next to the one from the night before, he leaned against the counter, still lost in thought. For a moment, he saw himself as Frost's stranger—pausing, just for a second, at the edge of the woods while time marched on around him. The stillness of that moment was deceptive, he knew. Momentum was an illusion, but it was the absence of it that allowed time to creep in, to expand and fill the space around him.

There's something the dead are keeping back. The words clawed at him, words he had first encountered, not in his studies, but in Mikal Gilmore's book about the execution of his brother—a rare foray into the fiction of true crime. A shiver ran down Jack's spine as he remembered. He felt a sudden jolt in his body, as if he had slipped momentarily out of consciousness, like a driver nodding off at the wheel. His knees bent involuntarily, and he steadied himself, his eyes catching the nearly empty bottle of whiskey above him. It loomed there, a silent reminder of something he tried not to think about but couldn't escape—a date that hovered in his mind like the narrow fellow in the grass, always there, waiting. Jack's thoughts circled around it, a growing agitation stirring in his chest. The obsessions came creeping in, like the whiplash of a sudden turn. They unbraided themselves in the summer light, twisting and coiling around his mind, pulling him back toward that fateful date, that inevitable reckoning.

He drew in a deep breath, trying to compose himself as the familiar pressure behind his eyes pressed harder. He glanced at his watch. Late again. The ticking of time, relentless as ever, offered no mercy. He walked back to the bedroom, searching for a fresh shirt, trousers, his jacket draped over the chair in the corner—it was all rote, a daily ritual performed with mechanical indifference. His movements, like the metronome's ticks, were precise, measured, but hollow.

In the bathroom, he brushed his teeth, watching his reflection in the mirror. The face that stared back at him seemed distant, almost as if it actually belonged to someone else, someone caught in a moment he didn't recognise.

Back in the living room, he grabbed a pen from the coffee table and scrawled a note on a scrap of paper, leaving it under the empty glass he'd just set down. The black-and-white photographic print on the table remained untouched, unseen—a fragment of some forgotten moment that held no significance. The metronome, steady and indifferent, continued to mark time, each second bleeding into the next without meaning. Jack's headache pulsed in time with its rhythm.

When he finally stepped out of the apartment, the heat hit him like a wave, thick and oppressive. His car, parked on the street, shimmered under the sun. The metal of the door handle burned his fingers as he grasped it, a sharp, stinging reminder of the world's indifference. Inside, the air was suffocating, the kind of stifling heat that made his head pound even harder, turning his thoughts into a swirling mess. He stumbled into the driver's seat, barely aware of how he'd gotten there. For a moment, he just sat there, staring blankly through the windscreen, his mind adrift.

These were the days when Jack cursed himself for not retiring when the chance had come. He could have escaped all this—the grind, the meaningless repetition, the endless ticking of time. But he had stayed, ploughing forward like a farmer too intent on his soil to notice that he had wandered into a bog. There was no grass now, no clear path. Just the stench of decay and the slow, steady pull of something unseen beneath the surface. A home for snakes, no doubt.

The veins in Jack's head felt like serpents, coiling tighter, constricting his thoughts. His eyes fell to the passenger seat where Gibbard's *Wise Choices, Apt Feelings* lay—a recommendation from Haggard, something meant to guide Jack deeper into the recesses of his own emotions. A futile endeavour, Jack thought. His emotions were a tangled mess, long since buried beneath the weight of too many days like this one. Still, he had tolerated others' anger, internalised the values expected of him, delivered results as was required. And somehow, despite everything, he was admired. It was a mystery to him, this admiration. His mind, sharpened by experience in some ways, felt dull and dead in others. Without Ed by his side, Jack knew he wouldn't have lasted this long.

Ed had carried him through, day by day, keeping things together when Jack could not. Seniority didn't matter between them. Friendship was the thing that made it all work. Jack had never quite understood what he had done to deserve such loyalty. Perhaps friendship wasn't something one deserved. Perhaps one day he would repay Ed, though how, Jack couldn't say. Ed was climbing higher, poised to outpace Jack in every respect. It seemed inevitable now that the roles would reverse, that Jack would be the one supporting Ed someday, if the fates had any say in it. But then, what did the fates know?

Each day was the same, the metronome marking the seconds, one exactly like the last. It was Jack's personal atomic clock, marching on with military precision, never missing a beat. It didn't care about the pain, the empty moments, the choices not taken. It just kept going, leaving everything in its wake, pain and all, unmarked and forgotten by the roadside. Time, Jack thought, wasn't something you escaped. It pursued you, doggedly, like Frost's stranger.

He couldn't remember when it had started—when time had begun to chase him. There was no point to recall, no moment to pinpoint. Time had always been there, circling, encroaching, a pursuer without end. It had no future but itself, no purpose but to continue, infinitely, through realms Jack could barely comprehend.

Time stretched before him, a vast expanse that flickered in and out of Jack's awareness as he sat there, hands on the wheel, eyes staring ahead. It was there, as it always had been, lying in wait, patient and unhurried. Time had been waiting for Jack from the moment he first faced the world, as if it had always known he would one day return to this moment, this interminable pause before action. The road ahead, cutting through the earth like a scar through the grass, twisted and unfurled, a narrow fellow winding toward some unknown destination. The grass itself—cool beneath, hot above—was unforgiving, a path not meant for bare feet, not meant for rest.

How could Jack notice anything else? The car behind him, parked across the street, was just another fixture in the blurred landscape of his life, something neither to be seen nor remembered. No one got out of it, and no one seemed to follow him when he drove away. The vehicle existed merely on the edge, unnoticed, like so many other things in Jack's life. He had become too accustomed to seeing without observing, too busy surviving the moments that passed to concern himself with what lay behind him.

Driving was no different. Another dimension, another rhythm for Jack to move through. Behind the wheel, he became the metronome once more, the steady pulse of the city beating with each turn of the tires. Life flew by on either side, scattered like the wind over the tall grass, bending the blades until they fell, flattened and indistinguishable. Jack drove, not in pursuit of anything, but merely to stay ahead of the relentless ticking of time. The road stretched out before him, indifferent and unmoving, while the world slipped away behind him.

If Jack had looked in his rearview mirror, he might have seen the driver of the parked car pull out a mobile phone and make a call. That would have been all—just a small, insignificant gesture in the flow of time. But Jack's eyes were on the road, and his mind was occupied by the mechanics of work, not the details of the street behind him. The metronome continued to tick within him, marking the seconds, the minutes, the hours—each one falling into the next with the same quiet, indifferent precision.

He was working now, and that was all that mattered. The world could rush by, and cars could follow, or not, but Jack's mind was already elsewhere, caught in the steady rhythm of the task ahead. There was no room for distractions, no space for the things that might have mattered once. Time stretched on, and Jack, like the metronome, moved within it, a small, ticking pulse in a world that never stopped.

2
'The Mysteries of Pain'

It was only a little while after Jack had left the apartment that the woman he had been next to stirred, perhaps roused by the distant hum of traffic creeping in through the gaps in the window frame. She turned, blinking at the empty space beside her, her eyes drifting to the metronome. The smooth, silver ball swayed with infuriating precision, and for a moment, she imagined tearing it from its delicate perch. Unlike Jack, she felt no comfort in its mechanical rhythm. To hold time in your hand, to freeze it there, would be like pulling the heart from the very fabric of the universe, she thought. But then, isn't that what we're all doing, anyway?

The thought of it twisted her stomach, but she let it settle. Things fall apart, she mused—who is the falcon, and who the falconer? The gyre widened with each passing year, perspective slipping away like the metronome's beat, impossible to reclaim. But today was Sunday, and for once, she felt a strange anticipation for it.

She sat up, ignoring the protest of her muscles, and rose quickly, a battle of wills between body and mind. She had grown accustomed to drinking more than she ever had before, and the nausea that had lingered in her gut disappeared just as suddenly as it had come. She put on some music, *WILDFLOWER*, by Billie Eilish, and it played softly in the background behind her.

Her head was surprisingly clear, save for the stale taste of last night on her breath, a problem easily remedied. In the bathroom she brushed her teeth with determined vigour, rinsing away the remnants of her indulgence, and glanced reluctantly at the mirror.

Her reflection had become something she often avoided. The face that stared back at her now carried traces of time she had once believed wouldn't touch her. Lines faint but deepening around her eyes, her mouth, her forehead—a map of her years traced in subtle relief. They reminded her of why she preferred not to look, why the mirror's gaze felt like an interrogation she had long tired of.

The heat in the apartment built up quickly, it was stifling now, thick and oppressive, so she opened the bathroom window, letting in a faint, warm autumnal breeze. She considered removing Jack's shirt—it smelled of her now, not him—but it felt like him, and that sensation of his presence was one she missed more than she could admit. She lingered at the mirror again before stepping away, whispering softly to her reflection, "Face it, Charley. You're not a girl. You're a woman."

Returning to the bedroom, she noted the slight coolness there, a relief from the thick heat of the rest of the apartment. She hadn't left the window ajar when she went to bed, but Jack must have cracked it open when he came home. She glanced at the clock—8:07 a.m.—and made the mental correction: five minutes fast. Time again, always five minutes ahead, always a little out of reach.

Relentless, she thought, are our obsessions—how they consume every second we give them, and yet somehow, they keep us motionless, tethered in place in a way that can be almost comforting, reassuring. But today, the sickness in her stomach felt different, like the herald of a shift long overdue. These past few months had changed her. She was ready now, ready to move on, to move forward, but Jack wasn't. That, perhaps, was the source of her nausea—the familiar drag of his inertia, his feet sinking deeper into the bog while she felt the sky, wide and boundless, calling her name. Somewhere up there, the falcon circled.

It had something to do with a man who had shown her, in ways she hadn't expected, that despite the tension between her skin and bones, despite the slow wasting of her once-full flesh, she was still beautiful. It was the monochrome portrait that had done it, revealing a truth she had half-forgotten. Only a partial truth, of course—an image could never capture everything—but it had soothed something in her, the way a fleeting vice could momentarily quiet the ever-churning mind.

But the photograph carried another truth, one it couldn't display outright, though Charley had come to feel it more keenly with time. A truth not etched into the paper but hidden in a dimension far beyond the physical. What she saw, beyond the face she'd lived with for forty-two years, the face she'd both loathed and loved in turns, was a face others had loved more than she had ever understood—and still did. But now, more than ever, she knew that love was not enough.

The photo, in its stark simplicity, had shown her in the gentlest way that this apartment, with all its quiet corners and empty spaces, would never ring with the laughter of a child. It was a fact that cast shadows on her heart in ways she couldn't quite explain. Time, once again, seemed like a child—innocent, running ahead on an open road, the sun on its back, turning only to beckon her to follow. But she wasn't sure she could. It was a race she wasn't certain she could finish alone.

Lost in these thoughts, Charley drifted toward the coffee table, her feet carrying her without her noticing. The whiskey glass, Jack's note—they meant little to her now, caught in the swamp of her own internal turmoil. It was only when she found herself finishing her first glass that she realised she had already poured a second. And then, well, she might as well finish the bottle. After all, she was meeting Seth in the park soon, and after lunch, she could pick up another bottle to warm the evening that loomed ahead. A cold, quiet evening, like so many others.

Two more short glasses emptied the bottle, and Charley finally made her way back to the bedroom. She stripped off Jack's shirt, the cotton weighing on her aching body, and kicked away the lace of her underwear with a dismissive flick of her foot. Naked, she crossed to the bathroom for her morning shower, the ritual that restored her skin to some semblance of its once-bright radiance, even as time chipped away at it, recalibrating its decline. The water soothed her mind, too, washing away the lingering shadows that had clung to her since waking. When she stepped out, she felt brighter, more optimistic about the day ahead.

The phone had been ringing while she was in the shower, the sound muffled by the rush of water through her hair. Now, as she padded across the apartment, still damp and not bothering with a towel in the heat, she reached for the phone. But as soon as she picked it up, the line clicked and went dead. She shrugged, assuming she'd taken too long to answer. It didn't occur to her to check the caller ID. The call, like so many things, seemed insignificant.

She set the handset down on the coffee table next to the photograph, her eyes barely grazing its surface. Instead, she felt a sudden whim pull her toward the window, and without thinking, she drew back the sitting room blinds. The sunlight flooded in, sharp and merciless, lighting up the room, the photo, and the empty bottle beside it. It was Sunday, after all, and she was ready for whatever was left of it.

Sunlight poured into the room, painting her naked body in a soft glow. For a moment or two, she stood there, unhurried, letting the warmth wash over her skin. She didn't care who might see—her body was just that, a body. No more, no less. A simple, inert mass, a vessel of flesh and bone that once carried meaning but now felt like an object separate from herself. The sunlight refracted off her, giving her a kind of transient, ethereal beauty, but it was a beauty she no longer recognised as her own. She hung there in the window, motionless, like a marionette suspended by invisible strings, until the passing rumble of a car below snapped her out of the reverie.

She moved to open the two larger windows, though there was little breeze to be found. What wind there was, weak and fleeting, existed only because of the building's position, a kind of artificial air that barely stirred the room. Still, the breeze touched her skin and dried it, leaving only her hair damp, clinging stubbornly to the nape of her neck. It was almost dry now, tangled and knotted, reminding her that she would soon have to leave this space of fragile solitude and deal with herself, with the world outside.

Before she did, she flicked on the air-conditioning, the hum of the machine filling the quiet as she felt the room grow gradually cooler. For the first time that morning, she began to feel comfortable. She found her hairbrush and ran it half-heartedly through the tangles, just enough to make the worst of them manageable, and pulled her hair into two careless pigtails. She had kept it short over the past year, a symbol, perhaps, of control. But lately, she had neglected it, and it had grown longer, fuller, less something she could manage, more something she let be.

Her eyes drifted back to the coffee table, where Jack's note and the photograph still lay. A small, sharp pang ran through her, a mix of guilt and grief, though she couldn't be bothered to figure out which object sparked which emotion. It didn't matter, not right now. It was too much to confront, and yet it clung to her, that quiet pain. She let out a sound that might have been a laugh, but there was no humour in it—only fear. Fear of her own feelings, of the things she didn't want to face but couldn't shake.

She picked up Jack's note, opened it slowly, and read the words twice before they began to register. The first time through, she didn't even see the words, only the blurred, familiar shapes of his handwriting, the curves and lines that once felt like home. She remembered letters he had written her before, notes that had warmed her in ways she couldn't explain, words that had been a balm. But now, reading this note, she felt only a shudder. She wasn't cold, though she stood naked in the middle of the room—her shudder came from somewhere deeper, a ripple of regret. The kind of regret that doesn't announce its beginnings but lingers like an unwelcome guest, reminding you that its presence is all that matters.

By the time she left the apartment, it was ten past ten. She didn't need to look at the clock to know she was late; she had felt it, unavoidable, from the moment she woke. She only hoped it wouldn't matter. Jack's note, its meaning still unclear, lingered with her as she stepped out into the world, the sun blazing overhead, the heat pressing down. But it was the coldness of uncertainty that rasped at her, trailing behind her hurried steps like a shadow.

3

'As by the dead we love to sit'

On his way to work that morning, Jack Miller had no inkling he was being followed. Why would he? There had been nothing about the day to raise his suspicion. It was the same city, the same street, the same muted rhythm of the early morning, yet something imperceptible had shifted. Some subtle disturbance in the routine distracted him, pulling his mind from its usual track, the one that had guided him without deviation for years. It had led him to this place—one of two places Jack had haunted for the better part of a decade, always moving between them, never lingering in either for long. This place, a Godless sanctuary within a space consecrated to God, was a contradiction, much like Jack's own existence. Life in a realm of death.

Jack stood at the entrance of Highgate Cemetery, staring past the heavy wrought iron gates at the tangled, haphazard rows of gravestones. The cemetery spread out before him in a dense, uneven labyrinth beneath the swaying trees. It was a quiet day, the kind of morning where the sky hung low, a pale, indecisive grey, unsure whether to bring rain or sun. The ambivalence in the air suited his mood. He came here often, though not for solace in the traditional sense. Jack hadn't prayed, not in almost forty years, since He had failed to answer Jack's request that He return his parents. With each passing day, the thought of kneeling to some higher power became more impossible, not less.

He walked the familiar path, gravel crunching underfoot, past the dilapidated headstones that leaned at odd angles, some lost entirely beneath thick layers of ivy. The earth, slow and patient, seemed to be reclaiming its own. Jack had always found something curiously alive about this place, as if the dead beneath him hadn't quite given up their hold on the world above. There was a pulse here, faint but persistent, a whisper of the past that hummed through the air.

Karl Marx's grave had become a sort of waypoint for him, a place where he could retreat when the noise in his head became too much. It wasn't Marx's ideology that drew him—Jack had no interest in revolutions or manifestos. What he sought was the equilibrium the grave offered, a stillness after the storm of thought. Marx's stone bust, imposing and immovable, seemed to offer a kind of finality, a place where ideas came to rest, exhausted after years of battle.

As Jack neared the grave, he saw someone standing there—a figure, tall and unmoving, slightly bent forward as if in conversation with the monument itself. The man wore a dark coat, loose and well-worn, the kind of garment that had weathered years but still held its form. His long hair, dense and dreadlocked, was tied loosely at the back, thick and substantial, cascading down like a lion's mane.

Jack hesitated, unsure whether to approach. It felt wrong to disturb someone at a graveside. This was a place of contemplation, of tranquillity. Yet something about the figure was unsettlingly familiar, as if Jack had seen him before, or as though this moment had already happened in some forgotten dream. He cleared his throat softly, more out of habit than intent.

The man turned, slowly, deliberately, his dark eyes meeting Jack's with an expression that held neither surprise nor curiosity. It was a look of quiet acceptance, as though he had been waiting for Jack all along. The man's lips curled into a slow smile, revealing bright, but yellowing, teeth. It wasn't the smile of a stranger; it was the kind of smile that acknowledged something unspoken, something both men understood, though Jack could not have said what it was. In the stillness of the cemetery, between the living and the dead, it felt as though time itself had paused, holding its breath for just a moment.

"Ah," the man said, in a voice deep and resonant, "you come to pay ya respects to the old man, too, eh?"

Jack nodded, feeling a little awkward, but the man's tone was warm and inviting. "Yeah," Jack replied. "I come here sometimes. When I need to think."

The man extended a hand. "Jack," he said simply.

Jack blinked, taken aback for a second, then smiled. "Jack, also," he said, shaking the offered hand warmly. "Jack Miller."

"Ah, we two Jacks," the man laughed, the sound rich and full of life. "Call me Jamaican Jack," he added, the nickname rolling off his tongue with an ease that spoke of long familiarity. "People have come to know me how they see me, because part of what they see in me is what they recognise from inside themselves. I suppose what I'm saying, Jack, is that you and I are not so different. Perhaps you'd like us to be, though?"

"I very much like that we are not so different. But difference can be good too, wouldn't you say?"

"Aye man, that I would. Just so long as you don't use it as a means of making yourself better than the next man, and so you don't let him become your master either. It never hurt to remember it's the similarities that bind us though, Jack. However good or bad, we are all driven by the same motives, the same emotions at the heart of all our actions.

You see it in the times we celebrate together, and the times we reel back in horror."

"Well, it's nice to meet you, Jack," he said. "What brings you here?"

Jamaican Jack turned back toward the grave, his expression softening into something more serious, more reflective. "The dead, my friend. They always bring me here. There's something in sitting with them, you know? Like they keep your company, even when you don't ask for it. As by the dead we love to sit, yeah?"

Jack nodded, and the Jamaican gestured to him to sit on the bench by Marx's tombstone. Jack obliged, he knew that poem only too well, and he knew the feeling better. The dead, with their silence, often spoke more clearly than the living. "I come here for that too," he admitted. "There's something... steady about it. Even though it's all over for them, it feels like they're still part of something."

Jamaican Jack smiled, a glint of understanding in his eyes. "You got it, man... The dead, they don't bother with all this noise we carry around. They done lived through it all, seen it all. Now they just sit and listen. And we... We get to sit with them, share in their quiet." He gestured toward Marx's bust, towering above them. "And this old man, he's seen more than most, I reckon."

Jack looked up at the face of Marx, that familiar, unyielding expression of stone, staring out into the distance as if watching the world continue to spiral in the very ways he had tried to predict and reshape. But now he was silent, and that peace was what drew Jack here. The theories, struggles, ideas—none of it mattered anymore to the man beneath the stone. There was only the stillness of being; the long exhale after the effort.

"I think that's why I come here," Jack said quietly, almost to himself. "It's like a reminder that everything we think is so important eventually ends. And what's left is… well, this. Stillness."

Jamaican Jack let out a soft hum of agreement. "Yeah, man. But stillness isn't so bad, you know. It's peaceful. We get caught up in so much. Like we always running toward something. But maybe what we're really running toward is the stillness. Maybe that's the real endgame, eh?"

Jack frowned, considering the thought. He had always feared that idea, the idea that stillness meant an end to everything, the quiet that came after the struggle. But now, standing here beside another man named Jack, he wondered if this tall Jamaican was right. Perhaps there was peace in it, not defeat, but something more final, something inevitable. The dead knew it, he thought. They had already reached that stillness, that ultimate understanding.

Jamaican Jack glanced sideways at him. "You ever think about death, Jack Miller?"

The question, though simple, startled him. Of course, he thought about it. In his job, how could he not? It seemed impossible not to, especially in a place like this, surrounded by the constant presence of death. But to admit it felt like stepping into a darker place than he was prepared for. "Sometimes… More than you might think," Jack replied carefully. "I think about it when I come here. It's hard not to."

"Yeah, man," Jamaican Jack nodded, his tone easy, unpressured. "But you know, I think about it a lot, too. Not in a bad way. Just… like a reminder, you know? Like the dead, they remind us that life is short, and we waste a lot of time running from things that don't matter in the end. When we should be sitting with them, listening to them."

Jack stayed silent for a moment, watching the sunlight filter through the leaves, casting dappled shadows on the ground. Jamaican Jack's words settled into his mind, joining his own thoughts, his own unspoken fears. He thought of Charley, of the growing distance between them, of the strange, unresolved tension that gnawed at him daily. They had both been running, hadn't they? But toward what? Or away from what?

"You ever read that poem?" Jamaican Jack asked. "It's by an old lady named Emily Dickinson. She wrote, 'As by the dead we love to sit, become so wondrous dear.' I always liked that line. It's like, by sitting with the dead, we get a bit of their wisdom. Like they teach us, without saying a word."

Jack nodded. He knew the poem from long before this path he know trod, and the line struck him, hard, in its simplicity. As if only today he had heard it for the first time. The wisdom of the dead. He had never thought of it that way, but now, standing here, he felt it. There was a strange clarity in death, in the quiet presence of those who had lived, struggled, and then moved on.

"Yeah, I do know her," Jack said softly. "I like that. I think that's why I keep coming back here. To learn something, maybe."

Jamaican Jack smiled; his eyes were warm with understanding. "Yeah, man. We listen, and we learn. And maybe, just maybe, we start to see what really matters."

They sat in silence for a while after that, the two Jacks, beside the grave of Karl Marx, feeling the weight of the world lift just a little as they shared in the wisdom of the dead. Jamaican Jack's long fingers traced an absent pattern in the air as he considered Jack's last words. The breeze stirred the trees gently, the faint hum of the city beyond the cemetery walls just a dull murmur now, leaving them in the quiet embrace of history. Jack glanced at him, sensing there was more the man had to say, something deeper hidden beneath his easy demeanour.

Jamaican Jack tilted his head slightly, eyes narrowing as if in thought. "You see, my friend," he began slowly, "when I was a young man, back in Jamaica, I didn't know much about the world. My family, we was poor, like most folks round there, but we had pride, you know? We had roots deep in the soil, roots that went back to the days of slavery. My grandmother, she used to tell me stories, stories of our people, of how we come from Africa in chains, brought to these islands where they tried to make us forget who we was. They wanted us to be nothing, just bodies for labour. But you can't forget where you come from, no matter how hard they try to strip it from you."

Jack listened quietly, drawn into the rhythm of Jamaican Jack's words. There was a cadence there, a depth that hinted at pain but also strength, poetry even.

"I learned about oppression from a young age," Jamaican Jack continued, his voice steady, eyes fixed on the headstone as though communing with Marx himself. "You don't have to be a philosopher or some big man scholar to feel it. You feel it in your bones, in the way people look at you, the way they treat you different. In Jamaica, the memory of colonialism is like a shadow that never leaves. The British took everything from us—our land, our language, our names. Even when we was free, we wasn't really free, eh? The chains were still there, just invisible. And we carried them on with us."

He paused, his voice becoming softer, more reflective. "But, you see, oppression—it makes you strong, if it doesn't break you first. My grandmother used to say that the soul is like a tree. The more you try to bury it, the deeper its roots grow. And she was right. We took their language, their religion, and we made it ours. We found strength in resistance, in remembering what they wanted us to forget."

Jack shifted on his feet slightly. It was a perspective he had always tried to understand but could never fully grasp. The depth of history Jamaican Jack spoke of wasn't just personal—it was generational, an inheritance of pain and resilience passed down from ancestor to ancestor.

"When I first came to England," Jamaican Jack said, his voice now quieter, as if turning inward, "I thought things would be different. I was a young man, you know, full of dreams… I'd seen pictures of London—big, shiny buildings, all the history, all the promise. But when I got here… man, it wasn't what I thought. The weather, for one," he chuckled, though there was no real mirth in his voice. "But more than that, it was the people. The way they looked at me. Like I didn't belong. Like I was some kind of intruder… You know the first time I looked in a dictionary the only word I looked for was Rastafari. I wanted to find out what the white man, the scholar, thought we were. How he defined us, as a people. Do you know what I found?"

Jack turned to the calm, deep voice that had spoken to him. "No, what?" he replied, softly.

"I found nothing. The white man, in his exalted chamber, in his illustrious gowns and hats had decreed we were not worthy of his acceptance. The Buddhist, the Sikh, the Hindu, they had their place in his world, but we were denied one. I was angry, I was angry for a very long time about that. Then, I realised something, I realised many things, actually. And this man, he helped me."

Jack turned back from the tall, dark stranger and looked back upon the tomb. "Someone once described him to me as a Godless man."

"And to me. And to me. I have heard those words about him many times. God and Communism do not reconcile," he chuckled, loudly, from the depths of himself.

Jack felt a pang of recognition. The cold, distant gaze of England—the way it could shut people out, even those born within its borders. But for Jamaican Jack, it must have been worse, far worse. The feeling of otherness, of being alien in a land that had once claimed dominion over your ancestors. Jack looked at him, noticing the lines of his face, carved not by age but by the harshness of experience.

"In Jamaica, we knew what oppression was, but we knew it together. Here, it's different. Here, they make you feel small in ways you don't even realise. You walk down the street, and people cross the road to avoid you. You try to get a job, and they act like they're doing you a favour, even when you're more qualified than the next man. And all the while, they remind you—in small ways, in subtle ways—that you don't really belong."

Jamaican Jack let out a long breath, his eyes clouded for a moment as he stared down at the ground. "But you learn to live with it. You learn to find pride in yourself, even when the world doesn't want to give it to you. You have to… That's the only way you survive. You realise that they can't take everything from you, no matter how hard they try. They can't take your history. They can't take your soul, Jack Miller, eh?"

Jack remained silent, absorbing the enormity of what Jamaican Jack was saying. It was a perspective he had often wondered about, but hearing it firsthand felt different, heavier. The quiet indignities of daily life, the thousand cuts that added up over time. It was something he had never truly faced—his own privilege, his own place in the world, had insulated him from that reality. But standing here now, in the presence of this man who had lived through so much, Jack felt a stirring of something uncomfortable, something that gnawed at the edges of his mind.

"The funny thing is," Jamaican Jack said with a small, sad smile, "England thinks it's the centre of the world. But they don't realise how small they've made themselves by shutting the rest of us out. They don't see that their history is tied up with ours. They want to act like they not responsible for what they did in Jamaica, Africa, in India... But history won't go away just because you ignore it."

He looked at Jack, his eyes clear and piercing. "You ever read much about Haile Selassie, Jack?"

Jack shook his head. The name was familiar, but not much more than that.

"Haile Selassie was the Emperor of Ethiopia," Jamaican Jack explained. "He was the one who stood up to Mussolini when Italy invaded Ethiopia. The League of Nations wouldn't help him. England wouldn't help him. They all stood by and watched. But Selassie—he didn't back down. He fought. And he became a symbol, not just for Ethiopia, but for all of us who had been oppressed. He was our lion. He showed us that even when the world turns its back on you, you don't give up. You keep fighting."

Jamaican Jack's voice took on a new intensity, a quiet fire burning beneath his calm exterior. "That's why the Rastas look to him as a prophet, as a leader. He represents the strength of our people, the power to resist, even when it seems hopeless. And that's the thing about history, you see. It's not just about what happened. It's about what we carry with us, what we choose to remember."

"Many races believe they are the chosen ones, but only the white European has ever had the unrivalled nerve to act like it so damn despicable... You know many people have done many things, terrible and good, in the name of many, not least God, but not many have dared to place such a small price on a human life as the white European."

At this point, the Rastafarian rested back for a few seconds to take a gentle pause. Everything about him seemed gentle to Jack at the moment; his breathing, his limbs in respite and the gentleness, appeared magnified against the giant, physical presence. Jack how the Rastafarian seemed to fill the tiny space he occupied and dwarf his neighbour. Jack and the giant, and there was little doubt the giant could smell the blood of this Englishman. Engrossed in mythology, Jack had begun to understand the fairytale differently; the significance of those magic beans became paramount.

Jamaican Jack continued, "When I first read Marx, I thought him Godless too, for a while. But when I understood him, then I saw something different. The absence of God was all around me. It was in the history of the nations from which I was forged. If Marx was Godless, it was because he saw the absence of God in the actions of men... Tell me Jack, what race is there on Earth to better understand the motive of profit than the one with which I share my heritage, eh?"

Jack, still silent, looked back and considered that thought. He knew the Rastafarian didn't expect an answer. The understanding between them was unspoken. But Jack thought on, as he took in the features of the man next to him – how would such a man have been described in the great literary texts he had studied with such interest all those years ago at Kings College?

A wide nose, thick lips, teeth and eyes of ivory white. There would have been *that* word, too, used in that supposedly harmless, old-fashioned way. Jack could, if he searched, just about remember some of the characters, a term used loosely because character implied some sense of individualism. The *great* works. The heritage of the Empire. He remembered how students were encouraged to be sympathetic to the abuse these races had suffered, still suffered, but also how sympathy can simply create victims. He considered how, for all the Christian understanding and moral outrage, they had emerged beautifully from the dark jungles of Africa and the sands of Arabia as victims, exoticised. Victims of their own backwardness, victims of their own difference; different only because the system that had judged them was immoveable, beyond question. In His name. He, in whose name the system was practised and exalted until He was forgotten altogether, and the system became a deity in itself.

These thoughts that Jack knew would take ages to extract and to order on paper had passed through his brain clearly and fleetingly, almost untouchable, so that barely seconds had passed between them. Such was the thoroughness of his mind, one prone to analysis, the skill that made him a first-class honours student and an excellent policeman. It was as if such thoughts were layered, like lengths of one-dimensional string, concurrent in the space they occupied but with a visibility and texture which was hard to grasp and cling to. He nodded as he felt the tall Jamaican's words settle into his bones. It felt as if he had never thought of history in that way before—not as something that lived and breathed in the present, but as a force that actively shaped who you were in the present, how you saw the world, and also how the world saw you. Jamaican Jack's view of history wasn't abstract; it was personal, lived, a constant reminder of the struggles and triumphs of those who came before him.

For a moment, the two men sat in silence again, the gravestones around them standing as silent witnesses to their conversation. Jack felt the wind shift slightly, carrying with it the faintest scent of damp earth and old leaves. It was as if the cemetery itself had heard Jamaican Jack's words and was responding in its own quiet way, reminding them both that time, and history, were ever-present.

Jamaican Jack let out a long breath, his eyes softening. "You know, Marx had some things right," he said, glancing back at the bust of the philosopher. "He knew that the world is built on oppression, that those at the top will always try to keep us down. But what he didn't see was that it's not just about class, it's about race, too. And if you don't see that, you miss the whole picture."

Jack nodded, feeling the truth of that settle deep within him. He had always thought of Marxism in abstract terms, as a theory, a critique of capitalism. But Jamaican Jack had shown him something different—something more visceral, more immediate. The struggles of class and race were intertwined, and the history of one could not be understood without the other.

"Underneath, we're all scared children?"

"Maybe. Maybe just scared of always being children. It maybe that try as we might, we'll never be more than innocent."

We'll never be more than innocent? Jack paused to reflect on this for a second. He certainly didn't feel innocent. But then maybe he was. Maybe in this world innocence was a sin. The heat was searing now, and it would have seemed a dream if it wasn't for the tap of Jack's heart and the tightness of his breathing.

"In my line of work, I see little innocence."

"Oh, you're a policeman. I know. You all talk the same way, walk the same way and you think no one can tell. I know a policeman when I see one, sure as I know a criminal by sight too. I don't profess to have a gift… Although there is something different about you, Jack Miller, it's true."

Jack laughed, he had heard it said before, countless times, and the exhalation appeared to loosen his breath. "If we are as innocent as you believe, it seems strange we should be obsessed with punishing the guilty, don't you think?"

"Aye, sometimes. Other times it doesn't seem so strange. All of it Jack, it's just ideology. Yuh dun know really, same as me." He paused. "Otherwise, you'd be here with a camera."

Jack smiled, genuinely, at the thought, as the significance of what the Rastafarian said fell upon him gently, like a silk veil. He glanced at his watch, noting the time, and stood up. Work called, pulling him back to the world of the living. But as he looked at Jamaican Jack, standing tall and steady beside Marx's grave, he felt a deep sense of gratitude for the conversation they had shared. He had come here seeking quiet, but what he had found was something far more valuable—a new understanding of the world, of history, perhaps of himself.

"I've got to head to work," Jack said, his voice low. "But… thanks, Jack. For the conversation."

Jamaican Jack smiled, his eyes warm and knowing. "Anytime, brother. We Jacks, we got to stick together. Yuh dun know."

Jack gave a small nod, then turned and began walking back down the path, his footsteps slow and deliberate. As he left the cemetery, the remnants of the conversation lingered with him, wrapping themselves around his thoughts like the creeping ivy that covered the graves. History, he realised, was not just something to be studied or remembered—it was something to be lived, something that shaped every moment of the present.

And as he made his way through the city streets toward work, he couldn't shake the feeling that something had shifted inside him, some deeper understanding of the world and his place within it. The time was now 10:34 and the first officers had arrived at the girl's flat and forced open the front door.

4

'Troubled about many things'

Charley crossed the road leading to the park, her feet moving mechanically, yet her mind felt strangely detached. The heat from the early morning sun, abnormal for the time of year, was high but now fading, ready to give way to a downpour. The shadows were long, as if the day itself was trying to prolong something before letting it slip away. She clutched her purse lightly, her fingers tapping the leather absentmindedly, thinking about the message she'd received from Seth earlier that morning. He had asked to meet her, as he often did, but this time there had been a subtle shift in his tone—an urgency she couldn't quite place.

She entered Dulwich Park through the southern gate, where the path divided into two directions. To the left, families with children could be seen playing in the open fields; to the right, the woods spread out in a dense knot, more secluded. Without hesitation, she took the right path. She preferred the woods—their silence, the way the trees stood still and unwavering like old companions who kept their counsel.

Seth was waiting for her near the old oak, a spot they had chosen months ago for its quiet seclusion. Charley liked the tree; there was something about its ancient, twisted roots pushing up through the soil that reminded her of the way life continued, even in the most difficult of circumstances. But today, the sight of Seth standing there, his back against the trunk, filled her with an odd unease. His relative youth made her feel exposed in ways she couldn't explain. She wasn't old, not really, but next to him, she felt the years between them stretch out like the shadow of the oak, long and unyielding.

He smiled when he saw her, his face lighting up in that easy, unselfconscious way that belonged to someone with no real sense of time yet. "You're late," he teased, though there was no reproach in his voice. Seth had a way of looking at her as if he already knew why she was late, as if her life were some kind of intricate game he enjoyed playing along with.

"I was troubled by many things," she said with a smile that didn't quite reach her eyes, knowing he wouldn't press for details.

Seth shrugged; his hands stuffed into the pockets of his jeans. "Aren't we all?"

She stood still for a moment, the weight of his words settling in her chest. Aren't we all? How casually he said it, unaware of the layers beneath her own troubles. He couldn't know about Jack, about the anniversary looming just days away, or the ache that settled in her bones each morning as she woke alone. Her mind wandered to the words of Emily Dickinson: "I, too, am troubled by many things."

But she didn't say any of this aloud. Instead, she took a step closer to Seth, sitting down on the bench near the oak, her eyes avoiding his for a moment. She had always been careful with Seth, never letting the lines blur, keeping their meetings quiet and undemanding. There was no affair, not in the traditional sense—nothing physical had passed between them, but still, there was a connection, something that drew her to him in ways she didn't entirely understand. It wasn't romance, nor was it friendship in the purest sense. It was more like an escape—a space where she could be someone else, maybe, even if just for a little while.

Seth sat down beside her, close enough that their knees almost touched. He turned toward her, his face full of that open, unguarded expression that made her feel both comforted and disquieted at once. "You've been quiet lately," he said, more observation than accusation.

Charley nodded, her fingers idly tracing the grain of the wooden bench. "I've had things on my mind."

"Jack?"

She stiffened for a moment before relaxing again. Seth knew about Jack, but not everything. He knew there was a man, but he didn't know all of their history, the years they'd spent intertwined, sometimes lovingly, sometimes painfully. Jack was like the oak tree—deeply rooted in her life, immovable. Seth was something else altogether—transient, a breeze that passed through the branches and the leaves of her life without demanding anything in return.

"I suppose," she said, her voice softer than she intended. "Things are… complicated with him."

Seth leaned back, letting the sunlight filter through the leaves above, casting dappled shadows across his face. "You don't have to explain," he said. "Not to me, anyway."

And that was the thing about Seth. He never asked her to explain. Their relationship, if she could call it that, was defined by what they didn't say to each other. It was as if there was a mutual understanding that words would only complicate things. It was enough to meet here, in the park, under the oak, and let the silence between them speak instead.

Still, there was something different today, something she couldn't quite place. Seth seemed less like his usual carefree self, more subdued, as if he, too, was carrying something not yet shared.

"You know," he said after a pause, "sometimes I think about leaving this place. Just… going somewhere new.

Starting over." He glanced at her, gauging her reaction. "Ever think about that?"

Charley looked at him, surprised. "Leave? Why?"

Seth shrugged, his eyes drifting toward the horizon. "I don't know. Just feels like... there's something more out there, you know? Like we're all stuck in this endless cycle of the same conversations, the same routines. Sometimes I think we need to shake things up."

She didn't know what to say. The idea of leaving, of shaking things up, was both tempting and terrifying. She had spent so long building her life, her routines, that the thought of dismantling them now seemed impossible. But wasn't she already dismantling them, bit by bit, with Seth? Wasn't this secret—this hidden friendship—a small rebellion against the life she had built with Jack?

"I don't know if I could," she admitted. "Leave, I mean. There are too many things that tie me to here."

Seth nodded but didn't press. He seemed to understand, even if he didn't fully agree. "You ever think that maybe those ties are actually just holding you back?"

Charley let his words linger in the air for a moment. The things that tie you down. Jack's note from the previous evening came back to her, the way his handwriting had blurred before her eyes. She hadn't wanted to think about what he meant, but perhaps Seth, in his own way, was echoing the same sentiment. The ties that bound her to Jack, to this life—they weren't just ties of love. They were ties of guilt, of obligation, of fear.

"I've never been good at letting go," she said quietly.

Seth leaned forward, resting his elbows on his knees, his fingers clasped together. "None of us are," he said after a moment. "But that doesn't mean we shouldn't try."

His words were simple, but they stirred something in her. She had always thought of Seth as uncomplicated, a relief from the tangled emotions she carried with Jack. But now she realised that Seth carried his own burdens, his own secret longings, quiet obsessions. Perhaps that's why they met here, in the park, in the quiet shadows of the oak—because they were both troubled by many things.

She shifted in her seat, the silence between them growing heavier. She didn't know what to say, what she could say, to bridge the gap that seemed to have suddenly opened between them. The poem came to her mind again, unbidden: *Troubled by many things, but not one solved.* How apt it felt, the weight of Dickinson's words matching the weight in her chest. There was no solving this—no simple solution to the tangled mess of her life, her desires, her fears. But Seth, for all his idealism, seemed to believe otherwise. His presence was a quiet reminder that there were other ways to live, other paths to take. He wasn't tied down by the same things she was. He was still free; in a way she hadn't been for years.

She stood up suddenly, feeling the need to move, to shake off the strange melancholy that had settled over them. Seth looked up at her, surprised but not alarmed.

"I should go," she said, her voice firmer than she felt. "I have things to do."

Seth stood up too, his expression softening. "Of course. I'll see you later?"

She hesitated for a moment, then nodded. "Yes. Later."

As she turned to leave, she felt his gaze on her back, but she didn't look back. She walked quickly, her mind a swirl of thoughts, her heart full of too many things left unsaid. The park seemed quieter now, the shadows longer, as if the day itself had shifted in the time they had sat there. She made her way back toward the southern gate, her footsteps steady, her mind anything but. The poem's final lines echoed in her mind as she walked: *What shall be—shall be, but the smiles, they fade as fast.*

Leaving the park, her mind became clouded by the memory of smiles, both past and present, circling her like ghosts. The day felt heavier now, the sun glaring down on her shoulders, while in her chest, a strange coldness settled. *What shall be, shall be*, she repeated to herself quietly, out loud, or just in her mind, she couldn't be sure, but those simple words from Emily Dickinson's poem reverberated in her with a conviction she hadn't considered before. It was a phrase that had seemed to offer comfort, resignation even, but today, it struck her differently. It was not resignation she felt—it was fear.

The smiles between her and Jack had once been so effortless. She could picture him now, in the early days of their relationship, that crooked smile he gave her when she made some dry remark, or the way his whole face lit up in moments of unguarded joy. She had loved his smile. In those days, it had been a constant reassurance that despite everything—the world, their faults, their imperfections—they would make it work. The smiles had been promises in themselves, unspoken assurances that they would weather whatever storms came their way.

But those smiles had faded, slowly and without warning, like colours bleached by the sun. When had they stopped smiling at each other? She couldn't pinpoint an exact moment, only that one day, she'd looked at Jack and realised he was smiling less, and so was she. There was no longer that quiet exchange of joy or shared understanding. Instead, there was a creeping distance, a tension that neither of them acknowledged but both felt. And now, when they did smile, it felt forced, like a performance they both knew the audience had long since abandoned.

The smiles, they fade as fast, the same poem had said, and Charley found herself thinking about how right Dickinson had been. Smiles weren't eternal, no matter how much you wanted them to be. They were fleeting, like everything else in life—happiness, youth, time itself. Fleeting and fragile. And the more she thought about it, the more it unsettled her. She had spent so long trying to hold onto things—memories, people, moments—only to find that they slipped away regardless. Jack's smile had slipped away too, replaced by the stoic expressions of a man who seemed increasingly weighed down by something unspoken. Perhaps it had been her fault, perhaps his, but she no longer knew who to blame, and it didn't matter either. Maybe the passage of time itself was the culprit. The years had passed, and with them, the ease of their early days, the untroubled joy they had once shared. Now, their smiles were rare, precious, and burdened by the knowledge of all the things left unsaid between them.

And then there was Seth. With Seth, there were still smiles—younger, more carefree, untethered to the complexities of a shared history. His smiles came easily, as if the world hadn't yet taught him the price of happiness. They laughed together, and Charley felt lighter in his presence, as if, for a few hours, she could step outside of herself, escape her life with Jack. There was something intoxicating about Seth's youth, his optimism, the way he seemed to believe that life could still surprise him, that happiness was something worth chasing. But even as she laughed with him, even as she allowed herself to bask in the warmth of his attention, a dark undercurrent ran beneath it all. It was the same thought that now tugged at her mind as she walked away from the park, the words of the poem resonating like a distant bell tolling some inescapable truth. *What shall be, shall be*. The inevitability of it chilled her.

She had told herself that her relationship with Seth was harmless, that it was nothing more than a brief escape from the stagnation of her life with Jack. They didn't touch, didn't cross any lines that would betray Jack. But something inside her warned that lines could blur, and intentions could shift. Already, she could feel Seth's desire to be something more than just a friend, just a confidant. He hadn't said it outright, but there were moments—small, fleeting moments—when his eyes lingered too long, when his words held a note of something unsaid.

And Charley knew, deep down, that it wasn't just Seth. It was her, too. She had allowed herself to drift toward him, to bask in the easy comfort of his presence, because it was easier than facing the hard truths about Jack. With Seth, there was no history, no expectation, no years of shared disappointment. It was easy to smile with him, easy to laugh. But that ease, she realised now, was dangerous. It was a mirage, a fleeting illusion that couldn't last.

What shall be, shall be.

The inevitability of those words gnawed at her. What was she doing, really? Was she waiting for something to happen between them? Was she tempting fate, hoping that Seth might pull her out of the suffocating confines of her relationship with Jack? She didn't think she wanted that. She didn't want an affair, didn't want to betray Jack in that way. But at the same time, she wasn't sure she could keep pretending that everything with Jack was fine, that they could continue living like this—silent, distant, their smiles nothing but faded memories.

Charley paused in her walk, standing under the shade of a tree, her thoughts swirling like the rainclouds could now see forming above her. She thought back to the park, at the families and couples scattered across the grass. There were smiles everywhere—children laughing, lovers leaning into each other, sharing private jokes, friends enjoying the unexpected simplicity of a sunny winter morning. She envied them and their unburdened happiness, the transitory moments of joy they could still take for granted.

Of course, she knew better now. She knew how easily smiles faded, how quickly they could be replaced by silence, by resentment, by distance. And yet, she also knew that no matter how much she tried to guard herself against it, life would continue to unfold. What would be, would be, whether she liked it or not. The poem had always comforted her in its fatalism, but today it felt like a warning. What was coming? What inevitable path had she set herself on with Seth.

The dark and foreboding sense of what might be sat heavily on her now. She couldn't escape the choices she had made, the small betrayals of trust, even if they were only emotional. It was all leading somewhere, and Charley wasn't sure she liked where it was taking her. She thought about Jack again—about the man he had been, and the man he was now. Could they find their way back, or was that part of their lives gone forever? Could they repair the distance that had grown between them, or was it too late? What role did Seth play in all of this? Was he merely a distraction, or had she already let him become something more? The truth was, she didn't know. She was troubled by many things, but none of them solved, none of them clear. All she knew was that the path ahead felt uncertain, and the smiles that once anchored her to something solid now felt as insubstantial as shadows.

What shall be, shall be. The words echoed in her mind, and for the first time, they didn't feel like a surrender. They felt like a challenge.

5
'An everywhere of silver'

Detective Inspector Ed Marks stood at the threshold of the dimly lit apartment, the solid iron scent of blood mixing with the lingering dampness from the rain-soaked night before that the morning's heatwave had done little to dispel here. His gaze settled on the pale figure lying in the middle of the room, her blonde hair fanned out in a halo around her head, darkening in the low light. It was the same shade as Charley's—a coincidence, he told himself, though the thought stuck in his mind like a splinter.

The woman's throat had been slit, a clean, deliberate cut. Her eyes were still open, fixed on something far beyond the room, as if death had caught her mid-thought, mid-breath, and left her frozen in the moment. Her skin, washed pale by the blood loss, glistened under the weak light like the surface of a silver coin. One hand outstretched, grasping, just like the other three. Covered in a confetti of silver halide, just like the other three.

An everywhere of silver. The words came unbidden to Marks' mind, a line from a poem he had once heard Jack utter when they'd attended what now appeared to be the first of four very connected victims. *An everywhere of silver, with ropes of sand to keep it from effacing the track called land.* He wondered what this woman had been holding onto in her final moments, what track she had been following, now lost in the infinite silver of death.

Marks swallowed the thought. He didn't need Jack's poetry clouding his judgment right now. This was Jack in his head again, always in his head somewhere. He needed facts, details—anything to fill the empty spaces in the narrative before him.

"Detective," a voice called from behind him, pulling him out of this reverie.

It was Jens Kreicher, a forensic. A short, wiry man who routinely looked like he hadn't slept in days. He was crouched by the body, snapping pictures, his camera clicking mechanically in the otherwise silent room. The rain pattered faintly against the windows, remnants of the storm that had swept through the city last night.

"What do we have?" Marks asked, stepping further into the room. His shoes made no sound on the thick carpet, but the air felt stained, dense with the remnants of violence.

"Victim in her mid-twenties, name's Rosie Larkin, a student," Kreicher said, still focused on his camera. "Throat was cut, likely by a single-edged blade. The wound is clean, controlled. Silver halide as before. No signs of a struggle." He paused, looking up at Marks. "She knew her killer, or at least wasn't expecting to die."

Marks nodded, his gaze drifting over the room. Who truly expects to die until the moment is upon them, he thought. It was a small one room apartment, sparsely furnished. The girl had lived here alone. A battered sofa sat against the far wall, a coffee table cluttered with empty wine glasses and cigarette butts in front of it. A single lamp cast a dim, yellowish glow, leaving most of the room shrouded in shadow. There were no signs of a break-in, no overturned furniture or broken glass. Everything was just… still. Like time had stopped the moment her life had ended.

"What about in her hand… a quote?" Marks asked.

"What will survive of us is love," said Kreicher. "It's from Philip Larkin, apparently. I had to look it up."

"Time of death?" Marks asked, kneeling down beside Kreicher, close enough to see the details of the wound. The edges were sharp and precise.

"Rough estimate, around three or four hours ago, hard to be exact right now."

Three or four hours ago. That put the murder sometime just before dawn, when the streets outside were still wet, still gleaming under the streetlights, before the sun had come to burn it away. Marks glanced toward the window. Outside, the city had been waking up, oblivious to the death that had occurred within its walls. People were going to work, sipping their coffees, carrying on as if the world hadn't just lost another life. He imagined Jack was on his way to the station now, probably cursing the early start.

Marks felt the familiar tug of unease in his chest. He had been doing this long enough to know when something didn't sit right. This scene—this woman—there was something off about it. The way she lay so peacefully, just like the others, almost serene, despite the violence that had taken her. It was too composed, too intentional. Like a painting, carefully arranged to convey something deeper. He hated when killers got poetic.

"We'll need a full sweep," Marks said, standing and glancing at the officers milling around the doorway. "Check the building, see if anyone heard or saw anything. And get the neighbours. Someone had to have seen her with someone, even if it's just a vague description."

Kreicher nodded, already motioning to one of his junior colleagues to start bagging evidence. "We'll also run prints, see if anything comes up. But I wouldn't get your hopes up. Whoever did this seems to know what they're doing."

Marks ran a hand through his damp hair, the rain from earlier still clinging to him. He couldn't shake the image of the woman, her vacant eyes staring up at the ceiling, the hollow silence of the room enveloping them.

Another line of Dickinson's poem drifted through his mind, unwanted yet persistent: *A sea of stilled silver, a void where there was once breath.* He wondered if the killer had felt that same eerie stillness he did when they had stood over her, blade in hand. If they had paused for a moment, just to take in the finality of it all.

"You think this is connected to the others?" Kreicher asked, standing up and wiping his hands on his already stained trousers.

Marks glanced at him, knowing he was referring to the three other women they'd found in the last two months, all with similar wounds, all blonde, all young and laid out in the same, grasping pose with a quote linked to their namesake in their clenched fist. He didn't want to admit it, not yet, but the pieces were starting to fit together in a way that made his stomach churn.

"Certainly does look that way, doesn't it?" Marks replied sourly, irritated by what seemed like an obvious question given the details. Kreicher must have known as much himself.

Kreicher sighed, pushing his glasses up his nose. "We're chasing shadows, Marks. This guy's careful. Leaves nothing behind."

Marks didn't respond, he didn't have patience for Kreicher. His mind was already racing ahead, piecing together what little they had, trying to form a picture of who this killer was and why he chose these women. The lack of evidence didn't bother him as much as the lack of motive. There was no pattern, no clear connection between the victims except for their appearance and the way they were killed, the silver halide, the poems. And even that felt... superficial.

He looked back at the woman on the floor, her face serene in death, and felt a cold shiver run down his spine. There was something in the way she lay there, something that felt too deliberate, too staged. It wasn't just about killing her. It was about showing them something. Marks wasn't sure what that something was yet, but he knew they were running out of time to figure it out.

"Call me as soon as you get any new information," Marks called to Kreicher, turning toward the door. "I'll head back to the station and start going through the files again. There has to be a connection somewhere."

Kreicher nodded, already focused on his work again. Marks stepped out into the narrow hallway, the sound of the rain now tapping faintly against the window. The city outside felt distant, detached, like it was happening in another world entirely. He pulled his phone from his pocket and glanced at the time. Jack would be arriving at the station soon, oblivious to the fact that another woman had been added to their growing list of victims.

As Marks made his way down the stairs, the weight of the morning settled heavily on his shoulders. The killer was out there, somewhere in the city, blending in with the crowd, hiding in plain sight. And in the moments that followed, as he pushed open the door and stepped out into the sunlight, the only sound was the echo of his own footsteps on the wet pavement. A faint, silver hum in the air, like the ghost of something forgotten, or the shadow of something just out of reach.

**

Jack Miller arrived at the station, late, though he tried to appear as if he wasn't. That early morning sun had given away sharply to rain, which had slowed to a drizzle. The collar of his coat was damp, soaking up water like a sponge. He ran a hand through his hair, trying to shake off the lingering weariness from the night before. As he walked through the narrow corridors of the station, his thoughts drifted to Ed, his partner and closest friend. They had been through more together than most—nearly two decades on the force, countless cases solved side by side, and a bond that, until recent years, had seemed unshakable. But something had shifted between them in the last few months, something neither of them had the nerve to talk about. It was the unspoken tension, an invisible weight that hovered in the air whenever they were together. They avoided it, like people stepping around a crack in the sidewalk, pretending it wasn't there even as it grew wider.

Jack found Ed Marks in one of the small, cluttered offices at the back of the station. He was hunched over a desk, sifting through reports, his brow furrowed in concentration. He looked up when Jack entered, but there was no greeting, no acknowledgment beyond the slight lift of his eyes. Jack dropped his coat over a chair, then sat opposite Ed, the silence between them stretching just a little too long.

"Good morning," Jack muttered, breaking it, though his words carried little sincerity.

"Morning," Ed replied, his voice also flat, his attention on the papers in front of him. Jack could tell it was one of those days where Ed would avoid eye contact, would speak only when necessary, like he was holding something back. Jack didn't push it, though part of him wanted to.

"I just came from the scene," Ed said after a moment, his voice low but steady. "It's the same as the others, Jack. Young woman, throat cut, clean."

Jack felt the familiar pit form in his stomach. He didn't need Ed to go over the details; he'd been expecting this. The same twisted pattern they had been chasing for weeks. The same kind of victim, the same method. Still, hearing it confirmed made it worse.

"Where was it?" Jack asked, leaning back in his chair, trying to sound casual, though his mind was already spinning with the implications.

"An apartment. Not far from Camden. Quiet building. No sign of forced entry. Whoever did this, she let in."

Jack nodded, his jaw tightening. The killer was too careful, too precise. It was like they were playing a game, leaving no trace except for the bodies. And yet, there was always something… something strange.

"And the scene?" Jack asked, trying to keep his voice steady. "Anything new?"

Ed hesitated, just for a second, then said, "Not much. Same as the others. Clean. No prints, no fibres, no obvious signs of a struggle. But…" He trailed off, and Jack caught the shift in his tone, the way his voice dropped just slightly.

"But what?"

Ed looked up then, meeting Jack's eyes for the first time that morning. There was something in his look, something darker, something unsettled.

"The silver halide. It's there again. And the quote, a girl called Larkin with a quote from Philip Larkin clenched in her fist."

Jack felt his stomach twist. He had been hoping that this time—just this once—the killer might have slipped, might have left something they could use, something that wasn't this strange, inexplicable ritual. But the silver was there. It was always there.

"How much?" Jack asked, leaning forward now, his pulse quickening despite himself.

Ed sighed, running a hand through his hair, his fingers lingering at his temple as if massaging away a headache. "Same as the others. Sprinkled around the body, like confetti, an everywhere of silver, like you said... You know what the lab said last time—it's photographic. Used in film processing. It's deliberate. He's doing this for a reason, but for the life of me, I can't figure out why."

Jack sat back, allowing it to fully sink in. Silver halide. It was one of the only real clues they had, linking all four murders. The killer had sprinkled it like a grim offering, some bizarre ritual that neither Jack nor Ed could understand. There was no logical connection, nothing to explain why someone would do that, unless... unless it was part of something bigger. Something they weren't seeing. "What about the quote, what was the message?"

Ed looked down at his desk. "Oh, um, 'What will survive of us is love'..." He looked back to Jack. "You're the English grad, what does it mean? What is he trying to tell us?"

"He's leaving us breadcrumbs," Jack said quietly, more to himself than to Ed. "But I don't know if we're supposed to follow them or if he's just taunting us."

Ed was silent for a moment, his eyes dropping back to the papers in front of him. Jack watched him, noting the lines of tension in his friend's face, the way his shoulders were hunched, like the case was pushing him harder than usual.

"This one," Ed said finally, his voice low and tight, "she looked like the others, Jack. Young, blonde, same kind of victim. But it feels different this time. It's like he's accelerating. Getting bolder."

Jack frowned, his mind racing. "What do you mean?"

"I don't know," Ed said, sitting up straighter, his voice hardening. "Four victims."

Jack felt a chill run down his spine. If the killer was speeding up, that meant they were running out of time. But if he was getting sloppy, that meant he was also close to making a mistake. "We need to get ahead of this," Jack said, standing up and pacing the small office, his mind already working through the possibilities. "We need to figure out why he's doing this, why he's using the silver halide. What these quotes mean… There's got to be a reason."

Ed nodded, though his expression remained grim.

Jack paused, looking out the small window at the now grey, rain-soaked streets below. His mind drifted back to Charley, to the unease that had settled between them, how is had hastened in the past few months. He had tried not to let it affect his work, but it was always there, lurking at the back of his mind, making everything feel just a little bit off.

He turned back to Ed, determined to refocus. "We need to get the lab results as soon as possible. Maybe there's something in the silver halide we haven't caught yet. Some connection to the victims. And we need to check if there's anyone in their lives who might have access to, or have recently purchased, any old photographic equipment."

Ed nodded, already reaching for his phone to make the necessary calls. But Jack could see the strain in his friend's eyes, the weariness that came from chasing a killer who always seemed to be two steps ahead, or more. As Ed dialled, Jack sat back down, his mind still spinning. The silver confetti, the precise cuts, the methodical way the killer operated—it all pointed to something deeper, darker. But what? It felt like they were running out of time.

6

'Forever is composed of nows'

Jack Miller sat on the steps of St. Paul's Cathedral, the world of London quietly moving around him. It was just after lunch, the rain has eased, and a soft light from a low afternoon sun filtered through the city's skyline, casting long shadows that stretched wide across the cobblestones. His coffee, now lukewarm, sat untouched in his hand. He watched the tourists and the office workers hurrying across the square, their footsteps muffled by the sheer enormity of the space, of the history that lingered in every corner.

He came here often, to sit and think, to let the fabric of the city wrap around him like an old coat. St. Paul's, with its towering dome and stone facade, had always felt like a refuge, a place where time seemed to stretch and contract, where past and present met in unspoken conversation. London was an envelope of moments, he thought, each one slipping away as soon as you tried to hold it. *Forever is composed of nows*, he recalled, Emily Dickinson's words floating through his mind like a whisper.

The case had been gnawing at him for weeks. Four murders, all the same: young women, throats cut, bodies staged with a sick precision, and always, the silver halide. The same archaic substance, scattered like confetti, shimmering in the forensic lights like a taunt. Each murder seemed to blend into the other, the details blurring in his mind. The silver halide, the staging, the poetic quotes—it was as if the killer was trying to say something, but the message remained maddeningly out of reach, and yet somehow deeply personal.

Jack took a sip of the tepid coffee, grimacing at its stale bitterness. His thoughts drifted, unmoored, from the case to his own life. Charley. The woman who had once been the centre of his world, the axis around which everything turned, now felt like a stranger. Their marriage, once so full of laughter and warmth, had become something cold and distant. He could trace its unravelling back to small moments, the nows that had seemed insignificant at the time but had added up to something irreversible.

He remembered how she used to look at him, her smile lighting up her face. He used to know every nuance of that smile, the way it shifted with her moods. But now... now it was gone, replaced by something guarded, something he couldn't quite penetrate. *Forever is composed of nows*. Each moment, a piece of a life, a love, slipping away before he had the chance to save it.

Jack set the coffee down beside him, running a hand through his hair. It wasn't just the case, wasn't just Charley. The burden on his shoulders was heavier than that, a pressure that had been building for years. His mind drifted, as it often did, to the past, to a day twelve years ago that he couldn't forget, even if he tried. It had been one of those unbearable summer days, the kind that made the air shimmer with heat, the sun pressing down on the city like a physical weight. He and Ed had been partners then, chasing a suspect through the streets of East London. The man was dangerous, armed, and they had known from the outset that this pursuit was life or death.

He could still feel the adrenaline, the way his heart had raced as they tore through the narrow streets, sirens blaring. The city had flashed by in a blur of colour and light, the pavement shimmering with heat. He could hear Ed's voice over the radio, calm but urgent, telling him to cut the man off, to push harder. They had been so close. Jack remembered the suspect's silhouette, darting between cars, weaving through traffic like a ghost. And then—Jack felt his stomach tighten, the memory stopping short, as it always did. He remembered hitting that pothole, his coffee cup spilling across his lap, slamming on the brakes, the jolt of the car coming to a sudden, violent stop. But beyond that... nothing. He never allowed himself to go further, to remember what had come next. He didn't need to. The case had never truly been closed, at least not in Jack's mind. The suspect had disappeared, vanished into the city's labyrinthine streets, never to be seen again. But it wasn't the suspect that haunted Jack. It was the moment before the brakes, the split-second distraction that had changed everything.

Now, as he sat on the steps of St. Paul's, that memory seemed to hover just out of reach, like a shadow at the edge of his vision. London, with all its history, felt like a mirror of his own mind—layered, complex, filled with hidden corners and forgotten moments. Forever is composed of nows; but some nows never let you go.

Jack's phone buzzed in his pocket, breaking the reverie. He pulled it out, squinting at the screen. Ed's name flashed across it. For a moment, Jack hesitated. He knew that whatever Ed had to say would pull him back into the present, back into the case, and away from the stillness he had found here. But he couldn't avoid it. Not now.

"Yeah?" Jack answered, his voice rough from the cold city air.

"Got an update from forensics," Ed said, his tone clipped, professional. "You'll want to hear this."

Jack stood. "What is it?"

"The last victim," Ed continued, "they found something... strange."

Jack felt his pulse quicken. "Strange how?"

Ed hesitated, as if trying to find the right words. "More fragments of a photographic negative... Under her tongue."

Jack stopped in his tracks, the city around him suddenly feeling too loud, too close.

"They think the killer must have put it there."

Jack's mind raced, trying to piece together the implications.

"They can't tell what the photo is yet," Ed continued. "Too fragmented. But they're working on it. Matching it the other pieces."

Jack exhaled slowly as this new detail settled in his chest. A photo, silver halide... there was a connection here, a thread that tied all four murders together, but he couldn't see it clearly. Not yet. "I'll be there in ten," Jack said, ending the call and shoving the phone back into his pocket. As he descended the steps of St. Paul's, the city seemed to close in around him, history weighing down once more. London was an envelope of moments, sealed away in its streets and buildings, but this moment—this now—was all that mattered. Forever might be composed of nows, but this now, this case, was slipping through his fingers, and Jack wasn't sure how much longer he could hold on.

**

Charley had always liked the quiet moments in the city. They were rare and fleeting, hidden between the rush of traffic and the endless thrum of life that seemed to pulse through London's veins. But today, as she walked towards the school, there was a peculiar stillness in the air, as if the city had paused for just a second, waiting.

She'd offered to pick Christian up after school. Ed's younger brother was thirteen now, taller every time she saw him, but still carrying the kind of sensitivity that made him different from other boys his age. She worried about him sometimes, about how he was growing up without the kind of support most kids took for granted. His parents had passed years ago—Ed didn't talk about it much, but she knew it had been sudden, brutal. Ed had stepped up, taking Christian under his wing, but with his job and all that came with it, there was only so much time left for him. Charley, in her own way, had tried to fill in some of the gaps.

As she neared the school, she spotted Christian walking down the street, his backpack slung low over his shoulder. He was surrounded by a group of boys. They weren't friends. Charley knew the posture, the roughness in their movements. They were circling him like wolves, and even from a distance, she could hear the sneer in their voices.

"Oi, you think you're better than us 'cos your brother's a copper?" one of them called out, giving Christian a shove. He staggered slightly, but didn't fall.

"Yeah, what's it like, mate, living with a filthy pig?" another chimed in, laughing. They all joined in, the sound mean and sharp.

Christian didn't say anything. He never did. Charley's stomach twisted with anger, and without thinking, she sped up her pace.

"Leave him alone," she said, her voice sharp and steady as she approached. The boys turned, surprised by her sudden appearance. She wasn't tall or imposing, but there was something about her that made them hesitate. Maybe it was the look in her eyes—cool, detached, but unmistakably dangerous.

"Bitch, who the fuck are you?" one of the boys demanded, stepping towards her, but not quite as bold as he had been with Christian, instantly backing off slightly when he caught the look of casual violence that flashed across Charley's countenance.

"I'm the bitch who'll break your little nose if you touch him again," Charley replied calmly, her eyes locking onto the boy who had pushed Christian. There was a slight smirk on her lips, not of amusement but more like a dare.

The boys shuffled uncomfortably, exchanging glances. They weren't sure what to make of her—she was beautiful, small-framed, but something about her tone made them nervous. It was in the way she stood, the way she didn't flinch or look away. There was no doubt in her mind that if it came to it, she would take them all on, and they could see it too.

"Come on, this ugly, fat bitch ain't worth it," one of the boys muttered, over-emphasising the words ugly and fat for Charley's benefit, but grabbing his friend forcefully by the arm at the same time. "Let's go."

They backed off, slowly at first, but the one who'd confronted her wanted to push things further.

"Come on, man, let's fucking go!" called one of the others, and the bolder one followed, staring her out as she held her ground, then giving her the finger. Her stare never left them until they had finally disappeared around the corner, then she turned to Christian, who was still standing there, silent, his hands clenched into fists at his sides.

"You alright?" she asked, her voice softer now.

Christian nodded, but there was a tightness around his eyes, a flush in his cheeks that betrayed how much the encounter had rattled him. "Yeah," he muttered. "They're just idiots."

"Idiots can be dangerous," she replied, resting a hand lightly on his shoulder. "Next time, don't let them push you around."

He shrugged, looking down at his shoes. "It's just because of Ed. They think it's funny, that my brother's a cop."

Charley smiled wryly. "People are always afraid of what they don't understand." She paused, then added, "Come on, let's get you a coffee."

Christian glanced at her, some of the tension easing from his face. "And cake?"

"Why not? It's not like you've got homework, right?"

He grinned slightly, the first real smile she'd seen on his face since she'd arrived. "Alright. Coffee sounds good."

They started walking, side by side, the awkwardness of the moment slowly dissipating. The streets around them were busy with people rushing to catch buses or heading into shops, but for a moment, it felt like it was just the two of them. There was something easy about their silence, the kind of understanding that didn't need words.

Charley had originally found this small coffee shop a few blocks down many years ago, not long after Christian had first lost his mum. The building itself was old but the business then had been a new start-up run by an ambitious young man called Joe, who had an intense passion for coffee and travel. The walls had been adorned with photographs of his journeys and colourful, ethnic murals from the countries he'd visited, learning his trade and sourcing his beans. Although it had then been surrounded by newer, trendier places, Charley had instantly liked its rustic, worn-down charm, the smell of ground beans and the soft hum of conversation inside. Over the years it had become her regular spot, a hidden gem, a cherished secret. Now, *Cuppa Joe's* was the trendy spot.

They ordered their drinks and found a quiet table by the window. Christian leaned back in his chair, looking out at the street, but Charley could tell his mind was still on the boys from earlier.

"You know how important you are to Ed, don't you?" Charley said after a moment, stirring her coffee. "He's so proud of you, Chris."

Christian scoffed lightly, but there was a flicker of something in his eyes. "Proud of what? That I get pushed around at school? That I'm not as tough as him?"

Charley shook her head. "Ed's tough, on the outside, but you don't have to be like him. You're your own person... Standing up for yourself doesn't just mean being able to fight. It means knowing who you are and not letting anyone else take that away from you."

He glanced at her, his expression thoughtful. "Yeah, well, that's easier said than done."

"I know," she admitted, leaning forward slightly. "But the more you know who you are, the less what other people say matters. You've got time to figure it out... Don't let a bunch of idiots define you."

Christian nodded slowly, taking a sip of his coffee. "I guess. It's just hard, sometimes. Like... I don't know. I feel like I don't fit anywhere. At school, with Ed, even with myself."

Charley smiled softly, understanding more than she let on. "I think everyone feels that way sometimes. Even Ed, probably, though he'd never admit it."

"Yeah, right," Christian said with a half-laugh. "Ed's too busy being a hero to feel anything."

Charley's smile faded a little, her thoughts drifting to Ed, to the way he carried it all but never let anyone see it. "He's not as invincible as he seems," she said quietly. "He just hides it better than some."

Christian looked at her, his eyes searching hers. "You've known him a long time, haven't you?"

She nodded. "Yeah. Longer than you've been around, kid."

There was a moment of silence between them, not uncomfortable but charged with the things they weren't saying. Charley had always felt a deep connection to Christian, partly because of her history with Ed, but also because there was something about the boy that reminded her of herself at that age—a little lost, searching for a place in the world that made sense.

"You're important to me too, you know," Charley said, her voice soft, but serious. "If you ever need anything, you can come to me. No questions asked."

Christian smiled, a real smile this time, one that reached his eyes. "Thanks, Charley. That means a lot."

They lapsed into a comfortable silence again, sipping their coffee and watching the world go by outside the window. The sun was beginning to dip lower in the sky, casting long shadows across the pavement.

"Do you ever think about how everything is just… moments?" Christian asked suddenly, his voice thoughtful. "Like, right now, this is just a moment, but soon it'll be over, and we'll forget about it."

Charley looked at him, surprised by the depth of his question. "Yeah," she said slowly. "I think about that a lot. Life is just a series of nows. But sometimes, the small moments are the ones that matter most. They stick with you, even when you don't realise it."

Christian nodded, his expression pensive. "Yeah. I guess you're right."

Charley smiled at him, feeling a strange sense of peace settle over her. For all the chaos in her life, for all the uncertainty, this moment—this now—felt solid. It felt real. And that was enough for now. She reached out and ruffled Christian's hair, making him duck away with a mock groan.

"Come on, let's get out of here before Ed wonders where you've disappeared to."

Interview Transcript
Date: October 3rd
Location: Dr. Haggard's Office
Participants: DCI Jack Miller, Dr. William Haggard (Psychiatrist)

[09:33 AM]

WH: Good morning, Jack. Please, make yourself comfortable.

JM: Morning. Thanks, sorry I'm a bit late.

WH: Not a problem. How are you today?

JM: Tired... It's been a long week. Feels like I've been running on fumes.

WH: Running on fumes, that sounds familiar. Maybe we should start by taking a step back. Let's go back to the start of the week, Jack. How were things then? How have you been feeling in general?

JM: I guess it started like most others. I'm working a tough case right now. Charley's been... distant. Not that I can blame her. I'm not exactly the best company when I do come home. Feels like we've barely seen each other now.

WH: Do you feel guilt around that?

JM: Yeah, I suppose... Guilt's been building for a while, you know? We're like two people living in the same space, but there's no connection anymore.

WH: What does Charley need from you that you're finding hard to provide?

JM: I don't know. She needs more than just... more than me coming home, falling into bed, and leaving again before she wakes up. She deserves someone who's present. But I've been so caught up in all this mess, these cases. She's been patient. More than anyone else would've been.

WH: Patience can only last so long. Do you think she's reached the end of hers?

JM: Some days, it feels like she has. Other days, it's like she's still holding on, waiting for me to snap out of it. I don't know which is worse, really.

WH: Do you feel like things can get better?

JM: I hope so. But I feel like I'm... stuck. Like I'm in this never-ending cycle of work and guilt. Charley and I used to talk about having kids, you know?

WH: You mentioned children in one of our earlier sessions too. Do you think part of your guilt stems from that... your shared plans with Charley that haven't come to pass?

JM: Yeah. I think about that a lot... about what kind of father I'd be. And I'm not sure I'd be any good at it, not like this. There's just no space left for... anything else. Not for kids, not for Charley. Not even for me, really.

WH: You've been doing this job for a long time now, Jack. Sometimes, when people carry as much as you do, it feels like there's no way out of that cycle. You talk about not having space for anything, but what about for yourself? How have you been taking care of yourself through all of this?

JM: I don't really know what that even means anymore. You start with good intentions... balance, all that. But once you're deep in it, the lines blur. You stop thinking about it, and before you know it, the job's swallowed you whole.

WH: Well, we're sitting here, having this conversation. That suggests part of you knows something has to change, or you wouldn't be here at all.

JM: Yeah, I guess. Maybe I'm just tired of the mess. Tired of feeling like there's no way to fix things. But I wouldn't even know where to start.

WH: You're not alone in this, Jack, even if it feels like you are. You've got Charley, your team.

JM: I'm not so sure about that. Charley's got one foot out the door, and the team have got enough on their plates. I'm the one supposed to keep things together for them, not the other way around.

WH: Leaders don't have to carry everything alone. It's not a sign of weakness to lean on others. Do you feel like you can trust your team?

JM: I trust them to do the job. But as for trusting them with this? I don't know. I've always been the one they look to when things go wrong. It's hard to flip that dynamic... Hard to show them... cracks.

WH: It's not about flipping the dynamic completely. It's about balance, Jack. You give them strength, but you can also let them be a source of strength for you when you need it. That doesn't make you any less capable or respected. It just makes you human.

JM: Maybe... You know, I've been thinking a lot about something someone said to me earlier this week. A guy named Jamaican Jack. Strange guy... smart.

WH: What did he say?

JM: He said, "The thing about history, is... It's not just about what happened. It's about what we carry with us, what we choose to remember." He said it like... like we all have a debt to each other, whether we like it or not. Our histories, our pasts... they're all tied together. Even if we don't want to acknowledge it.

WH: That's an interesting way of looking at things. How did it make you feel, hearing that?

JM: The more I thought about it, the more it made sense. We spend so much time trying to move on from our pasts, but we can't, can we? Not really. We carry it all with us... regrets, our mistakes, the people we've lost. They're all part of us, and they shape everything we do. And that weight... it feels like a debt sometimes. A debt we owe to ourselves, or to the people we've hurt, or even to the ones we've left behind.

WH: And what debt do you feel like you owe, Jack?

JM: I've tried to push a lot of things aside over the years... stuff I didn't want to deal with, things I thought I could just bury. But it doesn't work like that, does it? It always finds a way back. A way through... like water finds a crack.

WH: What's bringing all of this up now, do you think?

JM: I don't know. Maybe it's this case, maybe it's just life. But it's like I'm seeing connections everywhere... Like the Jamaican guy said, everything's tied together, whether we realise it or not. And I've been thinking maybe we do owe each other something. Like there's this unspoken debt between us, between all of us, to acknowledge what's happened, what we've done... I've been running from that for too long.

WH: What would acknowledging it look like for you? What would it mean to face that history, to stop running?

JM: I don't know if I'm ready to answer that. I think part of me is still afraid of what that might look like. But maybe it means taking responsibility. For everything. For the way I've treated Charley, for the mistakes I've made at work.

WH: It sounds like you're starting to realise that the walls you've built between those parts of your life might not be as solid as you thought.

JM: Yeah, exactly. I thought I could keep it all contained. But it's like holding water in your hands... eventually, it all slips through your fingers.

WH: And you feel like the case you're working on right now is bringing this to the surface?

JM: Maybe. It's hard not to draw parallels, you know? You start seeing yourself in the people you're investigating, in the lives they've led. There's this sense that everyone's got their own version of history. And sometimes it feels like we're all just chasing ghosts... our own, each other's.

WH: Chasing ghosts. That's a powerful image.

JM: I don't know. Maybe it's just the past. Maybe it's just this idea that I can still make things right, somehow. But if I'm being honest, I'm not sure I even know what "right" looks like anymore.

WH: It sounds like you're searching for something—meaning, maybe, or resolution. But sometimes, the search itself becomes the burden, doesn't it?

JM: Yeah. I think that's part of it. I've always felt like it's my job to carry it, like I'm the one who has to bear the weight. And maybe that's why things with Charley got so bad. I've been so focused on carrying everything by myself that I've shut her out.

WH: And what would it look like to let her in? To share it, even just a little?

JM: It'd be hard. I'm not used to it... I feel like I've disappointed her... so much... too much.

WH: You don't have to be a solitary figure, fighting battles on every front. It's okay to lean on the people around you. And as for the debts we owe each other... acknowledging those connections doesn't make you weaker. It makes you more human. We're all tied together in ways we don't always understand, but that's part of what it means to live in this world.

JM: Yeah... Jamaican Jack would've liked that.

WH: Maybe that's why the idea of chasing ghosts is so powerful to you, Jack. They're elusive, malleable—you can't put your hands on them. They're just a trace of the past, stuck in the present, lingering at the edges of your vision. You never know when they'll reappear, or how. Is that how it feels for you? Like you're chasing something that's always just out of reach?

JM: That's exactly it. You think you're done with something, that you've buried it, left it behind. But it comes back, changes form, and suddenly it's there again... part of your present, even though it belongs in the past. You can see it, sense it, but it never quite becomes tangible.

WH: The more you reach for it, the more it escapes... Just out of your grasp... The ghosts we chase often aren't even what we think they are. They evolve. Sometimes, they're memories—shadows of things that once mattered. But sometimes... they're the stories we tell ourselves about who we are, what we've done, or what we should have done.

JM: The stories... yeah, that's it, isn't it? We rewrite things in our heads, try to make sense of what happened. But that narrative, it twists over time. You start to believe your own version of events. Maybe the ghost isn't what actually happened but what you keep telling yourself *should* have happened... And then you're stuck chasing something that was never really there in the first place.

WH: That's the thing about ghosts. They're not just reminders of the past... they're distorted memories, altered by time and guilt, by hope and regret. They morph into something more powerful than the events that created them. So, the question is, what are you really chasing, Jack? Is it the truth of the past, or is it something else entirely?

JM: I don't know. Maybe it's a bit of both. Part of me wants to believe I can still make things right, that I can go back and fix what's broken. I know that's impossible.

WH: The past is elusive because it's gone. Chasing it only leads to more frustration, more disconnection from the present. What we often don't realise is that letting go isn't the same as giving up.

JM: But if I let go... what's left?

WH: That's the hard part, isn't it? When we stop chasing, we have to confront what's left, what's now. It means facing the truth, not just about the past, but about the present—about who you are, who you've become. Who are you without that narrative?

JM: I've been in two car accidents in my life, Doc, and I've survived both where others haven't. That narrative feels inescapable to me... how and why?

WH: I've often found with patients that the meaning comes to them unexpectedly, in its own time. Not through their chasing it, but through their patience for it to reveal itself to them.

JM: What do you mean?

WH: Maybe you're not in possession of all the facts to understand it yet.

JM: Like there's more to come?

WH: In a way, Jack, yes. Perhaps there's a moment coming, in your future, where this will all fall into place. It might not seem wholly fair, but it will make sense. The circle will complete itself.

7
'A coffin – is a small domain'

The streets were growing darker earlier with the wintertime drawing in. The season had its way of creeping in, tightening its grip with every passing hour, pulling the city into a deep, perpetual twilight. Jack sat in the passenger seat of the unmarked BMW, staring out the window as the city drifted by him in a blur of headlights, taillights and fading sun. It was a cold, grey afternoon, the kind that made the world feel smaller, more claustrophobic. He sipped the bitter coffee he had bought before meeting Ed, hoping the warmth would shake off the chill that had settled into his bones.

Ed was driving. His hands were steady on the wheel, but Jack noticed the occasional sideways glance. He could feel Ed's eyes on him, the way they flickered over, holding questions neither of them wanted to address. The silence between them was familiar, almost comfortable, but not today. Today, it was thick, laden with the unspoken tension that had been growing for months now. Jack didn't know when it had started—maybe after the first murder, or maybe it had been building since long before then.

"How are things at home?" Ed finally asked, breaking the quiet. His voice was casual, but there was something off about the tone, something too careful. Jack didn't answer right away, watching as the rain started to fall, light at first, then harder, streaking the windscreen in erratic patterns.

"Fine," Jack said, his voice clipped. "Same as usual."

"Same as usual, huh?" Ed's tone was neutral, but Jack could hear the probing in it, the way it lingered just a little too long on each word. "You've been looking... off lately, Jack. Thought maybe something was going on. You know, with Charley or..."

Jack turned his head slightly, catching Ed's look in the dim light of the car. "Everything's fine," he repeated, more firmly this time. He hated the way Ed asked about Charley, the way his concern for her seemed to go beyond simple friendship. It prickled at him, a discomfort that gnawed beneath the surface. It wasn't exactly that he suspected Ed of anything—but there was something there, something too intense.

Ed was too quiet for a moment, his eyes fixed on the road ahead. "I'm not trying to pry, mate," he said finally. "Just... it's been hell lately, you know? These murders... it's got us all on edge. And I know Charley..."

"What about Charley?" Jack snapped before he could stop himself. His fingers tightened around the coffee cup, the lid crinkling slightly under the pressure. He immediately regretted the sharpness in his voice but didn't back down.

Ed shot him a look, eyebrows raised slightly, then returned his attention to the road. "She's my friend, too, Jack," he said, his voice low, calm. "I care about her, that's all. You know that. Like I care about you, mate."

Jack exhaled, trying to shake off the tension. He knew Ed was telling the truth, at least in part. Ed had always looked out for her, but there was something more in the way Ed talked about her these days, something Jack couldn't quite place. Concern, yes, but it felt... excessive, almost protective, in a way that unsettled him in its familiarity.

"Yeah, I know," Jack muttered, his voice softening. "I'm just... tired. We're all tired."

Ed nodded, his eyes still straight ahead. The streetlights flickered on as they passed beneath them, casting long shadows on the wet pavement. "You ever talk to her about any of it?" Ed asked after a pause. "About how you're feeling?"

Jack took another sip of his coffee, though the taste had gone stale. "Not really."

"Maybe you should," Ed said, keeping his voice neutral, nonchalant. "Might do you both some good."

Jack didn't respond. He wasn't about to have this conversation, not now, not with Ed. It wasn't that he didn't trust his partner—he did, more than anyone else—but there were some things that didn't need to be shared, some thoughts best left unspoken. Especially when it came to Charley.

The rain had picked up now, a steady downpour that made the streets gleam with a slick, oily sheen. The wipers worked furiously, but the view through the windscreen was still blurred and distorted. Jack glanced over at Ed, who was leaning forward slightly, concentrating on the road.

"Where are we headed again?" Jack asked, steering the conversation away from personal matters.

"Shoreditch," Ed replied, his tone shifting back to business. "Another one."

Jack felt the words settle over him. Another one. The fifth murder in as many weeks. He felt the familiar knot of tension form in his chest, the gnawing sense of something they were missing. He leaned back in his seat, letting the hum of the car engine and the sound of the rain fill the emptiness between them. Staring out of the window again, his thoughts drifted. The city around them was dark now, the streets lit only by the harsh glow of headlights and the occasional flicker of neon signs. It was a city that never stopped moving, never stopped changing, and yet, here they were, caught in the same brutal cycle, chasing shadows.

Jack asked quietly, more to himself than to Ed. "The silver halide… it's not random. It's like a signature."

Ed glanced over at him, his expression thoughtful. "It's deliberate, sure" he agreed. "But we don't know why. There's something we're missing. A connection."

Jack nodded slowly. It wasn't the only detail that tied the victims together, but it was a detail they couldn't make sense of. What kind of killer sprinkled a chemical used in photography over their victims? What was the message, the meaning behind it?

"It's like they want us to see something," Jack muttered. "But we're not looking in the right place."

Ed didn't respond right away, his face tense, focused. Jack could tell his partner was thinking the same thing, the frustration simmering beneath the surface. They had been chasing this killer for months, and yet they were no closer to understanding him.

As they approached the crime scene, the blue and red lights of police cars flashed ahead, casting eerie shadows on the rain-slicked street. Ed slowed the car, pulling up to the curb, and the two of them stepped out into the cold, damp air. The smell of wet asphalt and cigarette smoke clung to the night. They didn't speak as they walked towards the alleyway next to the apartment where the body had been found. Uniformed officers milled about, their faces grim, and the familiar hum of police radios filled the air. The forensics team was already there, setting up their equipment, their faces hidden behind masks. Jack could feel the same feeling he always got when they arrived at a murder. It was a feeling of inevitability, like they were walking through a nightmare that had already played out, their roles preordained.

The wind whistled through the narrow streets as Jack and Ed made their way toward the crime scene. It was a familiar procession by now, the hurried steps, the tight silence between them, broken only by the occasional murmur of radios from the officers stationed outside. The building loomed ahead, a decaying relic of old London, its bricks dark with grime and its windows streaked with rain. A low hum of voices filled the air, the quiet bureaucracy of death. Jack thoughts, circling his mind as they stepped past the police cordon, focussed on the smallness of the space. The minuteness of the moment. There was something confined about it, as if every murder scene compressed the city into a smaller space, the boundaries of life shrinking, its edges pressed too close. The alley they passed through seemed to narrow as they walked, its walls tightening around them like the walls of a casket.

"Same again, chaps," Kreicher muttered grimly, as they approached the entrance to the building where the woman had lived. "Young woman, mid to late twenties. Throat cut."

Inside the building, the warmth of the stale air hit them, a stark contrast to the cold outside. Jack and Ed moved silently through the narrow corridor, and their footsteps were soft on the creaking floorboards. The dim light cast long shadows, and the smell—damp, decay, and something else, something faintly metallic—filled the space. As they approached the crime scene, uniformed officers and forensics were already at work, the hum of professional conversation underscoring the moment.

Jack noticed Sergeant Collins, a broad-shouldered man with greying hair, standing near the doorway. Collins had been around for as long as Jack could remember, his face etched with the kind of tired lines that came from years of seeing too much. He greeted them with a curt nod.

"Another one, boss," Collins said quietly, his voice low, as if the dead woman could still hear them. "Same as the others."

Jack crouched down, taking in the scene. The body lay crumpled in the corner, something almost peaceful about her expression, like she had been caught between moments, unaware of the violence that had ended her life, her hair falling across her face like a shroud. Her throat had been cut, the telltale mark of the killer they'd been chasing for weeks now. Then he saw it—the faint shimmer of silver dust on her skin, just like the others. The halide, scattered over her like a sick parody of celebration. He felt a chill run down his spine, not from the cold, but from the familiarity of it all. The pattern, the ritual. It was deliberate, controlled. This killer knew exactly what he was doing, and they were playing right into his hands.

Ed was standing beside him now, his face set in a grim line. "We need to figure out what the hell this means," he said quietly, his voice tight with frustration.

Jack nodded, his mind racing. He could feel the pieces of the puzzle shifting, but nothing was fitting together yet. There was still something missing, that one vital clue that would unlock everything.

Jack said softly, "It's the second body now in two days. He's speeding up."

Ed didn't reply, but Jack could see the tension in his jaw, the same gnawing fear that had been growing in both of them. The fifth body in total, time was slipping away, and with each murder, the killer was getting bolder and more confident. And somewhere, in the shadows of the city, he was watching, waiting for them to make their next move. Jack gave a brief nod in return, his eyes scanning the room before him. He stepped back to allow the forensic team to do their jobs.

A coffin is a small domain, Jack thought, looking at the body, the room, the smallness of it all. Life reduced to this cramped, final moment. The last, gasping, terrifying moments before death.

One of the younger detectives, a Constable named Radcliffe who'd joined the team only recently, approached them, fumbling with his notebook. "Detectives," he said, desperate to inject some positivity into his greeting while simultaneously glancing nervously from Ed to Jack. "The forensics team is still working, but it's… the same. Silver halide dust, throat wound, no sign of forced entry. We're running the prints now, but obviously I don't think we'll find anything."

Jack barely heard him, his focus entirely on the woman in the corner. He moved closer, crouching down as the forensic photographer finished his work. The body was still, lifeless, her skin pale except for the faint shimmer of silver dust across her neck. It was as if the killer had taken his time, carefully laying out the pieces of his ritual, controlling even the smallest details. Every inch of this scene felt deliberate, orchestrated.

DS Martin, a small-framed, brunette detective in her mid-twenties came over to Jack and eyed him quizzically. Her eyes were of the most piercing blue, a domain small but deep, somewhere that all secrets would be locked away, or perhaps buried forever.

"What's her name?" Jack asked Martin softly, without even looking at her.

"Emily Isherwood," she replied, "twenty-three, master's student at Kings. Classics."

Jack nodded. It felt close.

"You okay, boss?" she asked. Her manner was direct, but almost nervous at the same time.

Despite being lost in thought, something in his brain picked up her concern and snapped him out of it. He smiled warmly at her. "Yeah, Martin. I'm okay… Any note with this one?"

Martin nodded, looking down at her notes. "Christopher Isherwood. I googled it. No one ever hates without a cause…"

"What's his cause," Jack said softly, to the room, not expecting an answer.

Ed stood nearby, his arms crossed, his face impassive. Jack looked over at him, he knew that look well—he'd seen it a thousand times; it was the mask Ed wore to keep the horrors of this job at bay. But there was something else there tonight, something lurking behind Ed's usual calm. Jack could feel it, like a splinter in his thoughts, distracting him, pulling his attention away from the case and back to their earlier conversation in the car.

"Any word on the photo pieces from the last victim?" Jack asked quietly, standing up and moving beside Ed.

Ed shook his head. "Team's still working on it, trying to reconstruct it," he said. "They can't figure out exactly what the image is yet. Too damaged, too fragmented."

Jack frowned. The photo was a cruel addition to the already sickening ritual. But they still had no idea what it meant. Who the women were, why they were chosen, or why the killer left these strange, fragmented clues behind.

"It's clearly a message," Jack murmured, almost to himself. "But for who? Us, or someone else?"

Ed didn't answer, his eyes still on the body. "Maybe," he said finally. "Maybe God… Or maybe it's just to see how far he can push it, push us. To see how much control he has."

Jack felt the edges of his thoughts fraying, the nagging sense that they were missing something, something crucial.

Just then, Detective Superintendent Carrick entered the room, his presence commanding in a way that only came with many years of experience. His sharp gaze swept over the scene, assessing, calculating. He acknowledged Jack and Ed with a nod, but his attention was already on the body, on the forensic team gathering around it.

"Anything new?" he asked, his voice clipped.

"Not much," Jack replied, stepping forward. "Same M.O. Silver halide, throat wound, no sign of forced entry. Still waiting on prints."

Carrick grunted, clearly unsatisfied but resigned to the lack of progress. "We need a breakthrough," he muttered, mostly to himself. "This cunt's getting bolder, and we're no closer to catching him."

The room felt even smaller now, like the walls wanted to squash them under the weight of their failure. Jack exchanged a glance with Ed, who had moved toward the window, his face half-lit by the dim light outside. Jack watched him for a moment, noticing the tension in his posture, the way his hands were clenched tightly at his sides. There was something wrong here, something deeper than just the stress of the case. Jack could feel it in the air, in the way Ed had been acting lately, the questions he asked, in the way he talked about Charley.

A coffin is a small domain whispered in Jack's mind again, but this time it felt different, more personal. It wasn't just about the bodies they found, the small spaces of death they encountered. It was about all of them—trapped in their own small domains, their own coffins of secrets, regrets, and unspoken things.

He cleared his throat, trying to shake off the uneasy feeling. "Ed," he said quietly, stepping toward his partner. "You okay?"

Ed turned; his face was unreadable for a moment. Then he nodded, a tight, controlled movement. "Yeah," he said. "I'm fine."

But Jack wasn't convinced. There was something between them, something unspoken that hung in the air like the halide on the dead woman's skin. He didn't push it, though. Not now. There was too much else to focus on, too many other questions demanding answers. As the forensic team continued their work, Jack found himself drawn back to the body, to the shimmer of silver on her pale skin, the strange, deliberate beauty in the horror.

Another young woman, another life stolen. And they were no closer to stopping it. He felt the cold touch of inevitability, the same feeling he'd had at every crime scene since this nightmare began. But now, it was different. Now, the walls were closing in, not just on the case, but on all of them.

8

'A brief but patient illness'

The house was thick with the kind of quiet that came only after the end of something immense. The kind of silence that lingers in the air like smoke, invisible but suffocating, as if the walls themselves had absorbed the grief and were now holding their own breath. Christian sat on the edge of his bed, his small legs dangling, feet not yet able to touch the floor. He was five years old, and his world had just ended.

From the hallway outside, he could hear the murmur of voices, low and solemn. The wake had begun hours ago, adults shuffling in and out of rooms, carrying cups of tea and plates of sandwiches that no one really wanted to eat or drink. The house was filled with strangers, people who had known his mother in ways he hadn't, speaking about her life in soft, reverent tones as though their words could somehow summon her back from the dead.

His bedroom door was slightly ajar, letting in the faint sounds of the wake—the creak of the floorboards, the clinking of cups, the occasional stifled sob. Christian's eyes were fixed on a small toy in his lap, a plastic bee with faded yellow stripes. He'd found it in the garden a few days ago, lying in the grass as if waiting for him. Now, he turned it over and over in his hands, his small fingers tracing its worn edges.

The bee didn't move. It was just a toy, but in his imagination, it buzzed softly, as if it, too, understood that something had changed irrevocably, forever.

He knew his mother was gone, of course. He understood that in the way children do, with a blunt, unvarnished clarity. She had been ill for a long time, bedridden for weeks, and now she wasn't here anymore. She wasn't anywhere. His father had died years before, though Christian barely remembered him—a distant, hazy figure from before he could form clear memories. His father had been older, much older than his mother, and had passed away quietly, like a page turning. Now his mother had followed, leaving Christian behind in a world that felt suddenly enormous and empty.

The bedroom door creaked softly, and Christian glanced up, his small face pale and blank. He didn't want to see anyone. He didn't want to be reminded that outside this room, there were people who were mourning, people who knew how to cry in the right way. He didn't know how to cry. His chest felt tight, like something was buzzing there, but no tears came. Maybe it was just a bee.

There was a soft knock on the door, and then a voice—a woman's voice, familiar and gentle.

"Christian? May I come in?"

It was Charley. She stood in the doorway, framed by the dim light from the hall. Her face was softer back then, less strained, though even then it held that quiet, knowing look she had always had. As if she saw more than most people and understood what she saw better than she let on.

Christian didn't answer, but she took a step inside anyway, pushing the door open a little further. She moved quietly, careful not to disturb the fragile peace that had settled over the room. In her hand, she carried a cup of tea, though it was clear from the way she held it that it wasn't for her. She crossed the room and sat down on the floor next to him, setting the cup on the bedside table with a soft clink.

"Your room is nice," she said, glancing around. "I like the way the light comes in through the window."

Christian didn't respond. He was still turning the plastic bee over in his hands, his small fingers tracing the wings.

Charley watched him for a moment, her expression thoughtful. She wasn't much older than Christian had imagined a mother would be—young, but with a kind of sadness around her that made her seem older than she actually was. She had known Christian's mother for a long time, had been there in the final days, helping with the things that no one else could bring themselves to do.

"How are you feeling?" she asked quietly.

Christian shrugged, his eyes still on the toy. He didn't know how to answer that question. How did anyone feel after something like this? He wanted to ask if it was normal, if this tightness in his chest was what people meant when they said they were sad, but the words wouldn't come. Instead, he just shrugged again, hoping that would be enough.

Charley reached out and gently took the toy bee from his hands, holding it up to the light. "This is nice," she said softly. "Did you know that bees are very patient? They work quietly, going from flower to flower, always knowing what they need to do."

Christian looked at her, his eyes wide. "Do they ever stop?" he asked, his voice small and hesitant.

Charley smiled, but it was a sad smile, the kind that didn't reach her eyes. "Not really," she said. "They keep going, even when it's hard. They just keep doing what they're meant to do."

There was a short pause, a silence that filled the room as Charley placed the toy back in Christian's lap. Her hand lingered there for a moment, resting on his small knee, as if she was trying to give him some of her strength, trying to help him carry the silence.

"Do they ever get sad?" he asked, softly, as she passed the bee back to him.

"I don't know, Chris," she replied, as if the silence in the room were louder than her voice.

Christian glanced up at her, his brow furrowed. "What do we do now?" he asked, his voice barely a whisper.

Charley's expression softened, and for a moment, she looked as though she might cry, but she didn't. Instead, she reached up and tucked a strand of her light hair behind her left ear, composing herself. "We keep going," she said gently. "One day at a time. That's all we can do. Like bees."

Christian nodded, though he wasn't sure he understood. Everything felt too big, too overwhelming. The world outside this room was filled with people who knew how to mourn, people who knew what to say and how to move forward. But here, in this small, quiet space, it felt like the world had stopped. The bee in his hands was still now, its buzzing gone, and Christian wasn't sure how to make it move again.

After a long moment, Charley spoke again, her voice soft, almost hesitant. "You know, Christian," she said, "I always wanted to be a mother. I think about it a lot. But... sometimes things don't happen in the way we plan."

Christian looked at her, his young face confused. "Why not?" he asked, his voice innocent, uncomprehending.

Charley smiled, but there was a sadness in her eyes that Christian didn't understand. "Sometimes," she said quietly, "life just doesn't work out the way we hope it might. And we have to find other ways to keep going."

He didn't know what to say to that, didn't know how to respond. He could feel the tightness in his chest again, the buzzing of the bee that wouldn't stop, wouldn't go away.

Charley reached out and took his hand, squeezing it gently. "It's going to be okay, Christian," she said softly. "I know it doesn't feel like it right now, but it will be. One day, things will feel better."

Christian stared down at his small hand in hers, his eyes tracing the lines of her fingers, the way they wrapped around his. It was a small thing, but in that moment, it weighed as an anchor to the world outside his room. They sat there together, and for a time no one spoke, the murmur of the wake drifting in from the hall, the voices of strangers mourning a woman they had known in ways Christian never would. The room was quiet, the light from the window casting soft shadows on the walls, and in the stillness, Christian felt something shift inside him, something small but significant. The buzzing of the bee in his hands had quieted, and for the first time since his mother had passed, Christian felt a flicker of something like peace. Outside, the day moved on, the funeral wake continued, but in that small room, time seemed to pause, just for a moment. And for Christian, that was enough.

The murmur from the hallway had grown a little quieter now; the voices of the mourners were fading into the background like a distant hum. Christian was still sitting on the edge of the bed, his small hand resting in Charley's, the toy bee lying forgotten between them. The silence that filled the room felt different now, less oppressive, as if it had loosened its grip on Christian's small chest. Charley's presence beside him, calm and steady, had softened the edges of his grief, if only for a little while.

The door creaked again, and Christian glanced up, his wide eyes watching as Ed stepped into the room. He looked older than his years—the funeral, the loss, the responsibility—had settled into the lines of his face. His tie was loose around his neck, his suit wrinkled, as though he had forgotten to care about how he looked the moment he'd stepped through the door.

"Hey, bud," Ed said softly, his voice thick with something he was trying to hide. He gave Christian a small, tired smile before turning his gaze to Charley, who sat beside him on the bed. "Mind if I join you guys?"

Charley nodded, her own smile just as tired. She shifted slightly to make room for Ed, and he lowered himself down onto the floor beside her, his knees creaking slightly as he did so. Ed reached out and placed a hand on Christian's shoulder, squeezing it gently. "How are you holding up, bro?"

Christian shrugged, his small shoulders rising and falling in a motion that seemed too big for someone his age. He didn't know how to answer that question any more than he had when Charley had asked him earlier. The words felt too big and too complicated for him to put together, he was learning their meaning now, for the first time.

Ed sighed softly, his hand dropping from Christian's shoulder. He looked at Charley, his stare lingering for a moment longer than it should have. There was something in his eyes, a question maybe, or a plea for something unspoken. Charley seemed to understand, though, and gave him a small nod, her lips pressed together in a thin line.

They sat in silence for a while longer, the only sound in the room the soft ticking of the clock on the bedside table. Ed's hand found its way to Charley's, resting on her knee, his thumb brushing lightly against her skin. It was a small gesture, one that might have gone unnoticed in any other moment, but here, in the quiet of Christian's bedroom, it felt like a lifeline.

"Jack's been struggling," Charley said quietly, her voice barely more than a whisper. "He's carrying so much…"

Ed nodded with eyes downcast. He understood what she meant. Grief had dug its claws into him a long time ago and showed no sign it would ever fully retract them.

"It's like he's sick," Charley continued, her voice trembling slightly. "Not physically, but… in here." She touched her chest, right over her heart. "He won't talk about it, won't let anyone in. And I don't know how to help him… Sorry, I know today isn't about him."

"It's okay, Charley," Ed exhaled slowly. He had seen it too, in Jack's eyes, in the way he moved, like every step was just another in a long, endless procession. Grief had a way of hollowing out a person, leaving behind only the shell of who they used to be. Jack was trying to hide it, but it was there, just under the surface, like an illness waiting to spread.

"Grief is a strange thing," Ed said, his voice low and thoughtful. "It doesn't go away, does it? It just… changes shape. Means the shape of the boxes we keep it in have to change shape sometimes, too."

Charley nodded, her eyes filling with tears. She turned her head away from Ed for a moment, as if ashamed of her emotions. But Ed reached for her, wrapping his arm around her shoulders and pulling her gently against him. She didn't resist, letting herself lean into his warmth, her head resting against his chest.

"I appreciate you both," Ed murmured, his voice soft but firm. "More than you know. I wouldn't have been able to get through any of this without you."

She closed her eyes, the tears slipping down her cheeks now, though she made no sound. She had always been strong, always the one who held things together when everyone else was falling apart. But now, in Ed's arms, she allowed herself a moment's vulnerability, to let everything wash over her.

"I'm scared," she whispered, her voice breaking. "I'm scared that that we're going to lose him, too."

Ed tightened his grip around her, his chin resting gently on the top of her head. He didn't have any answers for her. How could he? Grief was its own beast, one that couldn't be tamed or reasoned with. But in this moment, he was here, and that had to be enough. He'd been there too; it was his cup on the dash, after all.

Christian, who had been watching the exchange mute, suddenly stood up from the bed and crossed the room. Without saying a word, he wrapped his small arms around both of them, pressing his face into Charley's side. He didn't fully understand what was happening, didn't understand the complexities of grief or loss, but he knew that something was wrong, and he wanted to be there, to offer whatever comfort his small body could provide.

Charley let out a soft sob, her hand reaching down to stroke Christian's hair. Ed pulled them both closer, his arms a protective circle around them. They stayed like that for a long time, the three of them wrapped in a small moment of stillness in a big world that seemed to be spinning out of control.

It was strange, Ed thought, how grief could bring people together in ways that nothing else could. It was like the pain connected them, creating a bond that went beyond words. He looked down at Charley, her tear-streaked face buried against his chest, and then at Christian, who was holding onto them as if his life depended on it. He didn't know what the future held for any of them. Jack was spiralling, and Charley was carrying a weight that no one else could see. Christian was too young to fully understand what was happening, but even he could feel the shift in the air, the way everything had changed since his mother's death. But for now, in this small room, in this brief moment, they were together. They were holding each other up, in the way that people do when there's nothing else left to hold onto.

Ed kissed the top of Charley's head again, his lips brushing lightly against her soft, golden hair. "We'll get through this," he whispered, though he wasn't sure if he believed it. "All of us... We'll get through this together."

Charley nodded against him, her hand still resting on Christian's small head. She didn't say anything, but Ed could feel her body relax slightly, her tension easing ever so slightly. It wasn't a solution, it wasn't a fix for everything that was broken, but it was something. The room was quiet now, the sounds of the wake outside having faded more or less completely. Inside, the three of them sat in the stillness, holding each other close, as if the world couldn't touch them here. And for a moment, it didn't. For a moment, they were just three people, bound together by love and loss, and in that moment, that was all that mattered.

9

'What I see not, I better see'

The late afternoon light filtered weakly through the frosted windows of Jack Miller's office, casting a grey, almost spectral glow across the room. It was the kind of London winter's day that seemed to stretch endlessly, where the fog clung low to the streets, swallowing everything in its path. Jack sat hunched over his desk, his fingers idly tracing the edges of a single piece of paper that lay before him, its contents obscured by the tilt of the light. He stared at it, but his mind was far away, chasing threads of thought of which he couldn't quite catch hold.

The paper seemed to hold some unspoken truth, something that gnawed at him from the corner of his consciousness, like he couldn't quite see it for what it was. He hadn't been sleeping well—not for twelve long years, but especially since the first murder—and now the fifth victim, Emily Isherwood, hung over him like a fog all of its own. He could see her cold face, those lifeless eyes, staring back at him, an image that had become as familiar to him as the lines on his own hands.

He ran a hand through his hair, a sigh escaping his lips as he leaned back in his chair. On the desk, piles of papers and files threatened to spill over, reminders of all the cases unsolved, all the questions unanswered. But it was the photograph—the negative fragments they'd found inside the bodies—that haunted him the most.

What I see not, I better see. The line from Emily Dickinson's poem had been stuck in his head for days now, ever since the details of Ariana's murder had begun to unravel. He didn't know why it had surfaced, but the meaning was clear enough. There were things hidden, things he couldn't see—not yet. But the more they uncovered, the more the picture would come into focus. The thought gnawed at him as much as the hidden meaning in the paper beneath his fingers.

His reverie was broken by the sound of the door creaking open. DS Martin stepped in, her expression grave but composed, as always. She was a solid detective, dependable and methodical. Her dark brown hair pulled back tightly, carrying a folder under one arm, her stride brisk as she approached his desk.

"I've got an update on the case, sir," she said, her voice steady but low, as if the walls might be listening. She hesitated for a moment, glancing down at the paper he was holding, though she didn't mention it.

Jack folded the paper and slipped it into the top drawer of his desk, locking it with a soft click before gesturing for her to sit. "Go on, Martin," he said, his tone quiet, the weariness in his voice betraying his restless nights.

She sat across from him and placed the folder in front of him, sliding it over with an unspoken urgency. "Imaging managed to reconstruct most of the photograph with what we found inside Rosie Larkin and Emily Isherwood. It's... well, it's strange."

Jack's brow furrowed as he opened the folder and pulled out the contents. Inside were the reconstructed fragments, carefully pieced together by the forensics' digital imaging team. He stared at the image for a moment, the edges still jagged and incomplete, but there was enough of it to make out the general shape.

It was a photograph of a woman—dark-haired, standing in what looked like a dimly lit room, her face turned slightly away from the camera. More in silhouette, it was hard to make out her features, her race even, the quality was too grainy. Something about the scene felt profoundly unsettling, however, the kind of image that lingers in the back of your mind long after you've looked away from it.

"Do we know who she is yet?" Jack asked, though the question was mostly to himself. The woman's face didn't stir any immediate recognition in him, nevertheless there was something about the image that sent a chill down his spine.

Martin shook her head. "We don't know yet, we're still trying to identify her. It's too degraded—and without all the pieces we might never get a match, but we've sent what we have to the lab for further analysis anyway. They're hoping they can pull more from it."

Jack leaned forward, his elbows resting on the desk, staring at the photograph with an intensity that made Martin shift slightly in her seat. Five victims now, all with parts of a mysterious photograph hidden inside them. The first two were more like background, nothing to make any real sense of on their own, but now altogether—something like a face and a body was taking shape. There was enough here to see, but still not enough to understand.

"And this woman?" Jack pressed. "Any connection to any of the other victims?"

"Nothing yet. We're still combing through her life— contacts, her movements in the days leading up to her death. But so far, no obvious link between her and the others. They all come from different backgrounds, different parts of the city, no overlapping social circles. The only connection is the way they were killed... the photos."

Jack nodded, though the answer didn't satisfy him. "I need to find out who she is. This woman in the photograph. Make sure you show her to the victim's friends, families, anyone who might recognise her or this picture."

Martin glanced at the picture once again, her eyes narrowing slightly. She nodded. "What do you think it means, sir? The photo being put inside her like that?"

Jack rubbed his temples, feeling the beginnings of a headache forming. "I don't know yet. But it's deliberate, that much is clear. Someone's trying to send us a message. They want us to see something. She's the key. Whoever she is... she ties this all together."

Outside the window, the fog continued to thicken, the streetlights casting a dim, ghostly glow over the wet pavement. Jack sat back in his chair, the photograph still in his hands. He stared at it, willing it to give up its secrets. But there was something more than the image itself that bothered him, something lurking just beyond the surface of his thoughts. He reached into his drawer and pulled out the folded piece of paper again, the one he had been staring at before Martin came in. Jack's fingers hovered over the photograph for a moment longer, the jagged edges of the image catching the dim light in his office. His thoughts wandered, drifting between the case and the lingering sense of something else, something unspoken that had been clawing at him for days now.

Finally, Martin stood, her hand resting on the back of the chair. "I'll keep you updated as soon as we hear anything more from forensics, sir. There's still a lot to go through."

Jack nodded absently, "Thanks, Martin."

She hesitated for a moment, as if there was something else she'd wanted to say, but then she turned to leave the room. He'd been about to let her leave, too—her shoes already clicking towards the door—but a sudden impulse made him speak.

"Martin," he called out, his voice low but firm.

She stopped in her tracks, one hand already on the door handle. There was a pause before she turned, her expression neutral but her eyes watching him carefully, as if she had been expecting this.

"Yes, sir?" she asked, her voice steady, though there was a faint note of something else there—something unspoken, something they both understood, but hadn't acknowledged.

Jack waved her back into the chair across from him. She hesitated for only a second before walking back, her movements controlled, almost too composed, like she was wary of what might come next.

"Sit down for a minute, please," he said, leaning back in his chair, his fingers still absently playing with the edge of the picture. He wasn't quite sure where this conversation was going, but something inside him—something more instinct than reason—told him it needed to happen.

She sat down slowly, her posture straight but relaxed, watching him with that same steady gaze. There was a faint glimmer of curiosity in those blue eyes, but she didn't push him. She never did. She was just unflinching. It unsettled suspects, made her devastating in an interview room. Now, that was part of what unsettled him, part of what had made this thing between them linger just beneath the surface.

"I've been thinking about the case," Jack began, but even as he spoke, he knew that wasn't really what this was about. The photograph lay in front of him like a symbol, half-seen but incomplete, much like his life had felt for some time now. "About what we're not seeing."

Martin nodded, her eyes flicking to the photo. "It's not just about the murders, is it?" she said quietly. "There's something else here, something... personal."

Her words hung in the air, and Jack could feel the tension between them tighten, just a little. She wasn't wrong, but the personal part of this had nothing to do with the case and everything to do with the silent understanding that had been growing between them over the past year. It was the understanding that had made their conversations longer than they needed to be, their silences more charged, and their looks just a little too intimate.

The gap between them—age, rank, experience—had always been there, but lately, it felt like the edges were blurring. Jack had been aware of it but had chosen to look the other way. Martin, with her calm presence and sharp mind, had slipped into his life with ease, and now, even sitting across from her in this cold, grey office, he couldn't shake the feeling that she saw through him.

"What I see not, I better see," Jack murmured under his breath, the line from the Dickinson poem returning to him unbidden. It was as though the words had a life of their own, prodding at the deeper truth he hadn't yet acknowledged.

Martin tilted her head slightly. "What was that?"

Jack met her gaze, his eyes searching hers for a moment before he answered. "It's a line from a poem. About seeing beyond what's in front of you. About what's hidden… underneath."

She was quiet for a moment, as if considering his words. Then, in that soft but clear voice of hers, she asked, "Do you believe that? That there's more to this than what we're seeing?"

Jack hesitated. "I think… there are things we don't want to see," he said slowly. "Things that are easier to ignore because if we look too closely, we have to face them."

He didn't need to say what those things were. He knew, and Martin likely knew too. It wasn't just about the case. It was about the choices they both had made, the way they circled around each other without ever crossing that invisible line.

Martin leaned forward slightly, her hands resting on the edge of his desk. "I don't think ignoring them makes them go away," she said softly. "Sometimes… what we don't see is just waiting for us to acknowledge it. I used to think that, just bury it deep. Strangely, I think it might be you who've taught me otherwise."

Her words struck a chord, reverberating through the tension that had built up between them. Jack looked at her, really looked at her face, for the first time in weeks. There was no accusation in her eyes, no judgment. Just the quiet understanding that had always been there, lingering beneath the surface. She was offering him an opening, a chance to confront what had been growing between them. But Jack wasn't sure he was ready to face it.

"You're a great detective, Martin. Ed is, lucky to have you… in his team… we're lucky to have you," Jack said, his voice quieter now, more introspective. "You've always had my back."

"I still do," she replied, her gaze unwavering. "But I can't help but feel that there's something you're not telling me. Something you're not seeing for yourself."

The words cut deeper than Jack had expected. He turned the image over in his hands, his eyes tracing the faint, ghostly image of the woman they couldn't identify. The blurred edges of her face felt like a metaphor for everything in his life that had become hazy, indistinct. His marriage, his friendships, his own sense of who he was. It was the truth of it that stung the most. He'd been walking around in a fog for months now, maybe even longer, pretending that everything was fine when it wasn't. Pretending that his relationship with Charley was the same as it had always been, pretending that his partnership with Ed was rock solid, pretending that whatever was happening with Martin wasn't dangerous territory.

He could feel Martin watching him, her eyes searching his face for some sign of what he was thinking. He had never told her about the strain in his marriage, the sleepless nights where Charley turned away from him in bed, or the nights he didn't come at all until the sun was up again. Conversations that felt more like exchanges between strangers than the intimate talks they once shared. He had never told her about the guilt that had settled into his bones, the way it chewed at him every time he looked at her. Because deep down, he knew he had let things drift too far, let the distance grow too wide.

Martin didn't push him. She never had. But there was something in her eyes now, something that told him she knew more than he had ever let on. Maybe she had seen it in the way he avoided talking about Charley, or the way his eyes lingered on her just a little too long during their late-night conversations. Maybe she had sensed it in the way he deflected every time their conversations edged towards the personal.

"I'm not having an affair," Jack said abruptly, the words spilling out before he could stop them. It wasn't a confession, not really, but it felt like one. He wasn't sure why he said it, but the look on Martin's face told him that she'd considered it.

She didn't react, didn't flinch. She just nodded, as if to say, I know. And maybe she did. Maybe she had always known. "I didn't think you were," she said quietly.

Jack stared again at the photograph in his hands, the blurred image of the woman staring back at him. He felt like he was staring at his own reflection, seeing only fragments of himself, the rest hidden beneath layers of uncertainty.

What I see not, I better see.

He wasn't sure if he could. But he knew he had to try.

The phone on his desk buzzed, breaking the tension. Jack glanced at it, grateful now for the interruption. It was Ed.

Jack reached for the phone, lifting it to his ear. "Yeah?"

"We've got something," Ed's voice crackled through the line, thick with urgency. "You need to get down here. I'll text you the location."

Jack closed his eyes for a brief moment, everything settling back into place. "On my way."

He hung up the phone and stood, grabbing his coat. Martin stood as well, watching him closely.

"Duty calls," Jack said, offering her a faint smile that didn't quite reach his eyes.

Martin nodded; her expression unreadable again. "It always does."

10
'Forbidden fruit a flavour has'

Cuppa Joe's had changed a lot since those early days when Charley had first brought Christian there as a young boy, for a slice of cake, shortly after his mum had passed away. It had been much smaller back then, tucked into the corner of a narrow street near the park. The windows had been grimy, and the lighting dim. The tables used to be mismatched and chipped. But now, since Joe had expanded and franchised, the place had been renovated and rebranded. There were ten *Cuppa Joe's* in total, dotted around the UK, mostly in areas of London full of busy professionals, a couple in the north in Leeds and Newcastle, one in Brighton, and one in Eastbourne, where Joe had originally come from and grown up.

With expansion came brand identity, Joe filtering his passion for coffee through a new, more bougie, artisanal flavour to his décor. Every visit, Charley felt like she noticed something different, a photograph, a face in a photograph, a colour or a shape in the murals on the walls. The tables were sleek, modern, and uniform, and the once-faded walls had been repainted in a warm, neutral shade. The baristas wore matching aprons, and the faint aroma of fresh espresso filled the air, cutting through the stale smell of damp that once lingered by the door. In the background, quietly enough as not to be intrusive, she could hear *Armour Love* by La Roux playing on the radio.

Reflecting on those changes for a moment, Charley felt like a stranger. But the feeling passed quickly, replaced by a wave of familiarity as the barista behind the counter gave her a warm smile of recognition. She had come here often enough over the years that the staff knew her, even if the faces had sometimes changed.

"Flat white for you, is it, Charley?" said the new barista.

Charley nodded, offering a polite smile in return. "Yeah, thanks. And a black coffee, no sugar."

It had been their usual order when she had brought Christian here—the flat white for herself and the black coffee for Ed, or sometimes Christian as he'd grown older and started to copy his brother. She'd never taken Jack there, her strange sense of ownership of the place meant that as distance had grown between them, increasingly Charley had wanted to keep it as a safe space just for herself. Today, though, the black coffee wasn't for Ed, or Christian. It was for Seth.

She glanced around the café as she waited, noting how much time had passed since that very first visit. She remembered the day she'd first walked in with Christian, the small boy clinging to her side, eyes wide and hollow after his mother's death. The memory hovered at the edges of her thoughts, bittersweet now as she stood in the same spot, in a café that had been polished and rebranded but still held the same essence of quiet solitude.

The staff had changed over the years, but the corners of the place still whispered to her. The creak of the floorboards beneath her feet, the faint clatter of cups behind the counter—it was all so familiar. And yet, with the passage of time, it felt like something had been lost. The imperfections that had once given the shop its character had now been replaced with the sheen of progress, the rough edges smoothed out, much like her own life. But underneath the surface, there were still cracks. There was always something hidden.

Forbidden fruit a flavour has, the line from Dickinson's poem surfaced in her mind, Jack speaking to her through another's words. She caught herself smiling, though there was little joy in it. Forbidden. Was that what this was now, her quiet meetings with Seth? A flavour that lingered in the back of her mouth, sweet but tinged with bitterness. She hadn't allowed herself to consider it in those terms before, but the thought tugged at something inside her, a sharp awareness of lines crossed, and emotions she didn't want to fully understand.

"Here you go, Charley." The barista slid the two coffees across the counter, and Charley snapped out of her thoughts, thanking her with another brief smile before finding a table near the back, one by the window. She could see the street outside, the steady drizzle of winter rain turning the pavement dark and slick. She liked the view—it gave her something to focus on when she didn't want to think too deeply about what was happening inside.

Seth arrived not long after, his tall frame ducking through the doorway as he shook the rain from his jacket. His hair was damp, and he ran a hand through it as he spotted her, grinning in that easy, carefree way that had first drawn her to him. It was a boyish smile, innocent in its charm, though Charley knew well enough by now that Seth was not as naïve as he sometimes appeared.

"Hey," he said, sliding into the seat across from her. "Thanks for the coffee, mate."

His eyes, warm and mischievous, met hers as he picked up the cup. Charley watched him for a moment, unable to shake the subtle sense of guilt that always lingered when they were together like this.

"It's still the same old place, huh?" Seth said, glancing around as he sipped his coffee. "A little spruced up, but the same bones."

Charley nodded, her eyes following his. "Yeah. It's changed, but... it hasn't. Funny how that happens."

Seth raised an eyebrow. "Like people sometimes?"

She gave a soft laugh, though the sound didn't quite reach her eyes. "Something like that."

Armour Love gave way to Bastille's *Poet*, and they settled into an easy rhythm, the conversation light and familiar. Seth had always been good at that—making her forget, for a little while, the weight she carried. He had a way of slipping past her defences, of getting her to laugh even when she didn't feel like it. He talked about work, his plans for the weekend, some ridiculous story about a friend of his. It was easy, the way it always was between them. But as they talked, Charley couldn't help but feel the undercurrent, the unspoken tension that always hung in the air when they were alone. It was subtle, almost imperceptible, but it was there, like the memory of the coffee shop in its earlier days—a familiarity that couldn't be erased, even with time and change.

Seth leaned back in his chair, his eyes settling on her with a look she'd come to recognise, a kind of quiet intensity that often made her heartbeat just a little bit faster. It wasn't desire, in the usual sense, but there was something between them that felt dangerously close to crossing a line. She'd never let it, and neither had he, but the possibility always hovered, on the edge, just out of reach.

"Do you ever think about what would happen if things were different?" Seth asked suddenly, his voice soft, his eyes steady.

Charley blinked, caught off guard by the question. "Different, how?"

Seth shrugged, but his eyes didn't leave hers. "I don't know. If we'd met at a different time. If things weren't so… complicated."

She looked away, her fingers wrapping around the warmth of her coffee cup. "Seth—"

"I know," he interrupted, his tone gentle but firm. "I know, Charley. I'm not asking for anything. I'm just… wondering, you know? Sometimes I think about it, that's all… and I wonder if you do, too?"

Charley didn't answer right away. She couldn't. The truth was, she thought about it too—more often than she liked to admit. But there were lines she wouldn't cross, not with Seth, not with anyone. She'd made her choices long ago, and even though those choices sometimes felt like shackles, she wasn't about to break them. *Forbidden fruit a flavour has.* The words echoed in her mind again, and she understood now what they meant. It wasn't the fruit itself—it was the temptation, the pull of something that couldn't be. The sweetness was in the knowing it was out of reach, the sharpness in the understanding that tasting it would ruin everything.

"You know we can't," she said quietly, her eyes still on the rain-slicked street outside. "We can't pretend things are different when they're not."

Seth was silent for a moment, and when she finally looked back at him, his smile had softened, become something sadder, more resigned. "Yeah. I know."

They sat there for a while, the conversation drifting into safer territory, but the aftermath of what had been said lingered on. Charley could feel it, a reminder of all the things she couldn't have, all the paths she couldn't take. The coffee shop felt smaller now, more enclosed. The rain outside had picked up, tapping against the windows with a steady rhythm that matched the quiet thrum of her thoughts. Seth was still talking, but Charley's mind was elsewhere, lost in the past, in the echoes of this place, of the years that had slipped by unnoticed until now.

She remembered bringing Christian here when he had been much younger too, remembering the way he had always clung to her, scared and small, so lost in his grief that it had nearly broken her heart. She had tried to comfort him; to be there for him in the way no one had been there for her when she had needed it. But now, sitting across from Seth, she couldn't help but wonder if she had done the right thing. If any of them had. The past was like that—always creeping up on you when you least expected it, like the slow change of the seasons, the way the café had transformed around her almost without her even realising it had. And the way people changed in the same way, too, whether they wanted to or not.

"Charley?" Seth's voice pulled her back to the present, and she blinked, refocusing on him.

"Sorry," she said, offering a faint smile. "Just... thinking."

Seth studied her for a moment, his expression unreadable. "You're always thinking."

Charley laughed softly. "A curse of sorts, perhaps?"

He smiled at that, but there was something in his eyes now, something that told her he wasn't satisfied with her answer. But he didn't push it. He never did.

Seth leaned back, the conversation seeming to settle between them like the rain outside. Charley sipped her coffee, her thoughts trailing back to the words they hadn't said, the places they refused to go, both in their conversation and in their lives. She noticed how Seth's eyes lingered on the table, his fingers tracing the rim of his cup in slow, deliberate circles. There was something in his silence, an energy that felt coiled, waiting. But, as always, he let it go. That was Seth's way, after all—he never demanded, never intruded. And yet, there were times when his restraint felt like its own kind of temptation, inviting her to ask the questions she was too afraid to.

They'd known each other for a while now, meeting in these quiet corners of the city where they could pretend, for a moment, that everything made sense. She enjoyed his company, his wit, his ease with the world. But there was also something about him that she couldn't quite pin down, a shadow in his past that she'd never dared to explore. He was younger than her, by a good few years, and though their conversations often flowed effortlessly, there was always a line they didn't cross—a mutual understanding that what they had wasn't quite normal, wasn't quite right. It was the unspoken thing between them, the thing that made their meetings feel like more than just friendship, even though they hadn't crossed any physical boundaries. Yet, there was always a pull, a magnetic draw that made her want to push against the limits of what was acceptable. *Forbidden fruit a flavour has.* The words floated into her mind, unbidden, but they resonated. Wasn't that what this was? This strange connection with Seth, this covert coffee shop ritual, was their own version of forbidden fruit. It wasn't explicit, but it lingered in the way they looked at each other, the pauses in their conversation, the little touches that seemed to hold more meaning than they should.

"You ever think," Seth began slowly, as if picking his words with care, "that the things we aren't supposed to do are the ones that taste the sweetest?"

Charley raised an eyebrow, intrigued as if he was somehow reading her mind. "Like what?"

He smiled, a slow, easy smile that didn't quite reach his eyes. "You know. The stuff everyone tells you not to do. The things that feel wrong, or maybe just… unconventional. The things people would frown on if they knew."

She could hear the edge of mischief in his voice, the same playful tone he always used when he was trying to get her to admit to something. But this time, there was something more to his words. Something somehow darker.

"You mean vices?" she asked, tilting her head, studying him.

"Vices," he echoed. "Yeah, sure, if you want to call it that. But I don't mean just the obvious stuff. It's more than that. It's the things society tells you to keep hidden. The stuff people do in secret because they know if anyone found out, it'd be over for them."

She took another sip of her coffee, considering his words. There was truth in them, she knew. Everyone had something—something they hid, something they indulged in when no one was looking. Some part of themselves that didn't fit neatly into the box society had built for them. She'd seen it often enough, in people's eyes, in the little slips they made when they thought no one was watching.

"So, you're saying it's the thrill of breaking the rules that makes it sweet?" she asked, her voice light but probing.

Seth chuckled softly, shaking his head. "It's not just the thrill. It's the fact that you're living outside of what's expected. The rules are there, sure, but they're only rules because someone decided they were. Who gets to say what's right and wrong?"

Charley couldn't help but smile at that. It was an idea that appealed to her, the notion that the boundaries society set were arbitrary, that the so-called 'right' way of living was just one option among many. She had never been one to follow the rules too closely, though her life, on the surface, appeared to fit within them.

"And you?" she asked, leaning forward slightly, her eyes meeting his. "What's your forbidden fruit?"

Seth looked at her, his smile fading as his expression grew thoughtful. For a moment, she thought he wouldn't answer, but then he shrugged, looking away toward the rain-splattered window.

"I had someone once," he said quietly. "A long time ago. It was... complicated."

Charley felt a twinge of surprise. He rarely talked about his past, especially not his personal life. She'd often wondered about it—what kind of relationships he'd had, who had shaped him into the man sitting across from her now. But he had never volunteered the information, and she hadn't pried. Until now.

"What happened?" she asked, keeping her tone gentle, curious.

He hesitated, his fingers still tracing the edge of his cup. "We met in university. She was... different. Smart, driven. We studied medicine together."

Charley blinked. Medicine? She hadn't known that about him, either. Seth never talked about his time at university, and she had assumed he had taken a different path. But the fact that he had once studied medicine changed her perception of him. It was strange how someone you thought you knew could still surprise you, how the past could suddenly surface in ways you didn't expect.

"What was she like?" she asked, her voice soft.

Seth's gaze grew distant, as if he were looking back through a dim haze. "She was... special. We were young, and everything felt so intense back then. You know how it is, when you're in your twenties, you think that maybe you have all the time in the world."

Charley nodded, though she wasn't sure if she really knew. Her twenties had been a blur of uncertainty, trying to figure out what she wanted from life. She had never had the kind of intense, consuming love he was describing.

"And then?" she prompted, sensing that there was more to the story.

Seth smiled sadly, his fingers stilling on the cup. "It didn't work out. Fate intervened. I think, in the end, it wasn't meant to be. All over a cup of coffee, ironically."

There was a note of finality in his voice, a resignation that told her the story was over, at least from his perspective. But something about the way he spoke—so vague, so careful—made her wonder if there was more to it. More than he was willing to share, at least right now.

"Do you still think about her?" she asked, her curiosity getting the better of her.

Seth glanced at her, "Sometimes. But not in the way you might think. It's more like... a dream than a memory now. Like something that happened to someone else. You know when you wake up and you desperately want to recall what it was... but it's just slipping away from you... We were both different people back then."

Charley studied him for a moment, trying to read the emotions behind his words. There was a sadness in him, a kind of quiet regret, but there was also a distance, as if he had long since come to terms with whatever had happened. Still, she couldn't shake the feeling that he was holding something back, that there was more to the story than he was letting on.

She didn't press him, though. She knew better than to push when he wasn't ready to talk. Instead, she leaned back in her chair, taking another sip of her coffee as she considered what he'd said.

"Forbidden fruit," she murmured, more to herself than to him.

Seth raised an eyebrow, his smile returning. "What was that?"

Charley shook her head, a small smile playing on her lips. "Nothing. Just… thinking."

Seth chuckled. "You're always thinking, Charley."

She smiled, but this time it didn't reach her eyes. There was something unsettling about their conversation, something that left her feeling uneasy. Maybe it was the way he spoke about his past, so carefully, so deliberately, as if there were things he didn't want her to know. Or maybe it was the realisation that, despite how well she thought she knew him, there were still so many parts of his life that remained a mystery to her. Looking out of the window, she watched as the rain dripped down the glass in slow, steady rivulets. The street outside was quiet, the usual hum of the city muffled by the weather. It was a scene she had seen a thousand times before, but today it felt different, as if something had shifted beneath the surface of her world, something she couldn't quite put her finger on.

Charley found herself wondering, not for the first time, what it was about Seth that drew her to him. Was it the forbidden fruit? The allure of something she couldn't have, something that society—or her own conscience—told her was wrong? Or was it something else, something deeper, something she couldn't quite name? She wasn't sure. All she knew was that this added to her feelings of uncertainty. And that uncertainty, more than anything else, scared her slightly.

11

'These strangers, in a foreign World'

Ganta, Liberia 1935.

Emmanuel Kamara, twelve years old and as wiry as a young sapling, darted between the huts, his bare feet kicking up puffs of red dust as he went. He was in no hurry today, with nothing to do but lose himself in the small streets that crisscrossed his hometown. The sun, a harsh disc in the cloudless sky, beat down relentlessly, but Emmanuel had long grown used to its intensity. His skin, dark and smooth, shimmered with a light sheen of sweat as he moved with the easy grace of a boy who knew every dusty inch of this place.

The town sat like a forgotten jewel on the edge of the jungle, its red clay roads winding through a scatter of wooden houses and narrow lanes, all but swallowed by the thick green fingers of the forest. Dust clung to the hems of skirts and trousers, sticking to bare feet like a second skin, and the air was filled with the smell of wood smoke, cooking fires, and the damp earth. The heat pressed down with a weight that made even the simplest movements feel like a burden, and yet life here, as always, moved on in its slow, unhurried rhythm.

Ganta wasn't much of a town by the standards of the coastal cities—Monrovia, or even Buchanan. It wasn't a place where merchants or traders came in droves, nor was it a popular destination for the missionaries who preferred the more populated areas. But to young Emmanuel, it was the entire world. The houses, made from wood and thatch, leaned slightly as if exhausted from the heat. They were painted in faded hues of yellow and blue, though many were now just the colour of the earth, having surrendered to the elements long ago. Chickens scratched in the dirt, goats wandered freely, and here and there, small knots of women sat in the shade, their hands busy with woven baskets or grinding cassava.

In the distance, rising like a sentinel above the town, was the mission house. It was one of the few solid buildings, a sturdy structure of whitewashed brick and iron roofing that seemed out of place among the humble dwellings of the locals. The mission was run by the American missionaries, and its presence was both revered and resented in equal measure. Emmanuel had been there once, taken by his mother to see the doctor when a fever had nearly claimed him. The white man who lived there—a tall, serious-faced preacher with kind eyes—had given him medicine and laid his cool hands on his burning forehead. Emmanuel remembered the feeling of the man's fingers, as foreign and strange as the taste of the medicine he'd been given.

Emmanuel rounded a corner, the sound of laughter catching his attention. A group of boys, not much older than himself, were kicking a makeshift ball—nothing more than rags tied together with string—in the narrow alleyway between two houses. He paused, tempted to join them, but thought better of it. They were older, stronger, and he had no desire to be shoved around for their childish amusement. Instead, he continued on, heading toward the market square where the town's life seemed to gather in a single, bustling knot of noise and activity.

The market was small, a cluster of wooden stalls set up beneath the shade of large palm trees. Women sold vegetables, rice, and fruit—papayas, bananas, and pineapples that seemed to glow in the afternoon sun. There were chickens in cages, their feathers ruffled and eyes blinking lazily, and fish laid out on mats, already beginning to curl at the edges in the heat. Emmanuel weaved his way through the market, dodging between women with baskets on their heads and men carrying sacks of grain. He wasn't interested in the food or the wares today. He was looking for something else—something to break the monotony of the day.

And then he saw the stranger.

The man stood at the edge of the market, just beyond the stalls, near the road that led out of town. Emmanuel stopped in his tracks; his curiosity piqued. The man was white—one of the few white men Emmanuel had ever seen in Ganta. He was dressed in khaki trousers and a long-sleeved shirt, though it was clear from the way he tugged at the collar and mopped his brow with a handkerchief that the heat was getting to him. A wide-brimmed hat shaded his face, but even from a distance, Emmanuel could see that his skin was pale, almost pink, like someone who had spent too long under the unforgiving sun. His clothes were dusty, and he carried a small leather bag slung over one shoulder.

Emmanuel approached slowly, keeping to the shadows of the nearby stalls, his eyes never leaving the man. He wondered what had brought him here—this stranger, with his strange clothes and strange skin. Was he another missionary, like the preacher at the mission house? Or perhaps a trader, though he carried no goods that Emmanuel could see. The man didn't seem to notice him, too preoccupied with the road ahead and the heat pressing down on him.

The man moved to the side of the road and sat down on a low stone wall, taking off his hat and wiping his face with the handkerchief again. He looked exhausted, his face drawn and tired, as if he'd been walking for hours. Emmanuel, still watching from a distance, felt a strange pull of sympathy for him. The white man looked out of place here, like a bee caught in the wrong garden, buzzing aimlessly with no flowers in sight. The image struck Emmanuel as funny, and he almost smiled, though he kept quiet.

After a moment, the man reached into his bag and pulled out a small bottle of water. He took a long drink, his eyes scanning the market as he did so, though he seemed to be looking for something—or someone. Emmanuel hesitated, unsure whether to approach or stay hidden. But his curiosity won out, as it always did, and he stepped forward, making his way across the open space toward the white man.

When he was close enough, he stopped, standing a few paces away. The man looked up, his eyes locking on Emmanuel's with a mixture of surprise and curiosity.

"Hello there," the man said, his voice thick with an accent Emmanuel didn't recognise. It wasn't like the preacher's voice—this one was not as rough, more polished, though not unkind.

Emmanuel said nothing at first, just watching the man. He didn't know what to say, and besides, it wasn't often that people like him—small, unnoticed—were spoken to by people like the white man.

The man smiled, though it was a tired smile, "You from around here?" he asked, his voice softer now, as if he could sense Emmanuel's hesitation.

Emmanuel nodded, still not trusting his voice. He shifted his weight from one foot to the other, feeling the heat of the sun on his back and the rough earth beneath his feet.

"Good place, this," the man said, glancing around the market. "Busy. Lively."

Emmanuel nodded again, though he wasn't sure if the man really believed that. To him, it seemed the white man was lost, out of place, like someone searching for something they weren't sure they'd ever find.

The man looked at him again, this time more closely, as if seeing Emmanuel for the first time. "What's your name, boy?"

"Emmanuel," the boy said quietly, his voice barely more than a whisper.

The man nodded, as if satisfied with that. "Emmanuel," he repeated, testing the name on his tongue. Then, with a sigh, he stood up, brushing the dust from his trousers, and Emmanuel noticed the way the man's long, white fingers danced over the fabric, as if trying to erase not just the dirt but the very experience of having been in Ganta. The boy stared, feeling a mix of wonder and apprehension. In all his twelve years, he had never seen such a white man as this one before—at least not up close. There had been whispers of them, fleeting stories shared in hushed tones: white men who brought strange things, who came from places where the sun didn't beat down with such fervour, and where the people didn't share the same skin colour or language.

Emmanuel felt a curious pull toward this stranger, a fascination he couldn't quite articulate. The man looked ordinary in his dusty clothes, but to Emmanuel, he was extraordinary, an embodiment of a world he had only heard of in stories, a world painted in shades of adventure and discovery.

"Who are you?" Emmanuel blurted out, unable to contain the question any longer. It felt bold, a small act of defiance against the pull of the boy's own timidity.

The man paused, his brow furrowing slightly, as if considering the answer. "Just a traveller," he replied finally, his voice smooth but tinged with a hesitation that made Emmanuel think he was hiding something. "Exploring, seeing the world."

"Why Ganta?" Emmanuel pressed, unable to hide his interest. "What is there to see in Ganta?"

A faint smile tugged at the corners of the man's mouth, but it didn't reach his eyes. "You'd be surprised at what you can find in places like this. The heart of it all, you know?"

His words felt important, mysterious, and Emmanuel sensed there was more to this man than he was letting on. Yet he couldn't grasp it, the significance of the encounter felt like mist slipping through his fingers. Instead, he found himself looking down the road, half expecting a miraculous sighting of the woman he thought the man was searching for, but the road remained empty, lined with trees that whispered secrets of their own.

As they stood there, a breeze picked up, stirring the dry dust and lifting the scent of something sweet from the market. Emmanuel's stomach growled softly, reminding him of the cassava waiting for him at home, yet he couldn't bear to leave just yet. There was something captivating about this stranger—a spark of possibility in a world that often felt closed and predictable.

"What's that?" Emmanuel asked, pointing to the worn book tucked beneath the man's arm, his curiosity overcoming his shyness. "You have a book?"

The man glanced down, almost protectively, as if it were something precious. "Ah, this?" he said, lifting it slightly. "It's nothing special, just a collection of poetry."

"What's poetry?" Emmanuel asked, his brow furrowing.

The man's eyes brightened with a hint of interest. "Words that dance, words that capture feelings, moments…

life, even. It can make you see the world differently," he said, his fingers running lightly over the fraying cover. "This one is by a man called W.B. Yeats."

"W.B. Yeats?" Emmanuel echoed, slowly, precisely, his mind struggling to catch up.

The man regarded him thoughtfully. "Can you read, Emmanuel?"

"Yes," Emmanuel answered, pride swelling in his chest. "The missionary taught me English good."

"Good for you," the man replied, smiling and nodding approvingly. "What do you think of poetry?"

"I don't know," Emmanuel admitted, his voice trailing off. "I never read any."

"You should," the man said, an earnestness creeping into his tone. "It's like… like seeing the world in a new way. A way that's deeper, richer." He flipped through the pages of the book, the sound like a gentle rustle of leaves. "Do you want to hear a poem?"

Emmanuel nodded, enchanted by the idea. The man cleared his throat, and began to read, his voice low and melodic, drawing Emmanuel into the words as if they were a soft lullaby.

"The Second Coming," he began, and as he spoke, Emmanuel felt the words settle around him, passing into the air with an intensity that made the world feel different, almost electric. The man's voice rose and fell like the swell of the ocean, and Emmanuel imagined the scenes unfolding—the falcon soaring through the sky, the darkness that loomed over the land, the birth of something new, something powerful.

"And what rough beast, its hour come round at last, slouches towards Bethlehem to be born?" The man finished; his eyes distant as if he were still lost in the lines he had just recited.

"Is that one your favourite poem?" Emmanuel asked, his voice a whisper.

"Yes," the man replied, his look returning to the boy. "It captures the feeling of the world, doesn't it? The chaos, the change, the inevitability of things we cannot control."

Emmanuel nodded, trying to grasp the meaning of the man's words. "I don't understand everything," he confessed. "But it feels… important."

"It is," the man said softly, a flicker of something in his eyes—an understanding perhaps, or maybe a reminder of his own lost innocence. "Life is full of such moments. They're fleeting, but they shape us, define us."

A silence settled between them, as if they were both on the brink of a revelation neither could fully articulate, as one could never truly understand the other. Emmanuel felt the air thicken, laden with unexpressed feelings, the intensity of the moment swelling like the wind before a storm.

"Do you write poetry?" Emmanuel asked suddenly, the question spilling out before he could stop it. "Like Mister W.B. Yeats?"

The man laughed softly, the sound warm and rich. "No, I'm afraid not. I leave that to others—those who have the gift. Another famous poet once wrote that poetry is the best words in the best order… The best I can do… is simply put words in their best order. I'm more of a traveller, a seeker."

"Seeker," Emmanuel echoed, the word rolling off his tongue like a promise. "What do you seek?"

"Everything," the man replied, his eyes narrowing with an intensity that sent a shiver down Emmanuel's spine. "Truth, beauty, understanding. There's so much to see in this world, young man. So much hidden beneath the surface."

"What do you see?" Emmanuel asked, his heart racing with excitement.

The man paused, his expression shifting as he considered the question. "What I see is not always what I want to see," he admitted, his voice lower now, tinged with a heaviness that felt unfamiliar to Emmanuel. "It's a reminder that the world is often more complicated than it appears. There can be beauty in the darkness, too, though."

Emmanuel frowned, sensing the man's discomfort, the way his gaze drifted, lost in thought. "You're sad," he said, the observation slipping out without an adult's hesitation.

The man smiled sadly, a flicker of surprise crossing his features. "You're a perceptive one," he said, the warmth of his earlier tone now mingling with something deeper. "It's easy to feel lost when you're out here, far from everything you know."

"Do you feel lost?" Emmanuel asked, the question lingering in the air.

"Sometimes," the man admitted, and there was a sincerity in his voice that sent a chill through Emmanuel's bones. "But that's a part of my journey, too, I suppose."

Emmanuel nodded, though he couldn't quite understand what it meant to be lost. His whole world was small and simple, contained within the dusty streets of Ganta and the familiar faces that filled them. He had never known the feeling of searching for something beyond his reach. "What are you searching for?" he asked, the curiosity bubbling back to the surface.

"Answers," the man replied, his eyes piercing through Emmanuel as if he could see into the boy's soul. "I'm searching for answers to questions I can't even fully articulate."

"What questions?" Emmanuel pressed, his heart pounding.

The man hesitated, glancing around as if ensuring no one was listening. "The kind of questions that haunt you," he finally said, the deeper meaning of his words settling in the spaces between them. "About life, about purpose, about the choices we make. The human condition… Life is full of these journeys we don't have maps for."

Emmanuel felt a sudden kinship with the man, an understanding that transcended their differences. He wanted to reach out, to bridge the gap that separated them, but he didn't know how. Instead, he looked at the man, his eyes reflecting the warmth of the sun, a glimmer of hope hidden in the depths of uncertainty.

"You don't have to be alone on your journey, sir," Emmanuel said, surprising even himself with the words. "I'm here. We can search together."

The man's expression softened, the corners of his mouth lifting in a hesitant smile. "Thank you, Emmanuel. That's a very kind offer, young man."

But just then, the tranquillity of the moment shattered as a group of children ran past, laughing and shouting, pulling Emmanuel's attention. He turned to watch them, feeling the joy from their laughter, the carefree joy that filled the air. It was a reminder of the man's own childhood, of the days spent playing in the sun, before the shadows of the world crept in. His voice broke through his reverie, gentle yet firm. "You should join them. Don't let this moment slip away."

Emmanuel turned back, the sunlight catching the man's features, highlighting the lines etched into his face. He felt a pang of regret as he realised their time together was drawing to a close. "Will you still be here tomorrow?" he asked, his voice tinged with hope.

"I don't know," the man replied, a glimmer of something flickering in his eyes—perhaps a hint of regret, perhaps something deeper.

12
'We see — Comparatively'

London, England 1981.

The boy sat cross-legged on the threadbare carpet, his small body hunched over, eyes fixed on the television screen in the dimly lit living room. The flickering image was grainy, washed-out from the years of use, and the sound crackled with the occasional static, but he could still hear the voices clearly enough. The stern and measured tones of the newscaster announced the latest in a series of race riots that had flared up in Brixton. The word "riot" itself seemed to hang in the air like a dirty word, a whispered thing, but now it was being spoken openly, daily, as if it had become normal, accepted.

On the screen, the scenes were chaotic—smoke billowed in thick, dark clouds, rising from cars set alight, and crowds surged through the streets. The faces of young Black men, filled with anger and defiance, were captured in brief flashes between the flurry of baton-wielding policemen and the trembling frames of store windows being smashed. It was a world both familiar and far away. The boy, all of twelve years old, watched it all silently, his hands clutching his knees tightly, as though he might anchor himself to the floor.

The living room was small and cluttered, every corner filled with the signs of life in a modest council flat. A fraying sofa, where the springs creaked whenever anyone shifted their weight, dominated the space. Next to it, a low coffee table bore a half-read newspaper, a few unopened letters, and a cup of tea that had long since gone cold. The air smelled faintly of oil and onions, a warm scent drifting in from the small kitchen where his mother was cooking.

On the mantel above the gas fire, a collection of trinkets and photos stood like silent witnesses to their lives: a framed picture of the boy at six years old in his school uniform from home, beaming with missing front teeth; another of his mother, her expression serious but proud, holding him as a toddler. Beside the photographs, a small wooden cross leaned against the wall, its presence subtle, but steady.

The television droned on, the images of burning streets and clashing crowds reflected faintly in the window as the day outside darkened into evening. A single lamp flickered in the corner, casting long shadows that danced on the walls. He felt the noise, the images, dressing him like a too-tight jacket. It wasn't fear, exactly, that he felt, but something else—something almost inaccessible, like a question that couldn't quite form in his mind.

"Mum?" he called out, his voice tentative, unsure if he wanted to disturb her.

From the kitchen came the soft clattering of pots and the hiss of something frying in a pan. The boy listened to it for a moment, the ordinary sounds of home that felt so distant from what he was seeing on the screen.

He called out again, this time louder, "Mum?"

"Mm?" came her reply, distracted, but she didn't come into the room.

The boy pushed himself up from the floor and padded toward the kitchen, his bare feet making no sound on the worn linoleum. He hesitated at the doorway, watching his mother move about the small space with quiet efficiency. She was in her early thirties but might seem older, her face lined with worry and exhaustion that never seemed to leave, no matter how much she tried to hide it behind her smile. Her dark hair, pulled back into a tight bun, was streaked with early grey, and she wore a faded floral apron over her dress, the same one she always wore when cooking dinner.

She didn't look up as he entered, her hands busy stirring something in a pot. The light in the kitchen was harsher than in the living room, the overhead bulb casting a bright, clinical glow that made the room feel even smaller than it was. The countertops were crowded with jars of spices, tins of beans, and a bowl of ripening plantains.

"Mum," he said again, quieter now that he was closer.

"What is it, little one?" she asked, still not turning to face him.

"I was watching the television man," he began, unsure how to ask the question that had been forming in his mind. He wasn't sure if she'd want to hear it, if it was the kind of thing he should even be asking. But the images of the riots, the fires, the faces of those young men—they had stuck with him, unsettling something deep inside.

She paused in her stirring, her back still to him. "You shouldn't watch that stuff. It's not for children." There was a weariness in her voice, an edge that made him feel like he was intruding on something private.

"I know," he said, shifting his weight from one foot to the other. "But… why are they fighting? Why are they so angry?"

His mother sighed, a sound that seemed to come from somewhere deep within her, and finally turned to face him. She wiped her hands on the apron and looked at him, really looked at him, with eyes that were both tired and tender. For a moment, she didn't answer, just studied his face as if weighing up how much he could understand.

"Come here," she said, gesturing for him to sit at the small kitchen table. The table was old and wobbled slightly when he rested his arms on it. She sat down across from him, folding her hands in front of her. He could see the traces of flour on her knuckles, the small burns from years of cooking. She looked at him for a long time before speaking, as if trying to find the right words.

"They're angry because life isn't fair for them," she said slowly, choosing each word with care. "Sometimes people get treated differently because of the colour of their skin. And when that happens over and over again, people get tired of it. They want things to change."

The boy frowned, trying to make sense of it. He thought of his own life, the smallness of it, the routine. He went to school, came home, watched television, helped his mother when she asked. It was simple. He had friends, sure, but sometimes he noticed the differences—small things, little remarks. He remembered the time at school when one of the boys had called him "darkie" and the way it had made his chest tighten, even though he hadn't fully understood what that meant, why it meant something bad.

"Like... they're angry at the police?" he asked.

His mother's face tightened just a little, the corners of her mouth pulling down. "Yes, the police. And others. People in power. Sometimes the ones who are supposed to protect us... don't." She paused again, her eyes softening. "But not all of them are bad. It's just... complicated."

The boy nodded, but the answer didn't satisfy him. It only made more questions bubble up in his mind. He thought about the faces of the young men on the news, their rage, their rebellion. Was that how he was supposed to feel, too? Was that what was waiting for him when he grew older?

"But Mum," he began hesitantly, "what can they do? Can't they just talk to someone to make things better?"

His mother smiled, a sad, weary smile, as though she had been asked that question many times before and had long since stopped believing in easy answers. "It's not always that simple, love. People have been talking for a long time. Sometimes, talking isn't enough. Folks gotta hear too."

He sat quietly, absorbing her words, but they felt painful, like beach stones in his small chest. He didn't want to think that the world could be so unfair, so full of fire and fury. It made him feel small, powerless.

His mother reached across the table and took his hand in hers, her touch warm and familiar. "But you, my boy—you don't have to be like them. You can grow up to be better. You can change things; you don't have to do it with anger. You can use your mind, your heart, your beautiful soul."

The boy looked down at his hand in hers, he felt her words, but he wasn't sure he believed them. The world on the screen seemed too big, too overwhelming. How could he, just a small boy in a small flat in Haringey, change anything?

"Go and wash up for dinner," she said softly, giving his hand a gentle squeeze before letting go. "It's nearly ready."

He nodded and slid off the chair. He could hear the news continuing to drone on in the other room, but the images in his mind were louder—angry faces, fire, and the question of what his place in this world would be when he was older.

As he washed his hands under the lukewarm water, he glanced back at his mother, watching her return to the stove, her movements slow but deliberate. He dried his hands and stood there for a moment, watching her, feeling the warmth of the kitchen, the safety of home, and the uncertainty of the world beyond their door.

Isaac's father entered the flat like he always did—quietly, his presence felt more than heard. The door clicked shut behind him, and his tall frame filled the narrow hallway. He looked tired, as he always did when he came home from the long hours spent working at the factory. His shoulders were hunched, the once-pressed lines of his shirt rumpled from the day's work, and there was an air of resignation about him, as though each step he took required more effort than it should.

Isaac stood near the kitchen doorway, his small hands fidgeting with the hem of his jumper as he watched his father remove his coat and hang it on the peg. There was something about the way his father moved that made Isaac hesitate to speak right away. His father always came home with that same look—worn, distant, as if the weight of the world outside their small flat was on him, and he had to shake it off before he could face his family.

"Papa?" Isaac said quietly, testing the air between them.

His father glanced up; his eyes tired but softening when they landed on Isaac. "Ah, my boy," he greeted, his voice low and gravelly, touched with the remnants of their homeland's accent. "How was your day?"

Isaac shrugged, not sure how to answer that question. He wanted to tell his father about the news, about the riots, but he wasn't sure if it was the right time. There was always a tension in the air whenever the subject of what was happening in London came up—a tension that Isaac didn't fully understand but felt all the same.

His mother appeared in the hallway, wiping her hands on her apron. "You're home late," she said, not unkindly, but with the familiar tone that came from years of worry.

"Yes," his father said, sighing deeply as he entered the kitchen. "There was trouble at work again. Some of the men didn't show up, and they asked me to stay late." He sat down at the small kitchen table, running a hand over his face. "It's been a long day."

Isaac followed him into the kitchen. He wanted to understand—he needed to understand. He could feel the unease in the air, not just in their home, but everywhere, like a storm was brewing just beyond their reach.

His mother began serving dinner, placing a steaming pot of stew in the centre of the table. The warm, familiar smell of spices and meat filled the room, a comforting contrast to the tension that seemed to linger unspoken between them.

Isaac sat down across from his father, watching as the older man slowly unbuttoned his cuffs and rolled up his sleeves. His hands were rough and calloused, marked by years of hard labour, and Isaac couldn't help but notice the small cuts and scrapes that marred his skin. His father never complained, never spoke of the hardships he endured at work, but Isaac could see it—the quiet suffering, the way the world seemed to weigh on him more heavily since they had come to London. He watched as those same calloused fingers gently turned off the television, putting on the radio instead, where Cocktail Slippers' *St Valentine's Day Massacre* played quietly in the background.

"Papa," Isaac said again, this time more directly.

His father looked up, his eyes meeting Isaac's, and Isaac could see the weariness there—the same weariness his mother carried. "Yes, son?" his father asked.

"I... I saw the news," Isaac began, his voice hesitant. "About the riots. In Brixton."

His father's expression didn't change, but there was a flicker of something in his eyes, something guarded, like he had been expecting the question but was still unprepared for it.

"Ah," his father said, leaning back in his chair. Isaac's mother glanced between them, her hands still busy setting the table, but Isaac could see the way her brow furrowed slightly, as if she too was waiting for what would come next.

"Mum say they're angry. Why are they so angry?" Isaac asked, the question spilling out before he could stop it. "I thought we came here to be safe. But it's not safe, is it?"

His father's look hardened, just for a moment, before softening again. He sighed deeply, rubbing his eyes with one hand. "It's different here," he said slowly, carefully. "The things they are fighting for... it's not the same as what we left behind."

Isaac frowned, confused. "But they're angry at the police. They're fighting in the streets. Isn't that what we ran away from?"

His father shook his head, his expression pained. "No, Isaac. It's not the same." He paused, as if searching for the right words to explain something too big, too complicated for a twelve-year-old boy to understand. "In Liberia, we left because there was nothing left for us. We left to survive."

As Cocktail Slippers softly bled into *Night Games* by Graham Bonnet around him, Isaac sat absorbed into his memories of the long, arduous journey from Liberia to England, and the fear that had clung to their family like a shadow. They had left behind everything they had, everything they knew, to find themselves in this strange, foreign land, hoping to start over in a place that was supposed to be peaceful. But now, watching the riots on the news, Isaac didn't feel safe. He didn't understand how they could leave one kind of violence only to find another.

"But why are they fighting here?" Isaac urged. "What are they so angry about?"

His father's face tightened, and for a moment, Isaac thought he wasn't going to answer. But then his father sighed again, deeper this time, and leaned forward, resting his elbows on the table.

"They're angry because... because life here isn't fair for them either," his father said, his voice low. "They've been treated badly for a long time, and now they fight back."

Isaac frowned, still not understanding. "But... we're all safe here, right? It's not like home?"

His father smiled, but it was a sad smile, "We're safer here than we were there," he said, carefully. "But that doesn't mean everything is fair. It doesn't mean there's no injustice."

Isaac didn't fully understand what his father meant, but he could hear the seriousness in his voice, the way the words seemed to hang in the air much heavier than usual. He could feel the same tension in the air that he had seen on the news, the same sense of unease.

"What about us?" Isaac asked, his voice small. "Are we... are we going to have to fight too?"

His father's expression softened, and he reached across the table to place a hand on Isaac's shoulder. "No," he said gently. "We don't got to fight. We left all that behind. We're here now, and we'll make it a good life here."

Isaac nodded, but the answer didn't satisfy him. It felt like there was more, something his father wasn't telling him. His mind lingered on the riots, on the anger and confusion in the streets of London, and on his father's words, which seemed to hang in the air like the dark clouds on the horizon—threatening but distant.

He glanced over at the bookshelf in the corner of the room, where his father kept a small collection of books, most of them well-worn, their spines cracked, and their covers faded. One book, in particular, caught his eye—a small, tatty volume wedged between the Bible and a handful of other old texts. Its cover was faded, the title barely legible, but something about it drew Isaac's attention.

He stood up from the table and walked over to the shelf, reaching out to pull the book free. It felt fragile in his hands, as if it might crumble under the weight of its own age. The cover read, in faint gold letters: *Michael Robartes and the Dancer* by W.B. Yeats.

"Papa," Isaac asked, turning the book over in his hands, "what's this?"

His father looked up from his meal, his expression softening as he saw the book in Isaac's hands. A faint smile touched his lips, but there was something else there too—something wistful, almost sad.

"That," his father said slowly, "was your grandfather's special book."

Isaac blinked, surprised. "Grandfather's?"

His father nodded, setting down his spoon. "Yes. He carried that book with him wherever he went. That, and his Bible."

Isaac looked down at the book again, its worn edges and fragile pages. He couldn't imagine someone carrying such a delicate thing through all the hardships his grandfather must have faced. It seemed like a strange choice.

"Why?" Isaac asked, looking up at his father. "Why was it important to him?"

His father leaned back in his chair, his eyes distant, as if he were looking back through time to a memory he hadn't touched in years.

"It was given to him," his father said quietly, "by a man he met when he was just a boy. A white man, travelling through our town in Liberia, many, many years ago."

Isaac's eyes widened. He had heard many stories about the life his parents had left behind, but he had never heard this one before.

"What happened?" Isaac asked, his curiosity piqued.

His father smiled faintly, though there was a touch of sadness in it. "Your grandfather was only a boy, not much older than you are now. It was a difficult time, you understand—his mother had just passed away, and he was all alone in the world, except for the missionaries who looked after him. One day, while he was wandering through the town, he met this white man, a stranger. They talked for a while, though your grandfather had never seen a white man before and didn't know what to make of him."

Isaac listened intently, imagining the scene—his grandfather, a small boy in a dusty town, standing before a man who seemed completely foreign to him. He thought of himself arriving in London a year or so before and how strange that all seemed to him, even now.

"The man was carrying a book," his father continued, nodding towards the one in Isaac's hands. "That book. And after they had talked for a while, he gave it to your grandfather, told him to keep it. Your grandfather didn't know much about books then—he could read a little, thanks to the missionaries—but he held on to it. He kept it with him through everything that came after."

Isaac ran his fingers over the cover of the book, feeling its weight in his hands. "But why this book?" he asked. "What's so special about it?"

His father's smile faded, replaced by a more serious expression. "There's a poem in it," he said. "One that meant a great deal to your grandfather. He used to say it reminded him of home. Of how fragile everything is."

Isaac frowned. "Fragile?"

His father nodded, leaning forward slightly. "Yes. The poem… it talks about how the world is always changing, how progress—everything we think is solid and permanent—can fall apart so easily. It's all too easy to go backwards, to lose what we've built."

Isaac thought about that, about the riots on the television, about the fear he felt when he saw the anger in the streets. "But why did it remind him of home?"

His father sighed, his eyes filled with memories Isaac couldn't fully understand. "Because home is fragile too," he said quietly. "In Liberia, everything we had could be lost in a moment. The war took everything from us. And when we came here, to London, we thought we would be safe. But the world isn't as simple as that. Even here, progress is fragile. People fight for what they believe in, but sometimes it feels like we're always on the edge of something—like we could fall back into chaos at any moment."

Isaac shivered. He didn't like the idea that everything around them—their home, their safety, their future—was so fragile. It made him feel small, like a leaf caught in the wind, with no control over where he might land.

"What's the poem called?" Isaac asked after a long moment, his voice barely above a whisper.

His father smiled again, though this time it was a sad, wistful smile. "The Second Coming," he said softly. "It's one of Yeats' most famous poems. Your grandfather used to read it out loud sometimes, though I don't know if he ever fully understood it. I'm not sure anyone really does."

Isaac opened the book, carefully turning the brittle pages until he found the poem his father had mentioned. The words were printed in a small, delicate font, and as he read the first few lines, a chill ran down his spine:

> *"Turning and turning in the widening gyre*
> *The falcon cannot hear the falconer;*
> *Things fall apart; the centre cannot hold;*
> *Mere anarchy is loosed upon the world…"*

He paused, his heart beating a little faster. The words felt like they carried some terrible truth, something he didn't fully understand but could feel deep in his bones.

"What does it mean?" Isaac asked, looking up at his father, his voice trembling slightly.

His father didn't answer right away. He sat back in his chair, his eyes distant again, as if he were looking back through time, back into the old days when his own father had read those same lines to him.

"It means," his father said quietly, "that the world is always changing. That nothing stays the same forever. And sometimes, when we think we're making progress, when we think we've built something solid, it all falls apart. Just like that."

Isaac swallowed hard, the significance of those words pressing down on him. "That's what happened in Liberia, isn't it?" he asked, his voice small.

His father nodded. "Yes. And it's what can happen anywhere, at any time. We have to be careful, Isaac. We have to remember that progress is fragile, that it's all too easy to lose what we've built."

Isaac closed the book, his hands trembling slightly. He didn't like the idea that everything around him—his home, his family, even the city of London itself—was so fragile, so easily lost. But as he looked at his father, he could see the truth in his eyes, the same truth that had weighed on his grandfather all those years ago.

Isaac's father stood from his chair; his eyes still burdened with the conversation they'd just shared. He walked slowly over to the small wooden cabinet in the corner of the room, its edges worn from years of use, and pulled open the creaking drawer. Inside, nestled between rows of carefully arranged vinyl records, he selected one—a familiar, well-handled album that Isaac had seen him play many times before.

Isaac watched as his father slid the record from its sleeve, the black vinyl catching the dim light of the room. He recognised the cover, the face of a woman staring out with eyes that held stories of a life lived in deep sorrow and unrelenting strength.

His father moved with a quiet reverence, setting the record on the turntable with care, as if it were more than just music, as if it were a kind of sacred ritual. The needle hovered for a moment before gently descending onto the spinning surface, and then the familiar crackle of static filled the air, a prelude to what was to come.

Isaac knew the song before the first notes even played. It was one his father would play on nights when the world seemed heavier than normal, when the memories of displacement—all of it—came crashing down upon him. Tonight, after the conversation about fragile progress and the delicate threads of history that bound them all, it felt like the right song.

The haunting, slow piano began, and Nina Simone's voice followed soon after, low and soulful, her words cutting through the room like a knife.

Isaac's father stood by the record player, his head bowed slightly, his eyes closed as the music enveloped them both. It was as though the song had the power to reach back in time, pulling all the pain, all the history, forward into this small room in Haringey, binding together the past and present in one aching note.

> *"Black bodies swinging in the southern breeze,*
> *Strange fruit hanging from the poplar trees..."*

He didn't understand all of it—but he felt it. He felt the sadness in the music, the anger, the injustice woven into each word. He reflected on what his father had said about the fragility, the futility, how progress can slip away at any moment. Were those riots outside, across London, that rage, all part of that same endless struggle, that same battle for something that could so easily be lost?

His father stood still, the music washing over him, his face set in a quiet sadness. Isaac had seen this expression before, the way his father would withdraw into himself when things felt too much to bear. And as the final words were sung, her voice fading into the crackle of the record, Isaac knew that this wasn't just a song for his father. It was a reminder of all that had been, and all that could still be, lost.

The room fell silent, save for the soft hum of the record player, the needle still spinning in its groove. Isaac's father didn't move for a moment, as if he were trying to hold on to the last echoes of the song, the last traces of the memories it stirred.

Finally, he opened his eyes and looked over at Isaac. "Do you understand, son?" he asked quietly.

Isaac nodded, though he wasn't sure he fully did. But he knew enough to feel the force of it—the pain of history, the strange and bitter fruit that still hung in the air. The world was fragile, and it could fall apart at any moment. All they could do was hold on and hope that this time, the centre might just hold.

Interview Transcript
Date: October 3rd
Location: Dr. Haggard's Office
Participants: DCI Jack Miller, Dr. William Haggard (Psychiatrist)

[09:41 AM]

WH: You've been talking a lot about history, about how it ties us together... have you ever thought about that history in a broader sense? Not just what you've lived through, but also what you've inherited?

JM: What do you mean?

WH: I'm talking about generational trauma, Jack. The idea that the things have been passed down, long before we were even aware of them. We inherit the burden of our ancestors' experiences, their mistakes, their pain, even, in our genes, in our souls. And sometimes, without realising it, we let those things define our own lives.

JM: That sounds a bit... I don't know, abstract... Like blaming my issues on the past, feels like an excuse in a way.

WH: None of this is about blame, Jack. It's about understanding... Tell me again about your earliest memory.

JM: The sea... It always comes back to the sea.

WH: You were born by the sea, weren't you? When you still lived with your parents.

JM: Brighton, yeah... But I don't know if it's a memory anymore... or if I've imagined it. Sometimes it feels like it.

WH: Talk me through it. Refresh my memory.

JM: The sea is rough. It looks silver... Stretched out for miles... Forever... An everywhere of silver... I remember... being on the beach, the pebbles, hard, loud. I can just about picture my mother, like I can picture the scene, but I can't see her face... you know?

WH: Hmmm.

JM: Her hair is so long... brown, blowing in her face. I can't see my father, but he must have been there, it's like there's a presence there but not a person.

WH: What makes you so sure he was there?

JM: Nothing... really. I mean I don't... like just a sense of... where else would he be?

WH: Memories are funny things, Jack. However hard you try to secure them, they wrinkle, and they're gone. Do you catch my drift?

JM: I get the reference, yeah... It's like that...fleeting... just out of reach.

WH: Do you remember much else about them?

JM: Not really, no... It's too far back now... the wounds are closed up.

WH: Maybe the wounds aren't as closed as you think. Sometimes the only way to heal is to face what's been buried. And I don't just mean the accident. I mean everything. The patterns, the beliefs, the fears that have been passed down through generations. What you think of as strength—keeping your head down, not letting things get to you—might actually be a form of avoidance. A way of not dealing with what really matters.

JM: I don't know if I can do that... don't know if I want to.

WH: I'm not saying it's easy. In fact, it's probably the hardest thing you'll ever do. But if you don't, you'll keep carrying this load. You'll keep punishing yourself for something that goes beyond the accident. And you'll keep pushing away the people who love you, like Charley.

JM: I don't want to lose her.

WH: Then don't. But you have to stop punishing yourself for something that can't be undone. You have to stop running from your own history, from your own fear of loss.

JM: You think this is all tied together, don't you? The accident, the case, my past... you think it's all part of the same thing.

WH: I think it's connected, yes. I think the way you've been handling this case is tied to your own history, your own unresolved pain. And I think that's why it's getting under your skin so much. You're not chasing a killer—so much as you're chasing yourself... your own ghosts.

JM: I remember birds on the water that day. Just getting carried on the waves as they crashed in on the beach, you know?

WH: Looking for fish getting pulled in on the tide?

JM: Yeah.

WH: Which one are you, Jack? The bird or the fish?

JM: There's times I feel like the bird, just carried on the tide... Other times it's like I'm swimming just below the surface, waiting to be caught.

WH: And what do you think the waves represent?

JM: Time, I guess. Relentless.

WH: You mentioned once, briefly, that you studied literature at university. I remember you saying that Emily Dickinson was a particular passion of yours.

JM: Yeah, I did... I wrote my thesis on her, actually.

WH: Tell me about that. About Dickinson. What drew you to her work?

JM: Emily Dickinson was... is complicated. People think of her as this reclusive, odd woman... who wrote about death and flowers, and I guess that's true on the surface. But there's so much more to her. Her poems are like puzzles. They seem simple, but they're layered with meaning, with emotion. She wrote about things no one wanted to talk about... death, yes, but also longing, isolation, desire, doubt. And she did it in these brief, fragmented lines that just hit you in the gut... She was ahead of her time, I think. She challenged the norms of poetry, the norms of how we see the world. It's like she was trapped in this small, constrained life, but her mind, her words... they reached far beyond it. She had this ability to take something as small as a moment of stillness, a single thought, and turn it into something profound. That's what fascinated me about her. She saw the world in a way no one else did. Or maybe in a way no one else dared to.

WH: Sounds like she really spoke to something inside you, too. What was your thesis on?

JM: My thesis was about how Dickinson used ambiguity in her poetry. How she deliberately left things unsaid, or open to interpretation. I focused a lot on her use of dashes—those little interruptions in her lines that make the reader pause, reflect. It's like she was forcing you to stop and think, to sit with the uncertainty. And in that uncertainty, she found truth.

WH: Ah huh.

JM: People think of poetry as this neat, structured, orderly thing. But Dickinson's poems are messy in the best way. They're fragmented, full of contradictions. She didn't give easy answers. She made you work for it. And I guess that's what I loved about her—she didn't pretend life was simple or straightforward. She embraced the mess, the unknown, and in doing so, she made sense of it. Or at least, as much sense as you can make.

WH: You speak about her like she's still very much a part of you. Do you still read her work?

JM: Not as much as I used to, no. You know how it is... life... life gets in the way. But, yeah, sometimes I'll pull out one of her collections and just read a few lines. It takes me back, reminds me of why I fell in love with literature in the first place. There's something timeless about her words.

WH: So, with all this passion for literature, how did you end up becoming a police officer?

JM: I don't really know, to be honest. I thought I wanted to make a difference in the world, you know? Literature was great, but it felt... abstract, sometimes. It's one thing to read about human suffering or injustice, but it's another to actually get out there and try to do something about it. Maybe part of me wanted to feel like I was really doing something. Something tangible.

WH: But you don't sound convinced. Was there something else? Circumstances that pushed you away from academia and towards law enforcement.

JM: Yeah. I mean, I thought about teaching for a while. I loved the idea of inspiring people, passing on my love for literature to the next generation. But... things didn't work out that way. Life had other plans. After university, I needed a job. A friend of mine had joined the force, and he convinced me to give it a shot. Said it would be steady work, and... well, here I am.

WH: And do you regret it? Not following that path, I mean. Teaching, literature... do you feel like you lost something by not pursuing it?

JM: I don't know. Maybe. Sometimes I wonder what my life would've been like if I'd stuck with it, if I'd fought harder to stay in that world. But then, I think about the people I've helped, the cases I've solved. It's not like I regret what I do. It's just... sometimes, it feels like I lost my way a little. Like I'm not sure where I'm supposed to be anymore.

WH: Is a sense of purpose still there for you?

JM: I used to think I was making a difference. Early on, I believed in the work, in justice. But lately... I don't know. It's hard to feel like you're really making a difference when you're constantly up against the worst parts of humanity. It wears you down. And this case... it's different. It feels personal in a way I can't explain. Like it's connected to something deeper.

WH: So, do you feel like you've drifted from what you wanted? From the sense of making things better, whether through teaching or police work?

JM: Maybe. I didn't set out to be the person I am now. I thought I'd be someone who could look at the world and still see hope, you know? But now, it's like all I see is darkness. I'm not sure if I've helped anyone, really. At least, not in the way I thought I would. And maybe that's why this case is getting to me. It's like I've been chasing something for so long, and I don't even know what it is anymore.

WH: It sounds like part of what's driving you is this feeling of lost potential. Like you've been trying to make up for something. Do you think, deep down, you feel like you've failed somehow?

JM: Maybe, yeah. Not in the obvious ways—my career, my life, it's all fine on paper. But I feel like I've let something important slip away. I don't know if it's idealism, or the love I used to have for life itself... I think I lost track of who I am.

WH: Do you think part of that is because of the accident? Or has this been happening for longer than that?

JM: It was like... everything before that was leading up to it. Afterward, nothing seemed to matter as much. Charley and I... we just stopped. Everything stopped...

WH: Trauma affects us in different ways, Jack. I'm not sure if you're chasing ghosts or living as one.

JM: I know I'm not always... present. So maybe I am. Like sometimes I feel like I'm just a memory myself... Things feel *almost*, like I'm trapped by invisible lines. People, timings, everything almost lining up.

WH: Life can be frustratingly linear.

13

'My River Runs to Thee'

The night was soaked with rain, the kind that seemed to hang in the air, turning the streets of London into glistening rivers of dark asphalt. Seth walked with his friends, shoulders hunched against the cold, their breath mixing with the mist as they made their way through the crowded streets of Soho. He kept his hands buried deep in his jacket pockets, the fabric wet to the touch, clinging uncomfortably to his skin. The city was alive, pulsing with a nervous energy that seemed to vibrate through the pavements, and into his bones.

They walked as a loose pack of shadows moving through the neon-lit streets. Around them, the city roared—laughter spilling from pub doorways, the clatter of high heels on slick cobblestones, the low rumble of cars and buses fighting through the night-time traffic. But none of that reached them. Their purpose was unspoken but clear. There was only one destination tonight, *Tokyo*, the club, buried deep in the heart of Soho, the basement that would swallow them whole until the morning light.

Tokyo's entrance was almost secret, a hidden black door set into the side of a narrow alleyway. A bouncer, large and indifferent, stood beside it, barely glancing at them as they slipped inside. The air changed immediately as they crossed the threshold—warmer, thicker, infused with the heavy scent of smoke and sweat, the low hum of bass vibrating through the walls.

Seth's friends moved ahead of him, weaving their way through the small crowd that had gathered near the entrance. No words passed between them, only nods and brief glances exchanged in the dim light. It wasn't necessary to speak here. The music would soon take over, drowning out everything else.

The stairs led them down, deeper into the belly of the club. Each step seemed to take them further from the surface, away from the wet streets above, into a world of shadows and sound. The walls were bare, painted black, lit only by the occasional flicker of a red bulb overhead. As they descended, the music began to grow louder, the steady thrum of a beat that pulsed in time with Seth's own heartbeat.

At the bottom of the stairs, the club opened up into a cavernous room, the ceiling low and oppressive, the air thick with cigarette smoke and something else, something sweet and cloying. The crowd was already thick, bodies pressed together, moving in a slow, hypnotic rhythm as the music washed over them. Faces appeared briefly in the haze—indistinct, blurred by the shifting light and the smoke that swirled through the room like a living thing.

Seth lingered near the edge of the crowd for a moment, his eyes scanning the room, taking it all in. There was something almost surreal about the atmosphere—the way the people moved, the way the music seemed to wrap itself around them, pulling them deeper into its spell. He felt the pull too, a slow, seductive force that tugged at his chest, urging him to lose himself in the rhythm, to forget everything but the here and now.

And then the song changed.

A new beat cut through the air, sharper, faster, the first notes of *Sinnerman* pounding through the speakers. It was the Felix Da Housecat remix, a pulse of house music and Nina Simone's earthy, soulful voice, raw and unrelenting, rising above the chaos. The effect was immediate. The crowd surged forward, bodies pressing closer, moving with a new urgency, a hunger that filled the room.

Seth let himself be carried by the wave of bodies, drifting toward the centre of the room where the lights were dimmest, where the music hit hardest. His mind began to empty, his thoughts dissolving into the beat. He was lost in the moment, a fleeting sense of freedom washing over him as he closed his eyes and let the music take him.

But then, through the haze, something—or someone—caught his attention. He opened his eyes, and there she was.

At first, it was just the movement that drew him, the way she seemed to float through the crowd, her body in perfect sync with the music. She wasn't like the others. Where they moved with a kind of desperate energy, a need to forget, she danced as if the music was hers, as if it belonged to her, as if it was something dwelling deep inside of her, giving her life, giving her power.

Seth couldn't look away. His breath caught in his throat as he watched her, the way her arms moved through the air, her hips swaying in time with the beat, her eyes half-closed as if she were lost in a world of her own making. She was beautiful, undeniably so, but it was more than that. It was the way she seemed to command the space around her, the way the crowd parted just slightly to make room for her, even though they didn't seem to notice. She was the centre of the storm, the eye of the hurricane, calm and powerful.

The flashing lights caught her face for a brief moment—a glimpse of dark, glossy hair, full lips curved into a slight smile, eyes shadowed but so alive. She moved with a grace that seemed effortless, her body flowing like water through the press of bodies around her.

And then, as if sensing his gaze, her eyes opened fully, and they locked onto his.

Seth's heart stopped.

For a moment, everything else disappeared—the noise, the people, the club. There was only her, and those eyes, dark, unfathomable, unreachable, holding him in place. Time seemed to stretch, the beat of the music fading into the background, until there was nothing but the connection between them, an electricity passing between them through the smoky air.

He wanted to move, to go to her, to close the distance between them, but he was rooted to the spot, caught in her stare, unable to look away. She didn't break the connection either. Her body continued to move to the rhythm, but her eyes never left his, as if she had seen something in him too, something that made her pause, which made her stay.

The crowd shifted around them, but for Seth, there was only her. He didn't know how long they stood like that, staring across the dark expanse of the club, the music rising and falling between them. Seconds? Minutes? It didn't matter. Time had ceased to exist in that moment. There was only now, removed, isolated, transcendent.

And then, just as suddenly as it had begun, the moment passed. She turned away, her body still moving to the music, but her eyes no longer on him. The spell was broken, and Seth felt a rush of something—disappointment, perhaps, or maybe it was relief. He wasn't sure. But he didn't move. He couldn't. He stood there, his breath shallow, his heart racing, as he watched her disappear into the crowd. She was still there, still dancing, still the centre of everything, but she was gone from him, and that left him feeling strangely hollow, as if something vital was taken from him without his knowing.

The music pounded on, but Seth remained still, a figure caught in the flow of bodies and sound, lost in the aftermath of a moment that he didn't fully understand. The relentless pulse, vibrating through the floors and walls of the basement club, left Seth standing frozen. His breath was shallow, his heart still racing in the aftermath of locking eyes with the woman. She had vanished back into the crowd, her body still moving to the rhythm of *Sinnerman*, leaving him hollow and restless.

A strange urgency surged through him—he had to find her again. The pulsating crowd blurred into a faceless sea of movement, indifferent to his desperation. Bodies pressed against him, swaying, dancing, oblivious to the fact that his world had just tilted irreversibly on its axis. Seth pushed forward, forcing his way through the throng, his eyes darting wildly in search of her, but it was as though she had evaporated back into the smoke and flashing lights like the otherworldly being she had appeared to be.

The music swallowed his shouts, the din overpowering everything else. People swirled around him, lost in their own worlds, not noticing him, not noticing anything beyond the beat. His frustration grew as he tried to navigate the undulating tide of dancers. The air was thick, suffocating with sweat and smoke, but Seth didn't care. He kept moving, kept searching.

He caught glimpses of her—just flashes. A dark figure, swaying hips, that intoxicating movement—but then she would disappear again, lost in the shadows and strobe lights. *Sinnerman* surged to its crescendo, the pounding bassline echoing his heartbeat. The song was almost over, and with it, Seth felt the moment slipping away from him. He stumbled through the crowd, his breath ragged, the sensation of loss growing heavier with every passing second.

Bodies brushed past him, jostled him, and yet the crowd seemed endless, indifferent to his need, his search. A hand landed on his shoulder, shoving him aside, and he nearly lost his balance. Someone shouted something at him, but the words were swallowed by the music. He looked again, scanning the room, searching desperately for her, but it was like she had never been there at all, just a ghost.

The song began to fade, its relentless rhythm giving way to something slower, something that seemed to dull the energy in the room. Seth stopped, chest heaving, a knot of frustration tightening in his gut. His pulse pounded in his ears, and the sensation of defeat washed over him. She was gone. Whoever she was, whatever that connection had been, it was gone now.

And then, just as he was about to give up, he turned, and there she was. Stood just a few feet behind him, the remnants of a knowing smile playing across her lips. She had been watching him, waiting for him. The lights flickered, casting her face into brief shadows, but her eyes sparkled, and her smile widened as their eyes met once again. His breath caught. She hadn't vanished after all.

Seth tried to speak, to ask her where she had gone, why she had disappeared, but the music had not stopped completely. The din was still too intense. His words were swallowed by the noise. She seemed to understand his frustration—her smile widened, amused, and she tilted her head, beckoning him to follow her.

Without waiting for him to respond, she turned and began to weave her way back through the crowd, her movements fluid and graceful, as if she knew exactly how to navigate the chaos. Seth hesitated for only a moment before he followed her, his heart pounding, a strange thrill coursing through his veins.

She led him away from the dance floor, past groups of people who barely noticed them, through a darkened hallway and into a quieter part of the club. They entered a dimly lit lounge area, where the music was a distant hum, the smoke thinner, the atmosphere far more intimate. Small groups sat huddled around low tables, talking in hushed voices or simply sitting in silence, the energy from the dance floor not quite reaching this space.

She slid into a booth in the corner, her back to the wall, and motioned for him to join her. Seth sat down across from her, his mind still spinning, the adrenaline of the past few minutes making it hard to catch his breath.

For a moment, they simply looked at each other, neither of them speaking. The silence between them was charged, like the air before a storm. When finally she spoke, her voice was soft but crystal clear.

"You were looking for me," she said, her lips curving into a smile once more.

Seth nodded, still trying to find his voice. "Yeah, I was." He leaned forward, resting his elbows on the table. "I thought I'd lost you."

Her smile widened. "I'm not that easy to lose."

They both laughed, and the tension that had been building in Seth's chest eased, replaced by something warmer, something electric. He couldn't take his eyes off her. She was even more captivating up close, her features softened by the low light, but her presence just as magnetic.

"That song," Seth said, gesturing back toward the dance floor. "You moved like it was your... anthem."

She nodded, her eyes lighting up at the mention of the song. "It is. It's my favourite."

"Really?" Seth leaned back, curious. "Why?"

Her expression grew thoughtful, her gaze flicking past him for a moment as if she were searching for the right words. "It's hard to explain," she said finally. "There's something about the way it builds, the way it moves, that feels... powerful. Like it's calling something out of you. There's this tension between what it's about and how it makes me feel. I lose myself in it. It's like... I don't know." She hesitated, then smiled, a little self-conscious that she'd spoken too much. "It's like the song gives me permission to be free. Like there's no choice but freedom."

Seth felt a shiver run down his spine at her words. He understood exactly what she meant, the contradiction, even if he couldn't put it into words. There was a kind of magic in that song, something raw and elemental that grabbed hold of you and wouldn't let go. And watching her dance to it had been like witnessing something pure, something untouchable.

She looked at him again, her eyes glinting with something mischievous. "My father named me after Nina Simone, you know."

Seth's eyebrows shot up in surprise. "No way. Really?"

She laughed at his reaction. "Yes way. He was a huge fan. He used to play her records all the time when I was a kid. It drove my mother crazy. But he loved her. Said she was a force of nature."

"Nina," Seth said softly, testing the name on his tongue.

"Simone," she said, laughing as she corrected him. "It's funny, I used to hate it growing up. Thought it made me sound old. But now..." She shrugged. "I don't know, I kinda like it."

Seth smiled, his chest tightening at the sound of her name. It fit her perfectly—strong, elegant, even a little bit mysterious. He couldn't believe how quickly he felt connected to her, like they'd known each other for longer than just a few fleeting moments in a basement club.

"And you?" she asked, tilting her head slightly. "What's your story…?"

"Seth."

"Seth, huh? The third son," she replied.

"Sorry?"

Simone laughed again, her face full of such joy and zero judgement. "In the Bible. Seth was born from tragedy, the third son of Adam and Eve. Good and heroic, Seth. But what is your story, my Seth?"

He paused, unsure of how to answer. His story felt small, insignificant, in comparison to hers, and his Biblical counterpart. But there was something about her that made him want to open up, to share pieces of himself that he usually kept hidden. He liked very much the idea of being her Seth.

"Nothing as interesting as yours," he said with a self-deprecating smile. "I'm just… a guy. A guy who wandered into a club and got lost for a bit."

She laughed, the sound soft and melodic. "Well, you found me. So maybe you weren't so lost after all."

Seth felt his heart skip a beat at her words, at the way her eyes lingered on his. He didn't know what was happening between them, but it felt important. It felt like something had shifted, seismically, like his life had just taken a dramatic, irredeemable turn. He wasn't sure where it was leading, all he knew was that he wanted to follow it, wherever it went. And from the way she looked back at him, he could just tell that she felt it too.

14
'A little overflowing word'

The lecture hall was almost empty now, with only a few stragglers lingering near the back, chatting in low voices as they gathered their coats and books. Seth and Simone stood near the front, the heavy silence of a post-lecture space settling around them, broken only by the occasional creak of chairs and the soft shuffle of footsteps. The large projector screen behind the podium had gone dark, but the image of Chinua Achebe still lingered in Seth's mind—a presence, much like the man himself, which was both profound and unshakable.

Simone, her fingers absently toying with a loose strand of her hair, was deep in thought. The talk had captivated her, as everything about Achebe did. She had sat through the hour-long lecture without moving, her attention never leaving the professor as he'd spoken about *Things Fall Apart*—its cultural impact, its subtle complexities, and Achebe's critique of colonialism. The words had flowed around Seth, carried by the guest speaker's soft, reverent tone, but Simone had absorbed them as though they were sustenance.

Seth, on the other hand, had found himself distracted. It wasn't that Achebe didn't interest him; through Simone he had not only discovered him but developed a strong appreciation for his work. But as the lecture had gone on, Seth's attention had wandered to Simone herself, watching the way she responded, her quiet, impassioned intensity. She was always like this when immersed in her studies and passions. She had a unique way of drawing connections, seeing the subtleties that others missed. She wholly fascinated him—her ability to lose herself so completely in something, to allow the text, the history, the words to envelop her. It allowed him to realise a love for someone else he didn't know had existed, or could exist, even.

Now, as they stood side by side, the lecture over and the room clearing out, Simone finally looked up at him, her dark eyes still burning with the fire of her zeal for Achebe's work. "What did you think?" she asked, her voice soft but expectant.

Seth hesitated, knowing he could never match her level of unbridled, unrestrained enthusiasm. "It was… intense," he said, offering her a smile. "I don't think I'll ever see the book the same way again."

Simone's eyes gleamed. "That's the point. Achebe didn't write *Things Fall Apart* to comfort us. He wrote it to challenge the way we see the world, to break apart those easy narratives that colonialism left behind."

She paused, shifting as if she was recalling a line from the lecture. "Remember what Professor Stephens said about the clash of cultures? It's not just the clash of Western and African civilisations. It's about the fracture within the soul, within the individual… Achebe deeply understood that."

Seth nodded, though it was her passion he responded to more than her words. She had that effect—making him want to care more about the things she loved. To protect them was to protect her.

They began to move toward the adjacent exhibition space, where artifacts, photographs, and original writings from Achebe's life were on display. The room was dimly lit, the walls adorned with images of Nigeria, old colonial maps, and typewritten pages preserved under glass. The soft murmur of other students and visitors filled the air, mixing with the subtle hum of the overhead lights.

Simone gravitated toward one of the displays, her fingers brushing against the edges of a glass case that housed a first edition of *Things Fall Apart*. The worn, yellowed pages seemed to hold the weight of history, the power of Achebe's words, and Seth watched as her expression softened into something almost reverential.

"I think this is why I chose Achebe for my thesis," she said quietly, her eyes fixed on the book. "He doesn't let you turn away from the truth. He forces you to confront it."

Seth stepped closer, standing beside her, feeling the gravity of the moment. He had always admired how deeply she cared about these things, how much she invested in her studies. For her, it wasn't just about writing a thesis—it was about understanding the world, understanding herself through the lens of history and literature.

"You're going to write something amazing," Seth said, meaning every word. He knew she would. Simone's mind was a sharp tool, capable of cutting through layers of complexity with grace. Not only would she find things in Achebe's work that others would miss, more importantly, she would make others see them; they would see them through her unique and beautiful eyes.

She smiled, a small, grateful smile. "I hope so."

They moved on through the exhibition, pausing at various points to take in the photographs and artifacts—images of Achebe in Nigeria, photographs of the villages that had inspired the novel, and handwritten letters that captured Achebe's thoughts on writing, on colonialism, on the role of the artist. Each piece seemed to add another layer to the man, another facet of his complicated legacy. But it wasn't until they reached the back of the exhibition that something truly haunting stopped them both.

There, framed in stark simplicity, was a photographic portrait of Chinua Achebe. The image was black and white, the contrasts sharp and striking. Achebe's face, aged and wise, stared out at them with an expression that was both serene and intense, his eyes penetrating, as though he could see straight through the viewer. His hands were folded in front of him, a posture of stillness that belied the inner turbulence of his thoughts.

Seth felt something catch in his chest as he looked at the photograph. It was unlike anything he'd seen before—there was a depth to it, a kind of quiet power that held him captive. The way the light fell on Achebe's face, highlighting the lines of age and wisdom, the shadows that curved along his cheekbones and jawline—it was a portrait not just of a man, but of a mind, of a life lived in contemplation and resistance.

"It's incredible, isn't it?" Simone's voice broke through the daydream.

Seth nodded, unable to tear his eyes away from the image. "Who took this?" he asked, his voice hushed.

"Steve Pyke," Simone replied. "He's famous for capturing these really intimate, human moments. You can see it in Achebe's face—the way he holds himself, like he's seen everything. Like he knows something we don't."

Seth could feel the consequences of that knowledge in the photograph, the sense that Achebe's understanding of the world was vast, and yet deeply personal. It reminded him of the way Simone had spoken about the clash of cultures—the fracture within the individual. Achebe's face, his expression, seemed to hold that fracture, that tension between tradition and modernity, between Africa and the West, between past and present.

"I don't know all that much about photography," Seth said, his concentration still fixed on the portrait, "but this makes me want to pick up a camera... it feels like so much more than just a picture. It feels like a conversation."

Simone smiled at his words, her eyes lighting up. "That's exactly it. Photography, when it's done right, is a dialogue... Pyke's captured something in Achebe that goes beyond what we can see on the surface. It's about what's underneath, like he's revealing his soul."

Seth nodded slowly, absorbing her words. He had always admired the way Simone saw the world, the way she could pull meaning out of things that others overlooked. He felt that same impulse now, standing in front of the photograph, wanting to understand, to connect with Pyke's vision.

"Do you ever think," Simone said quietly, "that Achebe's work is more relevant now than it's ever been? That we're still living in the aftermath of what he wrote about?"

Seth turned to her, surprised by the question. "What do you mean?"

Simone's attention drifted back to the picture of Achebe. "The world hasn't really changed. Not in the ways that matter. We're still dealing with the legacies of colonialism, of racism, of the destruction of cultures. Achebe wrote about it then, but it's still happening now. We just call it by different names."

Seth didn't know how to respond to that. He felt the truth of her words, but it wasn't something he had thought about in those terms. For him, Achebe's work, all art and literature had always been about the past, about history. But Simone was right—it wasn't just history. It was now. It was the world they were living in, the present they were trying to navigate.

"Do you think that's what your thesis will focus on?" Seth asked after a moment. "The idea that Achebe's work is still so relevant today?"

Simone nodded; her eyes were bright with the excitement of her ideas. "Yeah, that's part of it. But it's more than that. I want to explore how Achebe uses storytelling to challenge the narratives that we've been given—how he creates space for new voices, for different perspectives. The way not just trauma is passed through generations, but other emotional patterns too."

Her expression grew thoughtful. "Achebe believed that literature has the power to change the world. That's what I want to write about. How stories can shape the way we see ourselves, the way we see each other."

Seth smiled, feeling a swell of admiration for her. She always had a way of making everything seem larger, more important. She saw the connections between things, the way stories, art, history, all wove together to create something meaningful. It was one of the things he loved most about her. And as they stood there, side by side, gazing at the portrait of Chinua Achebe, Seth felt her words settle in his chest. Stories had power. They could change the way people thought, the way they lived. And in that moment, he knew that whatever Simone wrote, whatever she created, would be something that mattered.

"It's strange, isn't it?" Simone spoke softly, her words barely audible above the murmur of other visitors. "How someone can create something that doesn't just live in the past but keeps breathing in the present. Like this photograph. Like Achebe's words."

Seth glanced at the image again, then back at Simone. He felt the pull of her words, the way they wrapped around a deeper meaning, one he hadn't quite grasped yet. "Art does that, I guess... It's not just a record of the past, but a way of it living on, reaching forward into the future."

Simone nodded, her fingers brushing lightly against her lips as she thought. "Exactly. Achebe wrote *Things Fall Apart* decades ago, but his words still resonate. They still challenge people, still provoke thought, change minds. And this photograph... it's like he's watching us, reminding us that the struggle, the journey, the stories we tell—they never really end. They just keep evolving."

Seth stood beside her; his eyes now fixed on the same image. "I love that about photography actually. It captures a moment, but then that moment becomes timeless. It exists in the now, just as much as it existed then. You always have it. To cherish..."

"Or to haunt you?" she said, turning to him, a small smile tugging at the corners of her mouth. "It's like we're all part of something bigger. We're carrying it forward, like a thread connecting us to those who came before."

Her words seemed to linger in the air between them, drawing Seth in closer, not just physically but emotionally. He could sense that this conversation was more than just about Achebe, writing or photography. There was something else she was trying to say, something heavier, more personal. He wasn't sure if he was ready to hear it, but he also knew it was inevitable.

"That connection... it's not just through art," Simone continued, her eyes softening. "It's through us. Through our minds, through our bodies. Through what we carry, what we pass on. To others, to... to the next generation."

Seth's heart quickened. The next generation. The words hung in the air like a shadow, not fully formed but unmistakably there. He looked at Simone, studying her face, the quiet intensity in her eyes. "What do you mean by that?"

he asked, his voice gentle, though he suspected he already knew.

Simone took a breath, hesitating for a moment, as if she were weighing her words carefully, knowing they would change everything. "Seth..." she began, her voice faltering slightly before she found her footing again. "I've been wanting to tell you something. I've been trying to find the right moment. To find if there's a right moment."

Seth's pulse quickened, his mind racing ahead, trying to piece together what she was about to reveal. The exhibition hall around them seemed to recede into the background, the people, the artifacts, the very air itself fading into a distant hum. It was just the two of them now, standing in front of Achebe's portrait.

"I'm pregnant, you see," Simone said quietly, her eyes never leaving his. "And... it's yours. Of course."

For a moment, the world stood still. Seth blinked, the words echoing in his mind, not fully sinking in at first. Pregnant. It's yours. The simplicity of the statement struck him, as though it had been waiting there all along, just beneath the surface of their lives, unspoken but inevitable.

He opened his mouth to speak, but no words came. Instead, his mind whirled with a thousand questions, thoughts, fears, hopes. He looked at Simone, at the quiet determination in her eyes.

"You're... pregnant?" he finally managed, his voice barely more than a whisper.

Simone nodded, her gaze steady but her smile fragile, as though she wasn't sure how he would react. "Yes. I found out... worked it out... a few weeks ago."

Seth stared at her, his emotions swirling in a confused mass. Part of him felt an inexplicable joy, a strange warmth spreading through him at the idea of creating something with Simone, something that would live on beyond them, connecting them to a future they hadn't yet imagined. A future that only now became real. But then another part of him felt fear—a sharp, immediate fear of the unknown, of responsibility, of what this meant for his life, and for their life together.

"I... I don't know what to say," he admitted, his hands trembling slightly. "I really wasn't expecting this."

Simone reached out, placing her hand on his arm. "I know. Neither was I. I thought we'd been so careful, but... accidents happen, I guess? And now... here we are."

Her calmness surprised him, the way she seemed to have already processed this, already accepted it. "Are you... happy about it?" he asked, unsure of how to phrase the question.

Simone tilted her head slightly, her eyes thoughtful. "I think I am. I mean, it's terrifying, of course. But there's something about it... about the idea of us, creating something together, that feels right."

Seth exhaled slowly, his mind still trying to catch up. "I don't know if I'm ready for this, Simone."

She smiled softly, her fingers tightening around his arm. "No one's ever really ready. But that doesn't mean it's not the right time. Things happen for a reason, I'm sure."

He looked down at the floor, his thoughts racing. Parenthood. Fatherhood. The simple, overflowing word. It wasn't something he had ever imagined for himself, certainly not now, not this soon. Perhaps never. But as he stood there, the consequence of it all settling into his bones, he began to see it differently—not as a burden, but as a part of life's story, another chapter in the narrative that had brought them together.

Simone watched him, patient but expectant, as though she understood the storm of emotions now raging inside him. "We'll figure it out, Seth," she said quietly. "We always do."

He looked up at her, meeting her eyes, and in that moment, he felt a shift, a subtle but profound change. This wasn't just about him anymore, or even just about them. It was about something bigger, something that connected them to the past and the future in ways he couldn't fully comprehend yet. It was about life, in all its messy, complicated beauty.

"Yeah," he said finally, a small smile tugging at his lips. "We will."

Simone smiled back, relief washing over her features. She took his hand, lacing her fingers through his. "I'm glad I finally told you."

Seth squeezed her hand, feeling the warmth of her skin against his, the steady rhythm of her pulse beneath his fingertips. "Me too."

"You'd have just though I was just getting so fat otherwise." She laughed, "Maybe you wouldn't have loved me then."

They stood there for a moment longer, silent but connected, as the promise of something new settled between them. Something they would face together.

"I don't think it's possible that I could stop," he replied, turning back to the portrait of Achebe. The image—Achebe's eyes, shadowed but intense—held a depth that seemed to reach out across time. It was as if Achebe, through his quiet, knowing expression, was reminding him that the stories we live, the lives we touch, aren't just fleeting moments to be captured and forgotten. They stretch forward and backward, weaving a tapestry of time that connects and holds us all.

Seth felt that thread now, tightly bound between himself, Simone, and something greater. It wasn't just their physical selves, their meeting by chance, or their shared nights talking about books and dreams and futures. It wasn't just about the thrill of touching her skin, the magnetism of her beauty, or even the electric spark of seeing her dance in that dank and smoky nightclub. It was so much deeper—something far beyond the here and now, beyond the tangible. It was the kind of love that rooted itself in the soul, the kind that transcended time, history, and place.

He turned to look at Simone, standing beside him, her soft hand still in his. The gentle, dim, natural light of the exhibition hall playing across her features, casting delicate shadows across her face, highlighting the calm strength in her eyes. She was more than just the woman who had captured his attention all those months ago, more than just his lover or his companion. She was, in so many ways, an anchor to the world around him—his connection to something which felt timeless.

In that moment, Seth realised how much he loved her, but not in the way he'd ever thought of love before. It was as though he'd spent his entire life looking at the surface of things—at what could be seen, touched, or understood in a single breath. But now, standing in the commanding presence of Achebe's legacy, holding Simone's hand, hearing her words of life, creation, and parenthood echo in his ears, Seth understood that love was something that went far beyond the physical realm. It was a force that existed in the spaces between moments, in the silences shared, in the quiet understanding that they were part of something much bigger than themselves. Their love wasn't confined to this time, this place, or even to their own story. It was part of the same fabric that connected the past—and stretched into the future. It was part of the thread that had brought their ancestors together, that now led them to this very moment.

Simone's hand tightened around his, and he felt the pulse of life there, not just in her, but in the child growing inside her. That life wasn't just an extension of them; it was a continuation of a story that had begun long before they met and would continue long after they were gone, and that idea both frightened and comforted him in equal measure.

Seth had always been wary of the idea of permanence, of responsibility, of an inescapable bond tying him to another human being for life. But now, as he stood here, it didn't feel like a burden. It felt like something precious, something eternal. It was as if love, true love, didn't belong to the moment but to all moments, like a story written across time. He realised, with a sense of peace washing over him, that his love for Simone was just that—eternal. It was woven into the fabric of who they were and who they would become. It wasn't just about desire, or even compatibility. It was about knowing that no matter what happened, no matter where life took them, they were part of something much larger, something that surpassed their individual selves. He loved her in a way that went beyond anything he could explain or fully comprehend, a love that was as timeless as art, and as enduring as history.

And as he stood there, in that quiet gallery, with Achebe's eyes watching them, with the glorious potential of their future pressing gently against them, Seth knew one thing for certain: their love—like the stories that had come before them—would live on, in the child they were bringing into the world, in the connections they made, in the way they would leave their mark on the future.

He squeezed her hand, leaning in to press a soft kiss against her temple. "I love you, Simone. And I can't wait to see what we build together."

Simone smiled, her eyes filling with a quiet joy. She leaned into him, and for a moment, the two of them stood there, enveloped in what felt to them to be a timeless love, one reaching far beyond the white gallery walls and into the endless future ahead of them.

15

'A poor - torn heart - a tattered heart'

The café was warm, a sanctuary from the cold drizzle outside. Seth sat across from Simone, watching her stir her coffee, though he knew she wasn't really concentrating on the task. Her fingers traced slow circles in the mug, the light catching the faint curve of her growing belly, just beginning to show. He smiled, always quietly amazed by her. The city murmured beyond the glass, a steady hum of movement and grey light reflecting off wet streets. It was a familiar scene, ordinary in every sense, and yet the air between them felt heavy, as if every word had significance.

Simone looked up; her eyes were bright despite the rain-soaked gloom outside. "I'm thinking of changing the direction of my thesis a little. I've been reading more about Achebe's later work—there's something about the way he speaks of disillusionment, not just with the colonial past, but with what came after. The promises that were made to his people, to all of us, and how they were broken."

Seth nodded, leaning in, his elbows resting on the small table between them. He could listen to her speak like this for hours, her voice thoughtful, measured, but full of passion that was never far beneath the surface. She had a way of drawing him into her world, making everything she cared about seem vital, even urgent.

"Do you think they'll be open to that?" he asked, his voice low and rougher than usual, perhaps from the damp weather or perhaps from something else—a tightness in his chest he hadn't quite been able to shake recently.

"I don't know," Simone sighed, lifting her spoon from the coffee at last and resting it gently on the saucer. "But it's what I need to write about. It's not just academic anymore, not to me. It feels... personal." Her hand drifted to her stomach, a gesture that was almost unconscious.

Seth's gaze followed the movement, his heart tightening with a mix of emotions he couldn't quite name. There was joy, of course—an overwhelming sense of love for the woman sitting across from him, for the life growing inside her. But beneath that was something else, something harder, more jagged, that he didn't want to examine too closely. A fear, maybe, that the life they were building together was somehow fragile. As though, with one wrong move, it could tear, unravel like a poorly mended cloth.

"What about your parents?" Seth asked, his voice careful, trying to keep the conversation light. "When are we going to tell them about..." He nodded toward her belly, unable to suppress a grin.

Simone laughed softly; her smile easy but her eyes distant. "Soon. I need to. But you know how they are. My father will be thrilled, of course. My mother—well, she'll worry. She always worries. About everything."

Seth chuckled. He had met Simone's parents only a handful of times, but he knew exactly what she meant. Her father was a larger-than-life figure, a man who embraced change, life, and love with open arms. Her mother, by contrast, was a worrier, the kind of woman who saw the shadow behind every door, the danger in every opportunity. She loved her daughter fiercely, but it was a love that came with expectation, protective layers that could be suffocating.

"They love you., you've got nothing to worry about," Simone continued, reaching for his hand across the table.

"They're going to love you even more when they know we're getting married."

Seth smiled, though the warmth in his chest was tinged with something bittersweet. "I hope so," he said, his thumb brushing lightly over her fingers. "Your family—they're the closest thing I've had to that in a long, long time."

Simone's expression softened, her fingers tightening around his. She didn't need to ask. She knew about his past, the scattered fragments of it he had shared with her. He'd grown up with wealth, yes, but without the love that money couldn't buy. His parents had died when he was still young, leaving him in the care of an aunt who had never wanted the responsibility. She had raised him out of obligation, not affection, and Seth had spent most of his childhood feeling like an unwanted guest in his own life.

"I know it wasn't easy for you, growing up," Simone said gently, her voice low. "But you're part of our family now. My family. That's real."

Seth looked at her, something breaking open inside him, a soft tearing that he couldn't quite hide. It was a feeling he hadn't let himself acknowledge before, not fully. A kind of aching vulnerability, as if he'd been carrying a tattered heart all these years, one stitched together with silence and independence, too scared to admit how much he longed for something more. Something like this.

"I'm not good at this," he admitted, his voice rough. "Being part of a family. I'm used to being on my own."

Simone smiled, a little sadly. "You don't have to be on your own anymore, Seth. Not with me. Not with us. It's a cycle we can break."

Her hand rested on her belly again, and this time, Seth covered it with his own. The warmth of her skin, the softness of the gesture, made something shift deep within him. The realisation was slow, but profound. He wasn't alone anymore. He had a future now, one that was shared, one that was growing, and one that—despite all his fears—felt more solid, more real, than anything he'd ever known before.

He stood and slid his jacket over his shoulders. "Shall we go?"

Simone nodded, following his lead as they made their way out of the café. Outside, the rain had stopped, leaving the streets damp and shining in the faint afternoon light. The air was cold, crisp with the scent of wet pavement and fallen leaves.

As they walked, the conversation turned again to the future—where they would live, how they would balance her work on the thesis with the baby's arrival, what kind of wedding they might have. But as they talked, Seth found his thoughts drifting back, not just to the plans they were making, but to the distance he felt, the separation between the life they were building and the one he'd left behind.

They reached a corner, pausing at a pedestrian crossing. Simone glanced at him, noticing the faraway look in his eyes. "What are you thinking about?" she asked softly.

Seth hesitated for a moment, then smiled, pulling her a little closer to him as they waited for the light to change. "Just how lucky I am."

She raised an eyebrow, her lips curving in a knowing smile. "Are you sure that's all?"

Seth laughed, shaking his head. "Alright, maybe I'm thinking about your parents, too. How they're going to react when we tell them everything."

Simone chuckled, her hand slipping into his as they crossed the street. "Don't worry. They'll come around. Besides, my father's already halfway in love with you."

They walked in silence for a few minutes, the conversation trailing off as they reached a quieter part of the city. The sky was starting to darken, the early evening settling in, and the streetlights flickered to life one by one. There was something peaceful about this part of the day, the transition from light to dark, from the noise of the city to the softer, quieter moments that followed.

Seth glanced at Simone, his heart swelling with a strange mix of love and fear. He couldn't help but think of his own family—or the lack of one—and how different his life had been from hers. She had grown up with love, support, and security, things he had never known. And now, they were starting a family of their own, something that terrified him as much as it excited him.

"Simone," he said quietly, his voice almost lost in the sound of their footsteps on the wet pavement. "Are you scared?"

She looked at him, surprised by the question. "About the baby? About us?"

He nodded, dropping his eyes to the ground.

Simone stopped walking, turning to face him. She reached up, her fingers brushing lightly against his cheek, forcing him to meet her eyes. "Of course I am," she said softly. "But I'm not scared of what's happening. I'm scared of how much I love you, how much I want this. Us."

Seth's heart clenched at her words, the simplicity of them cutting through all the noise in his mind. He realised, in that moment, that the fear he had been carrying wasn't about the future or their relationship. It was about something deeper, something that had been gnawing at him for years. The fear of losing something so precious, so fragile, that he didn't know how to hold onto it.

But as he stood there, looking into Simone's eyes, he understood. He didn't have to hold on so tightly. Their love, their future, their family—it wasn't something he had to control. It was something that would grow, naturally, beautifully, in its own time.

He smiled, leaning down to kiss her softly on the lips. When he pulled back, his voice was steady, confident. "I love you, too. More than anything."

He held her close for a moment longer, the warmth of her body grounding him in the moment, despite the restlessness growing inside him. It was the sirens—he could hear them now, an unsettling soundtrack to their tender exchange. They echoed through the streets, distant but persistent, rising above the murmur of the evening.

He pulled back slightly, looking into Simone's eyes. "Do you hear them?" he asked, his brow furrowed. "There have been so many sirens today."

Simone listened for a moment, the noise registering in her expression before she turned back to him with a soft smile, trying to ease the concern in his eyes. "It's London, Seth. There's always sirens."

But Seth shook his head, glancing toward the street where the sound seemed to be coming from, his unease growing. "It feels different tonight. Louder. Closer. Sometimes I wonder…" He trailed off, his voice thick with the unspoken fears he had kept buried for weeks. "Is this the kind of world we should be bringing a child into?"

Simone's smile faded slightly, replaced by a quiet thoughtfulness. She took his hand in hers, her fingers warm and steady against his own. "Seth, this is the only kind of world there is. We act or we die. There will always be danger. There will always be things we can't control. Evil exists. Chaos exists. But that's not all there is. Love exists, too. Hope… Compassion. Without them we have nothing."

She squeezed his hand gently, her eyes steady and calm, like the eye of a storm. "We can't stop the world from being what it is. But we can do our part. We can love each other, raise our child with kindness, with hope. We can fight."

Seth wanted to believe her, to find solace in her words. And part of him did. But part of him, the part that had been hardened by his past, by his years of feeling alone in the world, still struggled to accept that love could truly be enough. That their small corner of the universe could resist the overwhelming darkness that seemed to grow louder with each passing day, like the sirens.

But as he looked at Simone, at the slight swell of her belly and the light in her eyes, something else became clear to him. She wasn't just talking about the world as it was—she was talking about the world as it could be. The world they could create, for themselves, for their child. It wasn't about shutting out the danger, the evil. It was about pushing through it, carving out a space for joy, for love, in spite of it all.

"You really believe that?" he asked, his voice quieter now, softer.

"I have to," she replied simply. "Because if I didn't, what would be the point?"

Seth nodded slowly, letting her words sink in. There was a logic to it, a wisdom that he had never fully allowed himself to embrace. The idea that hope wasn't about ignoring the darkness, but about believing that there was light strong enough to fight it.

Simone seemed to sense the shift in him, the way his shoulders relaxed, his grip on her hand loosening. Her smile returned, bright and playful, and without warning, she let go of his hand and took a step back, her body swaying lightly to a rhythm that only she could hear.

"What are you doing?" Seth asked, amusement tugging at the corners of his mouth.

Simone twirled once, her arms lifting above her head, her coat flaring out around her as she moved. "Dancing," she replied with a laugh. "Come on, Seth. Dance with me."

He shook his head, glancing around at the few passersby, who seemed oblivious to them, caught up in their own lives. "Here? In the middle of the street?"

"Why not?" she teased, stepping toward him and taking his hand again, pulling him into her orbit. "Life is too short not to dance when you feel like it. Especially now."

Seth couldn't help but laugh, the tension inside him dissolving as Simone's joy became infectious. She was right, of course. Life was short. And maybe that was the point. To seize moments of happiness where they could, to create their own light in the middle of the darkness.

He gave in, allowing her to pull him into a slow, easy rhythm, their movements out of sync but perfectly in tune with each other. For a few brief moments, the sirens faded, the city faded, and it was just the two of them, dancing under the dim streetlights, wrapped in the warmth of their shared future.

But then, the sirens came back. Louder now. Closer. Seth felt the pull of reality returning, tugging him back from the brief escape they had created.

"I need to tie my shoe," he said, stepping back and kneeling down to fix the loose lace that had come undone during their impromptu dance.

Simone, still smiling, continued to move, her arms swaying gracefully as she stepped further down the street, turning back every few steps to flash him a playful grin.

"Hurry up," she called, her voice light with laughter. "Or you'll miss all the fun!"

"Just give me a second," Seth called, crouching to tie his shoelace, fingers fumbling over the laces as if they, too, were caught in the rhythm of the city. He smiled up at Simone, her figure still moving gracefully in the dim streetlight, oblivious to the rush of the world around them.

Her laughter echoed softly, a brief, perfect note above the din of sirens in the distance, growing faint but never quite gone.

He glanced back down, pulling the lace tight as the infectious consequence of her joy settled deep in his chest. The world, which for his whole life has been so chaotic, so full of sharp edges and noise, had softened now because of her. Simone's joy seemed invincible, yet something in the air felt fragile, like the thin veil between this moment and whatever lay beyond it. The wind dropped momentarily, and the air froze along his back.

He stood, watching her dance ahead, her body carefree, moving with a grace that stirred something deep inside him—love, yes, but also fear. The kind of fear that comes with knowing how easily the beautiful things can fall apart. How fragile, he thought. How delicate. The threads between joy and despair, between love and loss, seemed so easily frayed. And yet, as Simone turned back to smile at him, her eyes bright, full of life, all Seth could do was run toward her—toward the fleeting, fragile beauty of it all.

Interview Transcript
Date: October 3rd
Location: Dr. Haggard's Office
Participants: DCI Jack Miller, Dr. William Haggard (Psychiatrist)

[09:54 AM]

WH: Tell me, Jack. Your feelings for Charley... have they changed at all? Or do you still love her?

JM: Of course... I always have... But... it's complicated now. Like... I don't know if it's enough anymore.

WH: Enough for what?

JM: Enough to fix things. Enough to make things right. To get back to... whatever we were before. Before everything went wrong.

WH: You say, "before everything went wrong." Are you talking about the accident?

JM: Yeah. The accident changed everything. For both of us.

WH: And do you think the accident ended your lives, Jack? Not physically, but emotionally, spiritually... did it become the end of you and Charley?

JM: I didn't think it would. Not at first. I thought we'd get through it. We're both strong people, you know? But... it just lingered. The fear, the guilt... it's like we've been stuck in the aftermath ever since.

WH: What's keeping you there, Jack? Why have you let it define everything?

JM: I don't know. I mean, it was traumatic, sure, but people go through worse and move on, don't they? I don't know why we haven't. Maybe because it wasn't just the accident. It was what it took from us.

WH: Took what?

JM: Children... The possibility of them, anyway. We never even really talked about it after. It was like we were suddenly on this different path, and having kids wasn't part of that anymore. I don't know if we chose that, or if it just happened to us.

WH: Do you regret it, Jack? Not having children?

JM: I don't know. I mean, it's not like we were trying before. And then the accident... After... it felt like we were frozen in place. Like moving forward with anything was impossible.

WH: Do you think it was important to you because you grew up in foster care? Like it would have broken a cycle to be a parent yourself?

JM: Maybe... I mean my childhood was good... Sad, obviously when they died. Not that I can remember much before then anyway.

WH: Just the sea?

JM: Yeah, just the sea... I mean there's snippets, but my foster parents were good. Kind. Gave me every opportunity they could.

WH: I'm not saying the accident didn't take something from you... Trauma has a way of altering everything... your perspective, your sense of safety, even your sense of identity. But I'm asking if you've let it become the defining moment of your lives. You said you never talked about children again after that. Why? Did the accident close that door for you, or did you close it yourself?

JM: I don't know. I guess part of me thought... it wasn't fair to bring a child into that. Into our mess. We were barely keeping it together ourselves. How could we raise a kid in the middle of all that?

WH: And do you think that was the right choice? Or was it a way of avoiding something deeper—something more painful to face?

JM: Maybe. Maybe it was easier to just... not deal with it. I don't know. Everything felt so fragile, like one more wrong step and we'd fall apart... it just seemed like too much. Like tempting fate.

WH: But now you're wondering, aren't you? If that was the right choice. If avoiding that fear might have cost you something more.

JM: Yeah. I am. But it's too late now, isn't it? That moment's passed.

WH: Not necessarily. Maybe you can't change what's happened, but that doesn't mean you can't move forward. The accident doesn't have to define your life forever. You're both still here. The future you want... it's not gone, Jack. It's just been waiting for you to stop chasing ghosts and start living again.

JM: Maybe... maybe you're right. Maybe that's where I should've been looking all along.

WH: Jack, I want you to consider something. You've been talking about making things right, about moving forward, but I can't help but wonder... do you think the underlying fear is that if you *do* make something real, if you actually build a future, then it becomes vulnerable? It becomes something that can be taken from you.

JM: Taken? I don't... I don't know. I guess I haven't thought of it like that.

WH: Maybe that's part of it, Jack. You're not just afraid of moving on from the accident. You're afraid of creating something real... something fragile. A future, a child, a life... because once it's real, it can be lost. It can be taken away from you, like...

JM: Like what? What are you saying?

WH: Like you took something away from someone else... do you think that's what this is about? Do you think, deep down, you're punishing yourself for what happened that day in the car? That you feel like you took something from someone, and so now you can't let yourself have something good in case the universe wants its pound of flesh from you?

JM: I didn't... I didn't mean to take anything. It wasn't supposed to...

WH: I know. But that's not the point, is it? Intentions aside, it happened. And you've been carrying it with you ever since.

JM: Maybe it's what I deserve.

WH: Do you? Or is that just an easy way to avoid facing something deeper? Punishing yourself for what happened... it might feel like justice, like you're balancing the scales. But is it?

JM: Like what? A test?

WH: Maybe. Do you feel tested?

JM: Yeah, definitely at times. Not sure I passed. Do you think these things are a test, Doc?

WH: I think we can learn from any situation. And there are probably lessons for everyone in a situation. It won't be the same lesson for everyone... think of it like an exam, but one where we all have different questions. Some pass, others don't.

JM: It's not personal?

WH: Do you see it that way, a personal test, or more as a punishment? The kind that might take something from you, something you actually care about, in order to make things equal.

JM: You think that's what this is? Do you think I'm... afraid of something bigger coming for me? For Charley?

WH: I think it's possible. You've been so focused on punishing yourself for the accident, but maybe that's just a way to shield yourself from the fear of something worse. Something beyond your control.

JM: You think if I have a kid, something will happen to them? Is that what you're saying?

WH: I'm not saying it *will* happen. Just that maybe that's your fear. That creating something as fragile and precious as a child is terrifying to you because it could be taken away. And deep down, maybe you believe that's what you deserve, to feel *that* pain.

JM: I don't... I don't know.

WH: Tell me about this case, you've said it feels personal in some way... why do you think that is?

JM: The victims remind me of Charley... the killer is leaving these weird clues... poetry.

WH: Okay, I mean tell me more, if you can... But can you see how that sense of persecution you're feeling could be related to what we've just spoken about?

JM: Yeah, that makes sense... Obviously I have to be careful what I say, but the bodies are laid out in a certain way, with their hands outstretched... and he leaves a written quote by a poet or author in their hand... and they just feel directed at me in some way.

WH: Okay, why?

JM: They'll be about justice or something.

WH: Can you give me an example?

JM: Okay, sure. So... all the girls have been selected, purposely I think, as they have the same surname as the person the quote is taken from... The first girl, her surname was Whitman.

WH: So, a Walt Whitman quote?

JM: Yes, exactly. Justice is not settled by legislators and laws. It is in the soul.

WH: Divine justice, the conscience...

JM: Yeah. Or... every man shares the responsibility and the guilt of the society to which he belongs.

WH: I don't know who that is.

JM: Henrik Ibsen, the playwright.

WH: Okay, so linking back to generational injustice, generational trauma. I see where you're coming from... but, Jack, I've worked with serial killers, in the past. They often have a type, some unique agenda, personality disorder, distorted perception of reality... Isn't it possible that's all that's going on here... they've got some twisted axe to grind, some 'truth' they want to reveal to the world through their actions?

JM: I guess, that's what I keep reassuring myself.

WH: It sounds like the judgment is coming from you, Jack. From the inside.

JM: I'm paranoid, in other words?

WH: No, not paranoia exactly. Look, how about I'll give you a quote this time, from Anais Nin... We don't see things as they are, we see them as we are.

16

'The Riddle we can guess'

Lauren Donne's body was laid across the floor next to the polished oak desk, one hand outstretched, reaching, wrists limp, just like her predecessors. Her head lolled at an unnatural angle, her chin pressed awkwardly against her chest, strands of blonde hair falling across her face like a delicate veil shielding the horror beneath. The soft glow of the afternoon sun filtered through the large bay windows behind her, casting an eerie light on the Thames below. Outside, the river flowed undisturbed, oblivious to the violent stillness inside the apartment.

Detective Sergeant Martin stood by the door, surveying the room with the kind of detached concentration she had learned to adopt over the years. It was a beautiful flat, tastefully decorated, modern but with enough personal touches to feel lived in. The kind of place someone like Lauren Donne could afford—an ambitious writer, a minor name in literary circles, known enough to get a deal, but not enough to avoid this quiet ending. The irony was sharp, Martin thought. A life lived for words, now silenced forever.

Ed Marks was hunched over the body, his gloved hands careful as he checked for any small signs, something to add to the mounting evidence they'd gathered over the last few months. Six murders now. And this one—like the others—had that same chilling signatures. His jaw clenched as he straightened up, pulling off his gloves and rubbing a hand over his tired face.

"Another one," Martin said softly, almost to herself. She had seen enough of these to know what the details would be before Ed even spoke.

He nodded grimly. "Same method. Literary quote. And then there's…" He hesitated, glancing over at the forensics team as they moved methodically through the room, dusting for prints, collecting fibres.

"What?" Martin pressed, sensing something heavier behind his pause.

Ed stepped back from the body, running a hand over his short-cropped, slightly curled hair, frustration etched into the lines of his face. "The silver halide again. Sprinkled like confetti, all over her body. Just like the others."

The reference to silver halide sent a chill down Martin's spine. She had read up on the compound after the second murder, its connection to old photography processes. Whoever this killer was, they had an artistic flair, something symbolic in their madness. But what did it mean? Why this?

Martin walked over to the desk, her eyes trailing the neat arrangement of objects around the body. A notebook, half-filled with handwritten pages, a fountain pen lying uncapped next to it, and a half-empty glass of wine. It was the kind of scene you'd expect from a writer in mid-flow, not from a victim in the final moments of their life.

"Any sign of a struggle?" she asked.

"No," Ed replied, his voice flat. "She knew her killer, or at least wasn't threatened by them until it was too late. Same as the others."

"Jesus," Martin muttered, folding her arms tightly across her chest as she surveyed the scene once more. The whole thing had an almost serene quality to it, the kind of quiet violence that left more questions than answers. But that detail—the silver halide—it was what tied these murders together in a way that made her stomach turn.

She walked over to the window, glancing out at the Thames, now glowing golden in the early evening light. It was strange how life outside carried on with such indifference, the river flowing calmly while chaos reigned in private moments behind closed doors.

Ed joined her, his hands shoved into the pockets of his coat. "Six victims," he said, his voice low. "Rosie Larkin, Emily Isherwood, and now her, all in the same week, and before them, Caroline Whitman, Hannah Ibsen and Ariana Lawrence."

"All women," Martin said, voicing the obvious but necessary observation. "Blonde, similar age range… and then the silver halide. What did the quote say?"

"Any man's death diminishes me, because I am involved in Mankind," Ed replied softly, his eyes narrowing slightly. "The press will run wild with it once they get wind there's yet another body."

Martin felt a tight knot of anxiety form in her chest. They both knew what that meant. The pressure would mount. The higher-ups would breathe even further down their necks, demanding answers, demanding a suspect. And with the media involved, the frenzy could spiral out of control. But right now, standing in the quiet of the apartment, surrounded by the residue of a life brutally cut short, it felt as though they were standing in the eye of the storm.

"We're missing something," Martin said, her voice edged with frustration.

"We're always missing something," Ed replied, his gaze lingering on Emily's lifeless form. His expression was dark, unreadable. "It's like he's staging these murders. There's a performance to it, a ritual even."

She glanced back at Emily, slumped against the desk. The pristine scene, the meticulous attention to detail. It wasn't rage; it wasn't random. The killer took their time, made sure every element was just so.

Martin sighed, rubbing her temples. "I hate to say it, but this is leading somewhere, isn't it?"

Ed didn't answer immediately. He looked out the window, the river's glimmering surface reflecting the fading light of the day. "Yeah," he said finally. "Yeah, it is."

Just then, one of the forensic officers, Shah, stepped into the room, holding a small evidence bag. "We've got something," she said, holding up the bag for them to see.

Inside, there was a tiny fragment of paper, yellowed with age.

Ed took the bag from her, his brow furrowing as he examined it closely. "Where did you find this?"

"Inside her mouth," Shah replied. "Not ingested like the others."

Martin's stomach churned slightly. She had almost forgotten about that detail—the killer forcing their victims to consume these strange, indecipherable fragments before death. It was a twisted signature, and one that only deepened the mystery.

Ed turned to Martin, holding up the evidence bag. "What do you make of it?"

She studied the fragment through the plastic. It was so small, so insignificant, yet it was somehow vital. "Another piece of the puzzle," she said softly. "Guess we just add it into the picture, see if makes our mystery woman any more recognisable."

They stood there in silence for a moment, the investigation wrapping them like a heavy shroud. Outside, the Thames continued its eternal journey, indifferent to the suffering and violence that unfolded on its shores.

Ed Marks leaned against the windowsill, his back to the dimming light of the river, flickering beneath the grey sky. The forensics team continued their meticulous work, moving silently around the room like ghosts. The evidence bag containing the paper fragment sat on the desk, casting a long shadow. Ed's eyes flicked from it back to Martin, his face drawn in hard lines of weariness.

"We need to talk about Jack," Ed said, his voice low, barely audible over the faint hum of the apartment. He didn't look at her directly, instead keeping his gaze on the river outside. There was something guarded in his tone, a restraint that told Martin this wasn't a conversation he wanted to have, but one he felt he had to.

Martin stiffened slightly, her hands resting on her hips. She glanced around, conscious of the forensic team nearby, though they were far too engrossed in their tasks to pay much attention. "What about him?" she asked, her voice carefully neutral.

Ed straightened, turning to face her. His expression was troubled, the shadows under his eyes deepening in the dim light. "I'm not sure his head is in the game."

Martin frowned. "He's been under a lot of pressure lately, sir. We all have. This case is… different to what we're used to."

"It's not just the case," Ed interrupted, shaking his head. "Something's… off with him. He's distracted. You've seen it."

Martin didn't respond immediately. She had seen it, of course. She'd seen Jack's mind drift during briefings, his sudden bouts of intense focus followed by long stretches of silence. But she also knew Jack better than most. He wasn't the type to let personal issues get in the way of the job. Or at least, he never used to be.

"Everyone has their moments," she said, choosing her words carefully. "He's just… dealing with some things. It doesn't mean he's not focused on the case."

Ed's eyes narrowed slightly. "You're defending him. But I know you've noticed it too."

Martin swallowed, Ed's words pressing sharply down on her. She shifted her stance, crossing her arms as if to guard herself against the direction this conversation was heading. "What are you trying to say, sir? You think he's not fit for this?"

Ed hesitated, then spoke in a quieter tone. "I think something's happening with him. Something in his private life."

The unspoken accusation hung between them like a fog. Ed didn't say it outright, but Martin understood the implication. He suspected Jack of having an affair, or maybe something darker—drinking, spiralling out of control in some way that was affecting his work. Ed wasn't the type to make baseless accusations, but the concern in his voice was undeniable.

"I don't know what you're implying," Martin said, a little too quickly. She cursed herself for the defensive edge in her tone. "He's so dedicated. He's always been dedicated. He's the reason I wanted to join this team, to work with the two of you."

Ed stepped closer, lowering his voice so only she could hear. "Dedicated doesn't mean infallible. I've seen it before, Martin. Men like Jack… bottle things up, and then it leaks out in ways you wouldn't expect. He's been distracted, he's been making mistakes, and you know it."

Martin's throat tightened. She could feel Ed's suspicion creeping toward her like a slow, inevitable tide. Did he know? Had he pieced together this subtle, unspoken connection between her and Jack? She had been careful—or so she thought—to keep their relationship strictly professional. They hadn't crossed any lines, hadn't even come close. But there had been moments, moments that Ed could have misinterpreted.

She forced herself to meet Ed's gaze, hoping her expression remained calm, unreadable. "Jack's personal life is his own business. Unless you have something concrete, we should stay focused on the case."

Ed studied her for a long moment, his eyes searching hers for something she wasn't willing to give. Then he sighed, running a hand through his hair. "I'm not saying he's not trying. I know Jack... we go way back. He's my best friend, after all. But lately... He's obsessed with this case. It's not just about catching the killer for him, it's spooked him. And there's something else... Something personal."

Martin exhaled, her shoulders relaxing just slightly. "You think the case is getting under his skin?"

Ed nodded. "It's more than that, though. He's been chasing something ever since the first body dropped. And now..."

His looked back to Lauren Donne's lifeless form on the floor. "Now, I'm worried he's lost sight of the job and we're six and counting."

Martin felt a flicker of guilt rise in her chest. She had seen it too—the way Jack's eyes lingered on the crime scene photos longer than necessary, the way his fingers traced the edges of the reconstructed photograph like they held some kind of answer only he could see. He had been distant, preoccupied, as if the case had opened up something in him that he couldn't quite close again.

"I'm not saying you're wrong," she said, choosing her words carefully. "But Jack's always been driven. That's why he's good at what he does."

"Being driven doesn't mean he's not a liability," Ed said quietly. "Not when it comes to something like this."

Martin's stomach twisted. There was a part of her that agreed with Ed, a small, insistent voice in the back of her mind that whispered Jack was walking a dangerous line. But another part of her—the part that cared about Jack as more than just a colleague—refused to accept that he might be losing control.

She glanced at the body again, her mind turning over the details of the case. The murders, the fragments of paper, the silver halide—all of it was connected, woven together in a web of mystery that seemed to be tightening around them. And Jack, whether he realised it or not, was tangled in it too.

"I'll keep an eye on him," she said finally, her voice steady. "But I don't think we should jump to conclusions."

Ed studied her for a long moment, then nodded slowly. "I hope you're right, Martin."

He turned away, walking over to the desk where Kreicher was photographing part of the crime scene. Martin remained by the window; her arms still crossed tightly over her chest. She watched Ed as he spoke to the officer, his face a mask of concern and frustration.

For a moment, she allowed herself to think about Jack, to wonder what was really going on beneath the surface. She had known him for years, had worked alongside him through some of the toughest cases they'd ever faced. He was brilliant, no question about it. But Ed was right about one thing: Jack wasn't himself lately. She thought about the late nights, the way Jack had started keeping things from her, the way his hands trembled ever so slightly when he thought no one was looking. He was unravelling, bit by bit, and she wasn't sure how to help him.

Ed stood by the desk, speaking in low tones with Kreicher and Shah. He glanced back at Martin, catching her watching him. For a moment, their eyes met, and something passed between them—an unspoken understanding, a shared concern for the man who wasn't in the room but loomed large in both their thoughts.

Martin turned away first, shifting her attention back to the river. The Thames moved slowly, steadily, like time itself, indifferent to the lives it touched. The silence in the room was punctuated only by the soft clicks of the forensic camera and the muted conversations of the officers.

**

Jack sat in the dim light of his office, the low hum of the station's fluorescent bulbs flickering overhead. The walls around him were plastered with crime scene photos, evidence tags, and notes scribbled in his rough hand. He leaned back in his chair, staring at the corkboard in front of him, where the faces of the victims were pinned like haunting reminders of the case he couldn't escape.

The photographs of Caroline Whitman and Hannah Ibsen were the ones his eyes kept returning to, side by side on the board. The two women were strikingly similar in appearance, though in life they'd had little in common. Caroline had been a librarian, living a quiet life in South London, while Hannah had been a lawyer, full of ambition and energy. But in death, the distinctions seemed to fade away. Their pale faces, hollowed out by violence, were frozen in time now, linked together by the same brutal fate.

His fingers tapped restlessly on the armrest of his chair. He picked up the folder marked *Whitman* and flipped through the images inside. The crime scene photos were cold and clinical, yet the horror behind them seeped through every image. Caroline had been found in her living room, laid out on the floor like the others. The same had been true for

Hannah Ibsen, found two weeks later in her South London home. The method, the positioning of the bodies, even the time of death had been chillingly consistent. Every time there had been no sexual assault, it was just murder, just about the kill. But it was more than just their ritualistic nature that unsettled him. It was the victims themselves—the way they looked, the eerie resemblance between them all, and Charley. Light hair, pale skin, delicate features. There was something about their appearance that had drawn the killer to them, more than just their names, Jack was sure of it.

He leaned forward, squinting at their faces, as if the photographs themselves might reveal the missing piece of the puzzle. His mind raced, trying to make connections between the women, but the truth remained elusive. They hadn't known each other, hadn't moved in the same circles. But still, there had to be something that tied them together. Jack stood abruptly, pacing the small confines of his office. His eyes flickered to the timeline on the wall, charting each victim's death, each clue, each dead end. Lauren Donne's name had just been added, her face still fresh in his memory from the crime scene earlier that day. Another woman, another life snuffed out, and the clock was still ticking.

He stopped in front of the board again, his eyes narrowing as he examined the crime scene photos side by side. Caroline and Hannah's deaths had followed the same pattern. But Lauren… there had been something different about her, though Jack couldn't put his finger on what. Perhaps it was the location—she'd been found in a well-kept, expensive apartment overlooking the Thames, while the other women had been killed in more modest surroundings. Or maybe it was the way her body had been positioned, just slightly off from the precise arrangement of the earlier victims. Something gnawed at him, a subtle shift in the killer's approach that he couldn't quite decipher.

His thoughts were interrupted by a knock at the door. Jack turned, his jaw tightening as he saw the young DC, Radcliffe, standing there, holding a file in his hands. Radcliffe had been shadowing him for the past few months, eager, but still too green for Jack's liking. The kid had promise, but this case was far from the training ground Jack would have chosen for him.

"Got an update from the latest crime scene, sir," Radcliffe said, stepping into the office and closing the door behind him.

Jack nodded, motioning for him to continue. He leaned against his desk, crossing his arms over his chest as Radcliffe opened the file and began to read aloud.

"Forensics recovered another piece of paper, this time from Donne's mouth. It's a partial fragment, like the others, but it looks like it might match the picture we've been piecing together."

Jack's eyes flickered to the corner of the desk where the evidence bag containing the reconstructed photograph lay. It had been painstaking work, but the image was slowly taking shape. Though they could make out the vague outline of a figure now, the details were still too obscured to reveal an identity. Another piece of the puzzle, another maddening fragment.

"And the scene itself?" Jack asked, his voice steady.

Radcliffe hesitated, glancing down at his notes. "It was similar to the others, sir…"

Jack's brow furrowed. "Go on."

"Well, for one thing, the apartment was immaculate. No signs of a struggle, no signs of forced entry. Everything was… in place. Almost too much so, if that makes sense?"

Jack's fingers drummed against the desk. "So, you're saying she let the killer in willingly?"

"Looks that way," Radcliffe confirmed.

Jack felt the knot in his stomach tighten. "Anything else?" he asked, his voice a little sharper than intended.

Radcliffe shifted on his feet, clearly sensing the tension in the room. "Forensics is still going over the place, but they haven't found anything that stands out yet. No prints, no fibres, literally nothing that can give us a solid lead at this point."

Jack exhaled through his nose, frustrated but not surprised. The killer had been meticulous from the start. He wasn't going to slip up now.

He pushed off from the desk and crossed the room to the evidence board, staring hard at the photos of Caroline Whitman and Hannah Ibsen again. Their faces stared back at him, pale and lifeless, their similarities more unsettling with each passing moment. He gestured toward them, not looking at Radcliffe as he spoke.

"What do you see when you look at them?"

Radcliffe blinked, caught off guard by the question, almost flattered someone as respected as Jack Miller wanted his opinion. He moved closer to the board, studying the images with a furrowed brow. "I see… two women who were killed in the same way. Two women who might've been chosen because of how they looked."

Jack nodded, though his jaw remained tight. "That's what I thought at first, too. But it's not enough. There's more to this. There has to be."

Radcliffe didn't respond, and Jack could sense the unease in the younger detective. He couldn't blame him. This case had wormed its way under his skin in a way no other had. It wasn't just the brutality of the killings, or the frustration of the dead ends. It was something deeper, something personal that troubled Jack in the dead of night, making sleep an impossibility.

"What was the quote?"

Radcliffe checked his notes again, "John Donne. Any man's death diminishes me…"

"…because I am involved in Mankind… And therefore, never send to know for whom the bell tolls; it tolls for thee," Jack concluded, cutting the young detective off mid-sentence.

Radcliffe gulped. "Yes, sir. But it was just the first part… Up to Mankind."

For whom the bell tolls, Jack thought. "It tolls for thee. Is he taunting us… taunting me?" he mumbled under his breath, barely conscious the sound had left his lips.

"Sorry, sir," asked Radcliffe, unsure if a reply was needed.

Jack turned to face Radcliffe; his tone sharp. "Just keep digging. I want every detail on Donne's life. Anyone she spoke to or had a connection with. There's a thread we're missing, and we need to find it before this bastard kills again."

Radcliffe nodded, his posture straightening. "Yes, sir. I'll get on it."

As Radcliffe left the office, Jack sank back into his chair. He stared again at the photos of the victims, his mind turning over the same questions again and again. There was a pattern here, a logic to the killer's madness. He just had to figure it out before it was too late. But as he sat there, alone in the dim light of his office, Jack couldn't shake the feeling that he was running out of time. The bell tolled, and with each passing day, its toll became greater, its chime louder, and the darkness seemed to grow closer, threatening to consume him whole.

17

'We grow accustomed to the Dark'

The rain fell steadily, soaking through his thin coat, and the dim, flickering streetlights cast long shadows that seemed to shift with every step. Ed Marks had never imagined it would come to this. He moved carefully, his footsteps soundless against the wet pavement, keeping a distance but never letting Jack out of his sight. Jack had left the station late, well past midnight, his face drawn, his usual steady demeanour unsettled in a way Ed hadn't seen before. Now Ed followed, not out of loyalty, but suspicion.

The streets of London, slick with rain, felt narrower tonight, darker. They'd walked these streets together for years—partners, friends, rising through the ranks of the force, solving cases that could have broken lesser men. They had been inseparable once, their bond forged in the crucible of shared danger and long hours spent chasing the ghosts of the city. But tonight, as Ed watched Jack move ahead of him, something was different. Jack's movements were too deliberate, too secretive, and Ed felt it pressing against his chest, heavier with each step. He couldn't shake the feeling that something was terribly wrong.

As they moved through the labyrinth of streets, Ed's mind drifted back to better times—days when trust between them had been implicit, unspoken. They had always worked in tandem, two halves of the same whole, knowing each other's thoughts before they were spoken. Ed remembered their early days on the force, green but ambitious, chasing down petty criminals and drunks in alleys not unlike these. It was the bond of shared experiences that had propelled them both forward. He smiled grimly, thinking of their first big case, a missing girl found in an abandoned warehouse by the docks. Jack had been the one to make the connection, to see through the smoke and mirrors and find the truth. Ed had been in awe of him then, a mentor and a friend. But now, that trust was eroding, crumbling like the wet pavement beneath his feet.

Ed kept his distance, careful not to get too close, but close enough to observe Jack's every movement. Jack walked with his head down, his collar turned up against the rain. He was heading toward the river, the shimmering lights of the Thames just visible in the distance. The route was familiar—one they had taken before—but there was something unnerving about Jack's solitude, the way he slipped between the shadows, avoiding the pools of light from the streetlamps.

As they turned onto a narrower street, the wind picked up, whipping the rain sideways into Ed's face. He pulled his coat tighter, blinking against the sting of the cold drops. Jack hadn't looked back once, his pace steady, determined. But to where? And why? These were the questions that had picked at Ed for days now. Jack's behaviour had become increasingly erratic, distracted. There were rumours in the station, whispers of things that Ed had tried to ignore, but now he wasn't so sure.

The rain was relentless, and the streets were nearly empty here at this hour. Ed couldn't help but think how often they had walked streets like these together—sometimes after a long shift, sometimes in pursuit of a suspect. And yet now, with every step Jack took, Ed felt as though he were chasing someone he no longer recognised.

He thought back to the last few months, how Jack had started to pull away, becoming more secretive, less forthcoming. They had always shared everything—no detail too small, no case too insignificant. But recently, Ed had noticed the distance growing between them, a widening gulf he couldn't have imagined or explain. Jack would disappear for hours without explanation, brush off Ed's questions, and then return to the station with a look in his eyes that Ed didn't like. It was as though Jack had become someone else entirely.

It was then, under those flickering streetlights, that Ed first allowed himself to entertain the possibility—an idea that had been lurking in the back of his mind for weeks. What if Jack was hiding something? What if Jack had crossed a line? The cases they were working, the brutality of the murders... Ed couldn't help but wonder. Had Jack gotten too close? Had the darkness of their work finally caught up with him?

Ed shook his head, trying to rid himself of the thought. This was Jack—his best friend, his partner. But the clawing doubt remained, and it was why he was out here in the pouring rain, following Jack through the shadowed streets of London instead of trusting him.

The rain eased slightly, though the streets remained slick and reflective, the pavement shimmering with the glow of streetlights. Jack had turned down another alley, and Ed followed, his heart beating faster. It was almost as if Jack knew he was being followed, as if he were leading Ed somewhere.

The narrow alley opened up into a small square, one of those forgotten corners of London where time seemed to stand still. Jack stopped, his back to Ed, his silhouette framed against the dark buildings. For a moment, Ed thought Jack might turn around, that he might catch a glimpse of the old

Jack, the man he trusted implicitly. But Jack didn't move. He stood there, his head bowed slightly, as if lost in thought, as if burdened by something far heavier than the rain-soaked night.

Ed kept to the shadows, watching, waiting. His breath was shallow, his mind racing with all the things he didn't want to believe. He wanted to confront Jack, to shake him and demand answers, but the time wasn't right. Not yet. He needed more. He needed to understand what was happening.

There was a noise behind him—a soft, scuffling sound—and Ed froze, his body tensing. He glanced over his shoulder, but the alley was empty, save for the rain pooling in the gutters. Still, the unease clung to him, a sensation he couldn't shake.

When he looked back, Jack was moving again, heading toward the riverbank. Ed followed, the distance between them shortening as the streets narrowed further. The river loomed ahead, dark and swollen, the steady thrum of water a constant backdrop to the city's distant noise.

Ed's mind wandered as he continued his pursuit. He thought about how the world had grown darker for both of them, how their friendship had once been a bright light in the dim corridors of the job. But now, it seemed that darkness had seeped into every corner of their lives, unspoken but ever-present. The cases they worked had left their marks, like invisible scars on the soul, but Jack had always seemed to cope better in the beginning. He had a resilience, a way of shutting out the worst of it. Until recently.

Was it the cases? Was it the pressure of everything they had seen, everything they had dealt with? Or was it something else, something deeper, something Jack hadn't shared?

As they neared the river, Jack's pace slowed. Ed hung back, staying in the shadows, watching as Jack stopped near the edge of the water, the Thames stretching out before him, vast and black. Jack stood there, hands in his pockets, staring at the water as if searching for something only he could see. The wind whipped around them, sending ripples across the surface of the river, and Ed shivered, though not from the cold.

For a moment, Ed thought about stepping out of the shadows, about confronting Jack right there on the riverbank. But something held him back, a deep, instinctual fear that stopped him in his tracks. Instead, he stayed where he was, watching as Jack stood motionless, lost in whatever thoughts haunted him.

Ed thought of the cases they had worked on together—the brutal murders, the victims whose faces still haunted his dreams. He thought of how they had always found a way to make sense of the madness, to hold onto their humanity amidst the chaos. But now, as he watched Jack, Ed couldn't shake the feeling that something had broken, that Jack had crossed a line he couldn't come back from. And as the rain began to fall again, soft and steady, Ed realised that the darkness wasn't just out there, in the streets and the alleys they had walked together for years. It was in here, between them, growing wider with every step Jack took into the night.

The rain hadn't let up. It fell in sheets, hard and relentless, blurring the edges of London's dimly lit streets. Ed Marks kept his distance, the collar of his coat pulled tight against the cold drizzle. His eyes never left Jack as he moved further down the narrow alley, his figure blending into the shadows like a ghost slipping through the cracks of the city. The thought had been probing at him for days now, but it had only solidified tonight, like a slow encroaching fog. What if Jack wasn't just hiding something—what if Jack was the thing they were hunting?

It was madness, of course. He and Jack had shared more than a decade's worth of cases. They'd tracked killers, thieves, liars. They knew each other better than anyone else in the world. Or at least, that was what Ed had always believed. But as Jack's behaviour had grown more erratic, the little things had started to add up. The late nights, the disappearing acts, the secrets. The likeness of the victims to Charley, the poetry. And then there was the way Jack had started to look at the evidence—disconnected, cold, almost methodical. The same way a killer might.

Ed's breath quickened as he moved cautiously after him. The alley opened up into a quiet side street, the kind of place only those familiar with the city's forgotten corners would know. There, at the far end of the street, was a small boutique cinema—its neon sign flickering, half the letters burnt out. *Empress Cinema.* The letters glowed weakly in the rain, casting a pale-yellow light onto the wet pavement.

Jack stopped, his hand on the rusted handle of the cinema's old-fashioned door, lingering for a moment. Ed watched from the shelter of a recessed doorway, heart pounding in his chest. What was Jack doing here? This wasn't the place for casual indulgence. It had a reputation—forgotten, obscure, catering to an audience that didn't want to be seen.

The thought that Jack could be hiding something like this, something worse than Ed had dared imagine, twisted in his gut. He pressed his back against the cold stone of the building behind him, waiting for Jack to enter before following at a distance. His feet moved almost mechanically, the rain slipping down the back of his neck, chilling him to the bone. He pushed the door open slowly; the sound of its creak swallowed by the hum of the rain outside.

Inside, the air was thick with dust and the faint smell of damp. The lobby was deserted, save for an old man at the ticket booth, his face half obscured by the hood of his jacket. He barely glanced at Ed as he bought his ticket. The place felt suspended in time, a relic of another era. Faded movie posters lined the walls, their colours washed out by years of neglect. The dim lighting cast long shadows across the threadbare carpet, the quiet was broken only by the occasional drip of water from a leaking pipe somewhere in the ceiling.

Ed's eyes scanned the room, but Jack was already gone. The only place he could have gone was inside the screening room, past a pair of substantial velvet curtains that led deeper into the darkened space. Ed hesitated for a moment, wiping the rain from his face. He thought of all the nights he'd spent with Jack, their banter, their shared frustrations over cases. But now, standing here in this shadowy cinema, the memories felt distant, unfamiliar. He pushed through the curtains and stepped into the dark.

The theatre was small, the seats worn and faded, the screen glowing faintly as an old black-and-white film flickered into motion. A few scattered patrons sat hunched in their seats, their faces barely visible in the dim light. Ed's eyes adjusted to the gloom, and there—two rows from the back— he spotted Jack. Alone.

The sight of him, sitting there in the darkness, sent a shiver down Ed's spine. Jack wasn't just watching the film— he was transfixed by it, his eyes locked on the screen with a strange intensity. Ed moved silently into the row behind him, his heart pounding, the feeling of unease thickening like the dark around him.

It was then that the words of a poem—half-remembered from a moment spent with Jack when they had first met, and he'd discovered Jack's academic past—floated to the surface of his mind. *We grow accustomed to the Dark—When Light is put away.* It was as if the shadows of the cinema had triggered something buried deep in his memory, a line that echoed the very feeling he had now. The dark had become familiar, hadn't it? The dark of the job, the dark of secrets, the dark that had been growing between him and Jack for months. It was the very thing Jack had warned him about in those early, early days on the beat. The thing that Jack, with his at times prophetic insight, had most feared about doing this job at all.

Ed studied Jack's profile from the shadows. There was something almost unnerving in the stillness of his form, the way he seemed to be absorbing the flickering images on the screen as though they held the answers to something Ed couldn't yet understand. What was he doing here? What was he thinking? Was he groping blindly, trying to make sense of something that was just out of reach? Or had he already hit a tree—had he missed something vital, something that would explain all of this?

For months now, the cases they had been working had weighed heavier than usual. Each victim, each scene, had felt like a new layer of grime settling into the cracks of his soul. And Jack had been the same, at first. They'd worked side by side, as always, sifting through the darkness. But then Jack had started to drift. And now, as Ed watched him in the flickering light of the cinema, he couldn't shake the growing suspicion that Jack might not just be drifting—but sinking.

The film on the screen played on, the characters moving in and out of the light, their faces shadowed in half-darkness. Ed strained to catch glimpses of the images, but his mind was elsewhere. He thought of the victims, of their broken bodies and hollow eyes, and of how Jack had looked at them with a detachment that had grown more pronounced with each case.

Ed's fingers tightened on the armrest. What if Jack wasn't just a detective following the trail of a killer—what if he was the one leading it? The very idea felt like a betrayal, like a knife twisting in his gut. But Ed couldn't ignore the signs anymore, couldn't shake the feeling that Jack was hiding something darker. The way he had distanced himself, the way he had begun to act—there was something there, something Ed had been blind to for too long.

The flicker of the film threw shadows across Jack's face, highlighting the hard angles of his jaw, the set of his mouth. Ed thought back to the days when he had trusted Jack with his life, with everything. Now, he wasn't sure if he could even trust him with the truth.

He watched Jack for a few more moments, waiting for some sign, some movement that would break the spell. But Jack remained still, his eyes fixed on the screen as if nothing else existed. The rain outside had become a faint patter, barely audible over the hum of the projector. Ed's heart raced, his mind spinning with questions he wasn't ready to answer.

His feet felt as though they were sinking into the floor, his heart pounding louder than the rain outside he could no longer hear. The darkness of the cinema wrapped around him like a suffocating fog, thick and inescapable. As Ed looked closer, he realised that the film playing on the screen was *Brief Encounter*. The flickering black-and-white image of Celia Johnson's face—strained with emotion, filled with the quiet tragedy of a love never fully realised—illuminated the room in soft bursts. It was a film Ed was at least familiar with, despite its age, a story of desperate, suffocated longing. Despite its age, it was still present, Ed could relate to that feeling. But what was Jack doing here, of all places, watching a film like this?

But as Jack sat there, his face illuminated by the soft glow of the screen, Ed saw something different. There was no malice in Jack's expression, no signs of the cold detachment he had come to fear in recent weeks. Instead, there was only a deep, unspoken sadness. A sadness so deep it seemed to echo the film playing before them, as though Jack's life had also somehow taken a dark turn toward an inevitable heartbreak.

Ed's shoulders slumped, the tension draining from his body, and he moved down the row of seats toward Jack. The dampness of his coat clung to him as he slid into the seat next to his friend, the familiar creak of the old cinema chair the only sound between them. He didn't say anything at first, just sat there, watching the film. The scenes unfolded with an aching familiarity, a melancholy that hung in the air like the lingering smoke of a cigarette.

On the screen, Celia Johnson's character gazed longingly at the man she could never have, her face a portrait of quiet desperation. Ed couldn't help but think of the cases they had worked together—the lives they had seen torn apart by violence, by loss. And now, sitting here in this forgotten cinema, he felt the true value of their friendship, and of all they had been through.

Jack didn't look at him, didn't acknowledge that Ed had followed him all this way. But he knew he was there, of course. Instead, he simply sat, his eyes fixed on the screen, lost in whatever private thoughts haunted him. For a moment, Ed wondered if he should say something—anything—to break the silence between them. But what could he say? How could he ask the questions that were burning inside him without shattering everything between them?

Instead, he leaned back in his seat and let the film wash over him, the sound of Rachmaninoff's Piano

Concerto No. 2 swelling in the background, as though it, too, were mourning something lost.

Finally, as the film reached its quiet, devastating conclusion, Ed spoke, his voice was low, careful, like a man testing the ice beneath his feet. "Why this one, Jack?"

For a long moment, Jack didn't respond. He just sat there, staring at the screen as the credits began to roll, the names of long-dead actors and filmmakers flashing across the darkness.

Ed turned to look at him, but Jack's eyes remained fixed on the screen. There was something fragile about him in that moment, something Ed hadn't seen in Jack for years. It was as though all the armour Jack had built around himself—the walls he had raised after every case, every trauma—had started to crack, and Ed was seeing the man underneath for the first time in a long while.

When Jack finally spoke, his voice was hoarse, barely above a whisper. "You ever wonder," Jack continued, his voice distant, "if we're all just waiting for a train that never comes?"

Ed frowned, unsure of what Jack meant, but something about the way he said it sent a chill through him. Jack turned to face him then, his eyes shadowed, his expression unreadable.

"You think you know someone," Jack said, his voice barely audible. "You think you know yourself. But one day, you wake up, and you're just… watching it all go by. Watching yourself become someone you don't recognise."

Ed swallowed hard. This wasn't just about the cases they'd been working, wasn't just about the strange behaviour Ed had been noticing. It was something deeper, something that had been festering inside Jack for a long time.

"Jack," Ed said, choosing his words carefully, "you've been… different lately. Distant."

Jack let out a bitter laugh, shaking his head. "Different? Yeah, you could say that." Jack leaned forward, resting his elbows on his knees. "I don't know, Ed," he said quietly. "I don't know what I'm doing anymore."

Ed felt a knot form in his throat, but he forced himself to speak. "You're still you, Jack. You've just... been through a lot."

Jack didn't respond. The cinema had emptied out now, the last few patrons slipping quietly through the exit doors. Outside, the rain had slowed to a drizzle, the streetlights casting long, flickering shadows on the wet pavement. Ed felt the urge to say something, anything, to reassure Jack, to pull him out of whatever darkness he had sunk into. But the words wouldn't come.

Instead, he reached out and placed a hand on Jack's shoulder, the gesture small but filled with a kind of quiet understanding that only years of friendship could offer.

"We'll figure it out," Ed said softly, his voice steady. "Whatever this is, we'll figure it out."

Jack didn't look up, didn't speak. But Ed could feel the tension in him start to ease, just slightly, as though the darkness wasn't quite so suffocating anymore.

The credits finished rolling, the screen going dark, and for a moment, the two of them sat there in the silence. And in that quiet, dimly lit cinema, with the rain still falling more softly outside, Ed couldn't help but feel that, despite everything, they weren't alone in the dark. Not yet, anyway.

18

'A Prison gets to be a friend'

The soft flicker of the cinema screen cast long shadows over the empty seats, and the hum of the projector blended with the faint patter of rain on the windows outside. Jack sat with his hands clasped in front of him, elbows resting on his knees. Beside him, Ed shifted slightly, the worn leather seat creaking beneath him. The credits had long since rolled off the screen, but neither of them made a move to leave. The space between them felt thick, not with suspicion any longer, but with years of shared history, memories like forgotten reels of film.

"How's it going with the shrink?" Ed asked lightly, finally breaking the silence. His voice was low, cautious, as if speaking too loudly might shatter whatever fragile thread was still keeping Jack tethered to reality. He didn't turn to look at Jack, but kept his eyes fixed on the blank screen ahead.

Jack sighed, leaning back into his seat. The air inside the cinema felt stale, like the past had settled into the fabric of the walls, refusing to be shaken off. "It's... going, I suppose," Jack said. His tone was distant, like he was answering a question about someone else's life, not his own.

"That's something, at least." Ed nodded, though Jack couldn't see it in the dim light. "Haggard's good at what he does. You're still seeing him regularly, yeah?"

Jack's hand moved to his forehead, rubbing at his temple with the same weary motion he'd used for years, a gesture that signalled an internal battle more than anything else. "Once every few weeks, give or take. But I don't know, Ed. Sometimes I wonder if it's doing anything at all. It's like…" He hesitated, searching for the right metaphor, something to convey the suffocating sense of futility. "It's like I'm locked inside my own mind, trapped in this… prison I can't break out of."

Ed's brow furrowed as he watched Jack from the corner of his eye. He didn't respond right away, but the words seemed to hang in the air between them, resonating in the silence.

"I guess that's what it feels like," Jack said finally, his voice quieter now. "This place—it's the closest thing I have to an escape. It's like coming here I'm… stepping outside of myself, for just a couple of hours."

"You mean watching these old movies?" Ed asked, a slight frown pulling at the corner of his mouth. "You've been coming here a lot?"

"Yeah. Davis, the projectionist—he knows me by name now. Always sets up these late-night screenings for me. It's an obsession, I suppose… Everyone's got a vice." Although he tried to make light, Jack's tone was resigned. The kind of acceptance that comes not with peace but with exhaustion.

Ed sat back, his eyes narrowing as he tried to gauge the depths of Jack's obsession. "It's not drinking, though?"

Jack let out a dry laugh. "No, not drinking. Haven't touched a drop in years actually. That's what people don't get. Everyone thinks it's the bottle that's going to do me in. Charley, especially. But it's not. I'm clean. My vice is this—sitting in the dark, watching old films. On repeat. That's my addiction now."

Ed paused, digesting the information. It made sense, in a way. Jack had never been the sort to give in to the usual temptations, but obsession? Obsession was something else entirely. "Charley thinks you're having an affair," Ed said, his words as blunt as a hammer.

Jack didn't flinch, didn't react at first. He just sat there, his eyes vacant, watching nothing. "Yeah," he said after a long pause. "I know she does."

"Are you?"

"No." The answer came swiftly, with no hesitation, but it was filled with a kind of hollow sadness. "No, I'm not. I wouldn't do that to her. I couldn't... Besides, who would take this on?" Jack chuckled to himself.

Ed watched him carefully, the shadows playing tricks on Jack's features, making him seem older than he was. "Martin. There's something there, isn't there... between you two?"

Jack laughed, "She's a good person... A friend, possibly."

"A lover?"

"More than that, but not that. Come on, Ed, you've seen her... me? She's set her sights higher than this, believe me." He rubbed a hand over his face, as if trying to scrub away the residue of his words, as if they sat on him, uncomfortably.

"Some feelings, then?"

Jack paused for a second. "You know, it's just a want, a need even, for her to just be... okay. If you know pain yourself, you learn to recognise it in others."

Ed nodded, lowering his head in thought. He understood that relationship, and knew those feelings, only too well.

"I've let things get... distant with Charley," he admitted. "It's almost like I don't know how to be around her anymore. Who to be... She's angry all the time, drinking too much. And I know it's because of me. She's convinced I'm hiding something, that I'm seeing someone. But the truth is, I think... I think she's been seeing someone. I just don't know who."

And there it was—a confession, of sorts. Ed felt the air between them shift, a tension easing as Jack allowed the truth to surface, piece by piece. "You think *she's* been having an affair?" Ed asked carefully, his voice softer now.

Jack shook his head, frustrated. "I don't know, man. I don't know anything anymore. All I know is that she's different. I'm different. And I don't know how to fix it."

Ed leaned back, his eyes drifting to the faded wallpaper on the cinema walls, worn and peeling from years of neglect. It felt like an apt metaphor for everything Jack had just described—the slow, inevitable decay of something once vibrant and full of life. "Do you want to fix it?" Ed asked quietly.

Jack was silent for a long time, his hands resting loosely in his lap. "Of course, there'd never be anyone else," he said finally, but his voice lacked conviction. "But I don't know if it's already too late."

Ed didn't press further. He knew Jack well enough to understand when not to push. Instead, he shifted the conversation slightly, though Jack's words lingered in the back of his mind.

"You've always had a way of escaping into your own head, Jack. Even before all this. I remember those long nights at the station when you'd just disappear into your thoughts. But this..." Ed gestured toward the empty screen in front of them. "This feels different."

"It is different, it's safe," Jack admitted. "I used to be able to switch off. Focus on the job, keep everything compartmentalised. But now... everything's bleeding together. The cases, Charley, this... void I'm in."

Ed frowned. "And Haggard hasn't been able to help with that?"

Jack shook his head. "Haggard's doing what he can. But it's not enough. It's like... I'm stuck in this cycle. Replaying the same scenes over and over again, expecting a different outcome. But it never changes. Just like the movies, just like history."

The cinema grew quieter, the rain outside now barely a whisper against the windows. Ed could feel the pull of Jack's words, the way they mirrored his own thoughts, his own doubts. But he couldn't afford to get lost in that. Not now. Not when Jack needed him to be the steady one.

"Maybe it's time to break the cycle, Jack," Ed said, his voice steady but gentle. "Maybe it's time to start doing things differently."

Jack didn't respond right away. He just sat there, staring at the blank screen, as if searching for an answer in the flickering shadows that no longer danced across it.

"Yeah," Jack said eventually, his voice barely a whisper. "Maybe it is."

The fog of it all was thick, deep and impenetrable. There was no easy solution, no quick fix, but Ed knew one thing for certain—he wouldn't let Jack go through it alone.

As the dim lights of the cinema flickered once more, signalling the end of the night, Ed reached out and placed a hand on Jack's shoulder, a gesture of silent solidarity. The darkness would always be there, lingering at the edges of their lives. But they didn't have to face it alone. The murmur of the projector winding down was the only sound in the room. The theatre had grown still, but Jack seemed trapped in his own thoughts, far from the faded velvet seats and empty screen before them. He hadn't moved since his last confession, his body coiled tightly, as if he were holding onto something that might slip away if he let go too soon.

Ed sat beside him, hands loosely clasped in his lap, the air between them thick with years of unspoken trust, unease, and now something else—something jagged and raw. He didn't rush Jack, didn't force him to explain further. He had known Jack too long for that. Sometimes, the only key was time itself.

Finally, Jack's voice cut through the darkness. "There was a time when I thought it was you, Ed."

Ed blinked, caught off guard by the admission. "Thought what was me?"

Jack's eyes stayed forward, fixed on some point far beyond the flickering shadows. "Charley. I thought you were the one she was seeing. I know how much she loves you... And Christian."

The words hung in the air like smoke, curling into the crevices of their shared past, tainting memories that had once seemed untouched by suspicion.

"I'm sorry," Jack muttered, his voice rough. "It was stupid. I know it's not true. But I wasn't thinking straight. I couldn't."

Ed's throat tightened, but he kept his tone calm, even. "What made you think that?"

Jack rubbed a hand over his face, a sigh slipping through his fingers. "I don't know. Maybe it was the way you were with her—how easy it seemed, how much she smiled when you were around. I started noticing things that weren't really there, maybe. You seemed to know how to act, what to say... That's what this job can do to you. You start seeing patterns everywhere. I thought, maybe, if she wasn't getting something from me, she was getting it from someone else. And who else but you... Who better than you?"

Ed didn't flinch, didn't show any sign of hurt. He had long learned how to carry Jack's suspicions, how to bear his friend's paranoia without letting it break them. He knew the nature of the work they did, how it corroded the mind, how it bent reality until everything looked suspect.

"You know that would never be true," Ed said quietly.

"I know." Jack's voice softened. "I know now. It wasn't you. It's no one, probably. Just my mind spinning itself in circles."

The rain outside tapped against the windows, like a clock ticking away the moments until Jack would seem lost again, sinking deeper into himself. His voice dropped to almost a whisper. "This case… It's pulling me apart. I keep thinking there's something, someone, always just out of reach. Like an invisible hand on me, guiding my every step, but I can't see who it belongs to."

Ed shifted in his seat. He could hear the exhaustion in Jack's voice, the weariness that no amount of sleep or therapy could touch. He wanted to offer something, some shred of comfort, but Jack wasn't done.

"You remember that movie?" Jack's eyes moved for the first time, glancing toward Ed. "The one I told you about ages ago, I saw when I was a kid? But it must be from the 1930s or '40s?"

Ed frowned, shaking his head slightly. "No, I don't think you've mentioned it."

Jack leaned back, his body sinking into the worn fabric of the seat, as if reliving the memory. "I must have seen it when I was, what, six or seven? Around the time my folks died… It's always stuck with me, but I've never been able to remember the title or find it again. It was about this man, trapped in time. Every time the clock struck twelve, in this room, everything around him froze—people, the world, everything. Except for him. He kept trying to figure out why, kept searching for a way out of the endless night. But no matter what he did, the clock always reset, and he was back where he started."

Ed listened, uncertain where Jack was going with this, but letting him talk. There was something feverish in Jack's tone now, a desperation beneath the words.

"For years, I tried to find that film again. I'd go to cinemas, libraries, ask old collectors. But it's like it never existed. Sometimes, I wonder if I imagined the whole thing." Jack paused, his breath catching. "But lately... lately I've started to think it's not about the film at all. It's a metaphor, Ed. It's a prison. The same damn prison I've been in all my life."

Ed's pulse quickened. "What do you mean?"

Jack exhaled, the sound heavy, as though every word he spoke carried the stress of a hundred sleepless nights. "The case, the murders, Charley... it's all part of the same cycle. I can't escape it. I'm trapped in time, just like the guy in the film. Every new body that turns up, every time I walk into a crime scene, it's like the clock strikes twelve, and everything freezes. No matter how hard I try, I can't move forward... can't get out."

The parallel Jack was drawing sent a chill through Ed's spine. He knew his friend had always been prone to brooding, to sinking too deeply into his work, but this was different. This was darker, more consuming.

"And the movies help, do they?" Ed asked carefully.

Jack nodded, but his gaze was distant. "Yeah, they help. When I sit in this dark room, watching the same old films over and over, it feels like I'm outside of time. Like I can pause the clock for a little while. But the moment I step outside, it all starts again."

Ed looked at him, taking in the strain etched into Jack's face, the deep lines carved by years of pressure and guilt. He wanted to say something, anything, that might pull Jack back from the edge, but the right words wouldn't come.

Instead, he leaned forward, resting his elbows on his knees, mirroring Jack's earlier posture. "You're not alone in this, Jack. You've got me, and you've got Haggard. We can help."

Jack let out a bitter laugh. "But what if this can't be fixed? What if this is just… who I am now?"

Ed met his eyes, refusing to look away. "That's not true. You're letting this case get under your skin, and I get it. We've seen some horrible things, but we've always come through. You'll get through this too."

For a moment, it seemed like Jack might argue, might push back against Ed's steady presence. But then his shoulders slumped, and the fight seemed to drain out of him.

"Maybe," Jack said softly. "Maybe."

Ed didn't push him further. There would be time to deal with Jack's unravelling mind later. For now, they sat in silence, the quiet, distant hum of the projector their only company. The prison Jack had built for himself wasn't one made of bars and chains, but of memories and fears, of guilt and suspicion. It was a prison that had grown familiar to him, a place where the darkness became a friend, even as it devoured him. Ed knew that prison well. He had his own cell in it, though he'd never admit it out loud. They all did, in one way or another. But there was still time, still a way out—if Jack could find the will to push open the doors.

Outside, the rain began to ease, and somewhere in the distance, the low chime of the great clock echoed through the night. Jack didn't flinch this time, but Ed couldn't help but notice the way his friend's jaw tightened, as though bracing for the invisible hand to take hold once more. The dim flicker of the projector cast Jack's face in a pale glow, as though he were part of the film itself—an actor frozen in some forgotten role, waiting for his cue to speak. But the room remained silent. Neither Jack nor Ed had spoken for what felt like hours.

Jack shifted suddenly in his seat. His voice when it came, was hoarse and low, as if dredged from deep inside. "You remember that day...?"

Ed didn't move. He didn't need to ask which day Jack meant. He nodded.

Jack stared straight ahead; his eyes fixed on the blank screen. "I've been thinking about it, Ed. Everything changed after... You know what I mean?"

He didn't need to elaborate. That single moment when everything in his world came crashing down. The event had frozen him, paralysed him in a way that neither of them could fully articulate. It wasn't about blame or guilt anymore. It had transcended that. It had become something bigger, something that permeated everything they did.

"That's when the clock stopped for me," Jack continued, his voice brittle. "For all of us, really. You, me, Charley... Everyone who was touched by it, in their own way. That's when I got stuck in this... loop. This prison of my own making."

Ed clenched his hands into fists on his lap, trying to find the words to respond, but nothing came. What could he say? They had talked about it before, in fragments, in moments of vulnerability that neither of them enjoyed. But Jack had never spoken of it like this, never framed it so clearly—as though he had been watching it all from outside himself.

"Do you know that line?" Jack asked, his voice quieter now, almost as though he were afraid of the answer. "That line from Dickinson? 'A prison gets to be a friend'?"

Ed nodded. He had heard Jack quote it before, years ago. Jack had been immersed in literature back then, long

~ 228 ~

before he had joined the force. Before everything had turned to blood and crime scenes and endless nights without sleep.

"I used to think it was just a metaphor," Jack said, leaning forward slightly. "You know, a clever turn of phrase. I thought it meant that our thoughts could trap us—that they could become a kind of prison. And I guess that's true, in a way. But it's more than that. It's not just that the prison traps you. It's that, over time, the prison becomes the only place you know. It becomes a source of comfort."

Ed swallowed hard; his throat dry. "You think that's what happened to you?"

Jack nodded, though his eyes never left the screen. "Yeah. I do. That's exactly what happened. That day—everything stopped. I couldn't move forward after that. I tried, but it was like walking through water. Every step just got harder and harder until eventually, I stopped trying altogether."

He rubbed a hand over his face, sighing deeply. "I've built a prison out of that moment. Out of the memory of it. And now, it's all I know. I've been trying to get back to… before. To the time when things were simple. But I can't. There's no going back, Ed. And I think, deep down, I've known that for a long time."

Ed's heart clenched painfully in his chest. He had always known Jack was struggling—had seen the signs of it in the long hours, the obsessive need to control everything around him, the way he shut down when things got too close to the bone. But hearing him admit it so plainly, so matter-of-factly, made the force of it all hit harder.

"There's no going back for any of us," Ed said quietly. "Not after something like that. But you're not alone in it, Jack. You never were."

Jack turned his head slightly, just enough to glance at Ed out of the corner of his eye. There was a flicker of something there—gratitude, maybe, or relief—but it disappeared as quickly as it had come.

"I know," Jack murmured. "But that's the thing, isn't it? Even though I'm not alone... I still feel like I am. Every fucking day."

Ed opened his mouth to respond, but Jack cut him off.

"It's like I'm stuck in that moment, over and over again. The sound of the impact, the way everything went quiet afterward. I replay it in my head, like a film reel that never ends. And the worst part is, I don't want to let it go. I can't let it go. Because if I do... what's left?"

Ed's chest tightened. He could see it now, clearer than ever. Jack had become a prisoner not just of his own mind, but of his guilt, his grief. The accident had been the catalyst, yes—but everything since then had built the walls higher and higher, until Jack couldn't see a way out.

"You have to find a way to let it go," Ed said softly. "For your own sake. For Charley's. She needs you, Jack. More than you know."

Jack's jaw clenched, and for a moment, Ed thought he might push back, might deny what was so plainly true. But then he sagged in his seat, the fight leaving him as quickly as it had come.

"I know," Jack whispered. "I know she does. But she thinks... she thinks I'm having an affair, Ed. She's convinced of it."

Ed's brow furrowed in confusion. "Why would she think that?"

"I don't know," Jack muttered, rubbing his temple as if trying to scrub the thoughts away. "Maybe because I always come here instead of going home. I don't know. But the thing is... I did think she was seeing someone. I've had this feeling for months now. The way she's been acting. The drinking. I don't know who it is, but I can't shake the feeling that there's someone else."

Ed was silent, processing Jack's words. He had noticed Charley's behaviour, too—the way she seemed to retreat into herself whenever they saw her, the way her eyes were always bloodshot, her movements slow, deliberate, like she was holding something back. But an affair? That didn't seem like Charley.

"You really think she's seeing someone? You think she'd do that to you?" Ed asked cautiously.

Jack shrugged; the gesture was half-hearted. "I don't know. Maybe. Maybe not. But even if she isn't… it doesn't matter. The damage is already done. We've grown so far apart, Ed. I'm not sure I'd even know how to fix it anymore."

Ed frowned, his mind racing. He had never seen Jack like this—so defeated, so lost. It wasn't just the case or the accident that had done this to him. It was everything. Years of unresolved pain, of guilt and regret, all piling up until Jack could barely breathe under it.

"You're not a prisoner, Jack," Ed said firmly. "You might feel trapped, but there's a way out. There always is."

Jack let out a bitter laugh, shaking his head. "And where exactly is this way out, Ed? Because I've been looking for it for years now, and I haven't found a fucking thing."

Ed reached over, placing a hand on Jack's shoulder. "Maybe it's not about finding a way out. Maybe it's about accepting that the prison is part of you now—but it doesn't have to define you. You can still live outside of it."

Jack glanced at him, his eyes dark and hollow. "And how do I do that?"

Ed squeezed his shoulder, his voice steady. "You start by letting go of the idea that you can ever go back. Because you can't. None of us can."

Jack didn't respond, but Ed could see the wheels turning in his mind, the slow, painful process of grappling with a truth he had avoided for so long.

Outside, the rain had now stopped, leaving the streets slick and glistening under the dim glow of the streetlights. The world hadn't changed, wouldn't change, but maybe Jack could. They sat together for a while longer, neither of them needing to say anything more. Ed was beginning to think, despite his words, that sometimes the only thing you could do was sit with the darkness and wait for the light to come.

19

'The fascinating chill that music leaves'

October announced its arrival with the seventh murder scene, a dismal replica of those that had come before it. DS Martin stood just inside the door; her arms crossed tightly across her chest as if to shield herself from the chilled atmosphere of the room. The air inside was thick, stifling, even—and laden with the scent of stale cigarette smoke and the metallic tang of dried blood. Her breath felt thick in her throat, her chest rising with shallow discomfort as she glanced at the pale form on the floor.

Yasmin Eliot. Blonde, like the others. Late 20s/early 30s, like the others. And dead, just like the others.

Martin's eyes hovered over the body, taking in the familiar, brutal details. She felt no surge of shock, no sudden jolt of horror. Not anymore. It had become routine—if such savagery could ever be called that. The vinyl records scattered across the floor, Yasmin's prized collection, were a strange counterpoint to the violence. Patti Smith, Bowie, The Velvet Underground, a smattering of jazz and blues, covers and sleeves smeared with fingerprints as the forensics team moved cautiously around them. The turntable near her body had long stopped spinning, but the needle was still poised as though ready to drop, waiting to fill the air with music that would never come. Outside, rain had begun to tap lightly on the windows, each drop a slow, deliberate drumbeat against the glass.

Martin's fingers twitched as she dug them deeper into the fabric of her jacket. She looked up as Ed and Jack entered the flat together. Today, they both moved with a certain weariness, she noted, as if the sleepless nights had finally caught up with them, but there was also a newfound solidarity in their steps. They walked in tandem, their eyes alert, and for the first time since Martin had started working with them, they seemed like partners—genuinely partners, no longer tethered to unspoken tensions.

Jack scanned the room, pausing at the record player, then drifting to the body. His face remained impassive, the weariness behind his eyes more apparent today than usual. He looked as if he had forgotten how to blink, his gaze fixed but somehow not present. Ed was the one who approached first, his shoes making a soft scuffing sound on the wooden floor. He crouched down beside the body, close enough to examine but far enough not intrude on the forensic team's work. His eyes, too, were heavy, but his hands were steady, as he reached out to gently lift a strand of Yasmin's hair away from her face, revealing the telltale wounds on her throat.

"Same as the others," he muttered, more to himself than anyone in the room. "Blonde. Late twenties. Silver halide. This one has a vinyl collection. It's like he's pulling them from some catalogue."

Martin nodded but said nothing. She had learned to wait with these two, to watch and absorb before speaking. Her role here was secondary, no matter her rank. Jack and Ed were the ones driving the case forward, tied to it in ways she had yet to fully understand.

Ed straightened up, rubbing the back of his neck as he stepped away from the body. His eyes met Jack's for a brief moment, something unspoken passing between them. Then, without looking at Martin, he spoke again.

"She's a music journalist, yeah?"

Martin nodded. "Yasmin Eliot. Worked freelance. Wrote for a few of the big magazines—Mojo, NME, that kind of thing. Interviews, album reviews. Lived alone. No sign of forced entry, but it doesn't look like she was expecting anyone. One earring appears to be missing. Her laptop's still here. Forensics haven't found anything on it yet."

Jack finally moved closer, stepping around the records with deliberate care. His eyes flicked from the body to the turntable and back again, as if trying to piece together a connection between the woman's death and the scattered fragments of her life.

"He took her earring," Jack murmured, almost to himself. He stared at the turntable, and his brow furrowed. He reached out to run a finger over the edge of one of the records, his touch lingering as though the vinyl held a secret which only he could unlock. "Maybe he's collecting memories," he said, more to himself than to them. "He doesn't want just to kill them. He wants to hold on to a piece of them. Something that matters."

Ed shot him a glance, his lips tightening slightly. "We don't know that yet," he said, his voice measured but tense. "And we don't think he took anything from the others."

Jack shrugged, not looking up from the vinyl in his hand. "No, we don't. So why now?"

Martin watched Jack, noticing the tension in his posture, the slight tremor in his hand as he let go of the record. He wasn't fully here. His mind, his thoughts—they were elsewhere, tangled up in something she couldn't quite grasp. She had always known Jack was deeply connected to this case, but this morning, something about him seemed different.

She glanced at Ed, but he gave nothing away. If he noticed Jack's unease, he wasn't showing it.

"The thing is," Martin said, her voice steady as she attempted to steer the conversation back to the facts, "we still don't have a motive. What's he getting from them? Why these women? It's not random, we know that much. But why this specific type? All blonde, all around the same age…"

Jack exhaled sharply through his nose, rubbing a hand across his jaw. "He's got a type, that much is clear. But it's more than that. He's looking for something in them. Something they represent, maybe. The music could be part of it, but I don't think it's just about the records. The last one was a writer, too."

"He takes his time," Ed added, his voice low. "He wants to be close. He's deliberate. That's important. He's not just in it for the thrill of the kill. He's careful, controlled."

Jack moved away from the turntable, his hands sliding into the pockets of his coat. "Whoever this guy is, he's methodical."

Martin nodded, though her mind was still racing. She'd attended enough homicide scenes now to recognise the particular chill of a case like this, one that lingered at the edges of her thoughts long after she left the crime scene. But something about this one felt different. It was as if they were moving through shadows, chasing after something they couldn't quite see. And Jack, whether he realised it or not, was being drawn deeper into the darkness.

The room fell silent for a moment, save for the muted clicks of the forensic team's cameras. Jack stood by the window, staring out at the rain-soaked street below. Ed lingered near the body, his expression unreadable as he bent down again, his fingers tracing a line near the victim's hand.

"What are you thinking?" Martin asked softly.

Ed glanced up; his brow creased. "She was reaching for something," he murmured. "Look at her hand. The way her fingers are curled—like she was trying to grab something just out of reach."

Martin crouched beside him, examining the body more closely. She saw what he meant. Yasmin's right hand was stretched toward the turntable, her fingers slightly clenched as if she had been grasping for something just before she died.

Jack turned from the window, moving toward them with slow, deliberate steps. His eyes swept over the scene, his mind working through the details. "What could she have been reaching for? The records? Or maybe the player itself? What was in her hand, a note for us again, I assume?"

Martin glanced up at him, then back at the hand. "History is a pattern of timeless moments."

"Did you google it?" Ed asked, his voice grim. He rose to his feet, brushing his hands on his trousers.

Before Martin could answer him, Jack chimed in, "It's T.S. Eliot." He remained focussed silent otherwise, staring down at the body with a look that Martin couldn't quite decipher. He seemed far away again, lost in thought, as if he were trying to step into Yasmin's shoes, to feel what she felt in those final moments. It was a look she had seen on him before—detached, yet deeply personal at the same time. As if the case was no longer just a case, but something more.

"What's it mean?" Martin asked to break the silence. "What's his message?"

Jack shook his head slightly, his hands still in his pockets. "I think, he's telling us that this inevitable."

Ed shot him a sidelong glance, a flicker of tension passing across his face. "We're getting closer," he said, though there was little conviction in his voice. "The earring marks a change of direction. We just have to keep looking."

Martin stood, glancing at both of them. "Maybe something in her record collection can tell us more."

Jack nodded absently, still looking at the turntable as if it held some secret, some unspoken truth. "It's always in the details," he muttered. "Always in the small things."

Martin watched him for a moment longer, then turned her attention to Ed. He looked tired, worn down in a way she hadn't seen before. But there was something else there, too—something she couldn't quite place. A tension, a distance, as if he were holding something back.

The rain continued to tap against the windows, while the room was still clouded by the presence of death. Jack seemed to gather himself, stepping away from the window with a resigned air. "We need to figure out what connects these women. Why them. And why now."

The penny gleamed faintly from across the room, a flicker of copper against the dull greys and browns of the scene. Jack's eyes narrowed, drawn to it with a sudden, inexplicable intensity. It was small, insignificant really, yet something about it caught his attention in a way the body, the vinyl records, and the methodical violence had not. He moved toward it without a word, the tension in his shoulders softening as if the room itself had paused for a breath.

He crouched down by the desk, his coat brushing the floor as he reached out to study the coin more closely. The penny sat just beyond the desk leg, as if dropped by mistake, forgotten in the chaos of death. Its simple presence seemed out of place among the ruin, a tiny piece of a much larger puzzle. Jack tilted his head, his mind clicking through the details.

Ed, still standing by the body, glanced over. "What is it, Jack?"

Jack didn't answer immediately. His thumb hovered over the penny, but he didn't touch it. There was something about it—something wrong. It wasn't just an ordinary coin tossed carelessly on the floor. He could feel it, the way you feel a gust of wind before the storm.

"Get someone to bag this," Jack finally said, his voice low but firm. "Run it for prints."

Martin, who had been watching silently from the corner, nodded without question. She motioned to Vaz Shah to oblige, who moved in with a small evidence bag and gloves, carefully placing the penny inside as though it were the most delicate item in the room. The officer glanced at Jack, curious, but said nothing. Jack straightened up slowly, brushing off his coat and staring at the coin now sealed in plastic.

"A penny?" Ed asked, his voice sceptical. "For your thoughts, mate?"

Jack didn't meet his gaze. Instead, he stepped away, letting the shadows near the window swallow him up once more. He needed to think, to turn this new detail over in his mind without interruption. He could sense Ed's curiosity, the way his old friend was watching him, waiting for an explanation. But there was none—not yet.

"Just a hunch," Jack said, his voice distant. "Could be nothing."

Ed raised an eyebrow, clearly unconvinced. "A penny? What's it supposed to tell us? People drop change all the time."

"Maybe," Jack replied, though his tone was noncommittal. He had learned over the years to trust these small, seemingly inconsequential things—the details that no one else paid attention to. They had a way of revealing the truth, in their own time.

He turned his attention back to the room. Her collection of vinyl records, now carefully dusted for prints, sat like ghosts on the floor—testaments to a life cut short.

The needle on the turntable remained poised, as if still waiting to play her that final song.

"What do we know about her?" Jack asked, changing the subject as he moved closer to Ed and the body. His eyes flickered briefly over the lifeless form of Yasmin, but he kept a distance, as though the proximity of death had begun to fray the edges of his control.

Ed shifted his weight, arms crossed as he considered the question, flicking through a file passed to him by Radcliffe. "Freelance music journalist, mostly covering indie bands and underground scenes. Known for her taste in vinyl and rare records. Worked from home, lived alone. No family in the city, but she had a tight-knit group of friends. No known enemies."

"Until now," Jack muttered under his breath. He glanced around the room again, taking in the small details—the disarray of the records, the scuffed floorboards, the smell of stale cigarette smoke that still clung to the air. The room fell into a tense silence as Jack's words lingered. There was something deeply unsettling about this case, the way the killer moved through these lives with such precision, such care, only to leave behind the hollow shells of his victims.

Ed sighed, rubbing the back of his neck as though trying to ease the tension. "We've got the same MO—no signs of forced entry. But it's still not enough to make sense of it."

"It's never enough," Jack replied, more to himself than anyone else. His mind was already moving, spinning through possibilities, searching for the thread that tied it all together.

He stepped away from the body again, his eyes drifting back toward the window, where the rain was coming down harder now, streaking the glass like tears. He felt the city outside pressing in on him, the constant hum of life and death, the pulse of the streets. Somewhere out there, the killer was walking among them, slipping through the cracks unnoticed.

"What about the records?" Jack asked. "Anything stand out about her collection?"

Martin glanced down at her notes, then up at Jack. "She had a pretty impressive vinyl collection—rare editions, first pressings. Looks like nothing's been taken, though. It's all here."

"She was reaching for the turntable," Ed said, nodding toward the body. "Like she was trying to stop something."

"Or start something," Jack replied, his mind turning over the possibilities. He moved toward the turntable, studying the needle, the stack of records nearby. His fingers grazed the surface of one of the albums, then stopped.

"Do we know what was playing?"

Martin shook her head. "The record was off when we arrived. Could have been anything."

Jack stared down at the stack of vinyl, his brow furrowing. There was something here—something he wasn't seeing. He could feel it, like a shadow just out of reach. The penny. The records. The body. It was all connected, but the pieces hadn't fallen into place yet. He stared at the turntable, then back at the body. His mind raced, turning over details, fragments, trying to force them into a coherent shape. But something was eluding him, slipping through his grasp like smoke.

Finally, he exhaled sharply, running a hand through his hair. "I don't know," he admitted, his voice low. "But I can't shake the feeling that this is bigger than we realise. He's not just killing them. He's playing a game with us. And we're not seeing the rules."

Ed frowned, glancing at Martin. "A game?"

Jack nodded slowly. "Yeah. There's a narrative here. He's building something, constructing something out of their lives. And we're missing it."

Martin stepped forward, her eyes narrowing as she considered Jack's words. "What do you mean?"

Jack turned toward the window again, he seemed distant. "They're part of something larger. We just haven't figured out what it is yet."

The rain outside intensified, pounding against the glass in rhythmic pulses. Jack stood there for a moment, lost in thought, his mind racing to catch up with the invisible hand that seemed to be guiding the killer's moves.

Ed exchanged a glance with Martin, concern etched into his features. "Jack…"

But Jack didn't respond. His eyes were fixed on the rain, his thoughts far from the room, far from the case. He was somewhere else now, chasing after a shadow he couldn't quite see. And in that moment, as the rain poured down it felt as if the city outside moved on without them.

20

'A Word dropped careless on a Page'

The room was dimly lit, the sterile fluorescent overhead casting a cold glow across the evidence board. Jack sat slumped at the edge of the table, staring at the faces of the seven women pinned up in neat rows. Beside each photograph, hastily scribbled notes and timelines connected the details like strands of a tangled web. It all led back to the same empty centre: seven lives taken, seven stories ended, and still, no closer to knowing why. Ed stood by the whiteboard, marker in hand, tapping it absentmindedly against his leg as they reviewed the fragmented evidence for what felt like the hundredth time.

"Caroline Whitman, thirty-four. The eldest victim. A nurse. Nothing stolen. Hannah Ibsen, twenty-eight. Similar method. Body found on the floor next to an open laptop. Ariana Lawrence, twenty-nine. An office cleaner. All with fragments of a photograph in their mouths, under their tongues."

He paused momentarily, glancing over at Jack's tired face. He could tell his friend was feeling the pressure of this case more than any other they had worked on, so much so he felt it was like it had pushed the burden of his long-held grief and regret to one side too.

"Then we had Rosie, Larkin. Victim number four. Another photo fragment that allowed us to create this image with the pieces we'd found," he said, pointing on the board to the haunting picture that DS Martin had first shown Jack three days ago. He checked his thoughts, had it really only been for three days that this dark and mysterious figure had started gazing at them from the evidence board, this wall of death.

Jack grunted, running his hand through his dark and greying hair. The fatigue had settled deep into his bones now, into his soul, dragging at his movements. He hadn't slept properly in days now. The cases ran together, the faces blurred. In them all it was like all he could see was Charley, and that scared him.

"Then Emily Isherwood and Lauren Donne, same cause of death. Two more photo fragments and, again, a shower of silver halide," Ed continued. "Most recently, Yasmin Eliot. Music journalist. Found near her record player, same signs of struggle, same silver halide." He circled the word "VINYL" on the board with a sharp, deliberate stroke of the marker. "This time he takes something personal. One earring."

"An earring... So we'd know that something was missing," Jack muttered, half to himself. His voice was thick with exhaustion. He leaned back in his chair, eyes narrowing as he studied the photos again. Seven women. Seven different lives, and apparently unknown to one another. But they were starting to feel the same, like they were all being absorbed into one long, endless nightmare.

Ed tapped the board again, drawing Jack's attention back to the timeline. "No discernible connection between the victims."

"Apart from the killer," Jack's eyes flickered over the faces again, looking for something—anything—that might tie them together. Caroline Whitman's gentle smile, Hannah Ibsen's bright eyes, Yasmin Eliot's cheeky smirk. They all seemed so alike, yet so different, and the killer had marked them all. It felt personal, but there was no obvious link, no thread to pull on.

"He's our connection," Jack said, standing up and moving closer to the board. "Maybe there's something we're missing… something about their routines, their habits. What if it's not random? What if he knows them, but not in the way we've been thinking?"

Ed watched him closely, his eyes narrowed in thought. "What do you mean?"

Jack pointed to the notes beside Yasmin's picture. "Music journalist. She covered underground scenes, indie bands. What if he followed her? Not just physically, but online. What if he's been watching all of them for months? Years, even?"

Ed rubbed his chin, considering the idea. "It's possible. But how do we find that?"

Before Jack could respond, the door to the office creaked open, and DS Martin walked in. She was her usual self—cool, composed, the perfect picture of professional detachment. But today, there was something different about her. Beneath the surface, behind the mask, there was a flicker of excitement. It was subtle, almost imperceptible, but Jack noticed. He always did.

"Morning," she said, her voice clipped, carrying that no-nonsense tone Jack had come to expect from her. "I've got something."

Jack turned to her; his interest piqued. "What is it?"

Martin glanced at the whiteboard, then back at the two of them. "CCTV. We finally have a lead."

She walked over to the evidence board and took out a file, pulling out a series of grainy black-and-white images. She spread them out on the table in front of Jack and Ed. Jack leaned forward, studying the first image. It was taken from a security camera near Yasmin Eliot's apartment. The angle was poor, the street partially obscured by rain, but there was a figure. A man, his face hidden by the shadow of a hood, wearing a waxed jacket.

Jack's eyes narrowed. "This was near Yasmin's apartment?"

Martin nodded, a hint of satisfaction in her eyes. "Taken less than two hours before we estimate the time of death. I've cross-referenced the footage with CCTV from the other crime scenes. It's not perfect—some of the footage is corrupted, or the cameras didn't capture enough—but I found something. A similar figure was spotted near Hannah Ibsen's apartment the night she was killed. And another, near Emily Isherwood's flat. Same jacket in all of them… See."

She pulled out another series of images, pointing to the familiar, shadowy figure. The same waxed jacket. The same deliberate posture, moving through the rain-soaked streets unnoticed.

Jack's heart skipped a beat. It wasn't much, but it was the first real lead they'd had.

"Have we been able to enhance the images? Run the footage through facial recognition?" Ed asked, his voice measured.

Martin shook her head. "Not enough detail in the face, apparently. Too obscured."

Jack stared at the images, his mind racing. The figure in the waxed jacket. The meticulous planning. He had a feeling they were closing in on something, that the puzzle was finally starting to take shape. But there were still too many missing pieces. Or it was the connection between the pieces that had that was missing.

"Anything else?" Jack asked, his voice tight.

And then, in the quiet of the room, the sound of rain began to tap gently against the window, as if marking the passage of the time which they could no longer afford to waste.

Jack's question had hung in the air. *Do we have anything else?* His voice was tired, ground down by weeks of insomnia and too many unanswered questions.

Martin could hardly contain it any longer. "We do," she said, her voice uncharacteristically animated. "It's your penny."

Jack turned sharply, his eyes narrowing. "My penny?"

"The one you found by Yasmin's desk," she continued, stepping closer, the excitement leaking through her usually calm demeanour. "Forensics ran it like you asked… And they found a print."

Jack felt a surge of something—hope, dread, perhaps a mix of both. "A print?"

"A good one," Martin said, her lips twitching into a small, victorious smile. "And better than that—we got a match. Guy called Roy Murray."

Jack blinked. The name didn't mean anything to him. "Who's Roy Murray?"

"Single guy, mid-50s," Martin said, flipping through her file with a practiced hand. "A man with a record, too. Indecent exposure 1997 and 2003. Indecent images on his company laptop when raided in 2003, but nothing too major, Cat B and C. And a couple of sexual assault allegations that got dropped. For being a bit handsy."

The room seemed to shift. Jack's pulse quickened as he took in the information. Finally—a name. A face. A suspect.

Martin's voice steadied now, slipping back into her usual, professional self. "But it's enough to take a closer look. The prints don't lie. He dropped that penny at Yasmin Eliot's apartment. And it's not the first time he's shown up on our radar."

Jack grabbed the file from her hands, flipping through the details. There, on the page, was a grainy mugshot of a man in his mid-50s. Thick, unruly hair, a permanent sneer carved into his face. The kind of face you wouldn't trust, not for a second. Jack's fingers traced the edge of the photo as though it could give him more answers.

"Roy Murray," he muttered, the name sitting heavy in his mouth. "Why wasn't he flagged before?"

"No reason to, he hasn't been active in years, as far as we're concerned," Martin explained. "His last conviction was nearly a decade ago. He's been quiet ever since... To us, anyway."

"Until now," Jack said grimly.

Ed crossed his arms, studying the photo with a critical eye. "We've had false leads before. This could just be a coincidence. He could've been in that apartment for some other reason."

Jack shook his head. "A man with this history? In Yasmin Eliot's flat? Feels like something, but not a coincidence."

"He's right," Martin added. "Maybe the penny wasn't just lying around. Perhaps he left it there. Deliberately, almost like he's mocking us."

Jack closed the file, his thoughts racing ahead. "What else do we know about him?"

Martin looked to Ed, a flicker of unease passing between them. "Not much. He's been quiet since his last arrest. He did a year inside for the images, on the register, but like I said, nothing coming up on his record since."

Jack took a deep breath. They had a name, a suspect. It wasn't much, but it was more than they'd had in weeks. The idea that this man could be the one responsible for these brutal killings troubled him. Something didn't feel right. But he couldn't shake the thought that maybe, just maybe, they were finally on the right track.

"I want surveillance on him," Jack said, his voice firm.

Ed shifted, glancing between Jack and Martin. "What's the plan? Pick him up?"

Jack pinned Murray's picture on the evidence board, staring at the grainy photograph as if willing the face in the mugshot to reveal more than it did. The room seemed to close in around him—seven victims, all young, all blonde, all brutally murdered. And now, for the first time, a suspect. Surely, it had to be Murray. Jack's gut churned, but he had learned to ignore that gnawing feeling, the one that told him there was still something more. Something still hidden.

"Do we have an address?" Jack turned to Martin, the weariness in his eyes giving way to purpose. "Do we?"

Martin flipped through her notes. "Yeah, ground-floor flat. Converted Victorian, nice leafy street in Dulwich. Murray's been living there for the past few years, apparently. Runs an import/export business online."

Jack raised an eyebrow. "Import/export? What's he importing and exporting?"

"Antiques, supposedly." Her tone was laced with scepticism.

"Of course," Jack muttered, a wry smile tugging at the corners of his mouth. "Antiques. Always the perfect cover for something shady." He didn't like it—this man, this convenient suspect who had surfaced out of nowhere after months of frustration. But a print was a print, and they couldn't ignore that.

Martin cleared her throat. "What do you want to do?"

Jack turned, the sharpness returning to his countenance. "Get Radcliffe on surveillance. I want someone on that flat, now. No one in or out without us knowing about it."

Martin nodded, already making notes. "I'll get him out there immediately."

"Thanks. And pull together a team," Jack continued, pacing the room now, his mind racing through the next steps. "We'll need a warrant to search. But if Murray so much as twitches, tell Radcliffe to take him in."

Ed, watching Jack closely, chimed in. "You think he's going to run?"

Jack stopped, considering the question. "Maybe. If he knew we were onto him, he could bolt. Unless his plan involves us staying."

An uneasy look passed between them.

Martin glanced at her watch. "I'll brief Radcliffe and get him moving. Collins is around too. We'll have eyes on Murray's place within the hour."

As she left the room, the tension eased slightly, but it was still there—hanging between Jack and Ed like the remnants of a storm that hadn't fully passed. Ed studied Jack for a moment before speaking.

"You don't seem to think this is it, do you?" Ed's voice was low, almost hesitant.

Jack didn't answer right away. He moved back to the evidence board, staring at the faces of the victims, the timeline of their lives cut short by violence and death. He wanted to believe they had the right man. He needed to believe it. But there was that nagging doubt, the one he couldn't shake.

"I don't know, mate," Jack admitted, his voice quieter than before. "But we don't have a choice. We have to act on it."

**

An hour later, Radcliffe was on his way to Dulwich, the young detective eager to prove himself. The leafy street, lined with Victorian terraced houses, felt almost too idyllic for the grim business they were dealing with. Radcliffe checked his watch as he pulled up a few houses down from Murray's flat, careful to park discreetly. The sun had dipped low in the sky, casting long shadows across the pavement. It was the kind of street where nothing ever seemed out of place, where quiet families lived quiet lives, and where the idea of a serial killer lurking next door felt completely absurd.

Radcliffe adjusted the small camera mounted on his dashboard and settled in for what he expected would be a long, uneventful night. He radioed into Martin, letting her know he was in position.

"Eyes on the flat," he said, glancing toward the building. The ground-floor window was dark, the curtains drawn. No movement inside. "No activity so far."

"Stay sharp," Martin's voice crackled over the line. "We're pulling together a team to move in once we've got the warrant. Shouldn't be long now."

Radcliffe nodded to himself, though no one could see him. "I'll sit tight."

"But if he moves, you can take him. Miller doesn't want him making a break for it."

"Got it," he said, reclining slightly in his seat, his eyes never leaving Murray's flat. The anticipation was thick in the air, the kind of tension that made the hours feel like days. But Radcliffe was patient. He had done this before—waiting, watching, ready for the moment when everything would shift.

Back at the station, Jack paced the briefing room, the ticking of the clock on the wall marking each passing second with cruel indifference. The evidence was laid out in front of him—photos, reports, maps. But it was that penny, that one small detail, that had finally led them to Murray.

"Do you ever wonder why they leave things behind?" Jack asked suddenly. His voice was distant, as if he were speaking more to himself than to his partner.

Ed looked up from his seat, where he had been reviewing a file. "What do you mean?"

"The killers," Jack continued, his eyes narrowing as he thought aloud. "Otherwise so careful, vigilant. Then they leave things. Little clues. Like the penny, the details they don't need to leave, but they do. Why?"

Ed shrugged. "Could be arrogance. They think they're smarter than us. Or maybe it's part of their game. He's wants us to find him, in a way."

Jack shook his head. "No, it's more than that. Like he's trying to tell us something."

Ed watched Jack carefully. "You think Murray's been trying to communicate with us?"

Jack didn't answer right away. Instead, he stepped closer to the whiteboard, staring at the victims' photos. Seven young women, each connected by a series of brutal, calculated acts.

"The poetry, the halide... He's been toying with us, with me," Jack said quietly. "Leaving us breadcrumbs."

"And now we've followed the trail to his door," Ed said, standing up. "The question is, what do we do when we knock?"

Jack's eyes hardened.

Martin entered the room, a file clutched in her hand which Jack knew to be confirmation of their warrant. Her voice was brisk. "We're good to go."

Jack straightened. "Radcliffe's in position?"

"He's just reconfirmed Murray's home now," Martin confirmed. "But no other movement so far."

"Good," Jack said, grabbing his coat. "We're moving."

21

'By a departing light'

Radcliffe sat in an unmarked Audi; his eyes trained on the darkened windows of the ground-floor flat. The night had grown colder, a fine mist settling over the street as the leaves rustled quietly in the breeze. He checked his watch—nothing unusual. No movement. Just the quiet, waiting, the kind that made hours stretch into eternity. His breath fogged the glass as he exhaled, and he wiped it absently with the sleeve of his jacket, leaning back, resigned to the long night ahead.

A tap on his window startled him, and he snapped his head to the side. It was Jack. He crouched by the car, gesturing for Radcliffe to wind the window down. The young detective did so, feeling the crisp air rush in, along with the gravity of what was about to unfold.

"All quiet on the Western front?" Jack asked in a low voice.

Radcliffe nodded, not fully understanding the reference. "So far, nothing, sir. Flat's been mostly dark since I got here. No movement inside. No one in or out."

Jack's eyes narrowed as he scanned the flat. "We're going to move in," he said, his tone final. He looked at the house with a kind of intensity, as though already calculating the possible scenarios that might play out in the next few minutes. "Keep your eyes sharp. If he bolts, I need you to be ready."

Radcliffe swallowed the dryness in his throat, feeling the rising tension. He adjusted his glasses, "I'm ready, sir."

Jack nodded, then rose to his feet, tapping his radio. "Martin," his voice crackled through the device. "Take a couple of uniforms round the back. Secure the rear exit. Ed and I will go in through the front. Radcliffe's staying put unless he runs. And please be careful, if he is our guy then he's definitely dangerous, and could be armed."

Martin's voice came back swiftly, professional and terse. "On it, sir."

Jack clicked the radio off and turned to Ed, who stood a few feet behind him, surveying the house with a grim expression. Together, they made their way up the path toward the front door. The house was typical for the area—an old Victorian terraced home, red-bricked with arched windows, high ceilings, and narrow hallways that whispered of a bygone era. The front garden was overgrown, weeds choking the remnants of what might have once been rose bushes or lavender, the iron gate hanging at an awkward angle, rusted at its old iron hinges.

The house itself had a worn beauty to it, the kind of structure that had carried the lives and loves of decades, if not centuries. The bricks were cracked in places, the mortar eroded by years of rain and frost. A substantial wooden door, painted in peeling green, sat at the top of a short set of stone steps, the knocker shaped like a lion's head, its eyes chipped and weathered by time. The windows, once grand and polished, were now grimy, their sills thick with dust.

Jack's hand hovered over the knocker for a moment, as if considering something, before he rapped it hard against the wood. The sound echoed through the quiet street, drawing out the seconds like a tightrope.

He glanced at Ed, whose jaw was set in a rigid line. They waited. And waited. No sound came from within the house. Jack raised his fist to knock again, but before he could, the door creaked open.

Roy Murray stood there, silhouetted against the dim light from inside, his face half in shadow. He was older than the mugshot suggested, his hair greying and receding at the temples, skin pale and loose with age. His eyes, though, were sharp, cold, and filled with an alertness that made Jack's instincts flare.

"Mr. Murray," Jack began, his voice measured, but firm. "I'm DCI Jack—"

But before Jack could finish, Murray's body tensed. Without warning, he pushed past Jack with a force that caught the seasoned detective completely off guard, his elbow knocking Jack sideways as he bolted through the doorway and down the steps.

"Oi!" Ed shouted, lunging forward, but Murray was already tearing down the street, his shoes pounding against the pavement.

Radcliffe, startled by the sudden movement, jerked his head up and saw Murray sprinting in the opposite direction. He twisted the key in the ignition, the engine of his car roaring to life. Tires screeched as he swung the vehicle around, his heart thudding in his chest.

"Martin!" Jack barked into the radio as he and Ed took off after Murray. "Suspect fleeing down the street towards the park!"

Martin, although at the back of the house, had heard the commotion and reacted instinctively ahead of Jack's order. She darted around the corner, catching sight of Murray just as he turned at the end of the block. She was fast—as a competitive runner, faster than most, and certainly faster than Jack or Ed. Without hesitation, she sprinted after him, her feet thudding rhythmically against the pavement.

Jack and Ed followed behind, their breathing heavy as they kept pace, but Murray was quick, his long legs carrying him swiftly through the narrow streets, past shuttered shops and parked cars. The wet ground shimmered beneath the streetlights, the mist clinging to the air in soft, swirling tendrils. Jack's breath came in ragged gasps, his focus narrowing to the figure ahead of him.

Radcliffe, in the car, accelerated down the road, catching up to the foot chase. He could see Murray in the distance, his waxed jacket catching the light briefly as he dashed across the intersection. Radcliffe floored the accelerator, the car jolting forward with a roar.

But Murray was slippery, weaving between parked cars, darting through alleys, his figure becoming a blur in the twilight. Martin was relentless, however, her speed impressive as she closed the gap between them both, her focus sharp and unwavering.

"Cut him off, Radcliffe!" Jack shouted into the radio; his voice strained.

Radcliffe swerved the car down a side street, attempting to head Murray off as he rounded the next block. The chase twisted through the winding streets of Dulwich, past the Victorian houses and established gardens, the quiet neighbourhood now filled with the sounds of mad pursuit— the slap of boots on wet pavement, the roar of the car engine, the occasional shout cutting through the winter night.

Murray, sensing he was being cornered, glanced over his shoulder, panic flashing in his eyes. His breath came in harsh gasps, his movements growing more erratic. He made a sharp turn down a narrow alley, his feet slipping on the slick cobblestones.

Martin was close now, seemingly just a few strides behind him. She could hear his laboured breathing, the way his shoes skidded against the ground as he tried to outrun her. But she was faster, and her training kicked in. With a final burst of speed, she lunged forward, tackling him to the ground.

Murray hit the pavement with a grunt, his body twisting beneath her as he struggled to break free, but so did Martin. She tried to pin him down, her knee digging into his back as she attempted to wrestle his arms behind him. Her breath came in sharp, rapid bursts as she pressed Murray into the wet pavement, her knee digging hard into his back. "Stay down!" she barked, her voice fierce and unwavering, the adrenaline coursing through her veins. But the man beneath her, for all his appearance of weariness, had strength left, was larger, and in an instant, he twisted with a force she hadn't anticipated.

In a blink, Murray had bucked upward, throwing the young detective off balance. She staggered, her knee slipping off his back, and before she could recover, he swung his elbow hard into her ribs. She gasped, the air leaving her lungs in a painful rush. Murray pushed off the ground and was on his feet, bolting down the street again before Martin could stop him.

"Cunt!" Martin yelled, elongated, guttural, animal, as if she needed the fast and roaring expulsion of sound to refill her lungs, before struggling to her feet as the figure of Murray disappeared into the shadows ahead.

Jack and Ed, just behind her, saw the commotion unfold in what felt like slow motion. Jack's instincts kicked in first—he knelt by Martin, checking her over quickly, his hands firm on her shoulders. "You're okay?"

"I'm fine," she snapped, grimacing but shaking him off, already back on her feet. "Go!"

Without another word, Jack and Ed resumed the pursuit, their legs pounding the pavement in the direction of Murray. Radcliffe, forced to abandon his car as Murray made his way into the narrow, pedestrianised alley—one of those winding, twisting lanes known as twittens in the old towns of England—now joined the chase, jogging to catch up with the others.

Martin's eyes darted around the darkened streets. "Radcliffe, with me," she ordered, sensing an alternative route. "We'll cut him off."

Radcliffe nodded, his body moving automatically into the rhythm of pursuit, following Martin's lead as she veered down a side street that ran parallel to the twitten. Her mind raced—instinct and training guiding her through the maze of alleyways and streets. If she could guess where he was headed, they might be able to outflank him.

Jack and Ed, meanwhile, stayed on Murray's heels, their focus singular, the sounds of the chase reverberating around them—the thud of shoes on pavement, the distant sounds of traffic, the echo of their own breath. The mist hung in the air, dense and oppressive, obscuring everything just enough to make the night feel unreal, like they were chasing a ghost.

Murray's figure darted through the narrow passage, his old coat flapping around him in the night air, his feet skidding on the slick cobblestones. He was fast, but Jack and Ed kept pace, determination pushing them beyond their limits. They couldn't let him escape.

Ahead of them, a distant light flickered—the soft glow of the train station coming into view. Murray must have realised his only chance was to catch a train, to blend into the night, to disappear.

Martin, approaching from the other direction, could see where the road bent toward the station. "We've got him," she muttered to herself, pushing harder, her muscles screaming in protest. Radcliffe, just behind her, was silent and focused, but his face was pale with the exertion.

As they reached the end of the alley, they emerged onto the road just as Murray was making his way toward the station entrance, his breath visible in the cold night air. Martin caught sight of him just as he vaulted over the barriers, the electronic turnstiles too slow to stop his momentum. Her heart lurched—he was so close to slipping through their fingers.

"We've got him," she said, breathlessly, sprinting now with everything she had.

Jack and Ed arrived at the station from the other direction at almost the same moment, witnessing Murray's desperate attempt to escape through the barriers. Jack didn't hesitate—he threw himself over the turnstile with surprising agility for a man of his age, following closely on Murray's heels. Ed, the fitter and stronger of the two men, vaulted the barrier with a grunt, both of them landing on the other side, eyes locked on their quarry.

Murray, sensing the noose tightening around his neck, darted through the station crowd, weaving between the startled commuters, his body moving with the erratic, desperate energy of a trapped animal. His eyes flicked to the nearest platform, his only chance of escape—but the warning chime was ringing, it was approaching fast.

Jack pushed through the crowd, tunnel-visioned on Murray. "Stop!" he bellowed, though he knew it was useless. Murray was far beyond reason, utterly consumed with the need to flee.

Martin and Radcliffe entered the station from another side, converging on the same platform, watching as Murray made his final dash toward some semblance of safety.

Martin, running parallel to him, knew they were out of time. She leaped forward, her body slamming into him once more, knocking them both to the ground with a vicious jolt. The crowd gasped, startled by the sudden outbreak of violence, as the commuters stumbled back, wide-eyed.

"Get off me!" Murray snarled, his voice raw with desperation, as he wriggled violently in Martin's grip. For a split second, she tightened her hold, digging her knee into his side again in an attempt to keep him pinned to the ground. But Murray was slippery—an animal cornered, thrashing with an uncontainable force born from sheer panic, fear. With a sudden burst of energy, he twisted sharply, again breaking free from her grasp.

Martin, momentarily thrown off balance, grabbed at the air where his arm had just been. Murray staggered to his feet, his body jerking awkwardly, clearly unsteady from the struggle. He stumbled backward, arms flailing as if he were trying to regain control of his limbs, but they seemed to betray him. His foot caught on the edge of the platform just as a train's horn blared in the distance, a haunting sound that echoed through the station, signalling a train that would pass straight through.

"Watch out!" Jack's voice rang out, sharp and commanding, but it was already too late.

Murray, still off balance and dazed, fell backward, his arms flailing wildly, eyes wide with terror. His body teetered on the edge of the platform, just as the roar of the approaching train filled the station, drowning out the gasps of commuters who had gathered at a distance. For a fleeting moment, time seemed to freeze—the whole scene suspended in a grotesque tableau.

Martin lunged forward, her hand outstretched, her fingers grazing the back of Murray's coat as he fell. But it was no use. His body tipped over the edge and fell helplessly onto the tracks below, his arms still grasping at the empty air as if reaching for salvation.

The train's headlights blazed; its engine roaring as it hurtled into the station at full speed. It was one of the express services—faster, louder, merciless. The sound was deafening, a metallic screech that vibrated through the ground. There was no time, no room for hesitation. The train didn't stop.

The impact was brutal. Sudden. The collision a blur of motion and noise, sickening in its swiftness. Murray's body disappeared beneath the monstrous bulk of the train, a flash of movement swallowed by steel and momentum. There was nothing but the grinding of wheels, and the sickening thud of flesh and bone crushed under tons of fast-moving weight.

The station fell into an eerie silence as the train passed through, the awful truth of what had just happened settling over everyone like a pall.

Martin froze, her heart pounding in her chest, the world around her shrinking into a narrow tunnel of shock. Jack and Ed were at her side in an instant, their eyes wide with disbelief, their bodies still in motion from the chase, but now immobilised by the horror of what had just transpired.

"Murray," Ed breathed, his voice barely a whisper. He turned his head slowly to look at Jack, his face ashen, his lips forming the unspoken question—What just happened?

Jack stood there, his eyes locked on the spot where Murray had fallen, his mind racing, trying to process the violent finality of it all. He had seen death before, many times, in all its forms—slow, sudden, expected, horrific—but this was different. It wasn't supposed to end this way. Not here. Not like this.

"We had him," Martin whispered, her voice thick with disbelief. She was still half-kneeling, her hand gripping the edge of the platform as if she could somehow pull the scene back, stop it from happening. "We fucking had him," she winced. But the train had already passed, and with it, their only chance of taking Murray alive. Without thinking, Jack instinctively wrapped an arm around her, whether out of comfort or protection even he wasn't sure.

A low murmur began to rise from the gathered crowd, whispers and gasps, commuters staring wide-eyed, their faces pale with shock. One woman pressed her hands to her mouth, her eyes wide and horrified. Another man turned away, unable to look.

Radcliffe, who had been just behind them, finally caught up, his breath ragged from the chase. He took in the scene, his eyes darting from Martin to the empty tracks, his expression slowly transforming from confusion to horror as he pieced together what had happened.

"Did he…?" Radcliffe asked, his voice trailing off as if he couldn't bring himself to finish the sentence.

"Yeah," Jack said, his voice flat, emotionless. "He's gone."

There was a heavy silence. The clatter of footsteps, the sound of the train fading into the distance—it all seemed muted now, as though the world had been draped in a thick fog of unreality.

Ed exhaled slowly, his hands resting on his knees as he bent over, trying to catch his breath. "We need to secure the scene," he said, forcing the words out, though his voice sounded hollow, mechanical. "Get the station shut down. Call it in."

Jack didn't move for a moment, his eyes still fixed on the tracks, on the place where Murray had been. His mind was racing, sifting through fragments of thoughts, trying to reconcile the sudden, violent end to their pursuit. For weeks they had been chasing shadows, and now, when they finally had a lead, it had been snatched away in an instant.

Martin rose to her weary feet, her legs unsteady beneath her. She was bruised and shaken but determined to keep moving. "I'll call it in," she said, her voice tight with suppressed emotion. She pulled out her radio and began speaking, her words clipped and professional, even as her hands trembled.

Jack finally tore himself away from the tracks and looked at Ed, his expression unreadable. "He slipped," Jack said quietly, as if trying to convince himself. "He slipped, and the train…"

"Yeah," Ed replied, though his eyes flickered with something—uncertainty, perhaps. Guilt, even. "It all happened so fast."

Radcliffe stood awkwardly, his face pale, clearly struggling to process what had just happened. He had only joined the team recently, and looked to Jack for some sort of reassurance, but Jack had none to offer. As the station lights flickered above them, casting long shadows across the platform, Jack straightened, taking a deep breath. There would be questions, investigations, statements to give. The case wasn't over, but something had shifted. The momentum had changed, and yet, Jack felt, they were no closer to understanding the truth than they had been before. He glanced back down the tracks, a deep sense of unease settling over him. This wasn't supposed to be the end. It didn't feel close to it.

Interview Transcript
Date: October 3rd
Location: Dr. Haggard's Office
Participants: DCI Jack Miller, Dr. William Haggard (Psychiatrist)

[10:03 AM]

JM: So... you're saying it's, the past, the past is affecting my judgment... on the case?

WH: In a manner of speaking, but it's not a criticism. The past affects us all in our judgment.

JM: But do you think it's throwing me off? Confusing things?

WH: Perhaps... Jack, you've spoken about the poetic clues, the way that it somehow feels personal to you... You've talked about this sense of, I don't know, divine retribution, or karma, possibly underlying in your choices. A fear of it, I mean...

JM: Yeah, but I mean I don't sit around and reflect on fate. I'm out there, in the real world, trying to solve real problems. There's no room for ambiguity when you're chasing a killer. There's no room for... poetry.

WH: But honestly, Jack, are you reflecting on it? The memory about the sea you recalled earlier. When did you last think about that, prior to this session?

JM: Ummm... Last night.

WH: What brought it to mind?

JM: I was contemplating the case actually...How far my life had come, that I was sat in my car, in the cold... Charley was out. I don't know where. I couldn't reach Ed, my partner, Ed...

WH: Detective Marks?

JM: Yeah.

WH: He's your friend, too?

JM: Yes, for a very long time. He talked me into signing up for the force after I finished my master's degree, instead of pursuing a PhD.

WH: But you've expressed concerns about that friendship in previous sessions?

JM: I had... doubts, about him... and Charley. I don't know why. It was silly. We talked the other night, for the first time in a long time... He, he found the cinema. The Empress. The place I've been going to when I haven't been going home... He followed me, didn't trust me because my behaviour has been so... distant, erratic. So much so, it bordered on suspicious.

WH: And did that help? Talking to him?

JM: Yeah, somehow sharing that space changed things. We reconnected... I think we both needed the clarity, somehow.

WH: Of course, it's human nature to want clarity, especially when we've experienced trauma. But you said something earlier about Dickinson's poems—how she used dashes to create pauses, to make the reader stop and reflect. What if you're in one of those pauses now? What if part of what you're feeling is that in-between space, where things aren't fully resolved, and you're being asked to sit with the uncertainty?

JM: I hate those pauses.

WH: Most people do. But they're where growth happens. Dickinson knew that, too. She didn't fill in all the blanks for her readers because she knew the value of the space between words. That's where we find meaning. Where we have to confront what's unsaid, what's unresolved.

JM: So, what are you saying? That I need to just... accept that I might never know the full truth? That there might always be loose ends?

WH: I'm saying that maybe part of finding peace is learning to live with the unknown. A view on Dickinson's work is that it's not about giving up on finding answers, but in recognising that not all answers come in neat, tidy packages. Some truths are fragmented. Some are ambiguous. And that's okay. It doesn't mean you stop searching for justice, but maybe it means you approach it with a different mindset.

JM: I don't know if I can do that.

WH: I think you've been doing it for years, Jack. You've lived with the uncertainty of the accident, with the guilt, with the unknowns of this case.

JM: I've been chasing justice my whole career... trying to make things right, to fix what's broken. But maybe I've been going about it the wrong way.

WH: Justice doesn't always mean finding every answer, Jack. Sometimes it's about doing the best you can with the information you have and accepting that some parts of the story will remain unfinished.

JM: Maybe I can stop letting it tear me apart.

WH: every day is a second chance, Jack. It's a cliché, but don't waste them... Another quote for you, a story has no beginning or end, it's arbitrary where one chooses to look back or look ahead.

JM: Okay. Sorry, I can't place it.

WH: It doesn't matter... But do you see what I'm saying?

JM: Yeah... it's hard, though. I've spent so long trying to make it make sense. Trying to find some reason behind it. But if I'm honest... it doesn't feel like there's a reason. Not in the way I've been looking for, anyway.

WH: And that's okay, Jack. But maybe it's your entry point that's the issue... Like, life didn't stop, or start, when the accident happened. That's an arbitrary point in time.

JM: To describe it as arbitrary is like saying it was meaningless.

WH: But the accident was arbitrary, in a manner of speaking. It was significant, terrible, lifechanging... certainly not meaningless, there may even have been some fate or destiny behind it, some spiritual reason or grand purpose... but you're making an arbitrary choice to define that moment a certain way. To define yourself a certain way because of it.

JM: That's deep, Doc.

WH: I'm not here for small talk, Jack.

JM: You know, I keep thinking about this old movie I saw when I was younger. I can't even remember the name of it, but it's come up in our sessions before... I was talking to Ed about it the other night... It's kind of haunted me, to be honest... It was about a man who... well, maybe he was a ghost... I don't know, it was like black and white, war-time maybe... He would go into this room, just like in a bar or something, and time would stop. Every night, midnight. I don't remember what he did when that happened, but it made me think maybe time doesn't work the way we think it does...

WH: Is that the source of your obsession with these old movies, Jack?

JM: Yeah, I want to find it. Recover that memory, find out what he did and why.

WH: How will that help you?

JM: I don't know... It won't, I guess. I'll just let it go.

WH: When did you see the movie?

JM: I think... I'm not sure. But my parents were still alive. It was in our house, by the sea... I remember the view from the window. I remember the carpet, the rug, I was sitting on. It's texture... Coarse.

WH: Is it the movie you want to let go of? Or something else?

JM: Like what... my parents?

WH: Why would you want to let go of them, Jack?

JM: I don't know... I didn't think I did.

WH: So, what's the significance of this movie, why is that part of your story?

JM: It's unfinished, unknown.

WH: Did a small part of you hold on to a hope that they might come back?

JM: From the dead? Come on, Doc. I knew they were gone. I knew death was final... even then.

WH: How old where you?

JM: Eight.

WH: Can I challenge that?

JM: That I was eight, or that I knew death was final?

WH: The second part... Might it be truer to say that you didn't know death was final until they died and didn't come back. Until then, it was just a belief.

JM: Okay... I see your point, if a little pedantic.

WH: I'm not trying to be pedantic. I think it could be an important distinction.

JM: I get that.

WH: Fair, or pedantic?

JM: Fair... Very fair.

WH: I'm not trying to suggest that a rational man of your age thinks he can bring his parents back to life by watching a movie... If I genuinely believed that then I should be the one in therapy... But if there was a tiny part of you, a vulnerable, emotional, child, scared and suddenly left alone in the world, that believed that they might not be gone forever, you might hold on to anything that kept hope in your heart.

JM: Because?

WH: Letting it go, means letting them go... Facing the world alone. Before you felt ready to.

JM: Okay.

WH: And that would be part of your psyche now. Consciously, or not. It would shape your judgment, your future. How you view your past... All of it, really.

JM: Including the accident?

WH: Especially the accident.

22

'How ruthless are the gentle'

The office of DCSI Carrick was a sterile, cold affair—much like the man himself. The walls were adorned with minimal decoration, a few framed certificates and commendations, reminders of his long tenure and exemplary conduct and credentials, while a sizeable mahogany desk dominated the space. Papers were strewn across it, but they were placed in a calculated chaos, as if to suggest a mind forever at work. The light from the overhanging lamp reflected sharply off his polished nameplate.

Carrick sat behind the desk, a man in his late fifties, his thinning hair combed meticulously, his suit tailored to the point of discomfort. His reading glasses perched at the end of his nose, just high enough to give the impression that everything beneath him—including the paperwork—was too small to merit his full attention. The corners of his mouth were drawn in perpetual disapproval, his lips thin as they pressed together before he spoke.

"It's... highly problematic, Jack," Carrick said, sharply emphasising each word as his fingers skimmed over Jack's report. His eyes, narrowed in frustration, finally rose from the pages and peered over the rims of his glasses, fixing Jack with a look that was as much accusatory as it was curious. His scorn hung in the air like the lingering scent of old tobacco.

Jack stood opposite him, the stress of the night clinging to him like the smell of damp from the streets. His coat was still draped over one arm, a thin layer of grime from the chase settled on his shirt. His eyes, red-rimmed from lack of sleep, met Carrick's briefly before lowering to the desk, waiting for the reprimand that was sure to come.

Carrick sighed, removing his glasses and placing them on the desk with deliberate care. "It's all about the optics, you see, Jack," he continued, the edge in his voice sharpening. "Optics, that's what they care about these days." He let out a humourless chuckle, more a short burst of air than anything else. "I've got this bloody media consultant—have you seen her? Always running around the station like she's in charge of something. And now she's breathing down my neck about 'perception.'"

"Yes, sir, I understand," Jack replied, his tone neutral, respectful. There was an exhaustion in his posture, but his voice remained steady.

Carrick mimicked a frown, mocking the situation. "Oh, the optics aren't good if one of your boys is found beating his wife," he sneered, his voice dripping with sarcasm. "Well, of course not, I'd bloody lock him up, wouldn't I?" His eyes flashed as he shot Jack a rhetorical look, seeking some confirmation of their shared understanding. "But I'd need to know about it, you see. I'd need evidence—just like with anybody else."

Jack remained silent, his jaw set. He had seen this before. Carrick was gearing up for his usual tirade, using sarcasm as a scalpel to dissect his officers' failings, or rather, the failings of the world that fell outside his control.

"And now," Carrick continued, leaning back in his chair, "we've got seven dead young women on our hands, and to top it off, a dead pervert splattered across the front of Tommy the Bloody Tank Engine!" His hands gestured vaguely in the air, as if the absurdity of it all hung there like a thick fog. "The press has already christened him 'Waxed Jacket'—England's newest serial killer. It's all over the front pages. How the hell did that happen?"

Jack could only shrug slightly, his eyes still fixed on the floor.

Carrick sighed, this time a deeper, more frustrated sound. His eyes returned to the report in his hands, his brow furrowing as he skimmed through the details again. "I'd like to be angry, Jack," he said, his voice softening slightly, though still tinged with irritation. "I really would. But despite the chaos, you did well."

Jack blinked, momentarily surprised. Praise from Carrick was as rare as it was begrudging. "Thank you, sir," he responded quietly.

"But the problem we have now…" Carrick paused, his hands folding on top of the report. He glanced back up at Jack, his eyes even more calculating now. "The problem we have… is one of containment." His voice dropped, as though he were confiding in Jack, but there was an unmistakable edge. "I know Murray was a bastard, Jack. But was he, our bastard?"

Jack hesitated, searching for the right words. "I don't know, sir," he finally said. "We found a print at the scene, and Murray matched the description of someone spotted nearby. It's the best lead we've had so far. But he doesn't fit the right profile. None of the dead girls had been touched, hurt. Sexually."

Carrick leaned forward, resting his chin on his folded hands, staring at Jack with an almost predatory intensity. "But he ran," he said, his voice flat, almost bored.

"He did, sir."

"Very bloody fast, by all accounts," Carrick muttered, his fingers drumming on the desk. "Marks and the others are turning over his flat as we speak?"

"Yes, sir," Jack confirmed. His mind was racing, but he kept his expression neutral. He could sense Carrick's impatience simmering just beneath the surface, but the man was too seasoned to let it boil over just yet.

Carrick's eyes narrowed. "You need to find something on him, Jack," he said quietly, but with a sharpness that made the hairs on the back of Jack's neck prickle. "If he's not our guy, you need to find something else that really justifies our being there. Something. Do you understand?"

"If it's there," Jack said slowly, "we'll find it."

The two men locked eyes for a moment, the pressure of the case settling between them like a leaden weight. Carrick nodded, satisfied—for now. He gestured vaguely toward the door, his dismissal wordless but clear.

Jack turned on his heel, his coat still slung over his arm, his mind already returning to the chaotic jumble of thoughts that had been swirling since the chase. But just as his hand reached the doorknob, Carrick spoke again.

"Martin did well today, didn't she?"

Jack paused, turning his head slightly but not fully meeting Carrick's stare. "She was exceptional, sir," he said quietly, his eyes fixed on the floor. "She always is."

Carrick leaned back in his chair, a wry smile tugging at the corner of his mouth. "Good," he said, a rare note of approval in his voice. "She'll have your job in a few years, you know. Then mine." He laughed, a short, barking sound, before waving Jack away with a casual flick of his hand.

Jack nodded, his face impassive, and left the office without another word. As the door clicked shut behind him, the cold sterility of Carrick's office was replaced by the noise and chaos of the station outside. But Carrick's words still hung around his neck, like a hangman's noose.

**

Murray's flat was a cramped, narrow space, the air thick with the musty scent of age. It wasn't the scent of time spent living but of time neglected. Dust clung to the surfaces, and the small rooms seemed to close in around them, as Ed and DS Martin moved carefully among the scattered belongings, eyes searching for anything that might speak louder than the man himself ever had. The flat's walls, once painted a pale shade of cream, had dulled to a grimy yellow, the windows too grimy to allow much light. Marks wore the expression of someone long accustomed to sifting through the detritus of other people's lives. Martin was her usual taciturn self.

Forensics' gloved hands were already at work, moving silently over bookshelves and drawers, dusting for prints, photographing anything that might hold even the smallest of clues. The quiet, methodical hum of the search was occasionally broken by the low murmur of voices, professional but strained. Uniformed officers in the hallway spoke to each other in whispers, as though unwilling to disturb whatever ghosts might linger in the corners.

Ed crouched down by a small desk in the corner of the sitting room, his eyes scanning the papers haphazardly strewn across its surface. Unpaid bills, receipts, and a few notebooks, their covers creased and faded, lay in disarray. It was the kind of chaos that was easy to overlook but spoke volumes if you knew where to look. His fingers hovered over a torn envelope, the return address from some antique dealer, but there was nothing about it that struck him as out of the ordinary. Nothing to connect it to the murders.

"Anything so far, sir?" Martin's voice cut through the silence, but not sharply—more like a question she already knew the answer to.

Ed shook his head, rising from his crouch. His tall frame seemed out of place in the cramped flat, as if he were always on the verge of knocking something over. "Not yet. Just the usual... clutter. You?"

Martin, who had been standing near the doorway watching the uniformed officers move in and out, turned her head slightly, her eyes dark and unreadable as always. "Neighbours have been questioned. Upstairs and either side. Most didn't know much about him, though the one upstairs mentioned they could hear often him moving about late at night. Nothing unusual, they thought, nothing suspicious."

Ed grunted, turning back to the desk, his brow furrowed in concentration. "Doesn't mean much. People like Murray—loners—they slip through the cracks. Keep to themselves. Even if they were planning something, nobody'd notice."

Martin gave a slight nod, her hands in her pockets. She shifted slightly, her stance careful but relaxed, as though she were always waiting for something without quite knowing what it was. "The neighbours on either side barely even knew his name. They just called him 'the old man in the waxed jacket.' Teenage daughter said she found him a bit creepy. Used to see him watching her from the window, half-dressed. Kids at school told her he was a pedo. But mostly kept to himself. Never had any visitors. No family."

Ed stood, moving toward the bookshelves, his eyes scanning the titles. Old paperbacks, mostly, some with cracked spines, others so yellowed they looked as though they might disintegrate at the touch. "What about his import and export business?" he asked, his voice casual but curious. "Anything come of that?"

Martin shrugged; her movement so slight it might have gone unnoticed. "Online, apparently. Antiques, mostly. eBay, that sort of thing. Nothing out of the ordinary on paper. But the records are patchy at best."

Ed picked up one of the books, turning it over in his hands. An old novel, battered, weather-beaten, spine nearly broken, pages loose. He flipped through the pages, more out of habit than hope. "Patchy," he repeated under his breath. "Seems to be a pattern."

Martin looked over his shoulder at the tatty book, "Things fall apart," she smirked. "That seems appropriate."

He set the book down, glancing toward the small kitchen that led off the sitting room. The door was slightly ajar, and the faint smell of something long since rotted wafted through. "What's the kitchen like?"

Martin frowned, stepping forward slightly. "Small. Looks like it hasn't been properly cleaned in years. Even found some mouldy food in the fridge. Nothing that tells us anything about him."

Ed crossed the room, peering into the narrow hallway that led to the bedroom. "It's like he was living in limbo," he murmured, almost to himself. "Just… existing. Waiting for something."

Martin didn't respond. She stood near the door, her arms folded across her chest, her expression expressionless as she watched Ed move through the flat with the deliberate motions of someone trying to solve a puzzle that refused to reveal its pieces.

A uniformed officer appeared in the doorway, glancing between them. "We've got everything you asked for bagged and ready, sir," he said to Martin.

Martin nodded. "Good. Make sure it's all logged. We want every scrap of paper and every print double-checked."

The officer gave a quick nod and disappeared down the hall. Ed could hear the faint rustle of plastic evidence bags being sealed, the quiet hum of a forensic camera snapping one last photograph before the scene would be cleared.

Ed turned back to Martin. "Do you think Murray's our guy?" he asked, his tone low, but there was something cautious behind the question, as if he wasn't sure he actually wanted to hear her answer.

Martin's expression remained steady, though her fingers tightened slightly where they rested against her arm. "I don't know. Maybe. He fits a certain profile—a man living alone, secretive, no social ties. Pervy."

Radcliffe had been methodically searching the antique bureau, a piece of furniture that seemed out of place in the grimy surroundings of Murray's flat. The wood was dark, aged, and worn smooth by years of use, but it still held a certain dignity in the midst of the dust and disorder. His hands moved carefully, trained eyes scanning the surfaces, his mind half expecting to find nothing more than the usual pile of irrelevant junk—old bills, receipts, the occasional letter forgotten in a drawer. It was a routine search, the kind he had done a hundred times before, but then his fingers brushed against something small, something smooth and cold to the touch.

He pulled his hand back slowly, his heart beating just a little faster, and there, nestled between some tattered old copies of Mayfair magazine, lay a single gold earring. It gleamed faintly in the dim light, catching his eye immediately.

"Hey!" he called out, his voice betraying the excitement he tried to keep in check. "Come and have a look at this!"

Martin and Ed were standing by the door, still exchanging quiet words when they turned toward him.

Martin's expression, usually guarded and serious, shifted as she walked over to Radcliffe's side, her heavy shoes clicking softly against the hardwood floor. Ed followed closely behind, his face a mask of curiosity, though his eyes remained sharp, always calculating.

Radcliffe held up the earring for them to see, the gold glinting under the dim light. "Could this be Yasmin Eliot's?" he asked, his voice carrying a sense of urgency.

Martin leaned in closer, her eyes narrowing slightly as she inspected the small piece of jewellery. For a moment, she said nothing, simply staring at the earring with a look of deep concentration. Then, a slight smile tugged at the corners of her lips, something almost amused, but also satisfied. "Well," she said, her voice dry but carrying a hint of amusement, "If I had to bet, I'd say that's Yasmin Eliot's missing earring. I'd recognise those anywhere."

Ed raised an eyebrow, a small smile playing at the edge of his lips. "Really, Martin? You're an expert on earrings now?"

Martin shot him a look, one eyebrow raised. "What? You think I don't know a nice set of earrings when I see one?" She glanced back at the earring in Radcliffe's hand.

Radcliffe chuckled, shaking his head slightly. "I'll take your word for it."

Ed folded his arms, his smile fading as he looked at the earring again, the significance of the find dawning on him. "If that really is hers, we've got something very solid. It could tie Murray directly to her murder."

Martin nodded, her gaze never leaving the earring. "It's a lead, at least. We've been looking for something like this." She paused, her face serious again. "Radcliffe, get someone over here to run prints on that thing immediately. We need to know if Murray's touched it—or if anyone else has."

While Radcliffe made the arrangements, Martin glanced back toward the bureau, her eyes flicking over the copies of Mayfair lying inside. "Why would he keep something like this here?" she murmured, more to herself than anyone else. "It doesn't make sense."

Ed, catching her question, stepped closer, looking over her shoulder. "The magazines?"

Martin nodded. "Yeah. It's like he was trying to hide the earring, but this isn't exactly the best place to conceal something so valuable. He's careless, but not that careless."

Ed considered her words for a moment, then shrugged slightly. "Maybe he thought no one would look too closely at something like that. People see a pile of dirty magazines, they move on. They don't dig."

"Except we do," Martin said softly, her eyes still on the bureau. "We always dig."

The room fell quiet for a moment, each of them absorbed in their own thoughts. The sound of Radcliffe finishing his call brought them back to the present.

"Prints are on the way," he said, looking up from his phone. "We should have an answer soon."

Ed nodded, satisfied. "Good. Let's hope we get something we can use."

Radcliffe gently placed the earring into an evidence bag, sealing it carefully before handing it over to Shah, who was waiting by the door. The room felt different now, the atmosphere shifting as if they were on the edge of something important. The discovery of the earring had given them momentum, a small piece of the puzzle that could lead them closer to the truth.

As the evidence bag was taken away, Ed leaned against the edge of the desk, his arms folded across his chest. Martin, standing beside him, watched the scene unfold with her usual cool demeanour, but there was a glint of something in her eyes—something like hope. She crossed her arms also, still transfixed by the antique bureau. "Do you think this was a trophy?" she asked, her voice low and thoughtful. She watched the scene unfolding around her with her usual cool demeanour, but there was a glint of something in her eyes—something like hope.

Ed glanced at her, his eyes narrowing slightly. "Maybe. Or maybe it was just a mistake. Something he took without thinking, something he didn't realise would come back to bite him."

"People like Murray don't think they'll ever get caught," Radcliffe added, stepping forward. "They think they're too clever for us."

"Too clever for *you*, maybe, Toby," chuckled Martin.

Ed laughed, nodding slowly, and pushed himself away from the desk, standing tall as he looked at his two colleagues. "This could be the break we've been waiting for," he said, his voice steady. "But let's not get ahead of ourselves. We need to see if the prints match. And even if they do, it's only part of the picture. There's still more to uncover."

He remained there, arms still folded, eyes thoughtful and distant. When he finally spoke again, his voice was low, almost quiet. "I think he's connected to all of this in some way. Whether he's the one we've been looking for or just another piece of the puzzle, I don't know."

They stood there for a moment, no one spoke, and the flat felt more claustrophobic than ever. The dust had settled in layers on every surface. It was a place where time had stopped, where nothing had moved forward for years. Just like their case, trapped in limbo, waiting for something to break it wide open. Maybe now they had finally found that crack.

The air outside was sharp and crisp, the kind of October morning that felt like a balm after the long, suffocating hours spent inside Murray's flat. The weak autumn sun filtered through the yellowing leaves, casting long shadows on the quiet, leafy street. It felt almost incongruous, this stillness, this beauty, against the dark undertones of what had just unfolded within. Ed, leading the way, took a deep breath, the cold air biting at his lungs, clearing the fog in his head. He turned to Martin, who had lingered by the doorway, her face still set in that impenetrable mask she always wore on scenes like this.

"We'll leave the rest to Radcliffe," Ed said, his voice low, almost reflective, as though the morning itself required a certain softness. "The uniforms can finish up. We've got statements to give about what happened last night."

Martin nodded; the same stoic understanding that had been etched into her features since the day she joined his team. She had always been solid like that—silent, dependable, but never unthinking. Today, though, something lingered in her expression, something more than the usual calculated focus she brought to the job.

Ed glanced at her again, frowning slightly, "What do you make of the neighbours upstairs hearing him late at night? Think it's something, or just him moving around?"

Martin's brow furrowed slightly as she considered the question. "Could be nothing. Or... could be everything. People like him, they're nocturnal. Restless. It's when they feel safe to move. To do whatever it is that they like to do," she said, unable to hide her distaste.

They moved down the pathway leading from the flat, the cracked concrete damp with dew. A scattering of leaves crunched beneath their feet. Ed's hand brushed against a low-hanging branch, the wet leaves brushing his skin as he passed. He stuffed his hands deeper into his coat pockets, his breath visible in the chill.

For a moment, the city around them seemed far away—dulled by the morning quiet, the distant hum of traffic barely touching them here in this quiet, leafy enclave of South London. It was as if the street was holding its breath, waiting for something to break the calm. Ed could feel it all pressing against his chest—the death of Murray, the discovery in the flat, and the nagging uncertainty about whether they were actually any closer to the truth or just further tangled in lies.

"Doesn't feel real, does it?" he murmured, his words floating in the cold air.

Martin glanced at him sideways, her brow slightly furrowed. "What doesn't?"

"Everything," he said with a vague gesture. "That flat, Murray's death…"

Martin's face remained impassive, though her eyes darkened slightly as she looked out at the street, her thoughts still circling the scene they had just left. "I guess we'll know soon enough," she said quietly, but there was an edge to her voice—something that told Ed she wasn't entirely convinced either.

They walked in silence for a while, the sound of their footsteps muted by the damp ground. Above them, the sky was pale blue, almost clear, with just a few streaks of thin cloud clinging to the horizon. The sun had risen higher now, but the air remained cold, the kind that made you want to pull your coat tighter around you. Ed did just that, adjusting his collar as they neared the unmarked car parked a little way down the street.

"I'll drive," Martin said abruptly as they approached the vehicle. There was something about her tone, something final. Ed wasn't about to argue, he was exhausted. He tossed her the keys, and she caught them with a quick flick of her hand. Despite everything, it surprised him that her reflexes were so insanely sharp.

As she unlocked the car, Ed turned back for one last glance at the house. It stood there in the clear morning light, the shadows of the trees shifting over its worn brick facade. From the outside, it looked like any other house in this quiet neighbourhood—old, respectable, the kind of place that might have stories but nothing sinister. Yet they knew better.

A curtain twitched in one of the upstairs windows.

It was a small movement, barely noticeable, but Martin had seen it. She paused, her hand on the door handle, her eyes narrowing as she stared up at the window. For a moment, it seemed as though nothing was there, just an empty room with curtains hanging loosely. But she had seen it. There had been someone watching them.

Ed followed her gaze, squinting against the sun, but by the time he focused on the window, it was still again.

"What is it?" he asked, already sensing that Martin's sharp instincts had picked up on something he hadn't.

She didn't answer immediately. Her eyes remained fixed on the window, her mind ticking over the possibilities. Finally, she shook her head slightly, as though dismissing the thought—or trying to.

"Nothing," she said, though her voice was unusually tight. She slid into the driver's seat, but the look in her eyes told Ed it wasn't nothing. Not to her.

"Want to go back?" he asked.

"Not now," she replied. "Let's get these statements over with."

Ed hesitated a moment longer, his hand resting on the top of the car door before he finally ducked inside. He glanced once more at the house as they pulled away, watching the shadowed windows retreat in the rearview mirror. There was something about this case—something that kept pulling them back, like a thread they couldn't fully untangle. And now, with Murray dead, it felt as though the answers were slipping further from their grasp.

As they turned the corner, Martin's grip tightened on the steering wheel, her mind still on that slight twitch of the curtain. Not surprising, under the circumstances but something about it stuck with her, like a splinter lodged in her thoughts.

23

'Because He loves Her'

The coffee machine hummed softly in the corner of the kitchen, filling the air with the earthy scent of brewing beans. Charley stood by the window, arms folded, watching the slow drips of rain gathering on the glass and rolling down in thin rivulets. The October morning was muted, the light a dull grey, casting long shadows across the hardwood floor. Outside, the trees were losing their leaves in great clumps, the branches darkened by the drizzle, their golden crowns wilting. She had always loved autumn—the way it signalled both an end and a beginning. But today, the world felt smaller, more confined. It was as if the rain, instead of refreshing the air, was slowly closing it in, folding the world into itself.

She poured herself a cup of coffee, hesitating a moment before turning on the television. The news flickered to life, the soft hum of a presenter's voice breaking the stillness of the room. She wasn't really listening at first—just the usual morning drone of politics, traffic reports, weather updates. Then, a phrase caught her attention.

"… in connection with the death of convicted sex offender Roy Murray, a key suspect in the recent string of murders in South London. Murray was killed late last night while attempting to evade arrest…"

Her hand froze, cup halfway to her lips. The name hung in the air like smoke. Murray. That was what Jack had been chasing, then. She glanced at her phone on the counter, where his last message remained unopened. He'd texted late—later than usual. Apologetic, of course, like always.

Sorry, something serious came up. Won't be home tonight.

Charley had stared at that message for a long time before finally putting the phone face down on the table and pouring herself a glass of wine. She hadn't replied. What was the point? It wasn't the first time. She had grown used to it, to the apologies, to the unspoken mass that hung between them—a fog they both navigated through in the dark. Jack's work had always been a part of their life, but lately, it felt like it had consumed everything. The phone calls, the late nights, the hollow words.

She reached for her phone now, brushing her fingers over the cold glass, the message still unopened. A thousand replies had come to her mind in the hours since she'd received it—some biting, others resigned, and still others that were softer, kinder. But in the end, she hadn't written anything. She hadn't even decided if she was angry anymore, or if that anger had simply dissolved into something else, something more fragile.

She sighed, sipping the coffee, the warmth filling her mouth, the bitterness grounding her. The sound of the rain against the window grew louder, as if the world outside was whispering all the things she couldn't say.

Her phone buzzed, vibrating lightly on the counter. For a moment, she thought it might be Jack again, maybe an update, a reason, an explanation. But it wasn't him.

Hey, can't make our walk today. Something came up. Can I see you later tonight?

It was Seth.

Charley stared at the message, her thumb hovering over the screen. She thought about their walks—those quiet, companionable strolls through the park, the soft conversation that never seemed to demand too much from either of them.

There was something easy about Seth, something she had come to look forward to in recent weeks. He was younger, by a few years, though not enough to feel like it mattered. And he was kind, thoughtful in a way that Jack had once been, but no longer was. There was something about the way Seth spoke to her—something attentive, as if he actually saw her. As if she were still the Charley she remembered, not just Jack's wife, or someone waiting in the background of his life.

She'd met him by chance, really—one of those unplanned encounters that somehow became a habit. He worked freelance, she gathered, something in design or marketing. He never talked much about it, and she never pressed. Their walks had begun as just a way to pass the time, to clear her head, to escape the emptiness of the house. But over the last few weeks, they had become more than that, hadn't they? She wouldn't call it an affair—no, not yet. There was nothing physical, nothing spoken that crossed that line. But there was something unspoken, something that flickered just beneath the surface of their conversations. She knew he was attracted to her. It was in the way he smiled, the way his eyes lingered just a little too long when they said goodbye.

And she was flattered. She wasn't naïve, of course. She knew what it meant for a man like Seth to spend time with her. He wasn't that much younger, but young enough to make her feel a little like the woman she used to be. Before Jack, before all the long nights and missed dinners, before the strain of pretending everything was fine when it wasn't. Seth didn't demand anything from her, not yet at least, and she liked that. She liked the idea that maybe someone still saw her as more than just the fading outline of a marriage.

She thought about what she might say in reply. Maybe something light, something casual.

Sure, let's meet later. How about that place by the river?

Or maybe she'd make an excuse—tell him she was busy, that another time might be better. She didn't want to lead him on. She didn't want to make promises she couldn't keep. But there was a part of her that wanted to see him, to feel that gentle pull of his attention, to step out of the fog of her life with Jack, if only for a few hours. Her fingers hovered over the keys, typing and deleting, her mind racing with all the things she couldn't say.

Outside, the rain was falling harder now, the sky darker than it had been moments ago. She stared out at the trees, the leaves shaking loose with every gust of wind. She wondered if Jack was out there somewhere, chasing down another lead, another clue in the tangled mess of his cases. She wondered if he ever thought about her anymore, really thought about her. Or if she had become just another detail in his life, something to be managed, something to be smoothed over with apologies and late-night texts.

She typed a quick reply to Seth before she could change her mind.

Later works. Let me know when you're free.

She hit send, and for a moment, she felt a strange sense of relief. It was just a walk, after all. Nothing more. And yet, the thought of seeing him later gave her something to hold on to, something to look forward to in the grey, endless hours that stretched ahead.

The news continued to drone on in the background, but Charley wasn't listening anymore. She set her coffee down on the counter and turned off the TV, putting on a playlist instead. She didn't recognise the song, *Like today is our last day*, by ULUV, it wasn't even in English. Something Jack had randomly added, as he was inclined to do. Something he had heard somewhere that had touched him. And now, as the rain continued to beat against the window, the sound of it filling the space where her thoughts lingered, she felt it, too.

Even though she had no idea what the woman was saying, it somehow reflected her pain. It occurred to Charley that maybe the indecipherability of the words was precisely why.

She glanced at her phone one last time. Jack's message was still there, still unanswered. And for now, she decided, it could wait. She leaned against the counter, her soft, long fingers tracing the smooth curve of the coffee cup, where its warmth was already beginning to fade. The rain continued its relentless patter against the window, like the ticking of a clock she couldn't stop hearing. Time moved forward, always forward, yet somehow, she felt stuck. Trapped in the same rhythms, the same silences. She thought of Seth again, but this time his face faded quickly, replaced by Jack's.

Her attention drifted toward the living room, where the photographs still hung on the wall—a small collection of snapshots from their early years together. Before everything had grown so complicated. She had been younger then, hopeful in a way that now felt foolish. They had both been that way, believing that the future was something they could shape, control. The smiles in those pictures seemed almost foreign now, like relics from a different life.

Charley wondered how things might have been different if they had ever tried for a child. They had talked about it, in passing mostly. She could still remember those late-night conversations, lying in bed beside Jack, his arm draped loosely over her waist. They would talk about names, about schools, about what kind of parents they might be. It had felt light-hearted then, abstract, like they had all the time in the world to make those decisions.

But they never did.

Jack's work had always come first, and over the years, those conversations had become less frequent, the possibilities slipping further away. Then came the accident—

though they never spoke her name anymore. It was as though everything had stopped that day, the world tilting off its axis. And in the years since, Jack had buried himself deeper in his cases, working late, chasing ghosts, and she had let him. She had told herself that she understood, and that it was his way of coping. But now, in the quiet of the morning, she wondered if that had been a lie. A way to avoid facing the truth—that Jack wasn't the only one stuck. That they were both trapped in the aftermath of that day.

Had they ever really tried for a child? Or had it always been an excuse—his work, the timing never quite right, the unspoken sense that something was holding them back? Time had kept moving, and they had never caught up.

She stared at the rain, feeling the mass of the years between them. Would she have been a good mother, she wondered? There had been a time when she believed she would. She had seen herself holding a small hand, brushing wayward hair back behind a tiny ear, whispering stories late at night. But those visions had faded, and now, when she tried to picture it, all she could see was the emptiness that had grown between her and Jack.

Maybe it was for the best. Maybe some part of her had always known Jack wasn't ready, that he might never be. His work had consumed him long before the accident, but after, it became his escape. His way of punishing himself, she thought. Jack carried guilt like a second skin. Even now, years later, she saw it in the way he moved, the way he avoided certain conversations. There were things they would never talk about. Things that festered between them, unnamed.

She had been the line that Jack couldn't uncross, the shadow that loomed over them both. Charley had watched him retreat after that day, watched him pour himself into his work with a kind of quiet desperation, as if solving someone else's pain might absolve him of his own. And she had let him.

But in letting him, had she also trapped herself? Had she allowed that guilt to seep into their marriage, to hold them both in stasis? She had wanted to ask him, more than once, if he had ever thought about what they had lost—what they had never even tried to have. But each time the words had dried up in her throat. There was a fear, she realised, that in asking, she might unravel something too fragile to put back together. So, she had stayed silent, and now the void between them felt too vast to bridge.

She wondered if Jack ever thought about it—about children, about the life they might have had. But when she looked at him now, all she saw was a man weighed down by a burden he couldn't name. He was good at his job, always had been. But somewhere along the way, he had become lost in it, as if solving murders could somehow erase the death he could never undo.

And what about her? Was she punishing herself, too? For not pushing harder, for not insisting that they try. She didn't know. It had been easier to let the years slip by, to let herself believe that they had made the right choices, that there was always time. But now, staring out at the rain-soaked world, Charley wasn't so sure.

She turned away from the window, setting her coffee cup down with a soft clink. Her phone buzzed again—Seth, probably. She didn't reach for it. Instead, she sank into the chair at the kitchen table, her hands resting on the cool surface. She felt tired, not just physically, but in a way that seeped into her bones, a kind of weariness that had settled over her like the autumn fog outside.

She closed her eyes, letting herself imagine, just for a moment, what it would have been like to have a child. Would that have saved them? Or would it have been another thing to lose, another fracture in the already fragile foundation of their life together?

In the end, it didn't matter. The past was the past, and the choices they hadn't made were just as irreversible as the ones they had. Jack's work had always been his way of keeping the world at bay, and she had let him. Maybe that was her prison—this life, this house, this endless waiting for something to change.

Maybe a prison does get to be a friend, she thought, a bitter smile tugging at the corners of her mouth. That was the problem with prisons. You grew so used to the walls that you forgot how to leave.

Her phone buzzed again, but she didn't reach for it. Instead, she sat there, eyes closed, listening to the rain and the soft, steady beat of time slipping away.

**

Ed sat at his desk in the station, the familiar hum of the fluorescent lights above him casting a faint buzz in his ears. The place had that worn, tired feeling about it that always came around this time of the afternoon—the streets outside were alive, but the station still felt like the last refuge of the night. His eyes skimmed over the reports in front of him, but they wouldn't settle. His mind was elsewhere, chasing something just out of reach.

He hadn't slept, not properly. None of them had. The case gnawed at him, burrowed under his skin in a way he hadn't felt in years. And then there was Jack. Always Jack. The look in his eyes when that train had done its job—he'd seen something there that unsettled him. Jack had seemed relieved, like it was all over. But Ed knew better. It wasn't over. Not for any of them.

His phone buzzed on the desk, and he reached for it absentmindedly, expecting another report or some procedural detail. Instead, Radcliffe's name flashed on the screen.

"Radcliffe," Ed said, voice gruff, still not quite ready for human interaction.

"It's the earring, sir. It is hers... Yasmin Eliot's. Forensics confirmed it."

Ed felt his heart lurch, a small victory in a war that had been dragging on too long. The earring—so small, so seemingly insignificant—had become the key. He could almost hear Martin's voice now, the certainty in her tone when she said it was a nice set. He knew it mattered to her in a way it didn't to him, the details of women's jewellery, the feminine eye for those things. But now, it mattered to them all. The earring had been found among Murray's things. One more link in the chain, one more piece of the puzzle.

"Jack needs to know," Radcliffe added, but there was hesitation in his voice.

"Where is he?" Ed asked, already rising from his seat.

"That's the thing, sir. I've been trying to tell you— he's not in his office. I haven't seen him."

Ed cursed under his breath, grabbing his coat and pushing out of his small, cluttered office. The station hallways felt narrower than usual, a sense of urgency pressing in on him. The case was breaking, and Jack was nowhere to be found. It wasn't like him to disappear like this, not in the middle of something so crucial.

As he made his way through the corridor, he ran into Martin. She was always around, it seemed, with her sharp eyes and even sharper mind. She spotted him before he had the chance to speak.

"Sir, what is it?" she asked, stepping into his path. There was that subtle undercurrent of energy in her, like she was always on the edge of something, her thoughts racing ahead of the situation.

"You were right. It was Yasmin's earring. Forensics just confirmed it," Ed said, his voice low, conscious of the empty hallway around them. The words felt inhibiting, even though they should have felt like a breakthrough. But then, nothing about this case ever felt clean.

"Where's the boss?" Martin asked, frowning, glancing over Ed's shoulder as though expecting to see him materialise.

"That's what I'm trying to figure out."

Ed could see the tension in her posture, the way she crossed her arms, defensive without meaning to be. He didn't blame her—none of them felt comfortable these days. Too much was hanging in the balance, and Jack was becoming unpredictable in ways that unsettled the whole team.

They stood quietly for a moment, the buzz of the station around them, voices distant but ever-present. Ed's thoughts drifted, as they so often did, to Jack and Charley. He hadn't really seen her in months—not properly. She was always just beyond the periphery of their lives now, a ghost of the past they never talked about. He wondered if she was okay, wondered if Jack even asked her that anymore, and a small rise of anger swelled in his chest.

Charley was always kind to him. In the early days, back when they all still spent time together outside of work, she had been so full of life, so quick to laugh. He'd seen the way Jack looked at her then, with a kind of awe. She was everything Jack wasn't—light where he was dark, open where he was guarded. But something had shifted. The accident, of course, and then the cases that kept coming, one after another. Jack had retreated into his work, and Charley had become a stranger. It wasn't his place to ask. Not really. But he couldn't help the sadness that tugged at him when he thought of her. Charley deserved more than Jack was giving her. Jack was too wrapped up in his own guilt to see it.

"You think he's okay?" Martin's voice broke into his thoughts, her brow furrowed.

"I don't know," Ed admitted, glancing toward Jack's empty office.

Martin studied him for a moment, something unreadable flickering in her eyes. She wasn't naïve. She'd seen enough to know when something was off. Ed admired that about her—the way she never asked questions she wasn't ready to hear the answers to.

"Should we wait for him?" Martin asked, pulling her phone from her pocket, her fingers poised to type.

"No," Ed said after a moment, shaking his head. "We don't have time to wait. I'll try to track him down, but in the meantime, you and Radcliffe keep on with Murray's flat. There's got to be something else there. There's always something."

Martin nodded, already turning on her heel, her mind back on the case. Ed watched her go, feeling a strange sense of detachment settle over him. He couldn't shake the feeling that things were coming to a head—that this case, with all its twists and dark alleys, was about to break in ways none of them could predict. And Jack was right in the middle of it, like a man teetering on the edge of a cliff.

As he made his way through the station, Ed found himself thinking about Charley again. He hadn't seen her in what felt like so long. Too long. He knew Jack loved her, in his own way, but love wasn't always enough. Especially not when Jack was buried under so much guilt, so much regret. It was as if Jack had convinced himself that the only way to atone was to throw himself into his work, to solve someone else's pain because he couldn't solve his own. Ed understood that, more than he cared to admit. He had seen it happen too many times before—officers who let the job become their life, who forgot how to leave it at the station door.

As he reached the exit, Ed paused for a moment, glancing back at the empty hallways, the quiet offices. The evening light was filtering in now, casting long shadows across the floor. He thought again about Charley, about the way her laughter used to fill the room whenever she was around. He missed that. Missed her, missed *them*, if he was honest with himself. But there was no going back. And there was no going there. Not for anyone.

With a sigh, Ed pushed open the door and stepped out into the crisp October air. The light was fading, the sky clear, but the chill cut through him all the same. He pulled his coat tighter around his shoulders, his mind still on Jack, on Charley, on everything that had gone unsaid between them all. And somewhere, deep down, he knew that this case wasn't the only thing that was about to break.

24
'A Secret told'

Charley stood beneath Westminster Bridge, her breath clouding the cold air as she looked out over the Thames. The evening had settled into a grey, sombre quiet, while the river moved sluggishly, dark and impenetrable, reflecting the city's yellow lights like shattered glass on the water's surface. The stone arch above her dripped moisture from the day's rain, and the wind, though soft, carried the bite of late autumn. She pulled her coat tighter, stuffing her hands into her pockets to ward off the chill now creeping into her bones.

The city felt distant tonight, as though it were holding its breath. There was something about the way London could feel so vast and yet so small at the same time, its millions of lives folding into themselves like secret stories only half told. Charley knew she should feel lost here, in the cold, in the dark, and she did, but there was an odd comfort in it. It was a sort of stasis, a pause in time where nothing was expected of her. Where she didn't have to answer the questions that she wasn't ready to ask herself.

Her phone buzzed in her pocket, breaking the stillness. She hesitated before pulling it out, knowing before she even looked at the screen who it would be.

It was Ed.

Are you with Jack?

Her fingers hovered over the screen. The truth sat heavy on her tongue, like it always did these days. I haven't seen him. She typed the words quickly, her thumb hesitating for a moment before she pressed send. She hadn't seen him. Not really. Even when he was home, he was somewhere else.

The message sent, and she slipped her phone back into her coat pocket. As she did, she caught sight of Seth walking toward her, head down, his face illuminated by the soft glow of his phone screen. He was typing something, but when he saw her, he smiled, sliding the phone into the back of his jeans.

"I was just going to text you to find out where you were," he said, his voice warm despite the cold.

Charley smiled, though it felt fragile, as though the wind could carry it away if she wasn't careful. Seth was always so at ease, so natural, even in moments like these. She wasn't sure if it was the casualness of his presence or the way he seemed to understand her silences, but he made her feel seen in a way she hadn't felt in a long time.

They started walking, side by side, along the edge of the river. The lights from the embankment danced across the water, and the sound of the city was distant, muffled by the river's steady rush. Seth kept his hands in his pockets, matching her pace, his footsteps soft on the wet pavement.

"Cold night, tonight," he said, glancing at her. "You should've brought a scarf."

She smiled again, this time more genuinely, and shrugged. "I didn't think I'd need one."

"Next time, I'll remind you."

His voice was light, teasing, but beneath it, Charley could feel something else. He had a way of slipping through her defences, of making her feel like the world wasn't quite as enormous as it seemed. She didn't know what to make of it, of him, or of the way his presence had begun to fill a space in her life that she hadn't even realised was empty.

They walked for a while, the sound of the river lapping against the stone, the city sprawling out in front of them like a landscape they could never fully explore. The Houses of Parliament stood dark and imposing on the opposite bank, and beyond them, the London Eye glowed faintly against the night sky. The air smelled of rain, and the wind tugged at her hair.

"Do you ever think about the future?" Seth asked suddenly, his voice quiet but steady.

Charley glanced at him, surprised by the question. She had been so caught up in the present, in the things that weighed her down, that the future felt like something far distant, and almost unreal.

"I guess," she said, unsure of where he was going with it. "I think about it less than I used to… There's less of it now, I suppose," she added, laughing awkwardly.

He nodded, his eyes fixed on the river. "I think about it sometimes. Where I want to be, what I want to be doing. The kind of life I want."

"And what kind of life is that?" she asked, curious now.

Seth hesitated, then smiled, but there was a hint of sadness in it. "I don't know. Something different from this, I suppose. Something simpler. Less complicated."

Charley felt a pang of recognition. She understood that feeling all too well—the desire for something simpler, something that wasn't weighed down by the past, by the choices they hadn't intentionally made but felt bound to anyway.

"What about you?" he asked, his voice soft now, almost hesitant. "Where do you see yourself?"

She thought about it for a moment, her thoughts drifting to the dark water. Where did she see herself? The truth was, she hadn't thought about it in years. Not since everything with Jack had started to unravel. She had always imagined a future with him, back when they were young and in love, back when things were straightforward, or at least seemed so.

"I don't know," she said finally. "I thought I did once, but now... I'm not sure."

Seth didn't press her. He just nodded, as though he understood. And maybe he did. They kept walking, the conversation hanging between them like a fragile thread, easy to break but hard to let go of.

"You and Jack," Seth began after a while, his voice careful, "You never had kids, did you?"

The question hit her harder than she expected. It was one of those things she had tried not to think about, had tried to bury deep down because it was easier that way. But Seth had a way of bringing things to the surface, of making her confront the things she had hidden from herself.

"No," she said, her voice quieter than she intended. "We never did."

"Why not?"

She hesitated, her fingers tightening around the strap of her bag. Why not? It was a question she had asked herself so many times, but never out loud. She wasn't even sure she knew the answer.

"I'm not sure," she said eventually, her words slow, deliberate. "I think... we just never got around to it. There was always something else. Jack's work, my job, the timing never seemed right."

"Jack didn't want them, but you did?"

"No, it wasn't all him. My body wasn't... receptive, either. And then, well... things just... changed. We never talked about it, but it felt like… like we were stuck. Like time stopped."

She stopped walking, turning to look at the river, the dark water moving slowly beneath them. The memory of that day, the accident, was always there, just beneath the surface, like a scar that had never fully healed. It was the thing that had frozen their lives in place, the thing that had made Jack retreat into himself and had left her standing on the outside, unable to reach him.

"I do wonder if I would have been a good mother," she said quietly, the words slipping out before she could stop them.

Seth stepped closer, his voice gentle. "Why would you say that?"

Charley shook her head. "I don't know. I think… maybe because I didn't have a good role model. Something happened to us, and I began to think maybe if I fell pregnant, I'd be taking someone else's child. Like I didn't deserve my own. Maybe Jack felt the same."

She looked at Seth then, his face seemed soft in the dim light, like he didn't judge her, or make her feel like she had said the wrong thing. He just listened, intently.

"I was thinking more, like, why would you doubt it… but you don't have to have all the answers," he said quietly. "Sometimes things just… don't happen the way we expect them to."

She nodded, though she wasn't sure if she believed it. It was hard to let go of the idea of what could have been, of the life she thought she was supposed to have.

As they stood there, side by side, the city stretching out in front of them, Charley realised how easy it was to talk to Seth. How easy it was to be with him. He didn't push her, didn't demand more than she was willing to give. And maybe that was why she kept meeting him like this, in quiet corners of the city where no one could see them. It wasn't about Jack, or the past, or the things they had lost. It was about this—this moment, this connection. Something that felt simple, even though it wasn't. She turned to face the river again, her fingers tracing the cold metal railing beside her. The wind had picked up, a slight breeze that tugged at her hair, brushing it against her cheek. The silence had settled, thick and powerful, as if the city itself was waiting for her to speak.

Seth stood beside her, his hands tucked into his coat pockets, eyes distant, watching the dark flow of the river. The bright lights from the city flickering on the surface of the water, their reflection as fractured and restless as her thoughts. She took a breath, deciding to break the tension that had been slowly building between them.

"You know," she began softly, "we've been talking a lot about me. But what about you?"

Seth turned slightly, his gaze shifting to her. His expression softened, but she could see the wariness in his eyes—the guarded look he always wore when the conversation turned toward him. It was as though he carried an invisible line in the sand, and Charley was always afraid of crossing it. But tonight, with the cold pressing in and the weight of everything between them, she found herself wanting to push just a little further.

"You've never really talked about why you haven't settled down," she continued, her voice careful, probing but not forceful. "You know, no wife, no kids…"

Seth chuckled lightly, though it was a sound that held more resignation than humour. He looked back at the river, his eyes tracing the distant shadows of the boats that drifted silently by.

"I'm not exactly the settling down type," he said, the usual playfulness in his tone absent now. There was something darker, something hidden beneath the surface of his words. "I'd never really thought of myself as... father material."

Charley frowned slightly, feeling the hesitation in his words. "But why? I mean, you're great with people. You're kind, thoughtful... you'd be a good father."

Seth let out a long breath, his eyes still fixed on the water, as if searching for something that wasn't there. For a moment, she thought he wasn't going to answer, that he was going to let the conversation fall into that easy silence they often shared. But then he spoke, his voice low and distant, as though he were telling a story that wasn't entirely his.

"I didn't exactly have the best role models either," he said. "I wasn't... close with my parents. And they died when I was young."

Charley felt a pang of sympathy, though she had suspected something like that. It made her think of Christian, and she prayed somewhere that he wouldn't carry the same sense of loss she always found in Seth, an unspoken sadness that hovered around him like a shadow. She had never known the details, and she had never wanted to push too hard. Now, hearing the confirmation of what she had suspected, she felt her heart ache for him in a way she hadn't expected.

"I'm sorry," she said softly, not knowing what else she could say.

Seth shrugged, but it wasn't the kind of shrug that dismissed the pain. It was more a gesture of acceptance, of someone who had learned long ago that there were some things in life you just had to carry, no matter how heavy they were.

"I was about seven when it happened," he continued after a moment, his voice calm, detached. "Car accident. I barely remember them, really. Just flashes, you know? My mum's laugh, the way my dad smelled of cigarettes and leather. They were gone before I could really know them."

Charley felt his words settle over her. She could hear the distance in his voice, the way he spoke of his parents as though they were strangers, people he had only glimpsed in passing but never truly known. And it made her think of all the things she had never asked him, all the layers of his life that he kept hidden behind that easy smile of his.

"That must have been unimaginably hard," she said softly. "To survive a thing like that, alone."

"I wasn't with them, when it happened. I'd been naughty that day, my mum often struggled to cope with me, I think. My dad was… not the patient type either. So they took my older brother and sister out for the day, and left me with our au pair… I went to live with my aunt after the accident," Seth said, a faint bitterness creeping into his tone. "She was… well, she wasn't exactly the nurturing type. Wealthy, sure. She had this huge house in the country, all marble floors and high ceilings, the kind of place you see in magazines. But she wasn't kind. She never really wanted me there. She made sure I knew it, too."

Charley's hand instinctively reached out, her fingers brushing against his arm in a gesture of quiet comfort. Seth didn't pull away, but he didn't acknowledge the touch either. His eyes remained fixed on the river; his expression was unreadable, distant.

"She sent me away to school," he continued, his voice flat. "One of those posh boarding schools where they teach you Latin and how to tie a perfect Windsor knot but don't care much about whether you feel like you belong. I didn't, of course. I never belonged anywhere."

The words lingered in the cold air between them, heavy and sharp. Charley could see it now—the boy Seth had been, lost and alone in a world that had no place for him. A child orphaned not just by death but by indifference, sent away to be raised by strangers in a place that only deepened his sense of isolation.

"I was just a burden to her, I think" Seth said quietly, his voice tight with old resentment. "She did her duty, paid for my education, made sure I had clothes on my back, but she never cared. She was glad when I was gone. Less of a reminder of her sister, less of an inconvenience in her perfect little world."

Charley's heart ached for him, for the boy he had been, abandoned and unloved. She wanted to say something, to offer him some comfort, but the words felt inadequate. How could she, with her own tangled mess of a life, offer him anything that could ease that kind of pain?

"After school, I just… drifted," Seth said, his tone resigned. "Never really found a place to settle. I guess that's why I shied away from relationships for so long. Never wanted to risk being like her. Never wanted to be responsible for screwing someone else up."

Charley shook her head. "You wouldn't be like her."

Seth smiled faintly, though it didn't reach his eyes. "You don't know that."

"I do," Charley insisted, her voice firm. "You're nothing like her. You care about people, Seth. You're kind. That's more than most people get growing up."

Seth finally looked at her then, his eyes softening slightly. For a moment, she saw a vulnerability in him that he usually kept hidden, a crack in the armour he wore so easily. It made her want to reach out to him, to pull him closer, but something held her back.

"I'm not sure I could ever settle down," Seth said after a long pause, his voice quieter now, more thoughtful. "It's not just about kids. It's about… belonging somewhere.

To someone. I've never really had that... Or had it taken away."

Charley felt a pang of sadness at his words. She knew what it was like to feel unmoored, to drift through life without any real sense of purpose or connection. But she also knew that Seth wasn't as alone as he thought he was. He had people who cared about him, even if he didn't always see it.

"Jack was orphaned, too, you know. As a boy. He was fostered, but his foster parents sound very different to your aunt..."

Seth reflected on this for a moment and his expression shifted a little, almost imperceptibly. "Funny, isn't it, same circumstances, different lives... makes you think."

"Like perhaps you're not so different? she said softly. "You do belong somewhere, Seth," she continued, after a short pause, "You just haven't found it yet."

Seth looked at her for a long moment, his expression unreadable. The wind picked up again, ruffling his hair and carrying the scent of the river. For a moment, Charley thought he might say something, that he might finally let her in, but then he turned away, back to the water.

"Maybe," he said quietly, but there was a note of doubt in his voice, as though he didn't quite believe it.

They continued walking along the river, the conversation fading into a comfortable silence. The lights of the city shimmered on the water, and the distant sounds of traffic and laughter echoed in the night. As they walked, Charley found herself lingering on Seth's last words, the doubt in his voice as he spoke about belonging. It stayed with her, clung to the cold air between them like a shadow. She thought about the Seth she had come to know over these past months, his easy charm, his quick wit. But tonight, there was something more—a glimpse of the man beneath the surface, a man who had carried the burden of his past for too long.

She felt a question rising, something she'd wanted to ask for a while but hadn't found the right moment. Now, with the night pressing in and the conversation circling back to the heart of things, she couldn't hold it back any longer.

"Seth," she began cautiously, glancing at him from the corner of her eye. "You mentioned once that you studied medicine. Why didn't you finish that?"

Seth's pace slowed, and she could see him tense, his shoulders tightening under his coat. For a moment, she thought he might brush the question aside, make a joke or offer some vague answer. But then he stopped walking altogether, turning to face her. His eyes met hers, and for the first time that evening, there was a flicker of something raw behind them—something he had kept hidden for too long.

He let out a long breath, his hands slipping from his pockets as he crossed his arms over his chest, like he was bracing himself for something difficult. "I don't talk about it much," he said quietly, his voice laden with the burden of the admission. "But... a couple of things happened around that time. Things that just made me... lose my way."

Charley stayed silent, letting him speak at his own pace. She could see the struggle in his eyes, the way the memories tugged at him, pulling him back to a time he'd rather forget.

"When my aunt finally died," he continued, his voice flat. "She'd been ill for a while, but even then, it was sudden. A stroke. One minute she was there, the next... gone."

There was no sadness in his voice as he spoke about her, no trace of mourning. It was as if her death had been just another event in his life, a marker of time but nothing more. Charley wondered what that kind of detachment did to a person, how it shaped them.

"She was the one who pushed me into medicine," Seth added, his tone more reflective now. "I think… I think I did it more to please her than anything else. She had these high expectations, and for a long time, I thought if I could just meet them, I'd be… worth something."

He paused, shaking his head slightly, as if to rid himself of the thought. "But when she died, that sense of purpose went with her. I didn't need to please her anymore, and I realised… I didn't want to do it. I'd never wanted to be a doctor. It was an old ambition for another life, shaped by people who were no longer there."

Charley's heart ached for him, for the young man he had been, lost and searching for meaning in a world that had taken so much from him. She understood now why he had drifted, why he had never found a place to settle. Without that anchor, without the pressure to be something for someone else, he had lost his direction entirely.

"I felt… adrift after that," Seth said quietly. "Like I didn't belong anywhere. And without her, there was no one left to impress, no one to care whether I succeeded or failed. So, I quit. Just walked away. From a lot of things. A whole other life really."

Charley looked at him, her eyes soft with understanding. "And you never regretted it?"

Seth smiled faintly, though it was tinged with sadness. "Sometimes."

Charley nodded, growing comfortable once more. They continued walking, side by side, their footsteps in sync, the load of the past slowly lifting as the night stretched out ahead of them.

25

'A Spider sewed at Night'

Jack woke with a jolt, the kind that leaves your heart hammering in your chest for reasons you can't quite place. His breath hung in the cold air of the car, his own reflection ghostly in the windscreen, made worse by the thin layer of frost creeping up from the edges. He wiped at his eyes, trying to piece together the disjointed fragments of sleep. His body felt stiff, the cramp in his neck a dull reminder of how long he'd been here, slumped in the driver's seat.

Night had crept in without him noticing. The faint remnants of daylight were gone, replaced by the deep blue-black of evening, the sky still clear but threatening frost. Jack shivered and rubbed his hands together, trying to shake the chill from his bones. He reached for his phone, noting the time—8:42 p.m.—and a flurry of missed calls and texts. Ed had called three times, Martin twice. He thumbed through the messages quickly, scanning their terse requests for updates.

Jack, where the hell are you? Call me.
We've got something from Radcliffe. Call.

His fingers moved automatically to type a reply, but before he could hit send, the screen flickered, then went dark. Battery dead. Typical. He cursed under his breath, fumbling around the front seat for a charger, but there was nothing. Not even the spare lead he usually kept in the glove box. The silence in the car pressed in on him, thickening as he debated his next move.

There was no way he could go back to the station without checking in with Ed first, and with his phone dead, he felt cut off, directionless. Without really thinking, Jack turned the key in the ignition and eased the car out onto the road. His mind circled back to Murray's flat—there might still be uniforms on site, maybe they'd have found something, anything, that could give him a lead. Something about that flat had stuck with him.

He drove slowly through the narrow streets, the dim glow of streetlights guiding his way. The air outside was biting, the sort that clung to your skin and made you want to retreat into warmth, into safety. Jack's thoughts churned as the houses passed by in a blur, faceless windows staring out at him from the dark. He tried to shake off the feeling of unease creeping into his chest—the sense that something was rapidly slipping through his fingers, something vital.

Murray. It kept coming back to Roy Murray. The man had felt wrong from the start, and now, with him dead, the case seemed even more tangled, more elusive.

When Jack pulled up outside Murray's flat, he parked a few houses down, cutting the engine and sitting there for a moment in the stillness. Across the street, a man was leaving the building, his shoulders hunched against the cold, a woollen scarf wrapped tightly around his neck. Jack barely noticed him, though something about the man's hurried gait seemed out of place. The moment passed, and Jack dismissed it.

He stepped out of the car, his breath forming a mist in the freezing air, and walked briskly toward the building. A uniformed officer stood at the door, nodding when Jack flashed his badge. The air inside the flat was stagnant, the faint smell of dust and something musty greeting him as he crossed the threshold. The small, converted space felt too quiet, as though the life had already drained from it the moment Murray died.

Jack glanced around, taking in the surroundings slowly, methodically. The furniture was sparse, old-fashioned, with a dark wood desk sitting against one wall, a couple of armchairs near the window. The place had the feel of someone who lived on the edges of life, not really part of anything. Murray had been that way—an outsider in his own story.

Pulling on a pair of gloves, Jack stepped closer to the bureau, the focal point of the room. He let his fingertips graze the polished surface, feeling the coolness of the wood, the smoothness worn in by years of use. The grain of the wood caught the dim light, glinting slightly as he ran his hand across it. He imagined Murray sitting here, day after day, his fingers tracing the same paths Jack's did now. It was the closest he'd felt to the man, this strange, invisible connection through touch and space.

The bureau's drawers were already open, their contents rifled through by earlier search teams. But something about the piece still pulled at Jack, as though it held more than just papers and old magazines. It was a relic, a symbol of something larger—Murray's life, his secrets, the pieces of himself he kept hidden from the world.

The flat around him seemed to close in, the walls pressing tighter as Jack's thoughts spiralled. He had to get back to the station, but the scene in front of him demanded his attention for just a little longer. He walked the perimeter of the room, brushing past bookshelves, records, the ordinary objects of a life. Yet something about them felt wrong, like pieces that didn't fit. This was a life out of place, out of time.

And then, he noticed something. It was ordinary. Meaningless, almost. And yet, it was out of place. It sat on top of the bureau, untouched by the chaos around it, as though someone had put it there deliberately. Jack's instincts stirred, that unexplainable feeling in the pit of his stomach that something was here, waiting to be found. He almost walked away, dismissed it as another scrap in a sea of accumulation and waste, but he couldn't shake the feeling. He picked it up.

Jack's fingers hovered over the envelope, his eyes tracing the torn edges, the empty expanse of its surface. It was a standard white business envelope, the kind that clogs up letterboxes with bills and notices, forgotten almost as soon as they're torn open. But there was something about this one, something that made him hesitate. He turned it over in his hands, feeling the weightlessness of it. There was nothing inside, no address, no letter, only a faint crumple where something had once been tucked in neatly behind the plastic window.

He glanced around the room, half expecting an answer from the silent walls, the suffocating air. The sound of the officer's footsteps from the hall outside punctuated the stillness, but even that didn't break the strange pull the envelope had on him. He leaned closer, holding it up to the light. The tear was jagged, rough, as though opened in a hurry, maybe without care. The envelope hadn't been thrown away, just left there, abandoned.

Jack ran his thumb over the paper, feeling its texture, searching for anything out of the ordinary. Nothing. It was completely blank—no return address, no sender, no indication of what had been inside. And yet, he couldn't let it go.

He stood up, his shoulders tense, as if the consequence of the discovery—or non-discovery—had lodged itself in his spine. With a final glance at the envelope, Jack walked toward the door, but before he crossed the threshold, something tugged at him again. He stopped mid-step, turning back. His breath came in short, sharp bursts in the chilly flat. He walked back to the bureau, picked up the envelope again, and stared at it with renewed curiosity.

He stepped out into the hallway, catching sight of the uniformed officer on watch. The man straightened up as soon as he saw him approach.

"Can you radio someone from forensics?" Jack said, his voice low, calm, but edged with urgency.

The officer nodded, already reaching for his radio. "What do you need, sir?"

"This envelope." Jack held it out, his gloved hand almost reverent as he passed it over. "I want it checked for DNA, prints, anything we can get to find out where it came from."

The officer gave him a quizzical glance but nodded all the same. "Yes, sir."

Jack watched him pick up his radio and make the request and felt the tension in his chest loosen just a fraction. He knew it wasn't much—an empty envelope in a dead man's flat. It could have been a receipt for a utility bill or a piece of junk mail. But the way it had been left there, carelessly torn, as if something important had once filled it, something that had been discarded along with the envelope—it didn't sit right.

He stood in the middle of Murray's flat, the cold air still clinging to his skin, the echo of silence pressing in on him. It wasn't the first time he had found himself in a place like this—on the edge of someone else's life, peering in through the cracks they had left behind. But tonight, it felt different. There was something about Murray's flat, its dull anonymity, its emptiness, which spoke to something deeper in Jack. Roy Murray had lived here, tucked away in this nondescript corner of the world, hidden from view, existing on the periphery of life.

Jack ran his hand over the edge of the bureau once more, his fingers tracing the smooth, worn wood. The earring was already bagged, the envelope was gone, but the feeling of something unsaid lingered in the air, like a breath held too long. He glanced around the room one final time—an empty chair, a cheap lamp casting weak light, the curtains drawn tightly across the window. He felt an ache in his chest, a low thrum of frustration, not just with the case, but with everything. With the dead ends. With the relentless pursuit of a truth that always seemed just out of reach.

He sighed, deeply, resigned. He needed to call it a night. There was nothing more to be found here, not tonight anyway.

His breath fogged in the cold as he stepped outside, the night air hitting him like a slap. The sky was a deep, unforgiving black, the stars obscured by the thick blanket of cloud that always seemed to hang over the city this time of year. Jack shoved his hands deep into his coat pockets and began the short walk back to his car. His thoughts drifted as he walked, the rhythm of his footsteps falling into sync with the beat of his frustration.

How had it come to this? he wondered. Not just the case, but everything—his life with Charley, their marriage, the slow erosion of whatever they had once been. He couldn't pinpoint the exact moment it had started, the unravelling. Maybe there hadn't been a moment. Maybe it had been like the spider in that Dickinson poem he'd scribbled out for Charley, weaving in the dark, barely visible until it was too late.

He reached his car and sat behind the wheel for a moment, staring blankly at the dashboard. The empty flat, the cold, the missed calls from Ed and Martin, it all weighed on him. His phone was dead, but he didn't care. Not now. He started the engine, the hum of it filling the car as he pulled out onto the empty street, heading back across town.

The drive home felt like a blur, while Skunk Anansie's *Infidelity* played softly in the background, a haunting soundtrack for the deserted streets of the city, muted under the weight of the night. Jack barely noticed the buildings slipping by and the streetlights flickering overhead. His mind was elsewhere, caught in the tangle of thoughts he couldn't quite shake. When he pulled up in front of the apartment building, he sat in the car for a long moment, just staring at the front door.

He had expected to find Charley when he stepped inside. He had hoped, maybe, to hear the faint sound of her moving about the apartment, or to see her curled up on the couch, the way she used to wait for him. But the apartment was dark, silent. Empty. The cold followed him inside, lingering in the corners of the rooms.

Jack wandered aimlessly through the flat, taking in the small signs of her absence—the empty wine glass on the kitchen counter, the jacket she had left draped over the back of a chair. He felt the loneliness of it all, of their life together, seeping into him like a slow poison. They were living in the same space, moving through the same rooms, but they were miles apart, each lost in their own silence.

He went to the kitchen and filled the kettle, watching as the water came to a boil, the steam rising in soft wisps. He made himself a cup of herbal tea—some blend that Charley had bought, the kind he never usually drank, but tonight it just felt right. Something about the warmth of it, the humility, offered a small comfort in the coldness of the evening.

Carrying the tea with him, Jack walked over to the coffee table and saw it—the piece of paper he had left for Charley days ago. It was still there, untouched, crumpled slightly at the edges. He picked it up, staring at the words he had scribbled down in a moment of quiet desperation. The first stanza of Dickinson's poem, A Spider Sewed at Night.

A spider sewed at night Without a light Upon an arc of white.

He read the words again, the rhythm of them sinking into his bones. He thought of the spider, weaving in the dark, working without light. It felt like a metaphor for their lives now, for the way he and Charley were moving through their days—blind, disconnected, barely seeing each other, barely speaking. They were trapped in their own webs, caught in a stasis that neither of them knew how to break free from. That was the way he had intended it, but now it felt like that symbolism was far greater. As he thought of the full poem, the way it circled back on itself, the way the spider continued to work, despite the darkness. There was something haunting in that image, something that felt too close to home. He sat down on the couch, sipping the tea, the warmth of it doing little to ease the coldness inside him.

As he set the cup down on the table, something caught his eye. A glint of light from beneath the edge of the furniture. Jack leaned down, reaching underneath the couch, his fingers brushing against something smooth and cool. He pulled it out—a photograph, slightly bent at the edges, as though it had been carelessly knocked to the floor and forgotten.

It was a picture of Charley, he couldn't be sure when it had been taken, but it was recent. She was standing in a park, bathed in soft autumn light, her light hair catching the golden glow of the setting sun. She was looking back at the camera, smiling, her eyes bright with a happiness that Jack hadn't seen in a long time. He stared at the picture for a long moment, his chest tightening with an emotion he couldn't quite name.

When had she stopped smiling like that? Had he been there? He couldn't be sure, only that he couldn't remember the last time he had seen her look so free, so full of life. Now, everything between them felt muted, heavy with unspoken words and unresolved tension. They had become strangers, moving through their days in parallel, never quite meeting in the middle.

Jack turned the photo over in his hands, studying it, searching for some clue, some answer to the question that had been plaguing him for months. But there was nothing. Just the image of Charley, frozen in time, another ghost of who they used to be.

He set the picture down on the table, next to the crumpled piece of paper with Dickinson's words. The spider, the darkness, the weaving. It all felt too familiar, too close to the truth of their lives now. Jack stood up, the tea now growing cold in the cup beside him.

He walked over to the window, staring out into the night, the city sprawled out before him in shades of black and grey. Somewhere out there, in the shadows, people were living their lives, moving through the darkness, weaving their own webs. And here he was, trapped in his own, waiting for something to change, for something to bridge the gulf had settled between him and Charley.

But nothing changed. Not yet.

With a sigh, Jack turned away from the window and walked back to the couch. He picked up the photograph again, staring at Charley's smile, the way the light had caught her just right, the way she seemed so far away now. He thought of the spider, sewing in the dark, and wondered if they were too far gone to find their way back to that light.

He sat back down on the couch. Charley's smile—so distant, so unreachable now—seemed to mock him, reminding him of everything they had lost and everything he was too tired to try and fix. The room was quiet, except for the soft ticking of the clock on the wall. It felt like the pulse of his own thoughts, counting down the moments of his life, each second slipping away without him ever making a move.

Ed's words from the other night came back to him, those well-meaning reassurances, the warmth of friendship that had been meant to lift him, but instead weighed on him like a burden. The gaps between him and Charley felt too wide, the silences too deep to fill. It was as if they had built walls over the years, and now neither of them knew how to tear them down.

He looked around the apartment, at the hollow spaces between their lives. It felt more like a house where two ghosts lived than a home. The kitchen with its half-empty wine glass, the couch with the indents of a body long gone, the table littered with reminders of the days that had passed without meaning. And in the middle of it all, Jack, sitting there like a man lost in his own life, unable to see a way forward.

He drained the last of his tea, the lukewarm liquid settling uneasily in his stomach. What was he doing here? He didn't know how to fix things with Charley, and maybe part of him didn't even believe it could be fixed. He had tried, hadn't he? But trying wasn't enough. Sometimes, trying was just another word for stalling, for avoiding the truth. And the truth was, he didn't know if he could go on pretending that everything would be okay.

Reaching for his phone, Jack cursed under his breath as he remembered it had died. He fumbled in the drawer for a spare charger, tucked away for moments like these when technology failed him, but life still demanded attention.

There wasn't anything else left to do. There never was. Charley was gone for the night, maybe further gone than that, and he didn't know how to bring her back. But the job? The job was always there. The cases, the suspects, the trails of clues that never quite added up—they were puzzles he knew how to solve, even if they never gave him the answers he truly wanted.

Jack placed the photograph back onto the table, its colours dulled in the dim light. Charley's smile, once radiant, now seemed to fade into the shadows of their past. He couldn't shake the feeling that she had slipped away from him, not tonight, but long before. The apartment felt colder, emptier, like it was waiting for a life that wasn't coming back.

He glanced at his phone, it was still dead, still waiting for a charge to bring it back to life. What was the point? Another message to Ed, another half-hearted attempt to connect with Charley, but he knew neither would fix anything. Not tonight. Maybe not ever. His thoughts drifted, restless. Work was all that made sense now, the only thing that had a pattern he could follow.

But not here. Not in this hollow space. He needed something else, a way to lose himself, to escape the suffocating stillness. And that's when the idea struck him, the one place that still brought him a sliver of peace, tucked away in a forgotten corner of the city, his sanctuary, of sorts. It wasn't the work. It wasn't the case. It was something older, deeper—something tied to the past he could never quite shake. He grabbed his coat from the hook by the door, the familiar weight of it a strange comfort against the growing chill of the night. Then, stuffing the charging lead into his pocket for later, he left without bothering to leave a note or send another message. Charley wouldn't miss him, he felt, not tonight, not realising, of course, that it was because she missed him that she wasn't there in the first place.

The streets were quiet as he drove through the city, the rhythmic hum of the engine and the darkened windows of sleeping houses passing him by. The world seemed distant, like it was happening to someone else. But as he neared the cinema, that familiar pull, that tug in his chest, returned. He wasn't sure if it was nostalgia, or something more desperate. Perhaps it was the hope that tonight he might finally find what he'd been searching for all these years. That old movie that had lingered in his mind since childhood, like a ghost that flitted in and out of memory—a film about a man trapped in time, where everything had stopped the moment that the clock struck twelve.

Jack parked, pulling up just outside the small, weathered building. The lights inside glowed dimly, welcoming him into the dark. He got out and stood there for a moment, the cold air biting at his skin. He thought of Charley again, the distance that had stretched between them, but quickly pushed the thought aside. This wasn't the time for her. Not now.

Inside, the lobby was empty, the scent of old popcorn and worn leather seats thick in the air. Davis, the projectionist, glanced up from his counter, recognising Jack instantly. He gave a silent nod, understanding without words that Jack was here to see something. The same something that always brought him back.

Jack made his way down the narrow hallway to the small screening room, the projector already humming to life, the faint flicker of an old black-and-white film starting on the screen. He slipped into a seat near the back, the familiar sounds and sights drawing him in like they always did.

The old movie began, its grainy images playing out in front of him, but Jack's mind was elsewhere. He wasn't watching the film; he was waiting for something to happen. For something to click. The man on the screen, caught in an endless loop of time, mirrored his own feeling of stasis. Maybe that was why he kept coming back, to hunt for this ghost of a memory, to find some answer in these reels of forgotten celluloid.

But tonight, like every other night, it eluded him. The movie was just a movie, the answers stayed hidden in the darkness. And yet, Jack kept coming back, kept sitting in that cold, empty theatre, chasing a film he wasn't even sure had ever existed in the first place anymore.

As the credits began to roll some hours later, he stayed seated until the very end, staring blankly at the screen long after the last frame had flickered away. The hum of the projector became a kind of lullaby, a way to drown out the thoughts, the regrets, the empty spaces that had formed around his life.

With a weary sigh, Jack finally stood, pulling his coat tighter around him as he made his way back to the door. Outside, the night had grown colder, the streets quieter still. He stood there for a moment, breathing in the crisp air, trying to clear his mind. He wasn't sure what he was searching for, or if he would ever find it. But for now, the old movies, the quiet, the chase of forgotten things—it would have to be enough.

Jack walked back to his car, feeling no closer to the truth than he had been before. But at least, for a little while, he had been somewhere else, somewhere that wasn't home. And the snow began to fall lightly around him.

26

'Faith — is the Pierless Bridge'

The snow fell softly outside the bar's window, casting a faint, ethereal glow on the streets as dusk turned into night. The light from the streetlamps flickered weakly against the descending flakes, the world outside cloaked in a muffled silence that seemed distant and unreachable. Inside the bar, the soft murmur of voices and clinking glasses filled the warm, dimly lit space, a contrast to the wintry world beyond the glass.

Seth and Charley sat by the window, watching the snow fall in a slow, rhythmic dance. The song *Sugar* by Editors played low in the background, its dark, pulsating beats giving the atmosphere a kind of brooding intimacy. Charley stirred her drink absentmindedly, her eyes following the drifting snowflakes as they gathered on the pavement.

For a moment, there was peace in the quiet between them, the kind of stillness that comes when two people are comfortable enough to let words fall away. But underneath it all, there was tension—unspoken, but palpable—like a low hum beneath the surface. Seth was watching her closely, his fingers tracing the rim of his glass as if he were waiting for her to say something that never came.

Charley shifted in her seat, feeling the need to escape, if only for a few minutes. She stood abruptly. "I need the bathroom," she said, her voice quieter than she intended, barely cutting through the claustrophobia of the song's steady beat.

Seth nodded, his gaze lingering on her a little too long, as if he could sense something in her tone. But he didn't say anything. He just watched as she turned and made her way through the dimly lit bar.

As Charley walked past the bar, the music seemed to intensify around her, the haunting rhythm of the song growing louder, pulsing in her ears like the beat of some unseen heart. The ambient noise of the bar at night became a distant echo, while the floor beneath her feet felt like it was sinking, as if the world itself was collapsing inward, as if she were walking deeper into the belly of the beast.

The bathroom was cold and quiet, the harsh fluorescent light bouncing off the stark white tiles, a contrast to the warmth outside. Charley caught sight of her reflection in the mirror and paused, studying the face that looked back at her. The lines at the corners of her eyes seemed deeper tonight, the fatigue more evident. She leaned in closer, running a hand through her hair, as if trying to shake off the load of the last few days. But the reflection stayed the same—tired, distant, someone she barely recognised anymore.

She splashed water on her face, the cold bite of it jolting her slightly, and then her phone buzzed in her pocket. For a brief moment, her heart leapt, and she pulled it out quickly, hoping—against everything—that it might be Jack. That perhaps he was reaching out from the other side, trying to find his way back to her.

It was Christian. She stared at the message for a moment, her stomach sinking as she read it.

I'm worried about Ed. I haven't seen him since I came home from school, is he with you?

The words blurred on the screen as a sudden wave of panic washed over her. She tapped the call button, her hands trembling slightly as she raised the phone to her ear. It rang once, twice, and then went straight to voicemail. She tried him again, then Ed, but the same thing happened.

Panic swirled in her chest, tightening its grip. Something wasn't right. She could feel it, like a black cloud settling over her, dark and oppressive. Charley stood frozen for a moment, staring at her phone, before finally forcing herself to move. She shoved the phone back into her pocket and hurried out of the bathroom, her heart pounding in her chest.

Seth looked up as she approached, his eyes narrowing as he saw the look on her face. "What's wrong?" he asked, his voice low, but filled with concern.

"I—I have to go," Charley stammered, reaching for her coat with shaking hands. "Ed—Christian, my friend's son, just texted me. He hasn't come home, and he's not answering his phone. Something's wrong."

Seth stood up, immediately sensing the urgency in her voice. "Do you need help?"

Charley shook her head, fumbling with her coat. "I don't know. I have to get to his place."

Seth grabbed his own coat, already pulling it on. "I'm coming with you."

"No, Seth, it's okay," Charley started to protest, but he was already moving. He pulled out his phone, calling for a cab.

"You shouldn't go alone," he said firmly, cutting her off. "I'll come with you. We'll figure it out."

Charley didn't have the energy to argue. The panic was tightening around her throat, making it hard to think, hard to breathe. She nodded numbly, grateful for his presence, even if she didn't want to admit it. It was the same dread she'd felt *that* day, when Jack had called to tell her what had happened.

They stepped out into the cold night air, the snow still falling softly, but the world around them felt thicker, more crushing. The quiet calm of earlier was gone, replaced by an anxiety that twisted in Charley's gut. She barely noticed the city lights reflecting off the snow, the beauty of it lost in the storm of her thoughts.

Their cab arrived, and they climbed in quickly, the warmth of the car offering her little comfort. As they sped through the streets, Charley stared out the window, her mind racing. What if something had happened to Ed? What if he was in trouble, and she wasn't there to help him? The guilt pressed at her, and her phone remained stubbornly silent in her lap. Seth sat beside her, glancing over occasionally, but he didn't say much. He knew better than to push.

The snow outside was falling thicker now, its soft descent growing into a heavier curtain that veiled the streets. As the cab pulled up in front of Ed's building, Charley's pulse quickened, a knot tightening in her chest. Her hand reached for the door handle, but before she stepped out, she turned to Seth.

"I can't be seen with you," she said, her voice hurried, almost pleading. "Please, just wait here. Just… wait in the cab."

Seth frowned, his face shadowed by concern, but he didn't argue. "Are you sure?"

Charley nodded quickly, glancing toward the building as though the walls themselves might hold the answer. "Just… I'll be right back. I need to check on Christian."

The tension between them crackled, but Seth relented, watching her closely as she stepped out into the falling snow. He stayed put, his fingers clenching around the edge of the seat as he watched her figure disappear into the cold night.

Charley hurried to the entrance, her breath visible in the frigid air, her mind racing with worst-case scenarios. She stood outside the door, her fingers trembling as she rang the bell, expecting Christian's familiar face to appear behind the frosted glass. But there was nothing. No sound of footsteps, no faint voice from inside.

She pushed the bell again, her heartbeat rising in her throat as she leaned closer to the door. Still nothing. Panic clawed its way up her chest, and she crouched down, calling into the letterbox. Her voice echoed in the empty hallway beyond, swallowed by the cold emptiness of the house.

"Christian! It's me. Are you there?" Her voice wavered, but the stillness on the other side was unbroken.

She stood up, glancing over her shoulder. The cab was still there, Seth's silhouette faint in the dim light. But she couldn't wait any longer. Charley fumbled in her bag, her fingers brushing the cold metal of the spare key Ed had given her. She hesitated for a moment, feeling the key in her hand, and then she slid it into the lock. It turned with a faint click, and the door swung open with a groan.

The air inside was colder than she'd expected, a chill creeping through the dim, shadowed hallways. The house felt abandoned, empty—nothing like the warm, familiar space she'd visited so many times before. Her voice felt small in the vast silence as she called out again, stepping into the house.

"Christian?"

There was no answer, only the muted sound of her footsteps on the wooden floor. Her breath hitched as she glanced around, feeling the weight of the darkness press against her. She walked further in, her eyes scanning the familiar surroundings—the faded wallpaper, the framed photographs on the wall, and the mess of shoes by the door.

Everything was in its place, and yet, something was terribly wrong.

"Seth," she whispered to herself, half-turning toward the door. She knew she had asked him to stay behind, but she also didn't feel like she couldn't bear the growing dread alone.

As if on cue, Seth appeared in the doorway. He'd sent the cab away, the look on his face resolute, his concern etched into every line. He stepped inside, his presence grounding her, though the anxiety didn't leave her.

A sudden gust of wind slammed the door shut behind her, the echo reverberating through the house. She jumped, her pulse quickening as she looked toward the windows, the snow outside thickening into a swirling storm.

"It's okay," he said, reassuringly. "I'm sorry, I couldn't just wait," his voice soft but firm, "what's going on?"

"I don't know." Charley's voice broke slightly as she took a step back, shaking her head. "Christian's not answering, and the house feels... wrong."

She glanced around the hallway, his eyes narrowing as he tried to piece together what had happened. The cold, the emptiness—it all felt off. Seth followed her into the heart of the house, his footsteps cautious as though the silence itself might crack underfoot.

"Christian?" Charley called out again, her voice trembling. They moved down the narrow hallway, peering into the small kitchen, the empty living room, and the echoing spaces that had once held life. But each room they entered was void of sound, of movement—like the whole place had been frozen in time.

They stopped in front of Christian's bedroom door. It was slightly ajar, the faint light from the hallway spilling into the room beyond. Charley's heart pounded in her chest as she pushed the door open, her hand trembling. She braced herself, fearing what she might find, but as the door swung open, all she saw was an empty room. The bed was unmade, a heap of blankets tossed carelessly to the side, and Christian's schoolbag lay discarded on the floor, along with his blazer.

"He made it home," Charley murmured, her eyes scanning the mess of schoolbooks and crumpled paper. "He must have."

Seth crouched down, picking up the blazer, his brow furrowed. "Yeah, but where is he now?"

Charley's hands shook as she reached for her phone again, dialling Christian's number with trembling fingers. The call went straight to voicemail once more, her heart sinking deeper with each failed attempt. She redialled frantically, pacing the room as if somehow, moving would force an answer. But again, there was only the hollow, mechanical voice telling her Christian was unavailable. She clutched the phone in her hand, her knuckles white, and stared at the scattered remnants of his day—the blazer, the bag, a few scribbled notes on torn bits of paper.

"Where are you?" she whispered, half to herself, half to the empty room. Her mind spun, thoughts colliding—was he out with friends? Lost? Worse? The dread that had been slowly gnawing at her began to take a firmer hold, spreading like frost across her chest.

Seth stood up, placing the blazer back on the bed. His face was drawn, his eyes scanning the room as though searching for something they might have missed. "He's probably just out with mates, Charley," he said, though his voice lacked the usual confidence, as if he didn't quite believe his own words. "We'll find him, try not to worry."

Charley didn't reply. She knew, between how late it was, and who Christian was, this was unlikely. She moved to the window, drawing back the thin curtain, and stared out at the swirling snow. The street beyond was blanketed in white, eerily quiet, save for the occasional passing car or the distant sound of laughter passing by—laughter that only heightened the isolation inside the house.

The snow fell heavier now, thick flakes swirling in the yellow glow of the streetlamps. It made the world outside seem distant, unreal, as if they were trapped in some glassy snow globe, waiting for someone to shake it, to let them out. But there was no one to do that. Only the cold, pressing in.

Under the streetlamp, a spider had woven its delicate web, strands of silk glistening faintly in the dim light. It was a quiet, methodical work, each thread placed with purpose, connecting, intertwining, creating something fragile yet resilient in the biting cold. The tiny creature had moved unhurriedly, oblivious to the storm incoming around it, spinning its web with a kind of patient precision, as if this were all it had ever known.

Charley paused for a moment, watching the sight of the web picked out by the streetlight, so intricate and fragile; she felt it like a strange reflection of her own life—delicate connections stretched taut between her and the people she loved, connections that could so easily break under the strain of missteps and misunderstandings. Each thread, like the relationships she held dear, was so vulnerable, so easily torn by a single gust of wind.

The spider had worked tirelessly, weaving its threads as the snow collected on the ground beneath. Charley felt a deep, hollow ache as she watched it. The web was beautiful, but it seemed lonely, hanging there in the empty, frozen night, its purpose obscured by the storm that surrounded it. The light from the streetlamp was the only thing that gave it form, that revealed its existence.

She thought of Ed, of Christian, of Jack, each of them a part of this fragile web that she had built and tried to maintain. But how long could she hold it together? How long before the cold or the wind or the storm simply tore everything apart?

Turning away from the window, her arms wrapped around herself as though to ward off the chill creeping into her bones. She thought of Ed, of how easily Christian could slip through the cracks in his brother's life. Ed loved him, of course—there was no doubt about that. But Ed was distracted, overwhelmed, right now. And Christian was nowhere to be found.

"We need to call someone," Charley said, her voice tight, almost hoarse from the panic she had been trying to suppress. "The police. Someone."

Seth moved closer; his expression was gentle but firm. "Let's not jump to conclusions yet. We'll keep looking, okay? He can't be far."

Charley bit her lip, torn between the rising panic in her chest and the urge to hold it together, to trust Seth's calm. But something about the dark, silent house told her they didn't have time to wait.

"I'm going to check Ed's room," she said, her voice shaky but determined. Without waiting for a reply, she turned and hurried out of the room, her feet barely making a sound on the wooden floors. She could hear Seth following behind her, his presence steady, but her mind was elsewhere—frantically piecing together what could have happened, where Christian could be.

She pushed open the door to Ed's bedroom, and a sudden draft hit her, colder than the rest of the house. The room was dim, the soft light from the street outside casting long shadows across the bed and the furniture. Ed's clothes were scattered across a chair, shoes kicked off haphazardly by the wardrobe. But the room was empty, just like the others. Christian wasn't here either.

Charley stood in the middle of the room, her heart thudding in her ears. Her eyes darted from the bed to the wardrobe, to the small desk in the corner. Then something caught her attention—a small, crumpled note on the bedside table, half-hidden beneath a book. She reached for it, her fingers brushing the paper gently, as if it might crumble in her hands.

She unfolded it slowly, her eyes scanning the words hastily scribbled in Christian's familiar handwriting. The note was brief, rushed, and it made her stomach lurch.

Gone to find you bro.

Charley's breath caught in her throat. She stared at the note, her mind racing. He had gone to find Ed. But where? It made no sense, where would he even look. Panic surged again, a tidal wave she couldn't hold back.

Seth appeared behind her, reading the note over her shoulder. His hand touched her arm gently, trying to anchor her to the moment. "He's out looking," he said softly. "That's all."

But it wasn't all, it was everything. It was the crushing mass of fear and uncertainty pressing down on her. Christian was out there, somewhere, looking for his brother in the middle of a storm, and Ed was unreachable, too. What had happened? Where were they? As the snow began to thicken again, she became driven by a need she couldn't fully name. Somewhere out there, Ed and Christian were waiting, caught in their own webs, and she had to find them before everything unravelled.

"I need to go," Charley said, her voice barely above a whisper, making her way swiftly back downstairs.

"Go where?" Seth called after her, his brow furrowed.

"To find him," she replied, her resolve hardening. "To find them both."

Seth hesitated for a moment, then nodded, sensing the urgency in her voice. "Alright. But I'm coming with you."

The snow fell like heavy but careless whispers, softly blanketing the street in a quiet way that muffled the world. The flakes were thick, swirling chaotically in the beam of the yellow streetlamp, their delicate shapes no longer disintegrating upon meeting the cold, hard ground. Each step Charley took felt harder, as if the snow outside was dragging her feet down, as if it had conspired with the silence in the room to slow her down, to make her stop and think. And the spider continued, oblivious to her thoughts, spinning and weaving, building something in the dark that no one might ever see. The snow fell, relentless and unforgiving, and the world grew dimmer with each passing moment. But Charley moved forward, leaving the spider to its work, the web shimmering faintly behind her in the lonely glow of the streetlamp.

27

'A great Hope fell'

The snow now fell in dense, spiralling flurries, each flake a tiny fragment of the silent night. It was late, the streets long abandoned, save for the occasional tire tracks now disappearing under the relentless white. Jack's car moved through the empty roads, the headlights cutting narrow paths through the dark, the soft sound of the snow against the windscreen almost soothing. He hadn't meant to spend so long at the cinema, lost in that familiar haze of old reels and forgotten stories, but time had slipped away, the way it always did when he needed it to stop.

Life on Earth by Snow Patrol played softly on the stereo, a melancholy accompaniment to the quiet, frozen city. The lyrics, half-whispered, tugged at something deep inside him—a sadness that felt like it had always been there. He thought of Charley, alone somewhere under this same sky, maybe watching the snow through some other guy's window. He hadn't spoken to her properly in days, or even seen her now in almost a week. Even when they were together, it felt like they were moving in parallel worlds, close enough to touch but always just out of reach.

He adjusted his grip on the steering wheel, fingers stiff from the cold that seemed to seep into everything. His phone sat lifeless on the passenger seat, and the car engine hummed low as Jack pulled into the station's car park, the snow muffling even that sound. The place was nearly empty, save for a few cars scattered under the growing blanket of white. He stepped out, feeling the cold bite at his skin, and for a moment, he stood there in the silence, watching the snow fall, coating the world in a strange, beautiful isolation. It was as if the city itself had been muted, its heartbeat slowed to a crawl beneath the snow.

Inside the dimly lit corridors of the station, Jack's footsteps echoed, the sound bouncing off the empty walls as an eerie quiet hanging in the air. He passed the reception desk, nodding to the desk sergeant as he buzzed himself inside, making his way deeper into the building, towards the office of his major investigation team. There was still activity, of course, the day never ended there, and yet, the place still felt dead, as if everyone had packed up and left long ago, leaving behind only the shadows of whatever they'd been chasing.

He turned the corner, his mind drifting as it often did, thinking of nothing and everything at once—of Ed, of Martin, of Murray's flat and that damned bureau, the cold touch of its wood still fresh on his fingertips. He hadn't found what he was looking for there, though he wasn't sure he even knew what that was. A ghost, maybe. Or something worse. Something still alive.

As he reached his office, Jack stopped, noticing a faint light coming from one of the rooms. He pushed open the door, expecting it to be empty, but inside, sitting at his desk, was DC Radcliffe, his face illuminated by the pale glow of a computer screen. The young detective looked up, startled for a moment before recognition set in.

"Sir?" Radcliffe said, leaning back in his chair.

Jack nodded, stepping inside and closing the door behind him. The warmth of the room was welcome, though it did little to shake off the chill that had settled deep into his bones.

"Where is everyone?" Jack asked, glancing around the empty office. "Martin? Marks?"

Radcliffe shrugged, rubbing a hand over his tired face. He looked like he hadn't slept in days, and Jack supposed he hadn't either.

"Martin left hours ago," Radcliffe said, the faintest hint of frustration in his voice. "She was on her way home, last I heard. As for Detective Inspector Marks, no idea. He was looking for you earlier—he had something important to tell you."

Jack frowned. "Tell me what?"

Radcliffe leaned forward, his voice dropping slightly, as if what he was about to say carried the entire case on its shoulders. "The earring. The one we found in Murray's flat… it is a match for Yasmin Eliot."

For a moment, Jack stood there, processing the words, feeling the cold inside him give way to something sharper, more focused. Yasmin Eliot. Another thread in the web, another piece falling into place—too late for her, but maybe not too late for whoever came next.

"How sure are we?" Jack asked, his voice low, steady.

"Positive," Radcliffe replied. "We've run the prints, cross-checked DNA, everything. It's hers, no question."

Jack didn't move, didn't speak. He just let the information settle into his mind, his body. The puzzle was coming together, slowly, painfully, but it was coming together. And yet, something troubled him still, something didn't sit right. Murray's face flashed in his memory—those final moments, the look in his eyes, the desperate, animal fear as he'd run, as he'd fought to escape.

Why had he run? Was it guilt? Or was it simply fear?

Radcliffe watched him, his eyes searching Jack's face for any sign of what he was thinking, but Jack gave him nothing.

"I don't get it," Radcliffe said, "if he's our guy, why leave something like that behind? Why keep it at all?"

Jack shook his head. "I don't know. Maybe he wasn't thinking straight. Or maybe he didn't care."

Radcliffe leaned back in his chair, crossing his arms. "Well, whatever it is, we've got him now. That's something."

"Is it?" Jack's voice was quieter than he'd intended, almost lost in the low hum of the room.

Radcliffe looked at him, confused. "What do you mean?"

Jack didn't answer right away. Instead, he walked over to the window, staring out at the snow falling heavily outside. The world beyond the glass seemed so distant, so removed from the chaos inside his head.

"Do we have him, Radcliffe?" Jack asked, more to himself than to the officer behind him. "Or do we just have a dead man who can't answer for anything anymore?"

Radcliffe shifted uncomfortably in his seat, not sure what to say. "We'll find more. We've got people digging into Murray's background. We'll get there."

Jack nodded, but it was a hollow gesture. He couldn't shake the feeling that they were chasing shadows, that the truth was slipping through their fingers like the snow outside. Murray had been a lead, maybe even a good one. But was he the end of it? Or just another piece in a larger, darker puzzle?

He turned back to Radcliffe, forcing himself to focus. "Has anyone heard from DI Marks?"

Radcliffe shook his head. "Not since this afternoon. Last I heard, he was looking for you. After that... nothing."

Jack frowned, glancing at his dead phone on the desk. "My phone died. I missed his calls."

Radcliffe stood up, grabbing his jacket from the back of his chair. "Want me to call him now? See where he is?"

Jack hesitated, then nodded. "Yeah. Let's try to get hold of him."

Radcliffe dialled Ed's number, the ringtone cutting through the quiet. Jack stood by the window, staring out at the snowfall. Something was wrong. He could feel it, like a cold hand gripping his chest. And the night was only just beginning.

The snow against the windows had grown more persistent in its purpose. Jack stared out, the city blurred through a veil of grey and white, a trickling mess of lights reflected from the streets. His phone remained silent on the desk, its stillness a constant in the background of his thoughts. The call from Ed hadn't come, not even a text. He felt the hollow ring of it in his chest, something too familiar by now.

Jack grabbed the phone, typed quickly.

Don't know if you're home yet, something came up at the station, not sure when I'm home.

Charley's absence felt sharper in moments like these. He hit send, then tossed the phone down onto the worn-out leather of his chair. It was late, and the station was quieter than it had been all day. Only the occasional shuffle of feet, the rustle of papers. It should have felt comforting. It didn't.

Radcliffe stood by the evidence board, his arms crossed, looking at it like a puzzle too dense to untangle. Jack joined him, his eyes tracing over the chaotic mass of pictures, timelines, scraps of text pinned haphazardly. Faces, all of them victims. A grim collage of lives cut short, frozen in time.

"Anything more on the CCTV?" Jack asked, more out of obligation than hope.

Radcliffe shook his head, the movement tired, almost resigned. "Still nothing. No ID on the figure. Could be anyone, for all we know. Matches Murray in size, though."

Jack clenched his jaw, the frustration swelling again. They had so little—too little. Every step forward only seemed to expose more fog, more shadows. His fingers grazed the most recent photograph Radcliffe had added to the board, Yasmin Eliot's face looking back at him, eyes wide with something like shock. The chill in the room seemed to seep into Jack's bones as he stared at her.

"We have to be missing something," Jack muttered, half to himself. "It's here, somewhere. We're just not seeing it."

Radcliffe didn't respond. His eyes were still fixed on the board, his thoughts clearly elsewhere.

Jack took a step closer, his attention shifting to the fragmented photograph that had been pieced together. Now, with Yasmin's death, the final piece had surfaced.

Jack reached up and carefully adjusted the most recent addition to the puzzle. Yasmin's fragment slid into place with the others. His breath caught in his throat. It was complete now, the edges jagged but unmistakable.

"What the hell does this mean? Who is she?" Jack whispered, more to himself than to Radcliffe.

Radcliffe, however, had noticed. He came closer, eyes narrowing as he looked at the picture. "Yasmin Eliot," he said, his voice low. "Does this mean she's the final victim?"

Jack didn't answer right away. His mind was spinning, fragments of thought slipping away as quickly as they formed. If Yasmin was the final victim, if this puzzle was now complete—then what? What was it all for?

The photo felt like a taunt, a clue left behind by someone who was always two steps ahead. Jack's fingers traced the image again, and he felt the familiar surge of frustration boiling beneath his skin. They'd been chasing shadows, and now, as the image began to take shape, the meaning seemed to slip further out of reach.

"What if—" Jack paused, uncertain how to articulate the gnawing thought that had crept into his mind. "What if this is more than just a trophy? What if the photograph means something? A message. Something we've missed."

Radcliffe's eyes flickered with interest, though scepticism lingered. "A message?"

Jack nodded, his voice growing firmer. "We have to know who this woman is. This isn't just about killing. Whoever's behind this—they're trying to tell us something. Something we're not getting."

Radcliffe stared at it, his face grim. "Then what's the message? What are we supposed to see?"

Jack didn't have the answer. Not yet. But it was there, buried somewhere in that photograph, in the twisted mind of whoever had put it together. He stepped back, crossing his arms, his exhaustion pulling at him. His body felt tight, his thoughts tangled.

He hadn't slept in days. Not properly. Not since this case had started devouring his nights, creeping into his dreams with the faces of the dead. Yasmin's face lingered now, haunting, as if she were waiting for him to figure it out, to piece together the puzzle she'd unwillingly become a part of.

"I think," Jack started slowly, "Yasmin was the final piece. But this doesn't feel over. It feels like it's just beginning."

Radcliffe's brow furrowed. "What do you mean?"

Jack's gaze drifted back to the photograph. "The photo's complete. But the message—it's not. They're not done. They've set their stage, it's like this is a warning, there's more to come."

Radcliffe gave a curt nod, his expression hardening with the same resolve Jack felt tightening in his chest. The room seemed to close in on them, the low hum of the station fading into the background as they both stared at the evidence board, at the photograph that held far too many unanswered questions.

Jack's phone buzzed suddenly, the sound cutting through the stillness. His pulse quickened. Finally, something from Ed. But when he glanced down, it wasn't Ed's name on the screen. It was Charley.

He hesitated, his thumb hovering over the screen, then tapped the message open.

Still at work? Hope you're okay. Let me know if you need anything.

Jack swallowed; his throat was tight. Charley's concern felt like a lifeline, a reminder that there was a world outside of this case. But he couldn't think about that now. Not with so much still unresolved.

He typed out a quick reply.

Yeah. Just trying to get through this mess. I'll call you later.

Jack slipped the phone back into his pocket and turned his attention to Radcliffe. "We need to go over this again. Every detail."

Radcliffe sighed but didn't argue. He knew, as Jack did, that this case had more layers than they'd initially thought. It wasn't just about the victims anymore. It was about the photograph, the message hidden within it, and the person pulling their strings from the shadows.

They worked quietly for the next hour, going over the evidence, combing through every scrap of information they had, hoping to find a link, a connection, that they might not have seen before. All the while, the weather outside continued its relentless assault on the windows, the rhythm becoming a monotonous backdrop to their work.

But Jack's thoughts kept drifting, despite his best efforts to focus. The image of Yasmin Eliot, the final piece of the puzzle, lingered in his mind, her face blurred in his memory but her presence unnerving. He wondered, briefly, what she'd been thinking in her last moments. If she'd known. If she'd seen the figure on the CCTV, the shadow that had stalked her before her death. The thought sent a chill down his spine.

And still, no word from Ed.

It wasn't like Ed to go silent like this. Jack trusted him, more than he trusted most people, but there was something unsettling about the lack of communication. He couldn't shake the feeling that something was wrong, that something was happening just beyond his reach.

Another hour passed, and still, they were no closer to answers. The photograph taunted them from the evidence board, its meaning elusive. Radcliffe stretched, his joints popping with the movement. "We're getting nowhere, sir. Maybe we need to take a step back, clear our heads. Come at this fresh in the morning."

Jack didn't respond at first. His eyes were still fixed on the woman's image, his mind running in circles. He knew Radcliffe was right. They weren't going to solve this tonight. But the thought of leaving, of walking away without answers, felt unbearable.

"Yeah," Jack finally muttered, though his heart wasn't in it. "Maybe you're right."

Radcliffe gathered his things, throwing a glance at Jack as he shrugged into his coat. "Don't stay here all night, sir. Please get some rest. We'll pick it up tomorrow."

Jack gave a noncommittal grunt, and Radcliffe left without another word. The station felt emptier now, the quiet more oppressive. He stood there for a long moment, staring at the evidence board. The sound of the station door closing behind Radcliffe lingered in the silence like a whisper, slowly dissolving into the soft hum of fluorescent lights overhead. Jack glanced up at the clock on the far wall. 3:33 a.m. It seemed a strange time, suspended between the late hours of the night and the approach of morning, a moment that felt unmoored from the rest of the world. He was tired. Beyond tired. The kind of exhaustion that settled deep into the bones, refusing to let go.

He stayed for a moment longer, eyes fixed on the board—the final piece of Yasmin Eliot's fragmented life, her face now an unwitting part of a larger, twisted narrative. The air felt packed with things unspoken, waiting to reveal themselves. He couldn't shake the feeling that the answers were just out of reach, hiding in the spaces between what they already knew. He gathered his things, movements slow and deliberate, his body moving automatically, though his mind was somewhere else. Somewhere darker.

Outside, the wind was howling through the narrow alleyways, sweeping up the loose litter and dead leaves of the city streets. The cold hit him the moment he stepped out of the station, biting through the thin fabric of his coat, cutting into his skin like a reprimand. He pulled his collar up, sinking into it, his breath visible in the air as he exhaled sharply. His shoes crunched against the snow-tinged pavement as he made his way across the dimly lit parking lot.

The car door creaked open, the engine turning over with a low grumble. For a moment, Jack just sat there, staring at the windscreen as the frost slowly melted under the heat, distorting the world beyond. The late hour pressed in on him, the weight of it suffocating. But sleep was the furthest thing from his mind.

He pulled out of the parking lot, the city slipping by in blurred streaks of orange and white. His thoughts followed the rhythm of the wipers, clearing snow incessantly from the windscreen. The roads were empty, barren, save for the occasional flicker of headlights in the distance, ghostly in the mist. The world outside seemed impossibly still.

It was that figure in the consumed and fragmented photo which haunted him tonight—her eyes, wide with something he couldn't quite place. He couldn't stop thinking about the way the photograph had come together like a cruel joke. All these victims, all these faces, tied together in a puzzle they still hadn't solved. He gripped the steering wheel tighter, the familiar sensation of anger rising up in his chest. Ed had always been so reliable.

The city thinned out as he drove, the lights fading into the distance, giving way to the darker roads that cut through the outskirts. The snow was heavier here, splashing against the windscreen in sheets, the wipers struggling to keep up. Jack squinted through the haze, his vision blurring as fatigue threatened to pull him under. The radio played *Bosco*, by Placebo, softly, low, barely audible over the roar of the rain. It was comforting in a way, though Jack couldn't make out the words. There had to be a pattern, a reason.

Jack's eyes flickered to the rearview mirror, catching a glimpse of his own reflection. The face staring back at him was hollowed, unfamiliar. For a moment, he didn't recognise himself, didn't know the man who had become so consumed by this case, by the dead that haunted him.

He looked away, focusing on the road ahead.

The snow fell harder. The darkness drew closer.

And somewhere, buried deep beneath the storm, was a truth Jack wasn't ready to face.

**

He woke to a muffled silence. The world outside his car had transformed under the fall of snow, thick and blinding in its quietness. He was cocooned under an old blanket, stiff from the cold, but grateful for its thin warmth. The windows of the car were fogged over, the windscreen coated in a dense layer of white, as if the entire night had settled on him, burying him in something both weightless and stifling.

His first thought was that he had probably slept too long, but when he checked the time on the dashboard, a jolt of panic rippled through him. He was going to be late. Damn it, he thought, fingers stiff and fumbling as he struggled to switch the ignition on. The engine sputtered before roaring to life, the heater kicking in with a blast of cold air before gradually warming. He could see nothing beyond the snow-packed windscreen, the world outside still wrapped in a frozen, featureless shroud.

Frantically, Jack grabbed the ice scraper from the glove compartment and stepped out into the bitter air. The snow crunched beneath his boots as he worked to clear the frost from the windscreen, his breath a cloud of steam against the cold. Every motion felt sluggish, as if the weight of the night hadn't just settled on the car, but on his very soul. His mind, still fogged from broken sleep, replayed the events of the past few days in fragmented images—Ed, Charley, Murray. The dead faces. The unanswered questions. The girl in *that* photo.

His fingers numbed quickly, biting into the ice as he scraped at the windscreen, desperate to clear a small patch, just enough to see through. Snow continued to fall, but so much more gently now, as if the sky itself had grown weary from the task. He wiped his brow with the back of his glove, feeling the cold sweat mixing with the snowflakes. It was a bitter, relentless chill that made him feel smaller, like he was shrinking under the weight of it all.

Once he had cleared the worst of the frost, he climbed back into the driver's seat, slamming the door shut against the cold. As Jack slid into the driver's seat, the cold leather biting through his coat, he fumbled with the car stereo. The silence in the car felt oppressive, too powerful to bear alone. His fingers, still stiff from the cold, finally landed on a familiar playlist, and before he could think twice, *Who Knows* by Marion Black began to fill the space. The soulful, melancholy croon of Black's voice seeped into the air, swirling with the remnants of snow on the windscreen. The song's slow, deliberate rhythm matched the quiet beat of his heart, as the lyrics reached deep into the sorrowful corners of his thoughts.

The heater had finally made the car tolerable, and he sat for a moment, fingers wrapped around the wheel, staring at the patch of road that had emerged from the white. A sigh escaped him, long and low, before he shifted into gear and pulled away from the curb. As the car rolled forward, Jack let the music take over, his mind drifting with the bittersweet melody. Who knows what tomorrow would bring? The words tapped into his own uncertainty, a steady reminder that no matter how far he drove or how much distance he put between himself and the past, the questions were always there. As he stared through the partially cleared window at the snow-covered streets, each turn began to feel like he was moving through a dream, Black's voice pulling him deeper into a dream he couldn't quite shake.

London stretched before him in its winter stillness. The snow-covered streets were less busy than he expected, the usual city chaos muted by the weather. Far above, the familiar landmarks stood against the white sky like sentinels: St. Paul's, with its spire glittering like pale gold; the defiant silhouette of Nelson's Monument; the Tower, half-lost in the fog of snow and time. It was as if the city had been arrested, caught in a moment of frozen eternity. Even the sound of the traffic, the distant hum of buses and taxis, felt dim and far away.

But beneath that silence, there was a different sound, one Jack couldn't ignore—a steady, relentless dripping, like the slow beat of a drum. He couldn't tell if it came from outside or inside his own head, but it followed him, unbroken by the weather or the passing of time. It was a grim metronome, ticking away with every second, each drop heavier than the last.

He turned onto the main road, the tires skidding slightly on the slick surface. The buildings blurred into the background as the car moved steadily through the snow-covered streets, the city passing by in a cold, distant dream. There was something about the snowfall, about the empty streets and the way the world seemed to have folded in on itself, that filled him with a sense of foreboding. As if London itself had been swallowed by something vast and impenetrable.

And with it, Jack felt swallowed too.

In the stillness of the car, the sound of *Who Knows* had long since faded, leaving only the hum of the engine and the occasional rattle of the heater. But inside his head, the music played on, repeating those words that troubled at him: *Another day, Just another day, I wanna live, To share the love that only she can give?* The lyrics seemed to drift in and out of his thoughts, not so much a question but a quiet accusation. It tapped into that part of him that had been awake longer than he had—the part that remembered too much.

How had it come to this? How, in the span of just a few days, had his past crept out from its hiding place and begun to wrap its cold fingers around his life again? He could feel it now, like the pressure on his forehead—a gentle, insistent tapping, a reminder that the ghosts he had buried hadn't stayed in their graves. His sense of dread grew with each passing mile, an unease that settled deep in his gut and refused to leave. He had hoped, or at least pretended, that the past could stay where it was, buried in the shadows, under lock and key. But he had known better, hadn't he? In the way a mourner knows that no amount of earth or distance can separate the living from the dead.

By the time he reached Haggard's office, Jack's thoughts had spiralled into a knot of confusion, fear, and something else—something he didn't want to name, but which lingered all the same. Guilt, perhaps. Or maybe it was simply knowing that everything was finally beginning to unravel. The therapy session was a formality now, a way to go through the motions, to tell someone the things that couldn't be said anywhere else.

He parked the car, the snow still falling gently around him, and sat there for a moment, staring at the building. Haggard's office was a modest place, tucked away in a side street, unremarkable in the way that most London buildings were. It was quiet here, removed from the busier streets and the noise of the world. But Jack couldn't shake the feeling that, once he stepped inside, everything would come crashing in on him again—the memories, the guilt, the questions he couldn't answer.

With a sigh, Jack opened the door and stepped out into the cold. The snow crunching beneath his boots as he made his way to the entrance, each step feeling heavier than the last. He wasn't ready for this, not really. But what choice did he have? The past was catching up with him, and he had no way of stopping it. The dripping sound followed him still, echoing in the back of his mind like the slow, inevitable beat of time running out.

Interview Transcript
Date: October 3rd
Location: Dr. Haggard's Office
Participants: DCI Jack Miller, Dr. William Haggard (Psychiatrist)

[10:12 AM]

JM: But I mean, surely my accident was just bad luck, right? Wrong place, wrong time?

WH: Then why blame yourself for it?

JM: I killed someone. It was my fault.

WH: So, you need to take accountability for that, accident or not?

JM: Of course.

WH: Of course. But tell me, Jack... Is there any such thing as luck?

JM: What do you mean?

WH: Do you believe in luck? Pure luck? What does that mean to you?

JM: Well, yes in a way. Like not in the corporate bullshit way that you can make your own... Like by being prepared or ready for opportunity... it's not just luck if preparation helps an outcome... You mean like actual chance, things beyond your control working in your favour?

WH: Yes, or against you. Obviously... Like do you believe in a fatalistic universe, like these things were always going to happen to you, or do you think you're altering the outcomes one day at a time, through freewill?

JM: Yeah, um, I mean I guess I would say that my definition of luck is the chips fall where they may, sometimes they fall on your plate, and sometimes they fall on the floor and a dog eats them.

WH: Amusing. Wrong kind of chips, obviously... but lucky for the dog, right?

JM: I guess I've never thought about the dog.

WH: The dog's perspective?

JM: Yeah... Like every circumstance has a ripple of consequences, obviously. But they can affect some people positively and others negatively.

WH: What might be perceived as good and bad luck? From your own perspective.

JM: Yeah.

WH: We have a tendency not to see the bigger picture, see things from our own perspective.

JM: How we are, not how the world is?

WH: Yes. So much of our reality is shaped by our own thoughts and feelings.

JM: And if we change those, we change the world?

WH: No, sadly the world is still there, full of falling chips. But if our internal self is grounded, we are better placed to take more advantage of the good and be more resilient to the bad.

JM: I think there are rules, if you like, that the universe follows, like cause and effect. So, outcomes can be determined to a certain extent based on actions. And actions can be influenced by outcomes, but freewill is part of that, determining which action we take individually from each outcome.

WH: So, you don't believe in a fully predetermined reality? God's plan?

JM: I don't think God's plan would involve us having no freewill. I don't think that would make sense either.

WH: Because he couldn't test us that way?

JM: I guess not.

WH: Do you think you're being tested, Jack?

JM: Sometimes.

WH: How do you think you're doing?

JM: Mostly failing.

WH: Mostly?

JM: I get some results... But, Doc, I don't believe having freewill means things don't happen for a reason.

WH: People have their reasons.

JM: Yeah, often complex. No two people react the same way to the same event or have access to the same opportunities. I don't think any of these ideas have to be mutually exclusive.

WH: And, Jack, I'm not looking for a way of saying the accident wasn't your fault.

JM: You're not?

WH: No, Jack. I'm happy for you to take responsibility for it.

JM: Thanks, Doc. I appreciate that... So where are you going with this?

WH: I'm just trying to understand your belief system... Sometimes things happen seemingly out of nowhere, but they're just ripples from someone else's story that present themselves to you as chance events.

JM: Yeah, I get you... You know, there's another detail with this case, a woman in a photograph. It's... hard to explain. There's this feeling I can't shake. Like I know her... the woman in the photo. I don't, of course. She's no one I recognise, but she feels... familiar. Like she's trying to tell me something, but I don't know what it is.

WH: Do you think that's why you've been so haunted by it? Because you feel like there's a connection?

JM: Yeah, maybe. There's this, this... personal edge to it. Like it's not just another case. It's more than that. And I don't know why it feels that way, but it does. Every time I look at the fragments, that image of her in the dimly lit room, it feels like she's waiting for me to figure it out.

WH: So, this woman... in the photo... you think she's speaking to you?

JM: Well, not literally, no. But it's like... she's haunting the case, haunting me. I can't put my finger on it, but I can't stop thinking about her, either. She's got this look in her eyes, this... sadness. It's like she's telling me she's not finished yet. That we're not finished yet.

WH: Could it be that this sense of familiarity, this feeling that it's personal, is what's making the case so difficult for you? Because you're trying to make sense of something that feels like it's been... intertwined with your own experience?

JM: Yeah, maybe. That's what it feels like. Like our histories are tied together somehow, even if I don't understand it. And that's the thing about history, isn't it? It's not just about what happened—it's about what we carry with us. What we choose to remember. Maybe that's what's happening here. It feels like there's something I should remember, something from... I don't know. It's like she's part of a story I don't know yet.

WH: So, tell me more about where you are with the case. Do you have any suspects?

JM: Yeah. A dead one, now, a low-level criminal. The evidence against him is circumstantial, really. Like I said, I've got this nagging feeling that there's more to it. His profile doesn't really match the killer's.

WH: Jack, I've always been impressed by your ability to see things from different perspectives. You often have a level of insight that surprises me. Usually, people come to me lacking that awareness about their own thinking or their situation. So, with all of that in mind, I'd like to ask you this: what is it that you actually feel right now? About your situation, the case, everything?

JM: It's... it's hard to explain. There's a feeling, a sense of dread, I suppose. Like... like my time is running out. I can't really describe it, not in a way that makes sense. It's just this nagging weight on my chest, this sense that something's coming, and I'm not ready for it.

WH: Can you pinpoint when that feeling started? Was it tied to this case, or something else?

JM: I can't help but feel that woman's story is unfinished, that she's trapped in this cycle of violence and pain. And it's like... I'm her only chance to make it right. It's almost suffocating, knowing that I might be the one person who can give her a voice. But what if I fail?

WH: That's a heavy burden to bear. It sounds like you feel this obligation to her... to see her as a person, to honour her memory in some way. But in doing that, you're also risking your own emotional well-being, aren't you?

JM: It feels that way. I keep thinking about how she's trapped, just like I am. I want to free her, to give her justice, but in doing so, I'm also exposing myself to all this pain. And maybe that's why I'm so scared. Because once you start digging, you never know what you might unearth... I just wish I could see a way out. I want to break free from this... cycle of dread... to feel like I'm in control again.

WH: And what would that look like for you? What would it take for you to feel in control again?

JM: Maybe it starts with finding a way to process this fear, to confront the ghosts instead of running from them. If I can acknowledge them, maybe I can take back some control.

WH: That's a powerful insight, Jack. Acknowledgment is the first step in reclaiming your power. You've always had the ability to see things from different angles. It's time to turn that lens back on yourself and face what's there. You might find that the answers you seek are closer than you think... Jack, before you go, I've been thinking about something... There's an interesting parallel between what you and I do. Both of us are trying to get to the truth, in different ways. You, with your evidence and suspects, piecing together what's real and what's not. Me, with my patients, trying to help them connect the dots of their own story... figuring out what fits, what's been misplaced, and what needs healing.

JM: Yeah, I can see that. We're both searching for something, right? A version of the truth, or at least a version that makes sense.

WH: Graham Greene wrote it, actually... That psychoanalysis is a bit like journeying without a map, but the terrain is the mind... And just like in your work, there are times when things seem chaotic, when the pieces don't seem to fit together. But eventually, with enough patience and attention, they start to form a pattern. It's not always about finding the truth right away... it's about finding the right order. And once you do, things fall into place.

JM: The right order? That's interesting... because sometimes that's exactly what it feels like. Like the pieces are there, scattered, but I'm struggling to see how they connect. How they tell a story.

WH: You'll appreciate this, being a poetry man—Samuel Taylor Coleridge once said that poetry is "the best words in the best order." That's what makes it resonate... It's not just the words themselves, it's the way they're arranged, the way they reveal a deeper truth. Maybe it's the same for evidence in your line of work. It's not just about the facts themselves but how they fit together. The story they tell when they're in the right order.

JM: Yeah, I know that quote... It's the difference between noise and meaning. But evidence? That's a bit messier. There's no poetic flow to blood stains or autopsy reports.

WH: Maybe not in the obvious sense, but there's still a rhythm to it, isn't there? A pattern. A body in a crime scene tells its own story, whether we listen to it or not. The difference between us is I'm trying to help people make sense of their internal worlds, and you're out there in the external one, trying to bring some kind of order to the chaos. But in the end, it's all about connections. We're both looking for them... In here, I help patients figure out which parts of their story they've repressed or misunderstood. Out there, you're doing the same, just with physical evidence.

JM: I guess you're right. It's like I'm always sifting through fragments... photos, fibres, fingerprints... and trying to see the story they're telling me. Just like you're trying to sift through someone's history, their traumas, trying to help them see what they've missed.

WH: Exactly. It's about understanding the connections between seemingly random pieces of information. Nothing is ever completely isolated, Jack. Everything's linked. Even when it feels like the threads are too thin to see, they are there. It's about finding the right lens to look through. The right perspective.

JM: Yeah... you're probably right.

WH: Let me ask you this: What do you feel when you look at that photo? What's the first thing that comes to mind?

JM: Dread. And... guilt, maybe. Like I'm missing something, like I've already failed. There's a sense of finality to it, but also that it's not over yet.

WH: Finality... or something unfinished?

JM: Both. That's the weird part. It feels like this case is the end of something, but also the start of something else. Like a chapter closing, but another one opening. I don't know, it's hard to explain.

WH: That's not uncommon, especially when you're dealing with unresolved trauma—whether it's from the past or something happening in the present. Sometimes our minds create narratives to make sense of things that are inherently difficult to process. But those narratives can also trap us. Keep us from seeing the bigger picture.

JM: So, you're saying I'm trapped in my own story?

WH: Not trapped, exactly. But maybe you've got so used to seeing things from a certain angle that you've missed the larger context. It's like looking at a photograph too closely... you see every detail, every flaw, but you lose sight of the whole image. Step back, and maybe it'll start to make more sense.

JM: Yes. Maybe.

WH: Think about the case in the same way. What's the bigger picture you're not seeing? You've got the details... the photo fragments, the silver halide, the woman in the dimly lit room... but what's the story they're telling you when you put them together?

JM: The right order... it's all about the order...

WH: And isn't that the same with everything in life? We get so caught up in the minutiae that we forget to step back and see how everything connects.

JM: You're right. The case, Charley, the past... I've been looking at it all like separate issues. But maybe they're not. Maybe they're all connected, just like the evidence... I need to go, Doc. It's...

WH: Something becoming clear?

JM: Yes... yeah, I think it is. I've been looking at this case all wrong. At everything all wrong.

WH: Well, that sounds like a breakthrough, Jack. But don't rush. Take the time to think it through... Just remember, it's not about solving everything at once. It's about finding the right order. The best words in the best order, right?

JM: Thanks, Haggard. I'll let you know how it goes.

WH: You know where to find me.

[End of Recording]

28

'Denial — is the only fact'

The door to Haggard's office clicked shut behind him with a soft finality, but the sound reverberated in his mind like a gavel. Jack's legs moved before his thoughts could catch up, carrying him down the narrow hallway toward the stairwell. His footsteps echoed against the bare walls, the sound hollow, distant, like someone else's footsteps in someone else's life. For a moment, the world felt paper-thin, as if it might tear at the slightest touch and expose something raw underneath.

Haggard's words lingered—sharp, like the cool edge of a blade, cutting through the fog in his mind. Jack had always prided himself on seeing things from multiple perspectives, always looking for the pattern beneath the chaos. But this time, he'd been too close, too immersed in the case to see it clearly. The order. The damn order. They'd been looking at the bodies, the victims, in the sequence they were found. But Emily Isherwood had been killed before Lauren Donne. It was the timeline that mattered.

He reached the stairs, pushing the heavy fire door with even more force than was really necessary. It swung open with a creak, and the cold darkness of the stairwell greeted him like a deep, waiting pit. The light above flickered briefly, casting long shadows on the chipped concrete steps, but Jack hardly noticed. He took the stairs two at a time, his mind racing faster than his legs, chasing a revelation that was only half-formed. Haggard's voice, measured and calm, continued to whisper in his head, piecing together fragments that he should have seen earlier.

The chill in the stairwell was oppressive, biting through his suit jacket and settling in his bones. He'd left the top buttons of his shirt undone, and his tie hung loose around his neck like an afterthought. As he reached the bottom of the stairwell, he slowed, the cold air seeping further into his skin, into his thoughts. He felt as though he were moving through molasses—each step deliberate, weighted, pulling him back. The fire exit loomed ahead, the door to the outside world. Jack hesitated for a brief moment, one hand resting on the cold metal bar, and then he pushed it open.

The morning hit him like a physical blow. The crisp air swept over him, sharp and biting, curling around his exposed skin like a reprimand. It was a cold that carried the scent of snow, though much of it had already begun to thaw. The world outside was bright, light from the morning sun gleamed against the wet and snowy pavements, giving the city an unnatural sheen, as if it had been varnished in silver. The snow that still lingered in patches was no longer the soft, clean white of earlier—it was hardening, turning grey and brittle underfoot.

Jack pulled his jacket tighter around him, but the cold seemed to have taken root inside, where no amount of fabric could reach. He made his way across the narrow parking lot behind Haggard's building, his shoes slapping against the damp concrete. His car was parked near the far corner, half hidden in shadow, a dark silhouette against the grimy snow. As he approached, his breath came in quick, visible puffs, the urgency returning to his step. He fumbled in his pocket for his phone, pulling it out with fingers still stiff from the cold. His first instinct was to call Ed. He needed to reach him.

Now. His thumb hovered over the contact list, and then he pressed Ed's name.

The phone rang once. Twice.

Jack clenched his jaw, glancing around the empty car park as though expecting someone to materialise out of the shadows. He shifted from foot to foot, his impatience a sharp contrast to the stillness around him. The phone rang again.

Pick up, damn it.

Voicemail.

The mechanical voice on the other end was like a slap. Jack cursed under his breath and hung up, dialling again, the sense of urgency swelling inside him like a rising tide. But even as he did, the weight of the realisation began to settle—a dreadful, inescapable feeling that he was too late.

The voicemail again.

He swore, louder this time, and shoved the phone back into his pocket, but it did nothing to stem the rising tide of panic. His breath hitched, his mind racing through the details, trying to untangle the knots that had tightened around the case, around him.

Emily Isherwood was killed after Lauren Donne. The timeline had shifted, and with it, the entire case. The bodies had misled them—found in the wrong order, presenting a false narrative. But if Emily had died after Lauren, then something else was at play. Something darker. Something more deliberate.

The realisation gripped him like a vice. He should have seen it earlier. He should have—

Jack slammed his fist against the car door in frustration, the metal buckling slightly under the force. The pain flared through his cold knuckles, sharp and immediate, but it didn't ground him. If anything, it only heightened the tension thrumming through his veins.

He leaned against the cold metal of the car, staring at the wet, gleaming pavement beneath his feet, his breath coming in sharp, irregular bursts. The silence moved in around him, its choking embrace broken only by the faint hum of distant traffic. His mind was spinning, trying to connect the dots, but every thought only led him back to the same place.

He couldn't shake the image of the woman in the photograph, her eyes looking straight into the camera, pleading, accusing. The woman who seemed to be reaching out to him, even now. He had felt something the moment he saw her—something beyond the usual sense of duty, of wanting to catch the person responsible. It had felt personal, in a way he hadn't been able to articulate before.

Jack opened the car door and slid into the driver's seat. The cold leather bit into his skin, but he barely noticed. His hands gripped the steering wheel tightly, knuckles white, the tension in his muscles coiled and ready to snap. He stared out through the windscreen, the snow reflecting an eerie glow that felt otherworldly.

He started the car, the engine rumbling to life beneath him, and for a moment, he sat there, staring at the empty parking lot. With a sharp breath, he pulled the car into gear and drove out into the snow-covered streets of London, the cold air pressing in from all sides.

Jack's hands gripped the steering wheel tight, the cold leather biting into his skin as he sped through the quiet London streets. His breath came in shallow, sharp bursts, each one fogging the windscreen for a split second before disappearing. The city outside his window blurred into a smear of snow-slick pavements, and the occasional passing silhouette—a world oblivious to the storm building inside his head.

He tried Ed's number again, his fingers trembling slightly as he hit the button on the hands-free system. The ringing tone filled the car, maddening in its insistence. Jack's thoughts raced, fragments of the case swirling in a tangled mess, each piece packed with a significance he hadn't fully grasped until now.

The order. The victims. It had all seemed random at first—a string of tragic deaths, each one cruel but unconnected beyond the violence. But now, the pattern was emerging. The pieces had started to fall into place back in Haggard's office, but they were sliding into focus now, hard and clear, like the sharp crack of a bone setting into place.

Caroline Whitman. The first. Her name had felt so incidental, so far removed from the others. A woman from Camden with a troubled past. He'd almost forgotten her until now. Hannah Ibsen. Ariana Lawrence. Rosie Larkin. Then Lauren Donne. Then Emily Isherwood. Finally, Yasmin Eliot. Each name, each life, carved into his memory. Each woman carefully killed. Each woman even more carefully chosen.

The ringing stopped suddenly, and Jack tensed, hoping for Ed's voice—hoping for something.

Voicemail. Again.

Jack let out a low growl of frustration, punching the steering wheel. He could hear his own breath quickening, the tension in his chest swelling. He tried to steady his voice, focusing on the message he needed to leave.

"Ed," he began, his voice low, tight. "Ed, you need to call me. There's something... something bigger here. The victims—it wasn't random. It was never random."

He paused, his mind racing to assemble the pieces. Caroline Whitman, Hannah Ibsen, Ariana Lawrence, Rosie Larkin, Lauren Donne, Emily Isherwood, Yasmin Eliot. The names rattled through his mind, one after another. Each a letter, each a part of a larger whole, a grotesque puzzle only now revealing its final form.

"Think about it, Ed," Jack continued, his voice barely above a whisper now, as though saying it out loud would make it real. "The first letter of every first name, in the right order. Caroline. Hannah. Ariana. Rosie. Lauren. Emily. Yasmin. C. H. A. R. L. E. Y."

The name hung in the air like a curse, sending a shiver down Jack's spine. But it didn't stop there. The killer hadn't stopped with first names. The last names, too, held their own grisly message.

"Whitman. Ibsen. Lawrence. Larkin. Donne. Isherwood. Eliot. W. I. L. L. D. I. E."

Jack's pulse quickened. It was as if the letters had rearranged themselves on the evidence board in his mind, spelling out a message that had been there all along but hidden in plain sight. Charley will die. The gruesome prophecy echoed in his head like a tolling bell, deep and resonant, each strike shaking something loose inside him.

Ed's voicemail beeped—cutting him off mid-thought—and then the line went dead.

Jack swore under his breath, his fingers clenching around the wheel again, harder this time. He took a sharp turn down a side street, barely registering the snow crunching beneath his tires or the way the world outside had gone eerily still. The cold had become secondary, the numbness of it almost welcome against the heat of his panic.

The killer knows me.

It wasn't just a hunch anymore. It wasn't just the feeling of being watched, or the subtle clues he'd been too slow to piece together. This was personal. The victims, the messages, the whole twisted game—it had all been aimed at him. The killer had been playing him from the start, moving pieces around on a board Jack hadn't even realised existed.

But why? Why now? Who was behind this, and how had he missed it for so long?

Jack's mind raced through the possibilities, but every theory only led him back to the same, terrifying conclusion. Whoever this was, they knew him intimately—knew how he worked, knew his weaknesses, and, worst of all, knew Charley. The one person who still meant something in this cold, fractured world of his.

He couldn't lose her.

The thought hit him like a fist in the gut, doubling him over as he pulled the car into an empty alley and slammed on the brakes. His heart pounded in his chest, his breath ragged as he stared outwards, hands trembling on the steering wheel. The name—her name—kept repeating itself in his mind, each syllable a dagger twisting deeper.

Charley will die.

It wasn't just a threat. It was a promise.

Jack fumbled for his phone again, the urgency rising with each second that ticked by. He couldn't wait for Ed anymore. He needed to reach Charley. Now. His fingers flew over the screen, dialling her number with a desperation that bordered on panic.

The phone rang once. Twice.

Jack's pulse raced in time with the ringing. He glanced around the darkened alley, his paranoia prickling at the edges of his awareness. Every shadow seemed to shift, every creak of the car settling felt like a footstep drawing closer.

Jack's mind churned as he tried to make sense of it all. The killer's message had been clear, but the motive was still murky. Revenge? It had to be. But revenge for what? Jack had put away plenty of people over the years—enough to have made enemies. But none of them had ever been this meticulous, this careful in crafting such an elaborate plan. There was something else, something deeper. His mind flashed back to the evidence board, to the letters and the names and the chilling message they spelled out. He could see them so clearly now.

His heart jumped when his phone buzzed, breaking the taut silence inside the car. He fumbled to grab it, his breath catching in his throat, half-expecting it to be Ed finally returning his call, but it wasn't Ed. It was Charley. Swiping at the screen, the glow of the message cutting through the shadows like a lighthouse beam in a storm. His pulse quickened as he read her text.

Help Jack, I need you to come and get me. Ed's gone missing. Christian went looking for him. I've found Chris but I'm stranded. I'll send my location.

For a split second, relief flooded him—she was alive, and she had reached out. But the relief was fleeting, replaced immediately by a wave of cold dread. Ed was missing. The situation was rapidly unravelling into something far more sinister, something darker than he had anticipated.

The next message came in almost instantly, a pin drop on the screen marking her location: an industrial estate near the Thames, a few miles away. The name of the place tugged at something in his mind, but he didn't have time to think. The sight of her message, her cry for help, consumed him.

"I'm on my way." Jack typed back hastily, fingers tapping the letters in sharp staccato, but as soon as he hit 'send,' the screen flickered and went black. The final traces of his half-charged battery had given up in the cold.

"Shit!" Jack cursed, slamming his hand against the dashboard in frustration. His breath came out in quick, frantic bursts as the implications of his dead phone hit him. No way to contact Charley again. No way to warn her if something went wrong.

The cold air from the outside still seeped into the car, the last remnants of snow clinging to the windows in melting patches. Every thought, every worry, blurred together in his mind as he tried to push through the mounting panic.

He yanked the car into gear, pulling out from the alleyway, the engine roaring as he sped down the narrow streets, the tires slapping against the slush that clung stubbornly to the asphalt. His eyes flicked between the road and the map burned into his mind. The industrial estate by the Thames. He knew it vaguely—a collection of forgotten warehouses and shipping containers along the river, a relic of London's industrial past. It was the kind of place that always felt deserted, long abandoned by the ebb and flow of the city's pulse. Jack's mind churned with questions as he drove. Why was she there? What had led her to this desolate part of the city, and how had Ed gone missing? The case, the killings—they felt so far away and yet right here, tightening around him like a noose. The killer's game was no longer abstract, no longer some distant mystery he could investigate at arm's length. It had become personal, an entanglement of names, faces, and lives that all pointed towards him. Towards Charley.

Blue lights on, he pushed his foot harder on the pedal, feeling the car shift beneath him as he tore through the winding streets. The city seemed to fold away into the distance, the familiar lights of central London fading behind him, replaced by long stretches of empty roads, industrial buildings, and cold, lifeless warehouses. The snow on the ground had melted into dirty slush, the remnants of the previous night's frost still clinging to the rooftops in patches.

It was then, as the car moved closer to the river, that the Thames came into view. The grey waters snaked through the city like a silent witness, its surface dark and rippling, glistening under the weak sunlight filtering through the clouds. The buildings around him were a patchwork of crumbling brick and steel, remnants of an era when this part of London had been alive with the hum of machines, ships, and men. Now, it was ghostly, empty, an echo of a city that had moved on, but not forgotten.

Jack pulled off the main road, following the narrow, winding streets that led toward the estate. The landscape became more desolate with each turn—rusted fences, broken windows, and graffiti-splattered walls stretched out on either side of him, the occasional flicker of a security light the only sign of life.

He glanced at his phone again, but it was useless now—a dead screen, a broken connection. He could only hope that Charley was still there, still safe, wherever she was hiding.

Finally, the industrial estate loomed in front of him, a cluster of low, squat buildings and storage units laid out like forgotten dominoes. Jack eased the car to a stop near a stack of abandoned shipping containers, the sound of the engine dying as he pulled the keys from the ignition. For a moment, he sat there in the cold silence—the fear, the uncertainty, and the urgency all pressed down on him.

Without wasting another second, he climbed out of the car, the sharp bite of the air hitting him again like a slap. His boots crunched against the frost-covered ground as he scanned the area, his eyes sweeping over the warehouses, trying to find any sign of movement. He checked the location on his phone again, but it was pointless. The last coordinates Charley had sent were etched in his memory, and he knew she was close. Somewhere in this maze of steel and concrete, she was waiting for him.

"Charley!" Jack called out, his voice echoing off the empty buildings.

Nothing. Only the low hum of the river in the distance, the gentle slap of water against the banks.

He cursed under his breath, his heart pounding in his chest. His breath was shallow now, each exhale a puff of white mist in the frigid air. He moved quickly, his footsteps purposeful but cautious, as he approached one of the larger warehouses. The door was slightly ajar, hanging on its rusted hinges like a broken promise.

Jack pushed the door open, the metal groaning under his touch. Inside, the darkness swallowed him whole. The only light came from the broken windows above, casting long, jagged shadows across the floor. The interior was a vast, empty expanse—rows of forgotten machinery, rusted and lifeless, stood like silent sentinels in the gloom.

"Charley!" he called again, louder this time, his voice breaking the heavy stillness.

A faint sound reached him—something shifting in the distance, like a footstep or the scrape of metal. Jack froze, his senses suddenly on high alert. He listened closely, his eyes narrowing as he scanned the shadows, every instinct screaming at him to be ready for anything. He stepped further into the warehouse, his boots echoing off the concrete floor. His heart thudded in his chest as he moved toward the source of the sound, each step measured, deliberate. The cold air clung to him, biting at his skin, but he barely felt it now. The tension was electric, the kind that made every nerve in his body feel like it was humming.

And then he saw her.

29

'Had this one Day not been'

The light was dim, filtering through the dusty windows high above, casting long shadows that crept like dark fingers across the cold, concrete floor. Jack's breath hung in the air, a cloud of white mist in the freezing warehouse. The silence pressed down on him, the only sound his own heartbeat drumming in his ears.

Charley was there, tied to a chair, her wrists bound tightly to the arms, her legs secured to the legs. A strip of dirty cloth gagged her mouth, and her eyes—wild, wide, and glistening with tears—locked onto Jack's the moment he stepped into the room. The plea in her face cut him deeper than any words could. She shook her head slightly, her movements frantic but restrained, as if she was trying to scream through the gag. He could see the way her body trembled, not just from the cold, but from the raw fear radiating from her like a current.

For a moment, the world narrowed to just that—the look in her eyes. She was terrified. Begging for help but without making a sound. His first instinct, a primal one, screamed at him to run to her, to tear the ropes from her wrists, to tell her it was going to be okay. His muscles tensed, ready to move—

But then, he saw Christian. Slumped next to her, tied in the same brutal position as Charley. His head slumped to one side, his face pale, his lips slightly parted as if he'd been knocked unconscious. A dark bruise bloomed on his temple, and the slow rise and fall of his chest was the only sign of life. The sight of him, so still, added a new layer to Jack's panic. Christian had gone looking for Ed, and now he was here, incapacitated, like a pawn sacrificed in some cruel game. Jack took a step forward, his mind already racing with ways to free them both, but before he could move any closer, a voice came from the shadows, low and calm, yet dripping with menace.

"Sorry, Jack, it won't be that simple, I'm afraid."

The voice sent a shiver down Jack's spine. He turned sharply, his eyes scanning the darkness that clung to the edges of the room.

Seth.

He stepped forward, his movements deliberate, slow, his face twisted into a smile that didn't reach his cold, calculating eyes. In his hand, the gleam of metal—the barrel of a gun, pointed casually in Jack's direction, as if it were just an extension of his hand, something he carried like a set of keys. There was no hesitation, no doubt in the way Seth held it. He was in control. He was enjoying this.

Jack's stomach churned as Seth's words hung in the air, heavy and final. He narrowed his eyes, trying to focus through the fog of adrenaline and fear. The figure standing before him, Seth, was familiar—too familiar. But something was off, something was making it difficult to place him, to connect the dots. He studied the man's appearance, his weathered face framed by a rough beard that seemed new, a recent addition. It threw Jack off. There was something deliberate about it, a disguise maybe, or just an attempt to change, to become someone else. But the longer Jack looked, the more he noticed, and then it hit him. Dark green. Brown corduroy collar. The waxed jacket. Just like the one Murray had been wearing the day he'd died.

Seth noticed the flicker of recognition in Jack's eyes, a smirk creeping across his face as if he could read Jack's thoughts. He looked down at his jacket and gave a casual shrug.

"Oh, this?" Seth's voice was low, with a trace of amusement. "Yes, Jack, Murray's not the only man to own one, you know. I liked Murray's sense of style so much that I went out and got my own."

Jack's mind raced, piecing together fragments of conversations, faces, moments. Murray. The jacket. Seth. It was all connected somehow, but the full picture still eluded him. He glanced over at Christian again, still slumped in the chair, his head lolling to the side, unconscious but alive. The bruise on his temple was dark, ugly, but the steady rise and fall of his chest gave Jack some small comfort. Seth, sensing Jack's concern, tilted his head in Christian's direction.

"Don't worry about him. He's okay. It's worse than it looks," Seth said, his tone oddly reassuring. "He's sedated, that's all... I didn't hit him that hard."

Jack didn't respond, but his jaw clenched. Christian's motionless body, Charley's terror-stricken eyes—this wasn't just some random act of violence. There was a purpose to this, a twisted design that Seth had been working towards. Jack could feel it in the air, in the way Seth stood there, calm but on edge, like a man walking a tightrope between control and collapse.

Seth's eyes flickered, something dark and wounded passing across his face. "Murray lived below me. I gave a statement to your colleagues the other night, actually, about his little night games... Sent him the earring by the way, Yasmin's, I left it outside his front door in a little envelope." He seemed in control, but there was an undercurrent of emotion running beneath the surface, something raw and unresolved. "The penny I got from him in change. Asked him to order me some camera stuff... Must admit though, when I led you to him, I never imagined he'd end up dead... He was meant to just be a distraction."

Jack could see it now—the tension in Seth's body, the way his grip tightened around the gun ever so slightly as he spoke.

"I'm sure you're wondering why you're here," Seth continued, his voice quieter now, almost introspective. "What it's all been for."

Jack's pulse quickened. The puzzle pieces were still shifting in his mind, but the outline was becoming clearer. This was personal. Jack could see it in the way Seth's eyes flicked between him and Charley, in the way his voice cracked just slightly when he spoke. He was a man at breaking point, a man who had been pushed to the edge and was now teetering, emotions spilling over.

"You have no idea, do you?" Seth asked, his eyes bristling with intensity, his voice almost trembling. "No idea what it's like to feel like this... to be this close to losing everything."

Jack's mind churned, trying to place Seth, to fit the pieces of this puzzle together. But the harder he focused, the more elusive the connection became. There was a familiarity in Seth's eyes, something buried beneath the weariness and bitterness, but it remained just out of reach. Jack's instincts screamed at him to stay calm, to wait for a clue, for something to tip the balance of his confusion into clarity.

Seth seemed to sense Jack's struggle, his mouth curling into a grim smile, one that didn't quite reach his eyes. He shifted his weight, lowering the gun just slightly but keeping it trained on Jack. His tone softened, as if speaking to an old friend.

"This has obviously taken a considerable amount of planning," Seth said, almost conversationally, but there was an edge to his voice, a hint of frustration buried beneath the calm. "I almost hoped you'd work it out beforehand. I know how good you are at your job." The last sentence was delivered with a sneer, it wasn't a sincere compliment. It was simply an acknowledgement that Jack kept his job because he delivered results.

Jack's chest tightened, a creeping sense of dread washing over him as Seth's words lingered in the air. The timeline slid into place like a dagger twisting in his gut. Whatever this was, it had been in motion long before Jack had any inkling of it. Seth had been biding his time, weaving this web with meticulous care, waiting for the right moment to strike.

"I'd say it's probably been about ten years in the making," Seth continued, his voice lower now, almost reflective. "Give or take."

Jack's breath caught in his throat as the creeping realisation began to sink in. His mind raced back through the years, scanning through cases, faces, moments that could have led them to this very point. A dark, gnawing feeling took root inside him. This wasn't just a random act of vengeance or violence—this was personal. And somehow, in the recesses of his memory, Jack had been part of it.

"I'd only stopped for a moment, you know?" Seth's voice trembled, a bitter laugh escaping his lips as he continued, his gaze suddenly distant, as if remembering something long buried. "To tie my shoelace."

The words hit Jack like a punch to the gut. The simplicity of it, the absurdity of what Seth was saying, made the force of it even heavier. Seth's laugh was strained, hollow, like a man laughing at his own tragedy because there was nothing left to do but laugh.

"That's all it took, you know?" Seth's voice cracked, the emotion creeping through, his mask of control slipping for just a second. "A shoelace. And a cup of coffee, apparently. Little things that cost me everything."

Jack's stomach turned. He could feel the truth looming in the darkness, pressing closer, suffocating. He still couldn't place the exact moment, the exact memory that would snap this whole thing into focus, but it was coming. Seth's eyes locked onto his, pleading yet angry, as if he wanted Jack to understand, to feel the depth of his grief, his rage. The moment Seth had lost everything was right there, hanging between them, just waiting to be acknowledged.

And there it was. The memory surfaced like a jagged rock breaking through still water, unstoppable now that it had started to rise. Jack's mind reeled back to that day—frantic, flashing lights illuminating the already bright streets. The chase. The wail of sirens in the distance, cutting through the tension as his foot punching harder on the accelerator. The pothole he hadn't seen until it was too late, the sudden jolt that rocked the car, sending the cup of coffee from the holder onto his lap. The burn, the scalding liquid soaking into his trousers. The instinctive reach to swipe it away.

And then—the sound.

That deafening, sickening thud. Flesh and bone against metal. A mass slamming onto the bonnet, followed by the impossible stillness that overtakes everything in the moments afterward. The breathless, horrible silence that filled the space where life had just been.

SIMONE.

The name ricocheted through Jack's mind like a bullet, tearing through whatever defences he had left. He hadn't said her name in years, hadn't allowed himself to even think it. But now, here, with Seth standing before him, it came flooding back with the force of everything he'd buried.

Seth's eyes narrowed, reading the shift in Jack's expression. He didn't need to say anything to confirm what

Seth already knew. The recognition had bloomed in Jack's face, and with it, the guilt that had been quietly festering beneath the surface all this time.

"Ah, there it is," Seth said, his voice low and cold, but tinged with something else—satisfaction, perhaps, or vindication. "You do remember her, don't you?"

Jack swallowed hard, his throat tight, constricting. His stomach churned with a sickness that clawed at his insides, threatening to rise. He nodded, but it was a weak, almost involuntary movement. The words caught in his throat, "I—" His voice faltered. "I've never forgotten her."

"Never forgotten?" Seth's anger flared, sharp and bitter. "And yet you never even utter her name." The tremor in his voice betrayed the calm exterior he was trying to maintain, the cracks in his composure widening. "I was wondering how many more clues you'd need, Jack."

Jack's mind spun, trying to grasp the full implication of what was happening. Simone. The girl on that street. The girl whose life he had taken in an instant of distraction, in a moment of careless reflex. It had been an accident, the court had said. No charges. No crime. He'd been allowed to continue on active duty. A tragic accident. But here, now, in the cold light of this moment, facing Seth, it felt like a crime all the same. He could see it in Seth's eyes—this was about revenge, retribution for the life that had been stolen, for pain that had never gone away. Jack realised with mounting horror that Seth had spent a decade waiting for this moment, weaving together this elaborate trap, every move carefully calculated to bring him to his knees.

Jack's heart pounded in his chest, the force of the past crashing into him like a tidal wave. His throat tightened as the name finally surfaced, a ghost breaking free from the prison he had kept it locked in for so long. His voice cracked as he spoke, tentative, barely audible, as if giving sound to it would shatter him.

"Seth... Seth Curtis." He stared at the man standing before him, the shadows playing cruel tricks on his familiar yet unfamiliar face. The pieces fell into place with a sickening clarity. "You were her boyfriend."

Seth's expression hardened. His lips twisted into something between a grimace and a sneer. "Fiancé," he corrected coldly, his voice steady, but with the unmistakable tremor of a man clinging to fraying edges of control. "We were going to get married, Jack. I bought her a ring. We were planning a life together. She was expecting our child... of course, you know that..." His breath hitched, words failing him momentarily as his grip tightened around the gun. "And then you... you—"

The air between them was electric with tension, thick with years of unspoken grief and resentment. Seth took a step closer, his boots grinding against the cold concrete floor with a chilling finality. He studied Jack's face with a calculating stare, his eyes burning with anger and something darker, something more dangerous.

"Who was she, Jack?" Seth's voice dropped into a low, taunting murmur. "The girl in that photograph. Last photo taken of her before she died. I have it up in my flat... I'd not long got my camera, started taking pictures... it was so blurry and grainy, but she looked beautiful to me anyway... Do you even remember her."

He took another step forward, his eyes piercing through Jack. "Because I see her every day. Laid out in the street like she was discarded by life. Her hand—" His voice broke, the emotional weight unbearable to him. "Her hand outstretched, grasping. Like she was trying to catch her soul, stop it from leaving her body."

Jack winced, the memory slamming into him again with brutal force. He could see it—her—Simone, crumpled on the pavement, her body lifeless, yet her hand reaching, reaching for something he would never understand. The sight of it had haunted him, waking him in the dead of night, but he had buried it deep, refusing to let it take him. And now Seth stood before him, dragging it back into the light, tearing open wounds Jack thought had scarred over.

"Just like you laid out every one of those girls..." Jack said, comprehending the detail in each of those seven crime scenes that had felt so very familiar to him.

Seth continued, his voice gaining momentum, feeding off Jack's guilt like a predator toying with its prey. "Just like it. A simple clue, each one of them a step closer to this moment. And you—" He shook his head, a bitter laugh escaping him. "You couldn't even say her name, could you? Not once. Not even to yourself."

Jack's breath was shallow, each word from Seth chipping away at the walls he had built around his shame. His heart thundered in his chest, and his lips trembled as he tried to speak, but the words lodged in his throat like stones.

"Simone..." He finally uttered, the name slipping from him like a whispered confession. Broken. Defeated. A name that hadn't passed his lips in more years than he could remember yet was burned to his mind like a hot-branded cattle. "Simone Kamara."

The sound of her name hung in the air between them, as if it had been waiting all this time to be released, to be acknowledged. Jack's voice cracked, and he felt the sharp sting of tears he had never allowed himself to shed. For a moment, there was silence, save for the shallow breaths both men took. Seth's face twisted into something raw, anguished, as he watched Jack crumble. And there, in the dimly lit room, the pain of twelve long years bled into the air like a wound that had never healed.

Seth stared at Jack; his eyes cold but gleaming with a quiet satisfaction. "See? That wasn't so hard, was it?" His voice was a twisted mockery of compassion. "Just to acknowledge her existence. Just to say her name." He stepped closer, and Jack could feel the weight of his presence, the tension humming between them.

Jack's throat was dry, his heart pounding with a mixture of dread and pity. He looked into Seth's eyes and saw a man broken, lost, consumed by an anger that had festered for a decade. "Seth, I'm sorry," Jack said, his voice low, almost pleading. "I'm truly sorry for what happened that day. But none of this... this madness... is going to bring her back."

Seth's lips tightened into a thin, bitter line. He shook his head, a hollow chuckle escaping him. "You think I don't know that?" He stepped back, pacing the room with a restless energy. "It's not about bringing her back. This was never about some impossible wish to undo what's been done." He turned sharply, his eyes locking onto Jack's with a fierce intensity. "This is about you facing it, Jack. Taking some accountability, in front of the world. About you standing in front of some kind of judgment for what you did."

Jack's stomach twisted as he tried to hold Seth's gaze. He could feel the desperation in his own voice as he spoke. "But surely... surely Simone wouldn't want this. She wouldn't want you to become... to become *this*. Not for her sake."

Seth paused, the words hanging in the air. His expression darkened, the tension building as if the walls themselves were closing in on them. "Become what, Jack?" His voice was dangerously soft. "What have I become?"

Jack's breath caught in his throat. He wanted to say it, the word hovering on the tip of his tongue—monster. But he couldn't. Not like this. Not when he could see the pain burning so raw in Seth's eyes. "You've taken the lives of seven girls, Seth," Jack said, his voice steady but filled with a quiet sadness. "You must know that's not right either."

Seth's jaw clenched, but he said nothing, his face a mask of controlled rage.

"I get it," Jack continued, his voice softer now, trying to reach whatever humanity might still be left in Seth. "You're angry. You're hurt. But this? This isn't what Simone would have wanted for you. It's not who she loved."

Seth's eyes flickered with something—doubt, pain, Jack couldn't tell. But it was there, a crack in the armour of his cold resolve.

"What do you want from this?" Jack asked gently, stepping forward, his heart pounding as he took a risk. "What do you want to come out of all this?"

For a moment, Seth stood still, his face unreadable, the weight of Jack's question pressing into the silence. His hand, still holding the gun, trembled slightly. The room seemed to close in, the cold air thickening with the grief and guilt that filled the space between them. Seth's eyes, for the briefest second, looked lost, as if he wasn't sure of the answer himself.

Jack took a slow breath, his mind racing as he gauged Seth's unreadable expression. He could sense the desperation in the air, the tension coiling tighter with every passing second. There was no way out of this without pushing Seth further into the truth he seemed to avoid. "What do you want from me, Seth?" Jack asked, his voice steady despite the gravity of the moment. "An apology? Is that it? Do you want me to say I'm sorry again? Believe me, I am sorry… So sorry… Or is it revenge you're after—justice?" He leaned in slightly, searching Seth's eyes for a flicker of clarity. "You want me to suffer, like you've been suffering all these years?"

Seth shook his head, "No, Jack. It's not really about making you pay... I get you're sorry. But those are your emotions... Your pain. I want you to understand mine, even just for a second." Seth stood still, his grip on the gun tightening as his words hit their mark. But his face remained expressionless, cold.

Jack pushed harder, "Then help me... I need to know what this has all been for."

For a moment, Seth said nothing, his face shadowed with a strange, quiet resolve. The faint sound of dripping water from somewhere in the room filled the silence, mingling with the low hum of distant traffic outside the warehouse walls. Then, in a voice that was almost eerily calm, Seth said, "I'm trying to, and I think you're starting to... I want you to make a choice, Jack."

Jack frowned, his heart skipping a beat. He watched Seth closely, every word from him now carrying the fear of something inevitable, something final.

"What do you remember about that day?" Seth asked him, his voice quiet but sharp, as if he was digging into Jack's memories with a scalpel.

Jack blinked; his mind thrown back to that hot, unrelenting afternoon. He had tried to forget it, tried to push it into the dark corners of his mind. But now, with Seth staring him down, it came flooding back, vivid and unbearable. "The heat," Jack said slowly, his voice distant as the memory unfolded in front of him. "I remember how hot it was. The brightness of the sun, glaring off the pavement. And then... after it happened..." He trailed off, his throat tightening. "It didn't feel real. Like none of it made sense. One minute everything was normal, and then..."

Seth stepped closer, his eyes burning with an intensity that made Jack's chest tighten. "Go on," Seth urged. "Tell me."

Jack swallowed hard, looking to the floor. "After it happened... it was like the world stopped. There was this... sadness. This crushing sadness that hit me, but nothing about it seemed real. It was all too fast."

Seth's lips curled into a bitter smile. "Of course it didn't feel real, Jack," he said, his voice tinged with sarcasm. "Because it wasn't you lying there in the street. It wasn't your body lying broken on the pavement."

Jack flinched at the harshness of his words. Seth took a step back, the anger creeping back into his voice. "But it was real for me. It's been real for me every single day since." Seth's voice softened, the edges of his anger melting into a brittle sadness. He looked at Jack, his eyes distant as he drifted back into the past. "It wasn't a sunny day, Jack, by the way. It was raining, gloomy. I remember her lying there... bleeding out on the ground, and the rain—it just kept coming. Washing her blood, her life, away... into the gutter."

Jack felt a lump rising in his throat. He had seen the aftermath a hundred times in his nightmares, but hearing Seth describe it like this—so raw, so immediate—made it unbearable. He checked his own memories. None of it made sense, it felt disconnected.

Seth's eyes darkened with the memory; his voice steady but cracked at the edges. "The ambulance took her... I went with them, sat in that sterile hospital waiting room, with its fluorescent lights that made everything look so lifeless... I remember being sat there with this little Korean boy... His mum had just gone into surgery, too. Same time as Simone."

Jack didn't speak. He couldn't. Any words seemed stuck in his throat, choking him.

"They gave me a choice," Seth said, his voice low, like he was talking more to himself than to Jack. "They came out, doctors, nurses, I don't even remember who said it. They told me, they could try to save Simone, or our baby, but not both. There were no guarantees... I didn't hesitate. I chose her." He laughed, but it was a hollow, bitter sound. "Perhaps that was a mistake."

Jack's heart twisted in his chest. He could feel the agony of that decision.

"She still died on that operating table, our baby, too." Seth's voice cracked, his face contorting with the memory of that final loss. "They told me afterwards—complications, internal bleeding, some other medical term I don't even remember. It doesn't matter." He took a sharp breath. "That's what I've been left with, Jack."

Jack felt himself breaking, unravelling. Every word Seth spoke was like a knife twisting deeper into his gut. He could see Charley's face—pleading, terrified, her eyes wide as she silently begged him to do something, anything. The emotional tension in the room was crushing him. He needed to defuse it somehow.

"What do you want me to do?" Jack asked, his voice rough, almost desperate. He didn't know how to fix this, how to make it right. But if Seth had some twisted idea of penance, Jack would give it. Anything to stop this spiral. As he waited for an answer, a strange sound began to filter through the tension, softly, almost imperceptible at first. The familiar opening bars of *Sinnerman*—that haunting, relentless piano. Jack blinked, thinking it must be in his head, an auditory hallucination brought on by the stress. But it was growing louder, more defined, echoing in the cold, empty warehouse.

Sensing his confusion, Seth confirmed it—the haunting melody of *Sinnerman* was real, and it was echoing through the warehouse for thousands of unseen eyes. "Have a look around, Jack... All eyes on you, baby!"

Jack felt a wave of nausea crash over him as Seth's words sank in. Glancing around at the dark corners of the room, he could see multiple little security style cameras set up, recording all of it.

"You're filming this?" Jack's voice was barely a whisper, hoarse with disbelief.

"Streaming," Seth corrected, his tone chillingly matter of fact. "To the world. Right now, sixty thousand people are watching you on the dark web. And that number's only going up. *Cop gets his Karma*. Turns out a lot of people will pay to see that… That's the world we live in."

Jack's mind raced, his thoughts a jumbled mess of horror and desperation. Sixty thousand people witnessing this twisted moment of reckoning. His moment of reckoning. He glanced at Charley, bound and gagged, her eyes pleading with him. Christian lay unconscious, vulnerable. Seth stood before him, a shadowy figure of vengeance, waiting for Jack to choose who would live and who would die.

"Here you go, Jack," Seth said sharply, tossing a second gun to Jack's feet. He stooped down to pick it up, the weight of the gun in his hand felt like lead, its presence demanding a decision—one that would echo far beyond this warehouse, far beyond the reaches of London.

"One bullet, Jack. Your choice… her, or him."

"I can't do *that*…" Jack's voice cracked, his attention shifting between Seth and the gun in his hand. He couldn't comprehend the magnitude of this choice; the enormity of what Seth was demanding. But time, like the haunting piano melody, played on without mercy.

"You have until the end of the song," Seth's voice was calm, almost gentle, a stark contrast to the horror of the situation.

Charley's muffled cries intensified; her eyes locked on Jack's. Christian lay still, unconscious, oblivious to the fate hanging in the balance. Jack's mind raced through every scenario, searching for a way out, a way to defy the cruel fate that had brought them to this moment. But there was no escape, no loophole. The choice was his alone to make. He had faced killers, solved cases that chilled him to the bone, but nothing had prepared him for this. His fingers trembled on the cold metal of the gun as he struggled to find clarity amidst the chaos.

The piano's melancholic notes filled the air, a relentless reminder of the ticking clock. *Sinnerman*—the song of reckoning—seemed to mock Jack's indecision, its rhythm urging him to act before time ran out.

Seth watched him with a cold intensity, his eyes unwavering. "Decide, Jack," he urged softly, though there was no kindness in his voice, only a cold resolve born of years of grief and anger.

Jack's heart pounded in his chest, a drumbeat of fear and sorrow. He closed his eyes, blocking out the warehouse around him, the cameras, the unseen audience. For a brief moment, he saw Simone's face—the girl who had been lost to him, to Seth, to a moment's distraction and a cruel twist of fate.

"I'm sorry," Jack whispered, his voice barely audible over the haunting melody. He raised the gun, his hand trembling as he took aim. His mind screamed in protest, but his body moved with a terrifying inevitability.

30

'Love can do all but raise the Dead'

"I'm sorry," Jack repeated, his voice thick with emotion. He could barely form the words, his throat tight as he raised the gun. But instead of turning it on either Charley or Christian, his trembling hands shifted the barrel toward Seth.

Seth's laughter broke the tension like a glass shattering on stone. It was a dark, bitter sound, echoing off the cold, metallic walls of the warehouse. The chilling melody of *Sinnerman* continued to play in the background, its rising tempo adding a haunting urgency to the moment.

"You can try, Jack," Seth said, his voice steady, unaffected by the gun now aimed at him. "But I'll take at least Charley with me. Maybe if I'm quick enough. Is that your choice?"

Jack's hands shook violently. He could feel his body betraying him, the consequences of any decision pressing down on his chest. His heart pounded, the thudding echoing in his ears, almost louder than the music. The gun felt cold, alien, as if it didn't belong in his grip. It wasn't his tool for justice—it was simply a death sentence, and he knew it.

"I… I can't do this," Jack stammered, his voice cracking under the pressure. He blinked hard, trying to force back the tears welling in his eyes. The knot of fear and sorrow in his chest threatened to undo him completely. His mind raced, searching for any possible way out, but Seth was right—there was no escape, no way of saving them all.

Seth smiled, sensing Jack's breaking point. His calmness, his eerie detachment, only fuelled Jack's despair. "And don't even think about turning it on yourself, Jack," Seth warned softly, stepping closer, his eyes cold. "If you do that, you all die. I'll execute both of them. One after the other." He tilted his head slightly, considering. "No, no, that won't do. I'll make you watch before I finish you off. You'll see them go first."

The words hit Jack like a physical blow, his knees buckling as if the weight of them alone could bring him to the ground. He blinked, desperately trying to hold back the flood of tears.

"There's no way out, Jack. No clever plan, no escape route. You *will* make this choice. You have to. It's the price you pay." Seth's voice was calm, but beneath the surface, there was a tremor, a deep, unshakable anger.

The song escalated in the background, Nina Simone's haunting voice rising in intensity, like a tide pulling Jack under.

"Please," Jack whispered, his voice barely audible as he took a step back, the gun still shaking in his hand. "This isn't what she would've wanted."

Seth's jaw tightened, his calm demeanour fracturing for the briefest of moments. "Don't you dare tell me what she would've wanted. You don't get to speak for Simone. You took everything from her—everything from me." His eyes blazed with fury, but the pain was there, raw and exposed, just beneath the surface.

Jack's vision blurred. He was nearly in tears, and his body trembled with exhaustion, guilt, and hopelessness. He wanted to collapse, to fall apart, but the weight of the gun somewhat ironically kept him standing.

Seth's voice took on a strange, detached tone, as if he were telling a story that had nothing to do with the chaos and violence around them. His eyes flicked toward Charley and Christian, then back to Jack. "This was her favourite song," he said, almost dreamily, as the haunting refrain of *Sinnerman* continued to fill the room. "Simone used to play it all the time. I never understood the song—until that night."

His gaze drifted somewhere far beyond the warehouse, beyond the present. Jack watched as Seth became momentarily lost in his memories. "We met at this little club in Soho," he continued, his voice softening. "I wasn't supposed to be there, really, but I wandered in after work. She was… captivating. You wouldn't believe it if you saw her, Jack. The way she moved, the way she looked at me like I was the only person in the room. Like no one else mattered." A wistful smile touched his lips, his eyes clouded with something close to affection. "She changed my life that night… All of our lives actually…"

Jack shifted uneasily, the gun still in his hand, but Seth didn't notice. He was deep in the past, his voice growing more distant with each word. "We talked for hours, danced until the lights came on. By the end of the night, I knew I'd never be the same. That kind of love, it burns you up, Jack. It consumes everything in its path. She was my light… and when she died, that light went out. Can you imagine that kind of love? Is that what you have with Charley?"

Jack's breath hitched at the mention of Charley. His eyes flicked to her, bound and terrified, her face streaked with tears. His mind reeled under the weight of Seth's words, his heart torn between guilt, fear, and the devastating realisation that there was no way out for them. The music swelled, quickened, its insistent rhythm hammering in his skull. He couldn't hide from it, couldn't escape the rising tension that surged in on him from all sides.

"What a shame," Seth said, his voice slipping back into its cold, emotionless cadence. "To have wasted all this time. To have wasted her time, feeling sorry for yourself." His eyes sharpened, locking onto Jack's with deadly focus. "You think you're the victim here, don't you? That you're the one suffering? What about her, Jack? What about Simone? Her death became my death. And now, I'm giving you the chance to feel what that's like. The weight of a life, of a choice. Isn't that what love is?"

Jack was wracked with pain, with a guilt so intense it seemed to crush him from within. He couldn't focus. He couldn't breathe. His mind spun, unable to grasp the reality that Seth was demanding a choice that no human being could make. "I... I can't... do what you're asking," Jack choked out, barely audible. "I can't choose."

Seth leaned in closer, his voice low, goading. "It's not the first time you've killed someone, Jack. Don't act like this is so hard for you."

"It's not the same," Jack stammered, the memory of Simone's lifeless body flashing in his mind. "It wasn't like this. It was an accident... a mistake."

Seth's eyes darkened. "You don't get to hide behind that. Not this time. Mistakes have consequences, too."

The music quickened again, Nina Simone's voice growing louder, the drums pounding like Jack's heart. The walls of the warehouse seemed to close in, the room filling with the horror of Seth's demands. Jack couldn't hide. He couldn't escape.

Seth's eyes narrowed as Jack's trembling hand raised the gun again, the barrel shaking as if it weighed a thousand pounds. "I really thought you'd figure it out, Jack," Seth said with a tone somewhere between disappointment and mockery. "Kinda made me angrier you couldn't. You love all those little details. The crazy, abstract connections. You're always digging into the minutiae, finding patterns where no one else sees them. Ed almost figured it out, you know." He paused, and Jack's pulse quickened. The name—Ed—cut through the fog of Jack's mind like a knife.

Seth reached into his pocket and slowly pulled out a mobile phone. Jack's breath caught in his throat. It was Ed's. The phone he'd been trying to reach, the one that had gone to voicemail again and again. Seth flipped it open, staring at it almost absently before turning his attention back to Jack. "He was on his way to find you. He really was. But then..." Seth trailed off, his voice lingering in the silence like a noose tightening. "He had a little detour."

Jack's heart dropped. He knew now, without a doubt, why Ed hadn't answered. A dull ache spread through his chest, and he felt nauseous, a wave of panic rising up to choke him. He wanted to scream, to deny it, but the truth had already settled deep inside him. Ed was gone. His friend was dead.

"Maybe it's not seven lives anymore, Jack," Seth continued, his voice cold, calculated. "Maybe it's eight. Add Ed to the list. Plus, Simone's... and my baby's." He stared into Jack's eyes; his expression unreadable but his words dripping with venom. "Ten lives, for that one moment."

Jack's grip on the gun faltered. Seth's words crushed him, pulling him down into a dark abyss where the lines between guilt and innocence blurred until they no longer existed. He tried to steady the gun, but his hands were shaking too much. He couldn't focus. The world was spinning. Seth stood there, unnervingly calm, watching as Jack crumbled before him.

"This is all you," Jack spat, his voice breaking, accusing Seth but also accusing himself. His hands shook uncontrollably, and he felt the bile rise in his throat. "You can't put this on me." His voice was a fragile thread, barely holding together as the enormity of the situation collapsed in on him. He gagged, dropping to his knees, and vomited on the cold concrete floor. The sound of it echoed in the stillness.

Seth didn't move, didn't react. He simply stood there, his eyes steady, watching Jack disintegrate with a gaze pitiless, blank. "There's a concept in law, isn't there, Jack?" Seth said quietly, his voice unnervingly composed. "Take your victim as you find him?" He paused, letting the words sink in, before adding with a bitter smile, "Well, you found me."

Jack's core collapsed, sobbing. His entire body shook as grief, guilt, and terror overwhelmed him. He couldn't do it. He couldn't make the choice. He couldn't carry the gun, the responsibility. With a hollow, defeated motion, he tossed the gun across the room, watching as it skidded away, into the shadows, lost from view.

Jack stood, barely able to hold himself upright, his arms open wide in a gesture of surrender. Every muscle in his body screamed in exhaustion, in defeat. His chest heaved with intense, ragged breaths, and his limbs felt like they might give way at any second. It took all the strength he had left to face Seth like this, arms outstretched, utterly exposed. He was broken. Destroyed. There was no way out.

The warehouse echoed with the haunting wail of Nina Simone, her voice cracking as she called out to the heavens. She was breaking too, as though the weight of all this sorrow, all this madness, was too much for even her to bear. Jack's voice was low, raw, almost unrecognisable as it scraped out of his throat. "Just do what you want, Seth." He stood there, vulnerable and beaten. "Do what you want." The words felt like shards of glass as they left his lips. "I'm not giving you the satisfaction."

Seth, standing just a few feet away, watched Jack with an almost bemused expression, the gun heavy in his hand.

"Satisfaction?" he repeated, a bitter laugh escaping him. "You think I'm getting any satisfaction from this? You don't evade responsibility by relinquishing, you know?"

Nina's voice scatted in the background, her melody unhinged, spiralling into the final chaotic moments of the song. The music throbbed, pulsing with the desperation and pain that filled the air between them. Jack's heart was racing, but he had given up trying to reason, to stop Seth. It felt like the end, and in some perverse way, he welcomed it.

Seth's voice cut through the music like a knife, cold and resolute. "I told you, Jack," he said softly, "it was never about revenge. Who would want this?"

Time slowed again as Seth raised the gun, aiming it at Charley's head. Jack's breath caught in his throat, his heart twisting painfully in his chest as their eyes met across the chill. Suddenly, twelve years vanished in a moment. They both understood, there was only now.

Then, in the death throes of the song, a gunshot rang out like a thunderclap, deafening all with the silence that followed. The sound reverberated around the warehouse, bouncing off the rusted steel walls, echoing endlessly through Jack's mind like a reflection in a hall of mirrors.

The world around Jack collapsed in on itself, and he dropped to his knees, the pain of impact on the cold concrete dulled by the overwhelming numbness that consumed him. His hands hit the cold floor, but he barely registered the sensation. His body felt like it wasn't his own. His vision blurred, tears streaking down his face, his hair stuck to his forehead.

And then, through the haze of agony, he saw it. Not Charley, Christian, but Seth—Seth, fell backward. The gun slipping from his hand as his body crumpled, hitting the floor with a sickening thud.

Jack blinked, his mind struggling to catch up with what he was seeing. His heart pounded in his ears, and for a moment, he couldn't process what had just happened. Seth's body, lying on the ground, motionless. His gun lay discarded beside him. The warehouse was silent now, but for those final, dying drumbeats and shimmering cymbals.

Out of the shadows, Martin stepped forward, her silhouette sharp against the cold, dim light. Her posture was unnervingly perfect, rigid as she advanced, the gun still raised and her grip unwavering. Her eyes, locked on Seth's fallen body, were filled with a mixture of disbelief and controlled fury. She stood momentarily frozen, the echo of the shot still reverberating in her ears.

She knew there had only been one bullet, knew there was nothing left in the chamber, knew Seth wasn't getting up again. Arriving not long after Jack, she'd heard most of the conversation, waiting patiently in the shadows while Radcliffe called for backup. Everything had clicked when she reviewed the neighbours' statements about Murray, then painstakingly connected the dots, the small details—and finally, searching Seth's flat that morning, finding the photograph of Simone, and then the warehouse's location, listed among his assets, inherited years ago from his rich aunt.

As the chaos had unfolded before her, she made the only choice she could. She knew how to shoot, she'd competed in the discipline, almost making the British Olympic team at one point. But she had never killed. Never fired a pistol in anger—or was it fear?

Now, having watched Seth fall, she released a long, trembling breath. But to lower the gun would be to lower her defences, to allow the full force of what had just happened to crash down on her. And so, she held it there longer, solid, steady, even though the threat was gone.

Jack, kneeling on the freezing concrete, looked up through the fog of his own exhaustion and grief. He saw her there, a solitary tear tracing its way down her cheek. For a moment, he felt a rush of air fill his lungs, as if he had been drowning and suddenly the water had drained from his chest. He could breathe again.

Martin's eyes met his through the haze, and slowly, painfully, she began to lower the gun. It was a deliberate act, like she was releasing the tension in her body inch by inch at the same time, as though any sudden movement might break her completely. Her fingers slid away from the grip, and her free hand trembled slightly as she wiped her eyes, then her nose, wiping away any evidence of her emotions with the same coolness she had brought into the room. But Jack saw her struggle, the cracks forming in the armour she had worn so tightly until now.

For those few seconds, it was just the two of them, standing amid the wreckage of something neither of them could fully comprehend yet. It felt like time had slowed, like the whole world had drawn back, leaving only the faint echo of Seth's body hitting the floor and the soft shuffle of footsteps in the background.

Then, like the breaking of a spell, Radcliffe burst into the room, rushing in with uniforms and paramedics on his heels. The flash of high-visibility vests caught the edge of Jack's vision as the medics made their way quickly to Christian, working to untie him, checking his vitals, cutting the ropes that had bound him so cruelly. Another officer was already at Charley's side, hands moving swiftly to release her from the chair, but Jack barely noticed.

In those few moments, as Radcliffe barked orders and the room filled with the sudden rush of voices and movement, something passed between Martin and Jack. It was a connection forged in trauma; in the shared madness they had just survived. Her eyes, full of unspoken words, pleaded with him to understand something deeper. Something beyond the violence. Her body trembled ever so slightly, and though she fought it, more tears spilled onto the cold concrete floor, her face flushed with the strain of holding herself together.

And yet, despite it all, despite everything, she managed the faintest, most fragile smile. Jack saw it, saw her effort, and it shattered him. He couldn't hold it back any longer. His emotions—everything—came flooding out at once. His body shook, and before he could stop himself, his face crumpled, his hands clutching at the air as the sobs broke free.

Once free, Charley rushed to him without hesitation, her arms wrapping tightly around him as if she wanted to shield him from everything that had just happened, from the chaos swirling around them. Jack felt her warmth, her strength, and for the first time in what felt like days, for what, in fact, was days, he allowed himself to sink into it. His face buried against her shoulder, his body trembling, they both let go. They stood there, entwined, clinging to one another as the world continued moving on around them—officers murmuring into radios, the distant wail of sirens still echoing faintly from somewhere outside.

When Jack finally opened his eyes, everything felt strangely still, as though the warehouse itself had fallen silent in reverence for what had just taken place. Through the haze, he saw Martin again, still standing near where Seth had fallen. The gun was no longer in her hand, but she remained rooted to the spot, her body taut with tension. One of the uniforms gave her a light pat on the back for a job well done, or in an attempt to comfort her, but she barely registered it. Radcliffe came over, speaking to her, his mouth moving quickly as he sought direction from his superior. But even as she responded, Jack could see that Martin was on autopilot. She remained fixed on him, eyes unfocused, as though trapped somewhere between what had happened and what was yet to come.

For a moment, their eyes locked again. Jack, still clutched in Charley's arms, mouthed the words that had been sitting thick in his chest since the gunshot rang out: *Thank you*.

Martin's lips twitched in response. Jack couldn't tell if she whispered the words audibly, or if she was just mouthing them in return, but he saw the briefest flicker of acknowledgment in her eyes. She nodded once, biting her lower lip as if holding back everything that was bubbling just beneath the surface. "Told you I had your back," she seemed to say, her voice soft, almost lost to the noise around them.

He wanted to speak, to say something more, but his voice caught in his throat, and all he could do was nod back, blinking away the tears that blurred his vision. Martin, still biting her lip, gave him one more glance before she turned to answer Radcliffe, the spell between them breaking as the harsh reality of the scene around them returned. Charley's hand tightened around Jack's, grounding him again. He felt the cold concrete beneath him, the sting of exhaustion in his limbs, and the overwhelming sense of finality that hung in the air like a thick fog.

As the chaos of the scene began to dissolve into the background, a gentle breeze swept through the warehouse, stirring the dust motes that danced in the final remnants of the morning light. Jack and Charley remained entwined, their breaths mingling in the chilled air, as the sound of sirens receded into the distance, swallowed by the rhythm of a busy city. The snowy expanse of London rumbled on outside, its intricate web of streets bustling with life.

The rooftops, draped in a thin layer of snow, glimmered like diamonds in the pale light, and the Thames glistened below them, winding through the city like a silver ribbon, capturing reflections of the frost-covered buildings that loomed above. Commuters hurried on to their destinations, their breath visible in the frigid air, forming fleeting clouds that dissipated swiftly into nothingness. Each figure just a thread woven into the fabric of the city, connected by their own stories, both tragic and triumphant. The distant sound of laughter emerging from a café where friends gathered, a young couple walked hand in hand, and children threw snowballs, bemused by the unusual October downfall, their joyous shouts echoing through the crisp morning air.

EPILOGUE

'Hope is the thing with feathers'

The sun hung high in the endless summer sky, casting a blanket of warmth over the rolling expanse of the South Downs. From the cliffs of Beachy Head, the world seemed to stretch out forever, with the sea gleaming like liquid sapphire beneath the golden light. There was a stillness in the air that only summer can bring, a quiet calm broken only by the rhythmic crashing of waves against the sheer chalk cliffs far below. The cliffs, brilliant white, stood out starkly against the soft blue of the sky, jagged and timeless, their ancient faces weathered by centuries of wind and sea spray.

Three figures cut a path slowly, meandering along the edge of the fields, all three bodies dwarfed by the vastness around them. Each step took them higher, toward the crest of the cliffs, the wind tugging at their clothes and sending whispers through the wild grasses that covered the hillside. The man moved steadily ahead, his eyes fixed on the horizon, his face marked by the passing of time and the quiet acceptance that had settled over him in the last few months. Behind him the woman walked, her hand resting lightly on the boy's shoulder. The boy, now taller and leaner, was growing into his teenage years with an air of quiet resilience. He had been through more than most at his age, and it showed in the way he moved, deliberate and reflective.

The path underfoot was mostly well-worn, a thin line cutting through the vibrant greens and yellows of the summer grass, which danced in the light breeze. Above them, the sky was a painting of blues and whites, the kind of perfect day where the clouds seemed almost too delicate to be real. They stretched out like thin wisps of cotton, tracing soft lines across the heavens, their edges tinged with the faintest hint of gold. The sun blazed down, casting long shadows along the chalk path, yet the breeze from the sea kept the heat at bay, its salty breath cool against their skin.

Far below, the sea sparkled, a dazzling array of blues and greens that shifted with every movement of the waves. From this height, the coastline seemed impossibly far away, a distant line where the earth met the water. The cliffs themselves were a masterpiece of nature, their brilliant white faces glowing in the midday light, cutting sharp and clean into the sky. Every crack and crevice telling its own story, carved out over millennia by the relentless force of the tides and weather. At their base, the waves crashed with a steady, timeless rhythm, sending up plumes of foam that glistened in the sunlight like tiny diamonds.

Jack paused for a moment, turning to look back at Charley and Christian, his breath catching in his chest. For the first time in what felt like a long while, he allowed himself to truly appreciate the beauty of the world around him. There was something about this place, something ancient and sacred, that seemed to ease the burden he carried. The past ten months had been filled with moments of doubt and darkness, but here, on these cliffs, with the world spread out before him, he felt more than a fleeting sense of peace.

Charley caught his eye and smiled, a soft, knowing smile that spoke of shared histories and quiet understandings. The wind lifted her hair, sending strands of it flying in the breeze, and in that moment, Jack felt an overwhelming gratitude for her presence. She had been his anchor through it all, the one constant in a sea of uncertainty.

They continued their climb, the sound of their footsteps muffled by the grass beneath their feet, the world around them growing quieter as they ascended. Seagulls circled overhead, their calls echoing faintly in the distance, carried away on the wind. Jack could feel the muscles in his legs burning slightly with the effort, but it was a good kind of pain, the kind that reminded him he was alive, still here, still fighting.

Christian walked beside Charley; his face turned upward toward the cliffs. There was a quietness about him, a stillness that had grown over the past months. He had changed, as they all had, in ways both small and profound. The boy who had once looked at the world with wide-eyed innocence had been replaced by someone older, wiser, someone who understood the fragility of life in a way few others his age could. Yet, despite everything, there was a resilience in him that shone through, a quiet determination that had carried him through the darkest of times.

Then the cliff edge came into view, a jagged line where the land dropped away into the void, and for a moment, Jack felt a familiar shiver of vertigo. The sheer drop, the vastness of the space between earth and sky, was both awe-inspiring and terrifying. But it was beautiful, undeniably so, in its raw, untamed nature. As they neared the edge, the sound of the waves crashing against the rocks far below grew louder, a steady, reassuring pulse that seemed to echo in his bones.

They stopped, standing at the edge of the world, looking out over the sea that stretched endlessly out toward the horizon. The cliffs beneath them were pure and white, their faces catching the light and throwing it back in a dazzling display. The grass at their feet swayed gently in the wind, the only movement in the otherwise still landscape. For a long moment, none of them spoke, each lost in their own thoughts, their own memories. The scene was timeless, as though nothing in the world could touch them here.

"This is it," Jack said, his voice low, almost reverent. He stood still, gazing out over the endless expanse of the English Channel, the sunlight dancing across the surface of the water like shards of broken glass.

Christian stopped beside him, glancing at Jack's face before turning his eyes back to the view. "Why'd we come here again, Uncle Jack?" he asked again, his tone filled with curiosity, a hint of confusion. He'd asked earlier, but Jack hadn't given a full answer.

For a moment, there was only the sound of the wind sweeping across the South Downs, carrying with it the tang of salt from the sea. Below them, the cliffs stretched away, jagged and white against the deep blue of the water. Far in the distance, the horizon melted into a blur of sky and sea, seamless and infinite. The light was bright and clean, the kind that made everything appear sharper, more alive.

Jack let out a long breath, feeling the full weight of the years, the weight of everything that had passed. His gaze swept the vista before them, the beauty and starkness of it all. It was easy to forget the world up here, to feel removed from it in a place so eternal, where the land met the sea in such a violent but beautiful collision.

"Friedrich Engels," Jack began, his voice steady but tinged with something deeper, "this is where his ashes were scattered. After he died."

Christian frowned slightly, the name clearly still unfamiliar, "Who was he again?"

Jack smiled faintly, turning from the sea to the boy beside him. Christian had grown up so much in the last ten months, matured in ways Jack hadn't expected. But there were still moments, like this, when the boy's youth shone through.

"Engels," Jack said, "was a philosopher, he was a close friend of Karl Marx. You've heard of Marx, right?"

Christian hesitated, then nodded. "Yeah, I think so. Like... communism, right?"

Jack nodded, a slight grin touching his lips. "Exactly. They wrote The Communist Manifesto together. Engels helped Marx with his ideas, and when Marx died, Engels became the caretaker of his legacy."

Christian looked out over the cliffs again, squinting slightly as the sunlight reflected off the chalk-white rock. "And he wanted his ashes here, why?"

Jack's eyes followed the boy's. "I don't know exactly. Maybe just to return to where we all started, generations ago... I suppose he wanted to be somewhere beautiful. Somewhere quiet. A place where you can think. This view—it feels like it belongs to everyone and no one."

Christian shifted on his feet, still looking uncertain. "But why did we come here?"

Jack chuckled softly, running a hand through his hair. "It's a place I've been wanting to come to for a while, I think maybe I'm completing a circle... Since everything that happened, I've found a kind of comfort in their ideas—Marx and Engels. They wrote about the nature of society, the nature of people. About how systems work, how people are shaped by them. It's heavy stuff, but... I don't know, it makes sense in a way. It explains why things feel broken sometimes. How things like what we went through can happen."

Christian's brow furrowed as he tried to piece it together. "You read that kind of stuff now?"

Jack nodded, his gaze turning distant again, back toward the water. "I've always been interested in philosophy, Chris, but... recently, I've needed it. I visit Marx's grave in

Highgate Cemetery sometimes, just to think. There's something about their work, their ideas, that… grounds me. It's like looking for answers to questions that don't have easy answers. Or sometimes, just sitting with the questions themselves."

Christian looked thoughtful, silent for a moment as the wind tugged at his hair. "But what does that have to do with us? With what happened?"

Jack was quiet for a long moment, considering how to answer. He knelt down, picking up a small stone from the ground and rubbing it between his fingers, feeling the rough texture. "I guess I've been thinking about fate, about control. Seth spoke about justice, about things being inevitable. Engels and Marx—what they wrote—it's about understanding the world, seeing the forces that shape people's lives. And I've been wondering if maybe some things really are out of our control."

He tossed the stone into the distance, watching as it tumbled down toward the cliff's edge and disappeared over the side.

"But what we do with what we've been given," Jack continued, his voice quieter now, "that's still up to us. We still make choices. We decide who we want to be."

Charley, who had been standing quietly beside them, took a step closer, her hand slipping into Jack's. "That's why we're here," she said softly, her voice barely audible over the wind. "To remember that. To let go of the past and decide who we're going to be now."

Christian nodded, though his expression was still distant, still processing everything Jack had said. He glanced back out at the sea, the vastness of it, the sheer, dizzying height of the cliffs, and he seemed to understand.

"It's pretty here," he said quietly. "I get why you like it… It's the right place."

Jack smiled faintly, feeling a surge of warmth towards the boy. He nodded, squeezing Charley's hand gently as they all stood there, the three of them, alone on the cliffs, with the sky and the sea and the endless, timeless wind surrounding them. It felt like a new beginning. The weight of the past still lingered, but here, in this place, it seemed lighter, less oppressive. There was hope in the air, like the breeze that swept in off the Channel, fresh and clean, washing away everything that had come before.

The cliffs rose and fell before them, a jagged line that stretched out toward the horizon, and beyond that, the unknown. For a while, none of them spoke. They simply stood there, breathing in the salt air, letting the beauty of the place surround them. The world felt so enormous from this vantage point, the cliffs like ancient watchmen standing guard over the meeting of land and sea. They had survived so much, endured things that would have broken most people. But now, standing here in the golden light of summer, it felt as though they had been given a second chance.

Abruptly, Jack's phone buzzed in his pocket, interrupting the peace. He fished it out, glancing at the screen. A chuckle escaped him, soft but genuine.

Charley, noticing the change in his expression, tilted her head with a curious smile. "What's funny?"

"Martin," Jack replied, eyes still on the message. "Her timing, it's always… well, perfect."

Charley's smile widened, "Luckily for us, thank God." She leaned in, peering at the screen as if trying to catch a glimpse of the text. "How is she?"

Jack opened the message, then turned his phone to show Charley the picture attached. It was of Martin standing in front of a makeshift medical tent with a small team of locals and volunteers, the Red Cross symbol stark in the background. She was smiling, though the backdrop of the arid landscape, with its dust-caked horizon and faded, scorching light, told of the hard work she was doing. Her face was sunburned, her hair tied back under a faded cap, but her posture was strong, her eyes determined, as they always were.

"She's in Africa," Jack said, the amusement still playing on his lips. "Working for the Red Cross now. Looks like she's in the middle of nowhere, but she seems... happy."

Charley took the phone from his hand gently, studying the picture more closely. "She does, doesn't she?" she murmured, a touch of admiration in her voice. "It suits her."

Jack nodded, taking the phone back and slipping it into his pocket. "She always was better at keeping her focus when everything was falling apart. I think this—helping people, being out in the world—maybe it's what she was made for."

Charley looked up at him, a thoughtful look in her eyes. "Do you think she'll ever come back? To the police, I mean?"

Jack smiled faintly, shaking his head. "I don't think so. Once she's made up her mind about something... well, I think that's usually it. If she's found purpose, I doubt she'd leave it behind."

Charley nodded slowly, her eyes drifting back to the horizon. "Yeah, I suppose you're right. It's funny, though. I always thought of her as part of this world... our world. But maybe she never really belonged in it." The wind picked up slightly, tousling their hair, but it was warm, carrying with it the scent of the sea.

Jack glanced down at his phone again, thinking about Martin. It was strange to think of her so far away, in a place so foreign, yet so fitting for her.

"Besides," Jack added after a pause, "I think she's finally found some peace out there."

Charley nodded, slipping her arm around his waist as they both stood there, letting the sea breeze carry away the lingering weight of the past.

Christian stood quietly for a moment, staring out over the endless blue of the Channel. The wind played gently with his hair, jostling it like the hands of an unseen friend. Then he spoke, his voice quiet but certain. "He'd like it here."

Jack turned to him, the depth of those words settling over him with a quiet finality. He studied Christian's face, saw the maturity that had crept in over these last months, the shadow of grief that had given way to a quiet resolve. Christian had changed—he had grown—but some part of him still remained that little boy Jack had sworn to protect.

"Shall we do it then?" he asked softly.

Christian nodded, his movements deliberate as he shrugged off his backpack and knelt down, unzipping the main compartment. Inside, nestled carefully beneath a towel, was a simple, unassuming, grey container. For a moment, he just stared at it, his fingers tracing the outline of the container. Jack couldn't see the boy's face, but he could feel the emotion beneath the surface, as if the waves of the sea below them mirrored the swell inside the boy.

Christian looked up at Jack, who offered a small, understanding nod. Carefully, he lifted the container out of his backpack, holding it in his hands. The sun glinted off its smooth surface, and for a second, Jack could almost imagine Ed standing there with them, grinning that crooked grin, his brown, almost curly hair being tossed around by the sea air, telling them to hurry up before the wind changed direction.

Jack stood beside Christian, resting a hand on his shoulder. Christian smiled faintly, there was a pause, both of them lost in their thoughts. Jack looked out at the horizon, the sharp, bright line where the sky met the water, and he felt a strange sense of calm wash over him. This place—these cliffs, the sea below, the brilliant sky above—it felt like the right place for Ed to rest. Jack bent down beside him, his own heart heavy but steady, reaching into his own bag. His fingers brushed the cool surface of a second container, smaller and darker, and for a brief moment, his hand hesitated.

He looked up at Charley, and their eyes met. There was an unspoken understanding between them, a shared sense of the gravity of what they were about to do. She gave him a small, resolute nod, her lips pressed into a thin line, but her eyes were calm. Jack straightened up, pulling out the second container, holding it with a reverence that felt different, harder given all that had come before. Inside it were Seth's ashes.

Jack had wrestled with this moment for months— whether it was the right thing to do, whether Seth deserved to rest in the same place as Ed. But something in him had shifted when he met Simone's family, and there was a kind of inevitability to this moment, a sense that it was the only way to close the circle.

He turned to Christian, offering him the chance to speak. "Do you want to say anything?" Jack asked, his voice quieter now, carrying the tension of what lay between them.

Christian shook his head, eyes downcast. "No," he said softly. Then, after a pause, he added, "Do you?"

Jack looked out over the water, the horizon stretching endlessly before them, a silent witness to all that had happened. He nodded slowly. "Yeah," he said, his voice firming with quiet resolve. "I'd like to, if I may?"

Christian nodded, so he knelt down, his fingers resting lightly on the container. He didn't open it just yet. Instead, he took a deep breath, gathering himself, and looked to Charley, then back to Christian. "There's something I want to read," Jack said. "It's a poem."

"By Emily Dickinson?" asked Christian innocently, not grasping Jack's obsession.

Jack laughed. "No, it's called… *The Second Coming*. It's by a guy called W.B. Yeats."

Christian's brow furrowed slightly, and Jack could see the question forming, but he didn't wait for him to ask. He needed to explain this first. "After everything happened with Seth, I went to see Simone's parents," Jack said, his voice soft, but clear. "Her father, Isaac, told me that this poem… it had been special to their family for generations. Something they carried with them. He said it marked moments when things felt broken, when everything seemed to be falling apart."

Charley stood beside him now, silent, her hand resting on his shoulder, grounding him. Jack swallowed, feeling the words build inside him like a rising tide. "Yeats conceived of the world as a series of widening gyres—spirals moving outward, with history repeating itself but always in more chaotic, more fragmented ways. A breakdown of communication, of understanding between people. That's what his poem is about."

He glanced at Christian, whose expression had softened slightly with curiosity.

"But today," Jack continued, "today has to mark a point of reconnection for us. For all of us. We've been through enough chaos."

Jack opened the container, the fine grey ashes within catching a flicker of sunlight. He held the open container in his hand as he pulled out a folded piece of paper from his jacket pocket. The edges were worn, the ink slightly faded, but the words were still legible. He unfolded it with care and began to read:

Turning and turning in the widening gyre
The falcon cannot hear the falconer;
Things fall apart; the centre cannot hold;
Mere anarchy is loosed upon the world,
The blood-dimmed tide is loosed, and everywhere
The ceremony of innocence is drowned;
The best lack all conviction, while the worst
Are full of passionate intensity…

Jack's voice was calm, each word imbued with its richest meaning. As he read, the limitlessness of the sky and sea seemed to close in around them, as though the cliffs themselves were listening, holding them in the embrace of the earth.

Surely some revelation is at hand;
Surely the Second Coming is at hand.
The Second Coming! Hardly are those words out
When a vast image out of Spiritus Mundi
Troubles my sight: somewhere in sands of the desert
A shape with lion body and the head of a man,
A gaze blank and pitiless as the sun…

Jack paused, his throat tightening as the words stirred something deeper in him, something almost too profound to name. He felt the connection between this poem and everything that had happened—the violence, the loss, the confusion. It was all there in the widening gyre, in the chaos that had gripped them.

… is moving its slow thighs, while all about it
Reel shadows of the indignant desert birds.
The darkness drops again; but now I know
That twenty centuries of stony sleep

Were vexed to nightmare by a rocking cradle,
And what rough beast, its hour come round at last,
Slouches towards Bethlehem to be born?

When Jack finished, there was a long silence. The only sound was the soft hiss of the wind against the cliffside and the distant cry of gulls circling overhead. He folded the paper again and slipped it back into his pocket, looking at Christian and Charley, who were both watching him with quiet intensity.

"It's not about what's been lost," Jack said softly, "but about what we do from here. Simone's father said this poem reminded him that even in the worst moments, when everything falls apart, there's still a chance to rebuild… like we have."

Christian nodded, understanding dawning in his eyes. Jack took a deep breath, steadying himself, and then tilted the container of Seth's ashes, at the same time, with a gentle motion, Christian did the same, releasing Ed. The wind seemed to hold its breath for a moment, as if waiting, watching. The ashes lifted into the air, caught immediately by the breeze. The grey dust caught a gust, mixed with the air, and lifted upward into the sky, spiralling ascendent. As if caught in their own gyre, in a delicate, swirling dance, the ashes were carried off over the cliffs and out into the vast blue expanse. For a moment, the three of them stood there, watching as they drifted away, disappearing into the sky, merging with the air and the sea, and each other.

As they paused on the ridge, Jack stood quietly, his eyes scanning the endless horizon where the sky met the sea. The afternoon light had shifted, softening into something silvery and warm. The water below shimmered with a kind of quiet brilliance, reflecting the sun in long, wavering lines like threads of silver thread woven into the earth itself. For a moment, it took Jack back to that memory, or what he had always believed to be his earliest memory, from when he was a small child—standing on a beach, watching birds ride the waves.

He could remember the birds circling and diving, their wings cutting through the air with a precision that fascinated him. They were hunting, fishing, but it wasn't the birds that captured his young imagination—it was the waves, the way they moved beneath the birds and the fish, endlessly rolling, never tiring. He'd thought himself the bird at times, or perhaps the fish that struggled below the surface. Now, standing here, the sea spread before him like a great silver mirror, he wondered if he hadn't misunderstood that memory all along.

Maybe he was the wave, not the bird or the fish. Or maybe it was his memories that were the waves, gently rolling and returning, over and over. Always shifting, always retreating to the depths before rising again. And like the waves, maybe they too were part of something larger, something that moved beyond him, beyond the moment, beyond all that had happened. His memories, his losses, his failures—they were all part of that constant motion, that endless return.

The thought gave him a strange sense of peace. The chaos of the last few years, the violence, the heartbreak—it hadn't been for nothing. There was a rhythm to it all, a natural cycle, like the sea and the wind and the sun above them now. Things returned. Maybe they didn't come back in exactly the same way, but they did come back, eventually, and perhaps that was enough.

Charley touched his arm, pulling him from his thoughts. "You ready to go?" she asked softly, her voice cutting through the quiet.

Jack nodded. "Yeah," he said, glancing once more at the sea. "I'm ready."

Christian had already packed up his things, his backpack slung over one shoulder. Jack knelt down and began to gather their belongings, slowly and methodically, feeling the roughness of the wild grass brushing against his hands. The sun hung low in the sky now, casting long shadows across the chalky cliffs and painting the landscape in a shimmering gold. It was beautiful, achingly so.

They began their slow descent, the three of them walking through the wild grass, the blades unbraiding themselves in the gentle breeze. Jack could hear the rustle of the grass underfoot, the distant call of birds circling overhead, and the whisper of the wind as it moved through the open landscape. It felt like they were walking through something eternal, something untouched by the chaos of their lives. The sun warmed their faces as they moved, but there was still a bite in the air, a reminder of how exposed they were to the elements. Jack could feel it in his bones, that sensation of being at the mercy of something larger than himself. It was humbling, in a way. Comforting, even.

They stopped once more, halfway down the path, when Christian crouched to tie his shoe. Jack and Charley exchanged a glance, standing there, bathed in the last light of the day. For a moment, Jack felt that same pull, that same sense of connection to the world around him, the elements that surrounded them. The earth beneath their feet, the wind at their backs, the sea stretching out endlessly before them— it all felt like part of something he could never fully understand, but somehow, that didn't actually matter anymore.

As Christian stood up, they began walking again, their footsteps silent against the soft ground. The grass swayed gently in the breeze, and when Jack turned to look back at where they had been standing, it was as if they had never been there at all. The place where they had paused, where Christian had stooped to secure his shoe, was empty now, swallowed up by the wild grass and a fading light. It was as though their presence there had been erased, carried off by the wind, leaving nothing behind but the faintest whispers of their journey.